C000039672

Also by Umberto Tosi

Our Own Kind

My Dog's Name

Satan, the Movie

Gunning for the Holy Ghost

Elvis and Marilyn Have Left the Building

Milagro on 34th Street

High Treason

"Lord, we know what we are,
but know not what we may be"

– Hamlet, Act IV, Scene 5

OPHELIA RISING

A NOVEL BY UMBERTO TOSI

By Umberto Tosi

OPHELIA RISING - By Umberto Tosi

Copyright © 2014 by Umberto Tosi
All rights reserved

Cover image©2012 by Eleanor Spiess-Ferris.

"Ophelia's Garden" – gouache on paper.
By permission of the artist.

Cover layout by Gabrielle de la Fair,
Herethics Publishing

Published by

LIGHT FANTASTIC PUBLISHING
CHICAGO, ILLINOIS, 2014

ISBN-13: 978-0692346181 (Custom)
ISBN-10: 069234618X
BISAC: Fiction / Historical

To Eleanor, Alicia, Kara, Cristina and Zachary

++++

Europe Main Map at the Beginning of the Year 1600

####

ACKNOWLEDGEMENTS

I wish to thank my dear Eleanor Spiess-Ferris, Chicago imagist *extraordinaire,* who provided the evocative cover image for this book, plus her generous encouragement, insight and support. I also thank my eldest daughter, Alicia Anne Sammons and her erudite husband Brian for their editorial acumen and support. In addition, I thank Gabrielle de la Fair, editor-in-chief of HerEthics Books, for her editorial and design expertise. Authors Signe (Jennifer) Radcliff and John Le Bourgeois provided keen-eyed comments and editing for which I am grateful. I send special thanks to song writer and fellow San Francisco improv player Deborah Parma, whose long-ago, *Life of Ophelia* monologue at the Blue Bear Theatre stayed with me. I nod gratefully as well to friend, writer and former *Los Angeles Times* colleague, Linda Gross, whose fascination with the Fair Maiden first stirred this writer's imagination on the subject.   – *Umberto Tosi*

By Umberto Tosi

Hamlet and Ophelia, a drawing by Pre-Rafaelite Daniel Gabriel Rosetti, 1858.

++++

PREFACE

The mystery of Ophelia may never be solved fully. Nevertheless, I hope that this accounting, may serve to answer many questions about this extraordinary woman that have beguiled us for so long – questions that have multiplied since the discovery of her papers in the Vatican archives.

Thanks to gaining access to those papers, I have been able to let Ophelia tell the story in her own words wherever possible, drawing from the fragments of her journals that were found with her poetry, drawings and other effects. Otherwise, I have reconstructed this extensive, personal biography from the papers and memoirs of contemporaries, family members and historians of the times in which she lived.

I give special thanks to all those who helped research and assemble this biography, including my dedicated assistants, Lorna Crabtree and Sean McGee. My gratitude as well to Adriana Colandiao, Hans Otto, Pieter van Winkle, and Lars Heisen who translated and helped me interpret many documents from fifteenth century Italian vernaculars, Latin, old Dutch, German and old Danish, and helped me to select and integrate their content into this story.

What came to light in the process of assembling and writing this biography is that Ophelia of Elsinore was a much more fascinating, complex and significant historical figure than could have been understood solely from the Shakespearian play that made her famous – the "fair maiden" who became a woman of passion, poetry and courage. Her story can now be told fully – of a life that touched so many – high and low – as she made her fateful journey through troubled European lands in a time of war, clashing empires, revolution, intrigue, religious hatred, unprecedented discoveries, sublime, literature, the birth of science and of the modern world.

– the author

-

++++

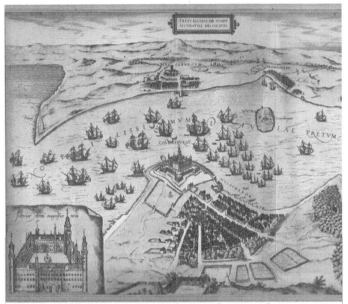

The real Elsinore - Danish Castle Kronborg:
depicted by 16th-century cartographers Georg
Braun and Frans Hogenberg, famed for their
bird's-eye view map drawings of 530 cities.

PART ONE

By Umberto Tosi

1. FALLING WATER

Out on a limb
for the sweetest fruit
the rarest bloom
the truest word.
And when the bough breaks
Cradles will fall
Down will come baby
dreams and all.
Out of my mind,
with violets and thyme
let swift current take me,
brook into stream
river to sea,
to be; not to be.

The plunge into cold water startles my body, hair-on-end awake. It brings back the childhood glee of summer frolics by the sea and the animal terror of falling, nothing beneath my feet as I go deep into blue whiteness. As quickly as I sank, I rise and break into cold sunlight, gasping, hands flailing. I see the broken bough above me recede. I see people, looking small in the growing distance, waving and shouting frantically on the shore. Then I go round a bend, still afloat, circular on the surface, rotating me slowly as the current takes me away. I feel my feet kicking on their own. I am like the daisies I used to drop into this stream as a girl and watch float swiftly away. But soon I feel my skirts soaking fast and heavy, pulling me down deeper into the numbing cold. I am gone, snaking with the current around another bend, then another skirts spread. The tops of trees wave me goodbye from the banks. Gone. Ophelia is lost. Ophelia no more.

15

They said I went mad and then drowned my silly self. I should leave it at that, letting people make what they will of my story. I would remain but a poor player – a doomed tragic maiden in the subplot of a legendary play. But let me sing you another song, maybe just as mad now, but mine own. It starts in the same place as the other, but takes a different path.

I did start to tell my story to the king once, as the Bard once quoted me:

Alack and fie, for shame!
Young men will do 't, if they come to 't.
by Cock they are to blame.
Quoth she, "Before you tumbled me,
You promised me to wed."
He answers,
"So would I ha' done, by yonder sun,
And thou hadst not come to my bed.

King Claudius did not heed my words. In truth, it was fortunate that his majesty heard only the babbling of a mad maiden.

King, queen, father and brother – they all believe that boys will be boys and maids will be credulous. It wasn't like that. The doomed royal pair, my melancholy prince and their courtiers – most of you as well – have only glimpsed pieces of Ophelia in the shards of Hamlet's shattered goblet. Now I hold up the glass for all to see.

Pansies for thoughts,
rosemary for remembrance.

How convenient to be considered unhinged when offering a murderous guilty king bunches of fennel and columbines – for that was the same as calling him a fool and an adulterer to his face.

And I let flowers speak for me as well when I proffered rue to the queen. Poor mad Ophelia, lamented Queen Gertrude. But unlike the king, she well understood the rue's intent: *Repent, your majesty. Have remorse.*

I had rue aplenty for myself too. And here's another flower more deadly – lacy, yellow henbane, growing in the forest, so delicate and innocent of its venomous nature. I know well the flowers, plants and weeds of these forests.

I speak in flowers when words won't do and truth cannot be told outright. I press and draw them into journals. You may think that strange, but it is no more uncommon than the practice of calling women mad when they speak their minds. I know my flowers and weeds by scent as much as by name – the pungency of rue, the merry lilt of pansies, the heavy sensuality of crocuses, the spicy mint of fennel.

What would you have me do? So many dangers, so few choices for a maiden – marriage, the madhouse or a brothel or a nunnery, No thank you. There are other flowers to pick – pansies, crow-flowers, nettles, wild daisies, and those long purple orchids that rougher folk call dead men's fingers.

A crimson flower danced out of reach on the twigs of a bough that overhangs a wide rushing stream. Its many colored petals spin in perfect circular symmetry like a rose window come to life. I climb and climb and shinny until I take hold of its green supple stem. I tell it: I will weave you into as fantastic a garland as the world has never seen, if I can. The flower says nothing, but the whirling water answers from below: Come, Ophelia. Let me take you into the whirlpool of death and creation from where you may begin anew.

2. SWIMMING LESSONS

The saddest, sweetest ballad floated into Fortunio Zannetti's reverie as he pissed in the stream. The voice was female, young and lilting. A siren, he thought, but then I am already shipwrecked, a fugitive player washed up on this cold Denmark shore. Her wavering tune sought out his own melancholy of love lost and reanimated its almost unbearable yearning.

"*Fa la finita! Fortuno!* Want me to come down there and shake it off for you?" Carlo's bass voice echoed through the white birches from the caravan wagons stopped on the embankment above.

"Too much ale last night." Rosa's contralto echoed off the bluff on the opposite side of the stream. Rosa sewed all the costumes and needled everyone. "The assassins will be upon us!" She looked up and down the road.

"Don't be foolish woman." Carlo motioned for Rosa to go back inside her wagon, but she stayed planted on the gravel road. "If that king wanted it, we would already be dead and buried."

Two of the roustabouts were nearly done with the broken axle on the troupe's lead wagon. Three other players loafed on the other side of the wagon, quibbling over a bet. The rest of the caravan, consisting of trade cargo bound for the harbor, had already pulled ahead of them on the postal road.

"We had no business interfering in royal affairs." Isabella stepped out of the show wagon for some air herself now.

"Now you blame me? The prince ordered us to do it." Carlo shrugged.

"And where is your prince now?" Isabella smirked. "Don't be so sure we're out of danger. The king favors stealth. We need to keep our eyes open."

Rosa nudged Carlo's broad dwarf shoulder with her hip, a tease to which he would have responded with a tweak of her rump if the two were alone. "Catch the conscience of the king?" she said. "Ha ha. We caught ourselves in the mousetrap instead."

Carlo rubbed his hands together against the morning's chill. "No more melodrama. From now on, we go back to performing comedies only! We are *i Comici*, from now on."

"Comedy can get us in trouble too. I recall more than one occasion..." Isabella stepped to the edge of the road and looked down through the trees to the stream herself. "Fortunio! Fa presto! We must make the harbor before the tide if we are to gain safe passage."

The wind picked up, rustling the trees overlaying the insistant rush of the stream.

Carlo yelled down, louder. "We're going, whether you're here or not."

They heard branches breaking down below them, but got no response from Fortunio.

Carlo yelled down. "We're leaving, whether you're here or not."

Isabella bent and nudged Carlo. "Go down there and get him."

They never wanted to stay this long in Denmark. They had planned to play only the Jutland port of Aarhus while the three-masted Dutch carrack that had brought them there unloaded cargo of silks and spices. While there, they entertained the duchess of Arhaus. Isabella presented her with a signed copy of her collection of plays and poetry, newly translated into Danish – and added the Duchess' name to the list of endorsements she posted to her printer in Antwerp. Afterwards, they had planned to catch the same Dutch carrack back to Antwerp when it sailed with a load of Scandinavian lumber. But Polonius invited the troupe to play for the royal family at Elsinore.

Carlo negotiated a generous fee, and Isabella jumped at the opportunity to secure Queen Gertrude's endorsement for her book. This meant missing their Dutch ship, and – as things turned out, catching a lot of trouble. Now they felt the hot breath of an offended king on their necks as they scrambled for whatever passage they could find out of that troubled land.

I Comici had been playing ports of call along ship routes for some time. Carlo had dreamed up the tour but Isabella had worked out the logistics – traveling by ship or riverboats wherever possible – always faster, though not safer than by land. With enough silver, cajoling and a little flirting, captains generally would provide them relatively comfortable passage wherever they wanted to travel.

Their plays, translated into half dozen vernaculars, had spread their renown. Carlo saw this tour as a way of cashing in on that renown, minimizing the hardships of travel that had proved its constant reality.
It has been nearly two years since they left Venice – full of brio – on their tour of northern Italy, France, England, Flanders and finally the Scandinavian kingdoms. They hawked newly printed translations of Isabella's verses and plays everywhere. They had played Catholic and protestant towns, avoiding the hazards of war and steering clear of the plague.
The fiasco at Elsinore was the last straw for Isabella. She demanded that they return to Italy forthwith. But Carlo had heard all this before. It would blow over. By now, they had become accustomed to the vicissitudes of the road. "We're here, and might as well make the best of it," he would always say.Down on the bank of the stream, Fortunio shook himself and buttoned his britches. Why must they talk to me like a child? He stood very still, and caught the eerie voice once again, blending with the stream's bubbling and wind ruffling the trees.

He listened intently to the voice, holding fast against its draw. Then the singing stopped. He saw something floating towards him – spread on the surface like a lily pad, fabric, purplish satin, perhaps, half submerged. He kicked off his boots. Perhaps some drunken lord had lost his cloak -- with luck, made of silk, perhaps bejeweled.

Unlike his fellow players, Fortunio knew how to swim – and very well. Water was his element. His father used to call him "Scombrino" – little mackerel – for how he could dart, silvery in the water. And indeed he had the physique for it, slender, smooth muscled, a comely rounded face bisected perfectly by an aquiline nose and sensuous, wide-set hazel eyes. His almost total lack of hair, head to toe, resulting from scarlet fever as a child – facilitated his aquatic glide and contributed to the exotic androgynous looks allowed for many roles on stage and off, male and female.

He had spent long days of his boyhood plying the treacherous currents of Venice lagoon in a single-oar *sandolo*, writing poetry, singing to himself, diving for mussels and crabs – pearls when he could find them. He salvaged trinkets, coins, sometimes jewelry and whatever else of value he could trade or sell. Not that he would have needed the money, being a wayward scion of one of Venice's richest merchant families.

He simply wanted to avoid asking his father, Antonio – master of Zannetti Glass works – for money, lest he endure yet another lecture. "*Mascalsone!* You'll never amount to anything," his father would harp. "You bring scandal upon us with your indolence. Enough! I'm cutting you off unless you finish your education, come to work in the foundry and learn the trade like I had to do.... When will you get married? Give us grandchildren?" On and on.

Young Fortunio, however, preferred the voluptuous, *dolce far' niente* life drifting on the lagoon, and eventually into the willing arms of Barnardo Levi, the lovely, equally diffident, curly haired son of a wealthy converso, merchant family living in the city's northern sector – the Cannaregio ghetto.

Bernardo's grandparents had fled Spanish persecution of Jews – including forced conversos – after the Christians drove the Moors from the Iberian Peninsula. The Republic of Venice, maintaining its independence, offered them relative safety from the Inquisition.

Fortunio and Barnardo were found out by a nosy servant, who denounced them to Fortunio's father.

Everything was handled privately between the families. Antonio rationalized that his son and Barnardo no doubt were simply engaging in horseplay – objectionable only because it demonstrated that these two spoiled youths needed discipline and putting to work. Bernardo's uncle – who was the Fortunio family glass works' lawyer, and offered to use his influence to secure Fortunio a commission in the navy. It was that or the galleys or worse.

When he was a boy, Fortunio recalled the burning of Pino Stelli, a defrocked friar, before a crowd in St. Mark's Square, for the ecclesiastical crimes of sodomy and blasphemy. The scandalous proceedings involved love letters between Stelli and Karl Klempt, an alchemist in Prague, denounced for "atheist writings" that promoted empirical observations in place of scripture as the basis for all thinking. The eccentric, Holy Roman Emperor Rudolf II – who surrounded himself with alchemists, astrologers, astronomers, magicians, natural philosophers and artists, stayed Klempt's sentence. But Stelli was not so lucky.

Thinking back on that, Fortunio offered no resistance to his father shipping him off to sea. Antonio exaggerated his son's maritime experience and convinced the Admiralty to commission Fortunio as a petty officer on one of Venice's newest, galleas warships, *Assunta*, pride of the fleet.

Bernardo's father, meanwhile, married him off, to the daughter of a rabbi. He dispatched Barnardo to Cyprus to manage one of his merchant banks. He was happy, at least, that on Crete, he could also keep an eye on his beloved younger sister, Anastasia – married to a maritime lawyer in Nicosia.

Bad timing. Soon after Bernardo's arrival, the Turks invaded the island with twenty thousand troops and captured its main cities at a cost many lives on both sides. Bernardo's family feared that he was among the twenty thousand Venetian prisoners slaughtered, not knowing of his survival – for that is another tale. Nor did Barnardo's family learn of his secret return to Christendom and travel, by circuitous route, to Denmark – becoming a sentry – and spy for the Turks – at Elsinore.

Meanwhile, Fortunio was getting his sea legs. "God has offered us glory. We are about to change history, men!" the Fortunio's captain, Julio Giunto exhorted his crew a month later when the *Assunta* sailed from Messina, Sicily. They led a squadron of the hastily assembled "Holy League" flotilla – almost three hundred warships from Spain, the Holy Roman Empire, the Papal States, the republics of Venice, Genoa, Florence, Padua and other Roman Catholic powers. Fortunio felt anything but glory as they headed into the Ionian Sea to meet the Ottoman fleet in what would, indeed, be history – the Battle of Lepanto.

Thanks to the new, Venetian galleas' superior maneuverability and firepower, the alliance ended up destroying the entire Ottoman fleet. Cyprus fell back into Venetian hands as part of a peace treaty that freed Spain to turn its guns northward onto Dutch rebels and their protestant ally, Elizabethan England.

The *Assunta*, however, sustained severe damage from cannon fire, with many dead. The wounded were transferred to other ships, including Fortunio who had been knocked unconscious and suffered a fractured arm when a powder magazine exploded. Spanish sailors took him aboard the *Marquesa*, headed back to its berth in Naples. The ship's doctor tended to him.

On the way, he got to know another sailor wounded in the fray, a sometimes playwright and struggling novella writer, a Castilian from near Madrid, one Miguel de Cervantes, who read one of Fortunio's poems, learned of his history and urged him to forget the Venetian navy and join a traveling theatrical group that had put on one of his plays in Naples – "*I Comici.*" With them, he felt at home for the first time in his young life.

"*Fortunio! Cretino!* Stop playing with yourself and get up here!" Carlo hollered again, but Fortunio had already dived into the water. The cloak swirled around him like a sea creature in midstream and would have carried him off had he not be a strong swimmer. The water chilled him more than he anticipated.

He grabbed one corner of the floating cloak and used an eddy to steer him back towards shore where he could get a toehold on the rocky bottom. He pulled hard, numbed by the cold and towed the heavy cloak onto a sand spit.

Something was wrapped in the cloak – a large bundle. Then he saw a face. The prince's maiden! He recognized the face immediately. She had been the one who liked to sing – her visage face chalky now, laced with translucent bluish veins. The maiden hair was matted like wet straw, and crowned with sodden flowers and weeds, like the soaked disarrayed garland around her neck. "The lass from the castle! *Jesu!*" He crossed himself and sank to his knees to see if she was alive.

"Fortunio! Where are you?" Carlo's rough nasal voice came toward him from upstream. Fortunio saw the dwarf's bearded bulk pushing and tumbling with difficulty though the brush until he stood next to him. "What in hell do you have there? ... A mermaid?"

Fortunio put an ear close to her lips. "Is she...?"

Carlo took a closer look. "Holy mother on a fork! It's Prince Hamlet's fair maiden!"

Fortunio pulled the girl onto the a flat rock near the stream's edge, and cupped his hand over her mouth and nose, unsure if he felt any breath. He shook his head.

"The king could have all our heads for this. They will accuse us of abduction."

"The lass may have expired."

"Our time in Denmark expired."

"I can't just leave the poor lass."

"This fish will bite you."

Also, unlike his fellow players, Fortunio knew what to do. He dragged her from the waterlogged cloak, then yanked aside her necklace of sodden nettles and daisies. He ripped her white embroidered blouse and loosened a rose bodice – no time for delicacy, or for prurience.

Carlo moved closer for a look. "Dio mio! What are you doing?"

Fortunio pumped firmly against her solar plexus with both hands, over and over. Fisherman friends back home had taught him this, and he'd seen one bring one of their own back to life this way.

He rocked back and forth pumping down on her as if to push the devil from her, the siren song he'd heard moments ago came into his mind, words forming – not a siren song, but an elegy – "gone, gone, gone to weeds my flowers, his breath of sweet regard … rosemary, violets, pansies and thyme..."

The girl coughed, gagged and spit water. The blush returned to her wide chalky lips. Fortunio helped her up to a sitting position and patted her back gently. She coughed again. Her eyes fluttered.

Carlo stepped closer to help, his own face as white as hers. "By the gods, she is beautiful – a pale Aphrodite risen from the waters.."

"I am a ghost," she whispered. She began to shiver violently.

++++

Fortunio recognized the raven amulet on the gold chain still on her white neck. "You are safe, Lady Ophelia." He rubbed her limp, icy hands.

"Let's get her up to the wagons where she can get warm." Carlo draped his leather jacket over her. "With permission, my lady." He nodded to Fortunio, who then lifted her into his arms and stood up.

++++

3. ISABEL

With one glance, Isabella could tell that the girl was at least six weeks along. She had suspected as much when she first saw her with Lord Hamlet at the performance, and felt that twinge of melancholy. Isabella had birthed four children of her own, none of which survived past a year.

She had no doubt that the girl Fortunio and Carlo brought up from the brook was Ophelia – and wearing no ring other than soggy weeds around her head. Why else would such a privileged lass have thrown herself in the river? Orphaned, jilted and knocked up – the old story, looking at the same miserable choices – brothel, convent or crazy house.

Isabella recalled how cheerful the girl had seemed at the castle – a pampered maiden on the surface, yet trouble in her eyes. That was when the troupe had played for the king and queen and that mad, troublesome prince who concocted that scene that brought the house down, and not in a good way. Disturbing the uneasy minds of kings was not healthy for traveling players.

The king had summoned Carlo and ordered the troupe to pack up and leave forthwith without paying them a ducat of what that toady Polonius had promised. It would be weeks before they could secure passage on a ship. Warily, they had played what Danish towns would have them, but these dour Danes rewarded them more with rotten eggs than coins.

Finally, in the past few days, mysteriously, they got word that "a friend" at Elsinore had arranged for a ship that could take them southwards away from Denmark.

A brief letter to that effect had been delivered to Fortunio by courier. Isabella guessed that he was from that guard captain Barnardo who had some kind of history together that neither would talk about.

They had to get themselves of the port of Aarhus on the eastern shore of the Jutland peninsula where ships passed through the strait to reach the North Sea. The letter ended by warning them about what they already feared. Be watchful for the king's assassins.

Ophelia – the poor girl, thought Isabella, could be the death of us all if we don't make haste. Shivering, subdued, her once flowing, golden hair clung damp and tangled to her neck and cheeks. She stared at Isabella, eyes as blue as a Botticelli sea.

As she stared at Isabella, Ophelia remembered her dead mother – a broad, open compassionate face with darker eyes than her mother's, with the same soulful depth – ebony hair, not red, but luxuriant as her mother's, cascading from a crimson velvet cap.

It took her a moment, but Ophelia recognized Isabella as one of the players she had watched at Elsinore. At that time, Ophelia had assumed Isabella was a young man, dressed in black, hair tucked under a page style straw blond wig it was the fashion for actors to wear on stage. Unlike the Italians and French, northerners continued to raise their pale eyebrows at women on stage, officially, at least. It was all a dance of pretense, Isabella observed.

Polonius and the royals at Elsinore knew very well that the actors were a mixed company, but looked the other way as long as *I Comici* discreetly put the women in pants and "passed" them off – ironically, even in comedic roles that called for "male" characters to dress as women, and "women" actors (who were really male), pretending to "pose" as women on stage.

29

Isabella and Carlo disliked having to limit themselves to stuffy adaptations of classical Greek and Roman dramas when performing for royal courts, but the money was good. In France and Italy, the troupe was famous for improvised, *commedia dell'arte*, class-crossing, gender-bending, custom-mocking farces, played in private suites to select nobles and to rowdy carnival and fair crowds where they could play could play right on the thin edge of respectability. "More baggage," Rosa chortled, coming up behind Fortunio. "As if we have not drawn enough wrath from king and queen upon us already!"

The other players climbed down from the second caravan wagon – larger of the two – halted a few paces back, whistled and gawked while Fortunio and Carlo dragged the soaked girl up the embankment and rolled her into Isabella's first show wagon, the one that opened out into a portable stage and doubled as bedding quarters on the road.

It became Isabella's problem, as co-director and unofficial mother superior of this squabbling, squawking, preening little band. She had looked forward to some measure of ease once they set sail, being a good sailor, knowing the herbs for seasickness.

I am getting too old for the road – and all this intrigue. I should be back in Venezzia .... I have stories and poems and a new play to write. Instead I chase coins with Carlo while golden pears fall to the ground unsavored, to rot in my garden at home.

Carlo and his gambling and this harebrained tour to make up for his losses: she could barely look at him lately, yet still felt the old urges when they performed – intuitively living their material, coming off as one, in that heady place where the fear turns golden, blood rising with the laughter and cheers of audiences caught in their moments, be they peasants or lords and ladies.

Privately, many often wondered how such a little bent man as Carlo – though handsome of face – had captured the heart of such a fair and stately woman as Isabella. She seemed glide across a stage, commanding it, long limbed and swan necked, catching onlookers with her feral eyes. She liked it that way. They had their moments. Isabella and Carlo had even been in love once, when they had eloped and he had saved her from the aging fop of a widowed duke that her parents had arranged for her to marry. But that's another story. Now they squabbled, but moved by second nature, their actions as instinctively synchronized as tumblers.

Carlo arched his eyebrows and smirked at Isabella – ever in character as the impish fool, the mocked dwarf with neatly trimmed chestnut beard and lively black eyes, who gets away with murder. He scrambled up onto high front seat with the muscular agility of a circus bear, and took the reins. Their patient team of giant dray horses snorted and clomped, rested enough by the delay.

Looking down on her – he liked that – Carlo shook his head. "We must take her back to the castle."

Isabella gave him a cross look. "Dangerous."

"We'll be in worse trouble if Ophelia's brother thinks we abducted his sister. They say Laertes is on a rampage, raising a mob to kill the king – and Prince Hamlet – for Polonius' murder."

Rosa interjected. "Why don't we just leave the wretch by the road? A royal patrol will find her."

Isabella snapped: "She's not a dog! Can't you see that this child has been sent to us as a test of our compassion?"

Carlo made a face, weighing the options. He squinted up the road, trying to see where it forked, one way leading back to Elsinore – brooding atop its crags like a bloody toothed dragon, the other towards the seaport.

"If we take her back to Elsinore now we will miss our boat. … and possibly lose our heads. If we take her with us to Arhaus, we will either catch our ship or lose our heads anyway."

Isabella, as if overhearing Carlo's thoughts, shouted to him through one of the caravan wagon's small windows: "There is nothing to decide, Carlo. We *take the lady Ophelia with us*, at least as far as the harbor. Let's go."

Carlo's shoulders sagged. He pulled himself onto the front seat with Fortunio and clicked the horses into motion along the rutted road.

Off they went, as before, the show wagon lumbered forward – painted cheerfully with caricatures of commedia stock characters and pinwheels and masks in yellows, reds and greens. Florid gold lettering on each side proclaimed: *"Compagnia Commedia e Dramatica Dell'Arte."*

Rosa already had the girl out of her wet clothes and into a plain tunic. Ophelia lay on one of the bunks, unresisting. The girl's eyes, shockingly turquoise, strangely alert and more knowing than Isabella would have guessed seem to size up Isabella and Rosa, following their slightest moves. Isabella took the girl's pale hand and stroked it softly.

The girl babbled on in Danish, slipping into French on occasion, talking of flowers, death and stones. Then she sat up and looked into Isabella's eyes. "Is this the road to heaven or hell?"

Isabella patted her hand. "A little of both, my dear." Rain tapped the wagon roof. "Sleep, child."

"You are one of the old gods, then." Ophelia said. "Freya leading me to Valhalla."

Isabella stayed quiet and close. She patted the girl's damp forehead with a cloth, like a mother with a sick child. After the girl had calmed somewhat, she pressed.

"What of your brother?" Isabella covered her with a velvet costume cape to keep her warm. The girl's own cape, still soaked, lay across two benches drying. "He will be searching for you..."

"My brother Laertes seeks only vengeance ...He raises a mob to kill the king, and the prince as well, for our father's murder."

Isabella blanched. "I'm sure he will be..."

"...Shamed!" Ophelia sat up, crying. "I have shamed him and myself... I can never return... from the land of the dead... "

Ophelia felt the wagon swaying now like a cradle. She heard the horses snorting and a dog barking from outside. She smiled. "...There are animals in Hades, at least, or I am dreaming... 'to sleep, perchance to dream,' he said."

The rain softened and the girl slept, her face blissful, reminding Isabella of Gina, the baby daughter, who would be the same age had she lived. Isabella lay near the girl and dozed herself for a time.

Rosa sat beside them for a while. "Saved from eternal damnation,"

Ophelia whispered back, almost inaudibly, with a smirk, "...and likely off to a new hell."

Isabella eyed Rosa and put a finger to her lips. She pointed to the girl's damp clothing. "No stones," she whispered.

Rosa looked puzzled.

"Had she meant to kill herself..."

"What?"

"She would have put stones in her pockets, or in the lining of her skirts."

Rosa nodded.

"In order to sink swiftly and not come up..."

"Sink..." Rosa's eyes widened.

"She sleeps now. We should tend to her things and decide what to do." They moved to the back of the wagon where they opened a trunk to find the girl fresh clothing.

Ophelia opened her eyes in the dimness and sat up. Silence. No more horses hooves and wagon creaking. The caravan had stopped. Rosa and Isabella slipped out. Ophelia heard low voices outside speaking incomprehensibly. I dream, perchance, she thought. Ah. Italian. Some variant, Venetian perhaps. She was good at languages, and at unexpected situations, but not at this one, awakening to an unknown reality.

By habit, she reached to her throat and felt the engraved onyx raven amulet still on its gold chain around her neck. She held it like a lifeline and ran her finger over its beak, wings, tail and felt its feathered grooves smoothed from care, but still distinct. The memories it evoked were not all welcome, but reassuring in their familiarity nonetheless.

4. SECRETS

Bernardo, sergeant of the queen's personal guard on duty that day, dismounted his horse like a sack falling from a broken shelf. He nearly lost his balance coming to attention. Barnardo cursed under his breath at Pressius, the battle scared captain, for assigning him this lumbering rouncey. The massive roan steed, with its white blaze, was more dray horse than bold charger, but chosen for its imposing dimensions rather than practicality. Standing at more than seventeen hands, his horse made the slender diminutive Barnardo look like boy playing soldier at attention, in ceremonial silvery breastplate and white-plumed helmet from which his black curls peeked.

Nevertheless, Barnardo had to admit this beat sentry duty or being a pike man doing bloody battle for the king. He missed nothing with his deceptively dreamy, eyes, green as the Venetian lagoon where he grew up.

Fortunio had been all questions, surprised, flustered, trying vainly for private moments, when the commedia troupe had first arrived at Elsinore to play for the king and queen. Barnardo looked older now than he did in their indulgent days in Venice, a touch of gray in his thick black hair. But Bernardo's subtle swagger, his rich, playful curls, the noble forehead and quick hands panged Fortunio like they had never parted.

If Barnardo felt the same, he didn't acknowledge it, except for the smallest hint of a smile.

"We gave you up for dead," Fortunio whispered to him in a private moment. "What happen...?"

"Not now!" Barnardo almost snarled it, eying for other guards in the passageway where they happened to encounter each other. "I am not the Barnardo you know." He tightened his lips, then hugged Fortunio furtively.

Fortunio stepped back and nodded.

"I will explain when the time comes, not now." Barnardo hissed and came to attention as two of the queen's servants hurried down the hallway where they stood.

That moment never came, after the stir caused by the Hamlet's "mousetrap" scene, which led to the players having to withdraw swiftly. But Bernardo, it turned out, intervened secretly to help players secure a neutral ship out of Denmark, a swift, Dutch cargo Flyut out to the North Sea and Amsterdam, where they might find passage back to Italy eventually. Barnardo also gave Fortunio a sealed letter to deliver, in secret, to someone there.

From his vantage point as a guard, rarely noticed, Barnardo had observed all that had transpired at Elsinore in the past months, most foul, heartrending and foolish: wars, the death of a king, succession, peace, rebellions, the inevitable challenge, a ghost, bloodshed, murderous intrigue.

He wrote pertinent details in periodic reports – invisibly with lemon juice or solution of vitriol. He covered the invisible writing with a normal correspondence that would not arouse suspicion, such as a commercial order, or bill of lading and would mail it to his contacts via normal post or courier.

He knew all his queen's moods. Though she always carried herself with dignity, today she had the furtive look of a wolverine pursued by hounds, evasive and dangerous as well. She had wanted to find the mad one, Ophelia.

Word was that her son had returned, secretly, from England, alive. Perhaps Ophelia had seen him. She found her. The queen and her retinue rolled up just in time to see the nymph, mad as ever, shinnied out onto the lean branch of a birch that hung out over a racing brook. Just as before, Ophelia's hair was tangled with weeds and flowers, and she was singing unintelligibly. Then, crack, splash, into the water she fell. They could see her come up and float, buoyed by her skirts, moving downstream, still singing, around a bend then out of sight.

The queen dispatched Barnardo to get her out. Too late. The girl appeared to go under as the swift waters carried her around a bend. The brook was running high this time of year and snaked rapidly into the Gudenå River emptying into Lake Nadal. The rocky banks kept him from riding his horse directly downstream after the girl. Instead, he took the winding road along the stream, and peered down through the trees at the water.

Better drowned than murdered, Barnardo muttered to himself. The mad, in their own way, can see more clearly than the sane. Better for Ophelia to throw her fate to the current than leave it in the hands of King Claudius. Evil was afoot at Elsinore. Everyone knew it even before the ghost appeared to Hamlet, before the players and his use of them to "catch the conscience of the king." Murder begets murder.

The prince had murdered Ophelia's father. He admitted nothing, but all in the queen's entourage knew that Hamlet had intended to kill his uncle, the king, not the hapless Polonius, and then been "sent to England." Betting odds among the servants, courtiers and guards were that Hamlet would not return – not alive, anyway.

And Ophelia, become an inconvenient nymph, roamed the castle corridors for days – singing brazen, accusatory verses, under cover of insanity – about the royal couple, assassination and the queen's errant son. Barnardo wondered what would be the king's order when and if he managed to "rescue" Ophelia.

Silence the maiden – who was not a maiden, he well knew – or send her away? He had seen her – and the troubled prince – growing up together, carefree, half-wild children that he watched over. He prayed that if they found Ophelia alive, the queen would not give him an order that would stain his soul and haunt his dreams evermore. He would find a way.

He traveled a ways more, lost in his thoughts. Then he spotted the player troupe's wagons around another curve and reined his horse to a stop behind a stand of willows. From there he saw Fortunio and Carlo dragging a bedraggled Ophelia up the river bank to their caravan, then, with the help of the women, taken her inside.

Barnardo then rode up to them. "Hail!"

"Ah, just the man..." Carlo began.

Barnardo held up a hand. "You haven't by chance seen a young woman...?" He stressed the "haven't" and shook his head subtly.

Carlo frowned.

Fortunio came up beside Carlo and looked, cow-eyed, still soaking wet, still holding Ophelia's soggy cape.

"We meet again, sir player. What was your name?" Barnardo continued his charade of never having seen Fortunio before the players appeared at Elsinore. Fortunio glared at him.

"Fortunio," said Carlo.

"Yes. Fortunio. The villagers, I hear, much enjoyed your playing the coquette, Zerlina, who tricks the old pedant in your play, then reveals he is a boy."

"The girl.... the maid Ophelia..." Carlo tried to steer the conversation back.

"Ah! There has been an unfortunate accident. I am sorry to say, she is lost. There will be great mourning, poor lass." Barnardo squinted, his wide mouth curved downwards. He lowered his pike at Fortunio, as if preparing for a joust. "I will relieve you of that cape, sir."

Fortunio stepped forward and draped it over the end of the pike. He started to point back to the wagon. "She is..."

"Thank you. That will be all. I will bring this memento back to the queen." He gestured back up the road with his free hand, then he raised the pike enough to let the cape slide into his reach. "It will serve as her remains to be buried with our prayers."

"I don't understand..." Fortunio found his voice, still hoarse though it was, from his dive.

"Our dear departed Ophelia was best gone from this place and all mortal dangers. Those who incur the wrath of a king, as she has, even in innocence, should stay in the shadows..."

"Like ourselves?" Carlo raised his eyebrows and pulled Fortunio back with one hand.

"The queen should not know of you on this road, my friends." Barnardo draped the cape over the horn of his saddle. "... nor that I have helped you arrange passage... That would be, shall we say, awkward..."

Fortunio half smiled, then nodded. "My Bernardo, we owe you. Thank you. "

"Be gone! Make haste for your ship, all of you – and your newest 'player' too ... a milk maid, I presume?"

"A milk maid, yes." Carlo half bowed, smirking, then walked back to the wagon with Fortunio and climbed up onto the driver's seat to take the reins.

"Safe journey." Barnardo waved and turned his horse back towards where he had left the queen's carriage. The players' caravan creaked as its horses strained ane got it rolling again, down the road in the opposite direction away from trouble, each occupant prayed.

5. GERTRUDE'S EYES

Barnardo breathed relief to see the queen's carriage where he had left it on the castle road on a rise overlooking a forest dell cut through by the stream. The carriage was stood, a fairytale image in the mist, its driver dozing on the high bench seat up front while a footman stood by, and guards on horseback, looking bored. Now he was close enough to see the horses' blowing hot vapor into the chill mist. On pleasanter days, the dell would be a place where the ladies of the court gossiped, played croquet, gathered flowers and let the children play while the men hunted – not where maidens drowned their sorrows.

He folded Ophelia's damp cape neatly into a rectangle and tucked it under one arm, snug against his black leather, chain mail reinforced doublet. He dismounted and knelt on one knee, awaiting her majesty's further instructions, stoic to the drizzle.

Her carriage stood out in its gray surroundings on this wooded road. It was a rolling work of art – a gift of King Claudius – with lacquered white, gold-leafed doors and panels painted with bucolic scenes and angels, slung like a cradle on leaf springs between high, red spoked wheels, liveried driver perched on his seat up front, pulled by a team of white horses. Barnardo could see the queen faintly through its window, keeping him waiting.

Inside, her majesty turned to Gilda, her confidante and lady in waiting, who, sat beside her. Gertrude gave a breathy laugh at the sight of her always polished guardsman with his shin armor in the mud.

"...a welcome moment of mirth in a day that has undone me, Gilda, as has each one before it." Her voice shifted from the publicly regal, to tearful tones, confiding in Gilda, dutifully by her side in the velvet, semi-darkness of the carriage.

41

Silently, Gilda let the queen's now familiar laments rush over her and then spill into the usual recriminations and self-pity.

"Better the fair Ophelia be swept from this madness in her grief, than wither in this place. My son cares nothing for her, now. Prince Hamlet has broken her heart, just as he has cleft that of his mother in twain."

Gilda shook her head. "Oh, the Lord Hamlet *does* love your majesty. Only his madness speaks words so harsh."

"It is our fate as woman to die to our innocence and youth as we grow old."

"You are far from old, my queen."

"We cling to our branches, but in the end fall – or let go – to cold deep – that or the nunnery, for poor lass."

Queen Gertrude broke into keening. "This is but one more consequence of my son's madness, his father's ire and my king's deceit all come to roost."

She recovered her composure then, and finally tapped the coach window for the footman to open its door. She had to stifle a laugh at the sight of the faithful Bernardo, swaying in the drizzle, his knee making a small cavity in the gravelly mud.

At last, she bid him to rise. "What news have you, Bernardo?"

"No sight of the fair maiden, your majesty."

"How far have you searched along this unfortunate brook?"

"Very far and very thoroughly, Ma'am." Barnardo pointed downstream. "Downstream to where it flows into the river."

"What have you there under your arm?"

"A cape, your majesty, that I believe belonged to the fair maid Ophelia. I found it on a dead branch in the water near the bank." He unfurled and showed it front and back.

"Let me see." She leaned for a closer look after signaling him to move forward.

Barnardo gingerly untangled strands of blond hair from the fur collar and showed them too her.

"Yes," she gasped. "Those would seem to be Ophelia's golden tresses." The queen looked away and shivered in the chill, suddenly anxious to be done with this. "Such woe."

"Daylight fades quickly now, your majesty, as does our hope of finding her..."

"...remains. You may say what you think, dear Bernardo..." The queen nodded to her footman to take the cape. "We shall take it back to Elsinore, for what memorial we can arrange."

"I am very sorry. It would seem the maid is lost."

"You may resume your position now, Bernardo."

"Yes, ma'am." Barnardo bowed instead of genuflecting this time. His face flushed, as if he were new to court ceremony.

Out of his peripheral vision – which he had sharpened for such situations – Barnardo examined his distressed monarch for signs of her next move. "Do you wish to return to Elsinore now, your majesty?"

"Yes. Before night falls." She signaled the footman to close her door, then muttered to Gilda. "... gone, then, she can bring no more grief upon herself and us."

"Beg pardon, Ma'am?"

She shook her head and waved one of her gold-embroidered pomegranate silken kerchiefs at her mock knight. "Home to our sorry castle, then. This brook overflows our tears."

Her footman shut the queen's door. He placed Ophelia's folded cape ceremoniously into the boot, then climbed onto the carriage running board. The driver snapped the reins and whistled the horses alert. The carriage lurched ahead.

Inside, the queen wept again to her consoling Gilda. The queen drew a deep breath, tearful, but recovering as the carriage resumed its familiar sway. "Oh, Gilda, this is my doing as much as my king's or that of my son. I am sick of heart."

"How unjustly you berate yourself, my queen."

"I cannot shed the burden, my Gilda. Only you can see my suffering."

Gilda took the queen's hand. "I know you grieve, but it will all be for the best, my queen."

"Wretched. What have we done? Her brother now, will seek vengeance, surely against my son, or the king."

Gilda handed the queen a fresh kerchief.

"These castle walls burst with secrets. And Ophelia carried one secret too many, I believe."

"My queen?"

"Better that her secret die with her, or be born elsewhere, away from this cursed place."

Gilda, squeezed her queen's hand and nodded in compliance. "And the players? The king seeks to bring them to account about their disrespectful play..."

"Let us hope, for their sake, they are well away by now."

"What can we say of Ophelia, my lady?"

"We will relate her watery end as a tragic misadventure, nothing more."

"Not a suicide?" With right of sacred burial then?"

"The pastor from the village will fuss and sputter, but can be trusted to comply."

"The good reverend – that Italian convert, Beppo? He is in your majesty's debt."

"... I will order the fair Ophelia's coffin sealed, in memoriam, and that nothing more be said of its contents – empty but for a few stones and poor Ophelia's sodden cloak ... her only remains.." The queen sat straighter now, drying her tears, regaining her regal composure.

"But what of Prince Hamlet, your majesty? Will his heart be broken?"

"He cared no more for the poor child in his own madness. Let us hope this will revive his compassion and let him bury his rage with Ophelia's coffin."

"When he returns from England, your majesty?"

The queen stiffened. "*If* he returns."

The carriage rumbled on cobble stones now as they approached the castle. She could hear Barnardo call out to the sentries, the old, oaken gates cranking open. The queen shuddered as the carriage wheels rumbled over the wooden drawbridge and into the castle grounds.

She spoke in low tones. "I am filled with foreboding, my Gilda. Last night I dreamed I rode in a carriage draped in black. I rose from my coffin, a ghost. I looked out the back window and saw a line of funeral carriages carrying my son and my husband, demons whipping the horses forward. I tried to jump from the carriage and flee, but the rough hands of King Hamlet, his face deathly, pushed me down into my coffin."

Dutch shipyards built hundreds of sailing ships like these for war and commerce during the 16th century.

6. OPHELIA'S CROSSING

Merciful seas allowed us on deck to take the air this morning after three bilious, storm lashed days below. I lean, hands to the rail like an old salt, steady on my sea legs at last. For the moment, I am no more the mad mournful maiden strewing flowers in distress – or in any dress, for that matter. I am one with the ship's motherly pitch, roll and yaw, attuned to her fluttering sails, to riggers' shanties and waves slapping her bottom.

The iodine mist evokes the summer palace on the Wadden Sea where the queen would take the prince, my brother and I, as children, to be safe from war and plague – joyful memories for us. No princes aboard here, only leathery seamen and wan passengers.

I can't tell – and care little – if we sail heaven or hell-bent, only that it smells of the salted herring I am sick of eating, when I can eat at all. I dare not take a bite or even think upon food this morning, lest my stomach remember violently again that I am at sea, and likely carrying a little passenger.

The only way to survive this journey, I have decided, is to say little and listen at lot. I thank the gods now for how Maritius, the royal tutor, who drilled me in Latin, French, English and German and guided me to so many books that a young girl was not supposed to be reading. I was a child of the royal court, and the tutor could not refuse the boy Hamlet's requests that I keep him company during the long hours of classical instruction. My father would have objected, if he had known. Most of it seemed frivolous to me then, but knowledge provides me rafts on which to float in heavy seas. I have little problem understanding the various Italian vernaculars that these players speak amongst themselves, thinking I do not understand.

47

They say, we make for Amsterdam, then Haarlem with a load of Swedish timber for the Dutch shipyards. Our good fortune was that this required sailing through the Øresund strait between the Baltic and North Seas and docking briefly to pay the Danish toll just when we showed up on the run.

I am relieved that the crewmen have taken scant notice of me in the squire's attire that Isabella provided from the costume trunk. As a precaution, I am listed on the ship's manifest as "Oliver Chenoit," a player with the troupe. These players seem to change roles – and gender – as casually off stage as they do on stage in their farces filled with mistaken identities and one sex posing as the other.

They say we could be at sea another week because of the storm. "God willing," the sailors add, stoic Dutch rebels, Scotsmen and French Huguenots. Best to savor the game. In my condition, I will not be able to maintain this charade for very long.

The morning fog thins, and a warship – four masted, square rigged, bristling with cannons, coming up by us. I look about for the captain. Why does no one shout sail ho or something? Pirates? The Spanish?

The freckled cabin boy who empties our slop bucks happens by, and as if reading my thoughts says, "Our privateers, sir."

My stomach knots up. "Then... whose? Will they...?" I'm expecting to hear shots, perhaps cannon fire, a boarding party, capture. But by whom. Ottoman Turks? Will I be discovered and sold as a slave?"

"Our escort, sir." He points at the flag fluttered from the main mast, a coat of arms in orange against white, with blue trim. The boy speaks in quirky German that I can barely understand, but I get that he is an orphan from Bremen.

"Sea Beggars, sir."

I remember the talk about them at Elsinore: The infamous Dutch raiders, have captured nearly every port along the Flanders coast, almost shutting out the mighty Spanish.

"Thank you. What do they call you, boy. I was too sick to ask before. "

He stifles a grin. "Jacob."

"I am Oliver."

"Yes sir, Lord Oliver." He gave me a mock salute.

Jacob can't be more than eight years old. He is on his way from the galley with a jug of grog for the night crew just turning in. He offers me a cup of it. I decline, but I ask him about the ship – more than I would have of a crewman or officer who might have questions of his own.

I know I am in another world when I discover that this muscular, three-masted cargo vessel, is one of five owned by a woman – a lumber merchant, Kenau Simonsdochter Hasselaer, called the heroine of Haarlem during the Spanish siege. Jacob gleefully, tells – and demonstrates – what has become an immediate folk legend. Mothers told their children of how Kenau was supposed to have stood on the battlements, braving musket fire. From there, leading a squad of Amazon farm women, she was said to have rained thousands flaming, pitch-coated wicker wreathes down upon the Spanish besiegers with pitchforks – a St. Margret sending devils back to hell.

Jacob withdrew with a bow. Now I have even more questions for Isabella. I need to press her, on their plans, if any. If they plan to cross into France, I am hoping they can take me from there south to Burgundy and Lyon, where I may find my mother's family.

I don't relish returning to the cramped cabin space allotted to us on this cargo ship. Carlo continues to complain about how much the sturdy Dutch captain of this three-masted fluyt is charging us for safe passage.

"... And every time I fart, he puts it on the bill." I know that privately, Carlo's complaints include me, though he is gentleman enough – despite his bawdiness – not to say so in my presence.

Isabella listens and goes about her work, sewing costumes and maintaining what props remain, for they had to leave all but one wagon and were allowed to take only two of the horses aboard. "This adventure was your idea. Remember, Carlo?"

"We're spending every penny those tightwads Norwegians and Danes threw at us."

"Just pray we arrive with our skins, my darling husband."

Today, without my asking, Isabella provided me with pen, ink and paper. There is a small table in the wagon lashed below decks where I can take a lantern in order to write in privacy. I cannot bear yet to write of the prince, my slain father and what is rotten in the state of Denmark, only poems and the dreams I have been having.

…Laertes toddles in baby breeches, giggling, his bony, rascally little frame, dripping across the marble floor of a palace room that I do not recognize.

Our mother – reanimated, ghostly white – runs after him – a ritual game of tag. I am running now with my brother down a spiral stone stairway and across a castle moat. We are on horses, children now, no longer babies, and the prince is with us, all in white, his blond hair long and flowing the way it did when he was 10. We ride through a moaning forest and dismount in misty clearing. It is a cemetery.

My brother holds my hand. I see a ruined temple, or church and suddenly we stand before my mother's fresh grave. Hamlet stands on a rise by the ruins. He is older now.

He draws a broadsword and cuts off our father's head. Laertes cries. I tell father to get up and put his head back on. Hamlet exhorts me about murders and sins and nunneries and death. I rise and try to run, but am rooted, my arms sprouting into daisies.

Is this *"the undiscover'd country from whose bourn no traveler returns?"* I can make little sense of these dreams, except that they seem so real. Are these merry actors – angels, demons, wise men, fools or knaves? Am I mad still?

"We can use a good madwomen in our plays." Isabella told me when my senses had returned enough to consider my situation. She, not Carlo, writes most of the troupe original plays. If I wrote a play I might cast her as the mother I wish for so often as a child after my own died.

Nymph, in thy orisons be all my sins remembered, lord Hamlet said to me out of his own madness. Thy sins I do remember, thy deeds most bloody, my fickle prince. But I have no prayers for you. The dead say no prayers.

Isabella helped me cut my hair. I saw myself in Isabella's glass and I like how my hair looks, short, with bangs, boyish and unburdened. A novice nun's cut, but I am no nun. And maiden no longer. I could be a lad, with fire, but for my circumstance.

By Umberto Tosi

PART TWO

By Umberto Tosi

7. OLIVER AND OLIVIA

It took a while to get their land legs and the rocking of the wagon on the road south from Amsterdam didn't help. The captain of the carrack that had brought them to Holland from Denmark told them he could take them no farther.

A big-faced man, weathered, beamed through a bushy beard with broken teeth. He waved a scrolled contract from the Dutch West India Company and explained that he would be carrying copper, textiles and muskets to West African slavers to trade for African slaves he would take across the Middle Passage for Dutch Aruba and Curaçao plantation owners, and from there, back home loaded with sugar and molasses.

"A fortune to be made! We can transport five hundred of them – males, females and their young – in a big ship like this." He spread his arms wide.

Oliver shuddered, thinking of the time they had just spent, bilious, below decks on their recent voyage. "But what of?... An abomination ... and ... slavery..."

The captain snarled. "Read your bible, sinner. Leviticus 25:44-46 says we may buy men and women as slaves from the nations around us...Commerce, my boy, commerce for the elect, as God chooses, my boy."

Oliver looked down at the deck planking feeling seasick again. The captain turned back to Carlo. "Good luck, in your travels" he told them.

They could find no passage to anywhere in the Mediterranean from Amsterdam, much less to Venice.

The war between the Spanish Habsburg Empire and Dutch rebels had spread. Plus, the undeclared conflict between Spain and Queen Elizabeth's England made passage through the North Sea, the English Channel and the Atlantic coast even more perilous than normally with its wild winds, choppy seas and pirates.

Isabella and Carlo opted to continue overland, playing in various towns, towards Lyon, Paris and eventually, farther south towards Italy.

But for Fortunio taking the wrong road, they would have played in Utrecht that day, and avoided disaster, perhaps even have been allowed to continue towards France on this fine October day. It was his turn in the coachman's seat, driving the horse with "Oliver" next to him. Inside the theater wagon, Isabella and Carlo took inventory of what remained of their props and continued to bicker.

"Her condition becomes more obvious each day." Carlo groused offhand. "We will be found out before we can get to Lyon." He moved closer to Isabella, pulled her to him, and tried to kiss her.

She pushed him back. "Enjoy your whores, Carlo."

"Sticking to girls, eh?"

He pressed on again.

She pushed him back and he lost his balance with the swaying of the wagon and landed on the floor by her makeup table.

"I have written a character for her, as 'Olivia,' a princess who disguises herself as a lad to find her husband who she thinks has been abducted by pirates, but is instead in love with a servant girl, who is really a boy hiding from enemies. She can play both the Olivia and the servant girl who turns out to be 'Oliver' the long lost brother of our heroine."

Carlo laughed. "But can she play the roles without stumbling?"

"Our Ophelia has a natural talent."

"...for eating our bread?"

"She helps me with my costume changes."

"Changeable as the wind, like all women, but worse." Carlo got up and sat by the table.

"She has more wisdom than her years, Carlo. You could not have held together through what she as seen."

"An unruly woman!"

"Do you mean me or her?"

"Both!"

"She makes a fine, convincing young man you have to admit, with her courtly manners, her height and classic features."

"It will be better for us when we are done with both!"

"You just want her Carlo, admit it."

"She has brought us nothing but grief."

"Don't forget, Carlo, that is was our 'Oliver' who talked that fanatical Calvinist sheriff out of arresting us as Spanish spies in Haarlem, while you were peeing your pants."

"Well, there is no need for her to disguise herself anymore. We are far from King Claudius' grasp." News had reached Amsterdam, where they had played last, about bloody happenings at Elsinore – the Danish king, queen, the prince and Ophelia's brother felled at once in a murderous fugue.

"We need to tell her, Carlo."

"She will go mad again, hearing of her brother's bloody end, and that of Hamlet."

"I'm going to tell her next place we stop."

"I thought you said we need her." Four of I Comici had defected to another troupe in Amsterdam after their Danish fiasco – the loss of half their equipment and most of their money spent for emergency passage.

"The girl has suffered deceit enough, Carlo."

"Ours is the art of deception, my Isabella."

They heard clattering and shouting outside, and Fortunio reining in the horses. Isabella and Carlo came out of the wagon. "What is happening? " Carlo shouted up at Fortunio, then looked ahead of them on the road.

A squad of armed irregulars on horseback blocked the way. The leader, a muscular, squat dark bearded man with a plumed helmet pointed a brass wheel-lock pistol at them.

"Sirs, please." Carlo started to address him.

He wagged the pistol. "Silence." He looked at his companions. "This one sounds Italian."

"Another cursed Habsburg agent, no doubt sir."

"Probably scouting."

"Sir, with your permission, we are but humble players." Carlo bowed and gestured towards the sign on the side of their wagon.

"You shall play the gibbet soon..." The leader snorted.

Ophelia, still outfitted as Oliver, spoke from the coachman's seat, in Danish, slowly enough and with gestures for the Dutchmen to follow her. "Sir! Please. We are players from the royal court of Denmark, come in friendship to your cause."

"You are on a States General road, forbidden to commercial traffic until further notice."

Oliver switched into a passable Low Country German. We come to lift spirits of your embattled people in our humble way, from town to town."

The leader sized Oliver up, then conferred with his cohorts in low tones that the players could not understand. Then the leader holstered his pistol and waved a hand. "Follow me, then. We will take you Burghermaster Adriaanszoon van der Werf."

Carlo looked over his shoulder as two of the squad brought their horse around behind the wagon so as to box it in. "Are we under arrest, then."

"Quiet, Carlo," Isabella hissed.

The squad leader grimaced and nodded for Carlo and Isabella to get back into the wagon. Then he turned his horse around and waved a hand forward for the procession to start. Fortunio flipped the traces and got the wagon rolling.

When they got inside Isabella stood in Carlo's way and pushed him back to a chair. "You see, Carlo, she is one of us, our Ophelia – our Oliver, our Olivia – a natural, as resourceful as you or I. We must do right by her."

They reached Leiden by sundown, more tired from traveling than fearful. In the remaining light, they could see star-shaped battlements as they passed through the city gates, over the Old Rhine, and entered a picturesque town of decorated facades, canals and bridges. To their surprise, the mayor welcomed them warmly and offered comfortable accommodations at his inn next to the town hall.

"Your show will provide our townspeople welcome diversion from the fear, as we await the Spanish to attack."

"Attack?" Carlo glanced out a window at the wagon in front of the inn, calculating how long it would take to get out of town.

"Do not worry, we are well prepared for the enemy. We had strengthened our outer walls in the *Trace Italienne* manner." Carlo knew that he referred to a ring of massive star-shaped bastions, which effectively kept enemy cannons at bay, conceived by Niccolo Machiavelli and now the standard for walled cities. "And the Iron Duke's men will drown trying to dig tunnels in our silted soil while we rain hell upon them." His eyes glinted with the hatred of the Spanish oppressors Carlo encountered everywhere upon returning to Flanders after many years.

"Your honor, we would not want to get in the way of your military preparations." Carlo smiled.

"Nonsense! We will repulse their siege in short order if they dare come. You will stay for October festival!

"I don't know..." Carlo cleared his throat.

"Nothing to fear! The Spanish are walking into a trap. William the Silent and the States General army will attack from the north as soon as we've pinned down the Spaniards.

Isabella curtsied. "In that case, we are most thankful, but we will not impose on your hospitality for long.. "

"You will stay the week and enjoy our harvest festival. We are amply supplied with fine beers and victuals of all sorts."

"Nothing like a siege to whet the appetite," Carlo smirked, looking green. They had all heard of the Habsburg Edict of Blood – endorsed by the pope, actively enforced by the Spanish Habsburg King Phillip II's authorities – condemning all heretics to death en masse – meaning most of the Dutch and north German populace.

"Fernando Alvarez de Toledo – the cursed Iron Duke – will break his shaft against our walls. You will be safe with our city, my fair players." The mayor kissed Isabella's hand.

Carlo whispered to Rosa, standing nearby, "If this William – the so-called Silent – ever shows up."

Rosa muttered back: "They the say Duke had six thousand townspeople – every man, woman and child – put to death at Naarden for resisting."

The mayor gestured to a clerk. "He will show you your rooms."

"This is a trap alright." Carlo and others followed the clerk, a spindly man with kind eyes, up a narrow staircase to two modest rooms the troupe was allotted.

After refreshing themselves and changing clothes, the troupe came down to a dining hall where they were greeted by the mayor, members of the town council and their wives and seated at a long table. Armed guards stood at the doorways.

They noticed, but avoided eye contact with an imposing gentleman seated next to the mayor, at the head of the table. The gentleman attended every word as he sat regally erect, in black with a wide white collar, in the Calvinist fashion, and a yellow silk sash he wore with ease, affecting at once, austere simplicity, wealth and high station.

Servants brought beer and food – hearty Dutch fare, beef and carrot stew, pork sausages, breaded fried eel, honeyed herring, and dark bread.

"You must tell us about Denmark." The mayor leaned towards Oliver. "What are we to make of this tragic news?"

"Tragic...?" Oliver's voice remained calmly boyish, but Isabella detected tremolo.

The man in black spoke. "We are hoping you players can clear things up." His short, pointed reddish beard and mustache contrasted to pale rose skin and gave him the comic look of The Captain character in their farces – as did his voice, which was nasal and high pitched. His eyes, however, dark, small and sharp as a jay's, missed nothing. "...if you please."

The mayor half stood. "This is Jules van Orange-Nassau, he is …"

"No need for the honorariums," pointy beard interjected.

Carlo nudged Isabella. She nodded. "Mind your words," she whispered to "Oliver," seated next to her.

Pointy beard looked at the mayor. "Perhaps our guests have not been fully informed."

The mayor looked at him quizzically, then turned to Oliver. "Why... the slaughter. Your king, the queen, Prince Hamlet, their chamberlain, they say, and his son Laertes..."

Isabella felt Ophelia tense, saw her jaw tighten, fists clench onto the chair under the table. "Dear brother … the fool," Ophelia muttered in a low voice that reinforced her male disguise.

Jules of pointy beard looked to Oliver. "Your brother?"

The mayor cocked his head, but went on: "None were spared, not even a maiden betrothed to the prince – all dead, murdered the same day."

Oliver seemed to disappear into her Ophelia persona somewhere deep inside. Isabella, Carlo, Rosa and Fortunio sat dumbfounded. The mayor went on to relate several versions of the Elsinore tragedy that had been conveyed thus far by courier, merchants and pigeon. Laertes had murdered the royal family to avenge his father. Hamlet had murdered everyone to avenge his father, the king had everyone put to death, but was poisoned himself. Fortinbras, the new king, had taken over by assassination.

A silence fell over the dining room. Oliver stared down at the table, breathing slowly, then looked up. "Not betrothed."

"What?"

"The maiden." She bit into the word. "She was the daughter – and she was not betrothed."

"Of the king?"

"No – the chamberlain's daughter, and she never betrothed herself to Prince Hamlet."

Pointy beard interjected. "The gentleman doth protest much. Was this maiden your betrothed? I pray not."

Oliver ignored the barb. "... and she was not murdered by anyone, except by grief. She drowned in a brook. They say she fell, but I say she leapt."

"Ah... terribly sad... " The mayor frowned, and considered this... "But the king... what of... ?

"... to freedom... I would hope ... Rosemary is for remembrance, violets for thoughts, and rue... there is much to rue..." Oliver recited in a flat voice, blinked back tears, trembled, but held steady in her chair.

"Freedom, yes." Pointy beard raised his beer mug. "Freedom from Spain, from Phillip's evil rule!" The rest followed except for the guests.

The mayor looked at them waiting. Finally they raised their drinks. "Freedom," they toasted with everyone. Then silence.

Isabella took focus. "We are still sorting this terrible news, your honor and do not have the full story ourselves."

Count Jules squinted at her. "We need to know one thing, madam. Will the new Danish king stand with us. Will our ships still be allowed passage through the strait?"

Ophelia recovered her Oliver voice: "Norwegian."

"What?"

"Fortinbras. He is a Norwegian prince who long coveted Elsinore, and now apparently has it in his grasp."

The mayor nodded. "We know. In fact, we have it that Fortinbras laid siege to the castle and killed all within."

Two servants came with more flagons of beer.

After a while, Carlo raised a toast to the mayor and Leiden. Afterward they had imbibed, he announced that i Comici would stage one of its best shows – a classic Venetian comedy of the sexes by Ruzante, which Isabella had translated into the German vernacular. Everyone applauded except for pointy beard. He continued to stare intently at the players.

"We must, regrettably, leave your fair city immediately after that, however, for we have engagements elsewhere."

Pointed beard kept smiling, but shook his head. "I'm afraid not, sir."

The mayor shrugged. "An unfortunate inconvenience... We are under military command of the House of Orange now," he nodded towards pointy beard. "The count, a cousin of William, has brought reinforcements and supplies."

Carlo started to object.

Count Jules smiled. "We trust you … Carlo, ... that is your name? … But Spanish patrols are everywhere, and attack is imminent."

As if on cue, they heard booming outside – beginning with a few at random, then steady drumbeats."

"Ah," count pointy beard stood up. "It has begun. You will excuse me ladies and gentleman." With that he exited the dining hall followed by the mayor, the council members and the guards, then the wives.

Isabella, "Oliver," Carlo, Fortunio and Rosa sat in silence for a time.

Oliver began to shake violently. "... wretched fools," she cried.

Isabella embraced Ophelia. "I am sorry. So sorry...."

"First water, now fire. I am condemned to die again and again."

8. THE SPANISH GAROTTE

Isabella scripted the ruse for us. I improvised from there – all of it a necessary madness that displaced my own disintegration. Looking back, I don't know what I would have done if Isabella had not called me out of my brooding over this new horror from Elsinore.

I had a reason to live now – arising from my belly. My body felt queasy, with a will of its own, impatient with grief, restless as an insomniac. I needed diversion from the black pit of helplessness, a new role in this play - and Isabella provided it. We would not get to Lyon anytime soon. We would have to be lucky to survive Leiden.

And I didn't know if my Aunt Clara and the haughty French nobleman whom she had married would accept me – with my child – even if we ever got to Lyon. From the letters I found in my mother's trunk, I knew the husband for a martinet, full of himself with little love for family. Convention dictates that I seek the protection of "my family" – a woman with child, out in the world. And there is always that nunnery.

In truth, Isabella, Carlo, Rosa and Fortunio had become my family, a clan of riotous women and raucous men like I had sinfully imagined but never known.

It turned out to also be a family in great peril at the moment, with no time for conventional niceties. If the monstrous Habsburg legions breaches the city's walls – no matter the mayor's boasts – we could in all likelihood face the torture, trial and punishment meted out to rebels, heretics and assorted sinners under Catholic canon and Habsburg law.

No matter that my friends were Venetian and I am a Dane, the punishments were all the same - the stake, hanging for men - and the stake or the garrote for the women.

We have only our guile and our props to deploy. Isabella gave me two roles – nothing unusual in popular comedies.

I am familiar with these arts. I have read and seen countless plays while growing up, and my father was Thespian during his university days, once played Julius Caesar. I remember, with a chill, that he often made light of being "stabbed by Brutus," little knowing that he would die by Hamlet's sword himself.

But the plays must go on – as must I in this new life. I play many roles, masculine and feminine. I'm often the young squire, Oliver, and then, his twin sister, Olivia.

Of course, as my belly grows big, I will play Olivia more – although Isabella has provided a loose-fitting tunic to hide my conditions as long as possible.

I play "Olivia" – a character Isabella gave, tongue-in-cheek, the same name as my present alter ego. In the first act, my Olivia character, fleeing an oppressive father who intends to put her in a cloister – disguises herself as a young man named "Oliver." Young "Oliver" befriends a nobleman, Antonio – played by Fortunio – becomes his valet, and secretly falls in love with him. Second act: Enter "Olivia's twin brother," the "real" Oliver – played, again, by me, but of course, lonely when my Olivia character is conveniently offstage. The twin brother has been lost at sea, and presumed dead. Third act: The Oliver character falls in love with Antonio's sister. The father of Olivia arrives at Antonio's house as a guest. Pandemonium follows.

Isabella said I was a natural at comedy, and at switching. She taught me all the best commedia dell'arte "Zanni" – classic pranks of physical comedy and masked hilarity – and coached me to perfection on the moves and voice changes required for changing genders and characters swiftly as the wind can change directions. She reminded me often of the line spoken by the valiant heroine of Moderata Fonte's *Risamante* – one of her favorites and whose lead I played, my first starring role – "It is custom and not nature that relegates timorousness to one sex and valor to the other." In all these turns, I found aspects of myself that I had never known.

But all of this, I realized, was no more than a reality we created for our audiences while on stage. We had been performing, by now, every evening in the warehouse near the town center that the mayor arranged for us to convert to a theater. I would feel better if I didn't know that there are kegs of gunpowder stored there among the other supplies. But this is war.

Pointy beard and the mayor suspect nothing. They commend us raising their citizens' spirits and will to fight. Which is good, but also bad, because now they would not release us even if the Spanish would allow us passage, and that's highly debatable. I wonder how long this besieged city can hold out if the Orange relief column fails to counter attack and food runs out.

I can't drop the charade now. Isabella is right. If they found out that I am not who I say, they will jump to the wrong conclusions and hang me for a spy before I can explain. So, for now, the game continues. The people applaud and shout and do not know that the real masquerading happens more off stage than on.

It is one thing to play a man – or a woman playing a man – on stage, and another to practice sexual inversion in every day life. Even with the dangers, I take pleasure in the easy leeway of being a young man – such freedom as I had not experienced since my childhood adventures at the summer palace, running with Hamlet, my brother, Rosencranz and Guildenstern.

Isabella established the story the very next day after our arrival. "Our young man, Oliver has a sister who travels with us," she told the mayor's wife that morning. "Olivia. But she was ill and stayed in our wagon last night – you understand, morning sickness, that as a mother well knows, can continue morning noon and night." Telling the mayor's wife assured that our story would circulate and become accepted as fact quickly.

"Oh. How far along?" The mayor's wife took the bait.

"Only a few months, possibly three."

That would be my cue to enter – demure in skirt, braided blond wig and bonnet to cover my cropped hair. It amused me that I felt myself such a fraud in my girl's get up, and not as a Oliver, though all the while conscious of the deep sea of my womanliness.

"Ah! Here is our Olivia." Isabella put out a arm to me. "Feeling better this morning, my dear?" She looked aside at our guest and whispered "She's had a time of it with the morning malaise." Isabella turned back to me. "This is the mayor's wife, Christine."

I curtsied.

The mayor's wife put out a hand, and I wondered if she was so pretentious as to expect me to kneel and kiss it. I took two of her fingers and milked them gently, smirking with a slight curtsy again.

In real life, Isabella conscripted Fortunio to play my husband – all very neat. I clung to his strong arm and kissed him liberally until he strained to stifle his laughter.

We thought that we would only have to carry on this masquerade a week or two until the William and his army rode to our rescue. But weeks turned into months the mood of the city had changed. Our audiences grew sparser and rations smaller.

The rosy Dutch faces of harvest time when the siege began set into cold winter granite that did not melt when spring arrived empty handed. The mayor tried to exhort increasingly sullen gatherings in the town square, and squabbled almost daily with his council. He tried to put a hopeful face on matters,

I knew otherwise. Frequently, I climbed to the roof of our inn where I could watch the carrier pigeon coup atop the town hall. I could see the grimness with which the mayor's officials unrolled and read incoming messages.

Though assured that they were in vain, the thunderous booming of Spanish bombardments, which could come anytime of the night or day never failed to put people on edge.

We welcomed the rains, then the snows of winter that silenced the invaders for long stretches, but failed to drive them away. As a child I would eavesdrop on my father in his councils with the king. I did the same now with the mayor's aides. I could have been hanged for spying, even though only for ourselves. I reported all I knew to Isabella, so we might plan an escape.

Fortunio went further. He dressed up as a watchman on night patrol to discover hoarders, then collected a "tax" consisting of what foodstuffs they could offer him, then disappearing.

Rations dwindled. The mayor had allotted a half pound of meat and bread per person, then it became per family, then it simply became a joke, as malt cakes were passed around, each taking a bite – and their "meat" rations because whatever vermin one could catch, skin and roast.

People thinned and sickened. Fortunio paddled around the city's canals in a skiff he found behind a house where all the inhabitants died of plague. He got to know every rivulet and bend, and would take me out in it to catch eels under the bridges to keep us all alive. Neither of us found a way for our troupe to escape even if we had wanted to take our chances with the Iron Duke.

The Spanish army – a collection of bloodthirsty mercenaries from Italy, Austria, Ireland and Catholic Germans and Englishmen, as well as conscripted Spanish peasants – continued their bombardments, none of which breached the town's massive walls. They sent squads and whole tercios against the battlements and gates over and over, met by deadly fire and musket and cannon volleys from above. Their bodies rotted at the watery base of the walls sending up vile odors for days before the Spanish could retrieve them.

I befriended Pieter, a nice enough Hollander, who had been a dairy farmer, and now was one of the quartermasters who drives a food wagon along the walls daily for the defenders. He let me ride with him on his rounds, where I learned of the men's vicissitudes first hand – so different from battles described in histories and romances I had read.

We talked a lot about his life – little about mine, though he was curious. He was highly regarded for actually having been a solider for the States General – a patriot, not in it just for the good pay, as many farm boys had been on both sides.

Defenders and townspeople gave him deference that led me to guess he possessed greater rank than his modest dress and easy ways would lead one to believe.

He was a handsome lad in a rough sort of way. He walked with authority despite his labored limp. I could imagine myself a milkmaid, marrying such a boy in buttery bliss – the first such stirrings I felt in a long time, as ludicrous as was my fantasy.

He told me he had joined the rebels at the beginning of the revolt and fought in several skirmishes inland well preceding the siege. He said he would be with his brigade still, but for his wounds. I imagined about running my finger along his scar from a Spanish musket shot through a shoulder, and another scar from a Neapolitan mercenary's pike down his right leg, the wound that made him limp along like a sailboat tacking to port in rough seas.

The battlements and terrain kept enemy cannons out of range. The Spanish occupied two forts with a mile of the city walls, one being the Duke's headquarters – again out of mutual range. Still, Spanish musketeers got close enough to fire volleys at those on the wall from time to time, often to cover raiding parties.

The proximity of battle made me heady and at the same time melancholy, but not frightened. Feeling the wind and smelling the gunpowder along the battlement conjured my childhood fantasies of Freya, although this was not game. There was real blood and the stink of fear and death in the air that my brother Laertes and my prince, Hamlet never experienced when they played soldiers out in the wooded palace grounds.

Still, I was drawn to it. I made up reasons to walk along the ramparts distributing what victuals Pieter and I could manage to bring.

I saw the faces of war – a missing eye here, a cut-off nose there, amputated fingers, hands and scars of every description. The defenders were either townspeople or from the dwindling contingent of States General mercenaries – battle hardened Scots, English and French Huguenots – all weary and wan. They livened when they recognized "Oliver" from having seen our show. Some managed whoops and cheers.

But I had to take care, as the weeks passed, even in my loose tunic, lest they discover the truth. With my height, Isabella said, I should be able to keep from showing much until near the end, if I survive it.

I met women on the battle line – assisting mostly, with suppliers – but all armed with daggers and Dutch hakebusses, hooked guns. The pretty ones and the ugly all flirted and teased at me for sport – in the first months at least before everyone turned gaunt from hunger.

One day on these rounds Pieter and I came upon a crowd gathered at the end of a star-shaped battlement looking out over a moat and a field of Spanish encampments. Some climbed up for a better view, oblivious of the risk. Pieter and I nudged closer to the edge for a better look. I wish we had never done so. A gallows had been erected in the center of the field, just out of our range.

Spanish soldiers had herded scores of people – young and old, women and men – close to it. All afternoon they sent people by tens to the gallows, hands bound, to be hanged, cut down and carted away. When the wind shifted towards us we could hear the wailing and the screams.

They put the entire population of a nearby village to death for our benefit, they said. Commander Francisco de Valdez sent Leiden a message that the mayor read aloud to the townspeople.

"People of Leiden, we have shown you our resolve. Tell your dog-eating rebels to lay down their arms and open your gates and we will show you our mercy. Otherwise face the same fate when we surely prevail, as it is the will of God."

"Will of God," Carlo repeated. "By that, that pernicious Spanish rat bane must mean all those milk-livered priests who stood by chanting pious prayers while soldiers hacked and hanged screaming children and their grandmothers."

The display and Valdez' ultimatum only stiffened the town's resistance.

Bands of townspeople came and went from the battlements and unfurled banners with blood-red letters: "NEVER!"

They shouted curses and obscenities at the enemy.

They chanted: "Butchers! We will eat every rat, cat, dog and cockroach if we must!"

Then: "We will consume our own dead, and still fight on!"

Then: "You will drown like rats fleeing Prince William's fiery orange sword!"

The time arrived all too quickly when I had to give up Oliver and be "Olivia" full time. I wondered if I would have the strength to survive what was to come. Here I was about to give birth in a city still under siege. Fortunately, in one sense, our hosts had become accustomed to "Oliver's" meandering and did not think to ask about his absence.

Then, good news! The Spanish began to withdraw. Everyone said they had lifted the siege and would all be gone soon – except for a few patrols. The mayor announced that a large rebel army under Prince William was at last marching to relieve us. The Duke of Alba pulled his troops from Leiden and sent a force under the notorious Gen. Sancho d'Avila to engage our rebels at Mookerheye.

It was already April -- my time too, and I began to feel the first pangs.

Isabella and Rosa made the wagon ready for departure as soon as the baby was born and ready for travel –- God willing that we survive, for childbirth is as perilous for a woman as battle for a man. Carlo went to the city stables were the horses had been quartered. He returned white faced. "Gone! The bastards commandeered our team."

Rosa came out of the wagon. "I could have told you that. Probably for food."

"More likely to haul cannons and supplies." Fortunio tried to smile. "We might find them."

The two marched to the mayor's office and were gone a long while before they returned, scowling. "Pointy Beard gave us no quarter. He's taking charge of supplies. Our horses now belong to the States General for the duration of hostilities."

"At least we didn't have them in our stew," Rosa shook her head. "Don't expect me to pull this wagon." She laughed.

"Could we buy a horse?" Isabella questioned. Carlo went to the square to try.

By evening this issue of horses became moot. The mayor called a town hall meeting. My contractions had subsided. Perhaps it was the distraction of the news. We walked next door to the town hall to hear the mayor, myself included despite my impending labor. The moment we arrived, everyone knew, seeing the mayor stooped figure and blanched face there on the small stage, that the news was not good.

"The Spanish have beaten our army at Mookerheyde. More than three thousand of our brave rebel soldiers have fallen, among them, two of our William's brothers – Louis and Henry."

The crowd shuffled, growled, moaned like a hive of angry wasps. People began to shout, the women louder than the men.

"Disaster."

"Incompetents!"

"Orange pig heads!"

"To hell with the Beggars!"

"We never asked to join this fight!"

Others pleaded, "Surrender!"

"We will starve here!"

"Plead mercy."

Patriots shouted them down: "Fight on!"

"Freedom or death!"

"God's glory! Death to the Papists!"

Still others: "Burn the city!"

"Take every bloody Spaniard to hell with us!"

The mayor pounded his gavel. "Order! Silence!"

One of the guards approached the mayor and handed him a small piece of paper.

A sullen stillness settled over the townspeople, curious about what possible new horrors this meant.

The mayor unfolded the tiny paper to a hand-sized note with fine writing on it. Everyone knew what these notes were. He waved it like a little flag. "We have another message, by pigeon, from Prince William himself this morning."

"Now what does he tell us?"

"Hope, citizens! The Watergeuzen – fearsome Sea Beggars – are coming to relieve us and turn their mighty guns on d'Avila and the Duke!"

The crowd remained quiet, not sharing his enthusiasm. Even I knew that the mayor referred to the formidable privateer ships of the Sea Beggars who had driven the Spanish from their North Sea coast, and had shepherded our ship to Amsterdam.

More shouting and nervous laughter.

"Have the Watergeuzen warships sprouted wings!"

"Will they sail their ships inland on the backs of oxen?"

The mayor hushed the crowd again, spoke slowly, but with some temerity.

Shouts again: "Speak up!"

The mayor straightened and gathered his confidence: "They mean to destroy the dikes, flood the polder land and sail right to our gates!" He spread his arms and forced a smile.

The crowd turned angry again. "They will destroy our land!" One yelled. Many were farmers and peasants who had left their rich land outside the walls to take refuge here.

"Sea water will salt our soil."

"It will take years to reclaim again."

"Surrender. Beg for terms," another farmer shouted and others echoed him.

Pointy Beard and his men closed ranks on stage next to the mayor. The mayor smiled feebly. "Stay calm. The incoming tides will flood only enough land to get the ships through to us and destroy the Spanish encampments."

A farmer in the back shouted. "Who will pay us for our lost crops and livestock?"

The mayor raised both his hands for calm... "The Sea Beggars have amassed hundreds of river boats, cannon and construction crews. They will only flood where necessary and we will be compensated for the damages by the William of Orange himself!"

The crowd quieted, but did not cheer. One yelled. "We're heard promises before."

"Promises from Don Luis de Requesens, you mean."

The new governor general – sent by Madrid to replace the Iron Duke and his heavy hand – had offered the citizens of Leiden full clemency – even gold – in return for surrender, conscious that his predecessor's brutal tactics had only hardened Dutch resistance. Few but papists among the rebels believed anything the Spanish had to say now, after their massacres and inquisitions.

76

Out of the silence that followed, one of the farmers' wives – a robust, apple faced woman – stepped onto a box and shouted. "Better to give our land back to the sea than ourselves to the Spanish!" She was joined by her family and neighbors and soon had the whole crowd cheering.

After the moment of bravado ended the mayor added, almost timidly."... We must hold out for only three months longer," the mayor added.

The crowd all seemed to gasp in unison. "Only?" No one needed to point out that food was already growing scarce in a city accustomed to plenty. The town had more than ample provisions when the siege had begun in the fall, shortly after harvest, along with rich gardens for vegetables and even a few small fields for dairy cows inside the walls. The mayor had not even called for "temporary" rationing until months later.

Through all these months of peril, I had not feared for myself. I had even resigned myself to the impending life-and-death passage of childbirth. But now image of a wasted, starving infant floated in my mind and filled me with dread for the first time. There was no exit, nowhere to hide from this, not in madness again, not in my flowers and dreams. I could not escape my body and the child I carried within it, soon to appear, either to live or die with me.

The contractions that had stopped for a while now returned with a vengeance. I turned to Isabella and grimaced with the next contraction, biting my lip to keep from crying out. I felt wetness stream down my legs into my shoes. She and Rosa took my arms, led me back to the town square and the caravan wagon that was home and soon to be my child's humble birthplace – if we both survived.

9. SON OF KINGS

"You have a little Danish-Dutch prince!" Rosa, who midwifed the birth, slapped the skinny, slime-covered pink newborn to squalling. She cut the cord and wiped him down gently with a damp cloth. "Every little finger and toe counted," she beamed, then swaddled and passed the tiny babe into my arms... my motherly arms... groggy, glowing, and exhausted. So this is what it was like! And we were both alive. Though for how long, I could not say.

The baby quieted in my arms, except for little whimpers and sudden little quivers. I gazed down into the mystery of its wide, startled eyes – a deep unfocused topaz that stared up at me in as much wonder as I myself felt in this moment. I did not need to think about it. I saw eternity in those eyes, felt it there, no matter what our impending fate would be.

All the terror around us! What world had I brought this sweet child into? I bent close to baby's face, smelling its sweet breath. I saw Prince Hamlet's strong brow and wide set eyes, but not his tortured bitterness. I did not want to remember the prince's sinuous body or his madness, or my father, bleed to death by his hand each time I looked at this child's face.

Rosa brought a ladle of water and watched intently as I sipped. How had an angel come from such grief? How had my Hamlet's evil come from good intentions and then such goodness as I held in my arms now, come from bloody misadventure? How had I been reborn from the rushing waters to give life myself? Was this another of what dreams may come?

I saw my tears wet my baby's tender forehead, christening him like new spring rain. He scrunched his little doughy birth-flattened face in a way that made me laugh.

"You see, Olivia, all that fretting!" Isabella had come into the room. "Your baby is perfect, your son. And you are alive. You even look well." Isabella, laughed,

"... For someone trampled by horses, that is." Rosa joined in.

"The play is, not so much the thing, now, eh?" Isabella touched the baby's tiny fist with one finger. "Rest now. You will need your strength."

For the first time since Fortunio pulled me from that streaming torrent, I felt that I had floated fully free from the grief of Elsinore. I offered the baby my breast and felt his wee lips touch my nipple briefly before he drifted into sleep.

"Patience, Olivia" Rosa, like everyone in the troupe, called me by the name now. No more Ophelia. "He will start to nurse, but it will take a little while."

Isabella touched my forearm. "Your wee one is as exhausted as you, my dear. Sleep now, you angels."

Rosa nudged me aside softly and replaced the sodden sheets from under and around me. She put them in a basket. Then Rosa pulled a fur blanket over the two of us.

Another death and rebirth. Had the Spanish breached the walls, and already slaughters all of us? Had God delivered me and my baby to the dim limbo inside this creaky wooden wagon, wind whistling through its cracks?

No fire this time. If not hell: perhaps I was a purgatory for what sins I knew not, but felt weighing upon me nonetheless.

In the days that followed, I slept and awakened, slept and awakened, fitfully, over and over to the tempo of my always hungry baby and became its great mother's teat and nappy changer – overriding discomforts until my little one and I seemed to finally arrive at a golden balance.

Fortunio provided for us best he could, and the troupe delegated their best provisions to me despite my protests. Hunger gnawed at me constantly – but better than the stupor of final famine. My milk flowed, but seemed thinner, as did my little "Aricin." I looked at his tiny round, pale face and was ready to slice one of my veins and feed him my blood if it came to that. My legs felt weak, my arms looked spindly. Isabella seemed to be wearing her own death mask. Rations were almost nonexistent. Plague and fevers ravaged parts of the city, mercifully sparing our inn thus far.

We would have starved for certain if not for Fortunio. He continued to poach eels and what he could snatch from gardens – at risk of hanging – but others had the same thoughts and pickings grew sparse. Fortunio joined one of the raiding parties. They would slip out through a side gate and were supposed to kill Spanish soldiers. The council offered "twenty florins" – in the form of promissory notes printed in heavy black over pages torn from old prayer books – for anyone of them who would bring back the head of a Spanish soldier. Fortunio preferred to bring back what food he could find – sacks of carrots, chunks of meat he stuffed into his shoulder bag, potatoes – all of which he brought to us. Where and when he fed himself remained a mystery – but he did will, keeping his strength for more raids.

"I'm worry every night about you, Fortunio."

"I have mastered the art of invisibility."

"I want to go myself!"

"There will be time for that. You tend to our little prince now." He patted the baby with his spidery fingers.

"You are truly a prince, Fortunio, as a prince should be." I took his hand, which that he somehow kept as fine as a lute player's.

"You honor me, my lady." Then whispered: "But truth be told, princess suits me more." He made small curtsy. We laughed, though hoarsely, for the first time in many days.

+++

The citizens of Leiden, grim but resolved, along with my new family, shuffled daily through a kind of limbo, awaiting either rebel salvation or Spanish hell. Weeks dragged into months. The mayor kept us all posted as news arrived by air. The Sea Beggars inched closer – by means not as simple as it had sounded. They had to blast through dike after dike, to inch towards us, not only one.

Each time they had to wait for the flooding while they battled clusters of Spanish holdouts. Spanish cannons kept them from sailing into a large freshwater lake that would have brought the Geuzen almost to our gates. They had to take a roundabout way instead.

Word came that William lay near death from a fever. The town turned as deathly quiet as a cemetery. Day after day, lookouts atop the town hall swept the horizon with their spyglasses and reported nothing. Then, a sail was sighted. Everyone cheered – weakly. Then came more bad news. Ships foundered when east winds held back seawater. The flooded fields were still too shallow for the Beggars' ships.

The townspeople nearly rioted at this news. They said the Geuzen sent in flat-bottomed riverboats to inch closer while the waters continued to rise.

All the while, we heard Spanish cannon fire and shooting and screams from behind the thick walls as the Spanish commanders continued to send tercios of ignorant soldiers to their deaths against our battlements.

Our hopes dwindled like a guttering candle, more each day. One night, suddenly, sentries on the walls reported seeing two of the towering Spanish siege forts aflame, a hopeful sign, but no one knew for sure if this had been the work of our rescuers, drawing closer.

Often with great effort on empty stomachs, Carlo and Isabella continued to put on plays each Sunday afternoon, on the mayor's request. The mayor ordered extra rations of beer and broth distributed, but audiences remained morose, barely able to muster a laugh. "Oliver" made appearances, starting a week after the baby was born, but only briefly while Rosa tended the baby.

In a now dead world long ago, this little boy would have been named Hamlet, after his father and grandfather, and grown up in princely adulation. But that was an unlikely outcome even before the trouble all started at Elsinore.

"What is your baby's name," they asked me.

"Aricin," I held him up for them to see. "It means 'son of kings."

"Ari," they would say. "A good name..."

I felt the regal raven pendant from his father that I had worn since that day long ago in the Jutland forest turn almost hot – as if aglow between my breasts. Someday soon I would relinquish it to Ari, the only memento he would have of his father.

10. LARA

Now I felt fear for the first time since we arrived in this city of the damned. Not for myself. I fear for my baby. I have been looking death in the face for nine months – since before the Spanish siege. It was like a death sentence to realize I was with child. It had been so for my mother.

I was no accident that I felt comfortable with Isabella from the start. Like Isabella and Carlo, my mother's family originated in the Republic of Venice. Though her parents had migrated to Lyon when she was a baby, my mother grew up speaking the Venetian vernacular. Her Danish was rounded and Latinized with her *Bourguignon* accent. She read stories to me in Italian and French and in her native Lyonaisse Occitan vernacular – *lenga d'òc* – from the prolific printing houses of Lyon, as well as Danish, as I grew up.

She was born Lara de Santille, the youngest of three sisters. Only one of the sisters survives now, my beloved Aunt Clara in Lyon. She and my mother were the daughters of a Venetian artist, miniaturist and toymaker Danilo De Santille, an exile in Henry III's French court. My father met her during his time as a diplomat in Paris – several years before he had become royal chamberlain. My father befriended Danilo and they became allies, so I gathered, exchanging information useful to their respective states.

I learned much this from reading my mother's diaries long after her death. I also read packets of letters in French and Italian, from mother's sister Clara with whom she had corresponded all of her years in Denmark.

Below the false bottom of a cedar chest, I discovered more letters – poetry and love notes from a young squire with whom she had apparently been in love before marrying my father. My father used to tell her that she really was a Dane, because after the fall of Rome, the region around Lyon had become the kingdom of invading Norse peoples from the Danish island of Bornholm in the Baltic sea – hence Burgundy – "people of Bornholm."

She would tease back, faking amazement. "Burgundians? Once barbarians of the north, like yourselves? That must have been before we taught them *cuisine Lyonnaise!*"

Indeed, my father took her with him to the island on their honeymoon. I remember a dreamy landscape oil painting of the island in my father's study.

Through these letters I came to know Lara as a poetic, often lonely, young woman, and not just my mother – things about her I only begin to comprehend now as a woman myself.

I dreamt about my Aunt Clara and her life in France, where I wanted to travel when I grew up. My father and mother did take Laertes and me to Lyon once when we were very young. It was for Clara's wedding – a fortnight of feasting celebrating her marriage to the comte Jean Paul de Talley, minor noble and wealthy textile merchant. I overheard my father joke that Clara would have done better with a husband of higher rank, but that his fortune would do nicely. My mother stiffened and looked away. I remember most of the wedding trip only vaguely, but Aunt Clara's tender voice and the lavish kisses she bestowed upon me and my little brother remained vivid.

I found a portrait of Clara drawn in pen and ink by an artist whose name I forget. She looked pensive in it, facing the artist boldly – unusual for such a portrait. How I'm thinking perhaps the artist was her lover.

Her voluminous black hair flows outward over the shoulder of an ornate gown instead of being swept up. She is a darker, more provocative version of my mother, with large wide set eyes, and high cheekbones. Her sensuous lips hint a smile – a darker-haired version of my mother. The artist – her lover she confessed – had drawn her as the water nymph Daphne – who drew the unrequited love of Apollo – with laurel leaves sprouting from her hair. My mother said that Clara had always inspired her to write and draw herself. That drawing of my Aunt Clara is the one thing I regret losing most of all that I left behind at Elsinore.

I still see her in my mind, sometimes in my dreams. My remembrance of her as a child blends with my recollection of the portrait. I have thought of her more often since my father, then my brother were killed – my only surviving blood relation now. I try not to dwell on these memories. My life is with Isabella and Carlo and the troupe now. But I do long to be welcomed into her arms when, God willing, I reach Lyon – if ever – at last.

My father and Lara were married in Paris, but soon he was recalled to Denmark. He announced that his Lara was with child. As a parting gift, her father, Danilo crafted an ornate castle siege game with hand carved soldiers and replicas intended for the grandson both he and my father felt sure was on his way.

I was born instead. My mother wrote bitterly about her husband's ire when his "son" turned out to be me. My father never gave the solider set to me. He gave it instead to old King Hamlet and Queen Gertrude a month later as a gift for their baby Prince Hamlet's first birthday.

The gift redoubled my father's favor with the king. The set showed the armaments, weapons, soldiers, rankings and "tercio" – division – formations of Spain's Army of Flanders in fine detail – a boon to King Hamlet and his military advisors.

Like my grandfather Danillo, my mother Lara took to artistic expression – in her case with pen and brush. My father, in the first throes of love, promised young Lara that she would be well situated and free to pursue her art if she returned to Denmark with him.

Truth was that my father proved an inattentive husband. Dark and drafty Elsinore oppressed my mother and sent her into moods. Courtiers and their wives looked askance at her. Worst of all, she discovered that my father told the king and queen that her family was French Huguenot, not Catholics from Venice – and of minor nobility.

Mother spent most of her time isolated in their chambers, except when she accompanied her husband to formal events.

She gave birth to Laertes a year after her arrival at Elsinore. The next year she died in childbirth, along with the baby. Not an uncommon event, but one that I had never realized remotely as possible in my child's mind.

I had hoped for a baby girl. I had imagined playing with a baby sister in the palace gardens. I remember overhearing my mother telling her maid that she feared that my father would fly into a rage again if the new baby turned out to be another girl. I shut my eyes tight and wished even harder for a new sister just to spite him.

My golden mother, in my last memories of her, large with life, she would kiss me and my rag doll good night and tuck us in every night. But she never said goodbye.

The night she died, I woke up and sneaked down a hallway and behind a curtain in my mother's bedchamber, from where I witnessed all the agonies and commotion of birthing gone wrong – midwife and servants coming and going, screams, pushing, crying, despair, my mother's voice weakening... panic when the midwife saw there was too much blood.

I knew from that tender age that the angel of death comes to the birthing bed as often as does new life. It is women's lot to face death giving birth, over and over, like soldiers sent to battle time and again. God so oft called upon, seemed to have nothing to do with it.

Even so, I thought, somehow, I must be to blame – perhaps as punishment for having wished a sister so spitefully – or for hateful thoughts about my pampered baby brother.

I refused to cry at my mother's funeral. I withdrew to my books, vowing I'd be more a seeker than a dreamer. No more foolish baby sister fantasies, nor girlish dreams of motherhood.

But now I have become a mother myself. And reality was not to be found in books or even in the war raging around us, but in my arms.

I think of my mother often these days, and all she bequeathed me - this life, of course, that I now hold tightly once again. And more. As I grew into my childhood loneliness, I discovered her journals and I devoured the collection of books I found among her belongings that father had stored away. I consumed books about chivalric adventure, legends and philosophies that took me away from the dark halls of Elsinore and set my passions burning.

Dreams that I had nowhere to put in my castle life, but carried me to other lives imagining myself as Bradamante, the warrior woman of Aristo's Orlando Furioso, and the daring heroines of Moderata Fonte. Women who did and wrote of what I would not dare. The Marquesa Vittoria Colonna's and Veronica Gambara's epics, a worn copies of Cornelius Agrippa's works on the occult and the "Declamation on the Nobility and Preeminence of the Female Sex," that made me wonder about her life with my father. I see Ouroboros – the eternal renewal of life and death – in my baby's clear eyes, unafraid

11. AN IMPROBABLE PRINCE

"We've seen terrible things, my good lady."

"I try not to dwell on them, Horatio."

"But I must – in the writing, to tell what is true."

"There is truth enough in our nakedness, my learned lover."

Horatio ran his fingers along Gilda's pearly cheek, slowly down her neck, shoulders, breasts, belly, hips, thighs, tracing the luscious curves of her beneath their silken sheets – memorizing her for when he would be gone – a solid country woman under that lady's finery, just as he was, in truth, a country boy come a long way.

She turned towards him again. "I know you do not love me, Horatio."

"Ah, but I do, Gilda. I am supremely..." He moved to kiss her, but she turned her head away.

"I am too wise a lady to be silenced by a man's insincere lips."

Horatio flopped back on his pillow and stared at the bed's crimson canopy. "You can believe these lips."

"Even when they whisper, 'Ophelia,' in sleep."

"I dream often of those who have died in this haunted castle..."

"I saw how you used to glance at her when lord Hamlet was not looking."

"I felt sad for her, the way he punished her so bitterly for his mother's sins...."

"You would not say such things if you had known the queen's heart as well as I."

"Let us be merry on our last day in this miserable castle, my lady. ... I do care for you, very much, you know."

"Yes, Horatio, but do not worry, my love is not the binding kind. I am happy enough with our amorous adventures … Go ahead. You may kiss me..." She slid against him and touched his lips with her index finger. He kissed it, then her hand and pulled her atop him.

They kissed for a long time, tussling sweetly, neither eager to leave the feathery embrace of the warm bed where they drank of each other one more time here, forgetting for a moment, the dark days. They breathed in unison for a long while – pressed like rose petals between the silken sheets, conspiring to steal a moment's more of bliss.

The rest of the castle was empty now, but for Gilda's elder sister and the servants downstairs, loading the waiting wagons. Soon the porters would be coming up for what remained. Gilda would have to slip back into her own bedchamber down the hall and pack to leave as well. Elsinore would be left to its ghosts.

Soon, she rose and used the chamber pot, then a pitcher and basin to do her ablutions while he watched, like a pasha, from the bed.

"If you don't arise soon, my dear Horatio, you'll find me next to you again." She flirted.

"I have arisen, woman."

"Again?"

"Alas, the time has gone."

She brushed her hair and donned stockings, shoes, a cotton shift, then her burgundy-and-emerald silken gown and coat. "My knight errant, already on your journey. I see Italy in your eyes."

"I am no knight."

"You were " She pursed her lips.

He got up, at last. "I take my leave only by royal command, my good lady."

She eyed his sturdy nakedness with that brazen pleasure he found so compelling about her.

"Have no fear, my lord. I lay no claims on you."

"...Ah, but your eyes do..." He brushed by her, stealing one more kiss – this one meant to last – before proceeding to get ready himself.

"You will do well in Italy with that charm, my dear." Fully dressed now, she threw him a sensuous, open-mouthed smooch with white velvet gloved fingers and slipped from the room. Gilda and her sister later would take their carriage southwest to her husband's manor in Jutland.

Horatio, dressed and sighed, surveying mist-shrouded ramparts of the castle one more time from his balcony, though he had little time to tarry. A royal coach awaited him at the main entrance ready for the two-day journey north to *Kronenberg Fortinbras*, the emperor's newly constructed fortress. Horatio would report there before embarking on a fortnight's voyage as an emissary to the Duchy of Genoa.

"He wants you far away." Gilda had seen the play immediately. "Fortinbras..."

"I will gain much by being in Italy – meeting great princes, artists, philosophers, studying antiquities."

"...And assassins. You are well loved by the people here – and thus a threat – but in Italy..."

"My eyes are open. Marcellus will be with me."

"I will pray that his eyes stay open as well."

Horatio stuffed the last of his notes and manuscripts into a heavy leather bag. His majesty had commended Horatio on the draft that he had provisionally entitled *Good Night, Sweet Prince*.

"It needs a stronger title, Horatio. The title should mention us," the new king remarked, which Horatio took to signify and that it should legitimize Fortinbras' right to the Danish throne. This was not part of Horatio's promise to a dying Hamlet that motivated him to write the book, but he could say nothing to his ambitious new tyrant for the moment.

That had been weeks ago. He had not shown Fortinbras the later revision that he would soon risk sending to Plantin, his printer in Antwerp, and that presented a less flattering picture of the new, self-styled emperor than he would have approved. He wondered about the consequences. But it would please others of the gentry grown restive under the new king.

Something stirred the motes filtering from the window in the morning light. Horatio felt a presence.

Buzz, buzz.

"Go away."

There, once again, the melancholy Dane appeared, sitting in a high backed chair by the hearth: his page-boy blond bangs as coiffed as the day they graduated Wittenberg University, still in mourning black tights and doublet, gold-and-silver medallion dangling.

Why do you ignore me, my loyal Horatio?

"I have sworn off ghosts, my lord."

Then, you prefer fishmongers?

"I prefer solitude." Horatio made a show of continuing to pack.

How goes your opus magnus, the story of my life that you promised?

"First my publisher, now you! It is close. Close. Nearly done!"

If thou didst ever hold me in thy heart,
Absent thee from felicity awhile,
And in this harsh world draw thy breath in pain,
To tell my story.

Horatio rolled his eyes. "Yes, my lord, with respect, I heard you the first time."

Report me and my cause aright. Remember that?

"There is more *amiss* than aright now, my lord. Have you seen Ophelia?"

Once. I think. I cannot be sure – in some other place, in times out of joint.

"Then what am I to make of Gilda's suspicions about Ophelia's death…?

You would do well to marry the lady Gilda.

"It's not like that... But, what about Ophelia? Tell me..."

A perfect wife – too old to bring sinners into the world.

"Me thought you spirits were privy to all things of this world and the next."

No revelations, good friend.

"... 'and in that sleep of death what dreams may come.' What about that, my lord?'"

Aye, there's the rub. Death is a bore, Horatio. No dreams – not so far – only wandering, brooding over my life, over and over, every sin.

"But Ophelia. We saw her coffin. You and Laertes fought over it.. Yet ..."

Sand, my friend, I believe, and a damp cape. My devious mother paid Yorrick to fill it, alas...

"You've seen your mother then – Queen Gertrude?"

She sends her regards, and says thank you for the nice funeral.

"The queen is alive, then?"

No, you nunce! Only Ophelia. Mother haunts Elsinore too. Always lurking about. She hounds me about the boy...

"What boy?"

Exactly! That's what I say to her, 'what boy, mother?'

"And Ophelia, if she did live, could you tell me where..."

Methinks, dear Horatio, that now you doth protest too much about the fair Ophelia. I saw once you had your eye on her when I first brought you to his castle.

"Only for your biography, my lord. If Ophelia lives, I need to speak with her – if I am to tell your story, as you wish, in full."

I have no control. One minute oblivion, the next, I find myself who knows where – or in what times. Just a moment before I appeared to you, I found myself walking the streets of Copenhagen, but not in our time. *A giant metal wagon with no horse pulling it nearly ran through me. I saw people in strange attire, with cords attached to their ears. I saw them talking to themselves like lunatics as they walked past towering glass palaces. Then, poof! I was back here.*

"And you saw Ophelia there?"

No. But I glimpsed her – or someone like her – on a cobbled street, in Flanders, I think. She walked past me. She was dressed as a young man.

"Did she see *you?* Did you speak to her?"

She stared right through me.

"Turnabout is fair play, considering..."

That a fishmonger's daughter did conceive...

"She was with child?"

*No. But with one in tow – born and the image of his father, I must say ...*The ghost smiled to himself.

"A footnote in your story, then, or a new, final chapter? I must inform my publisher."

My son, if he be real – would be crown prince of Denmark should he lay claim.

"... With respect, a bastard prince. Even so..."

Not precisely. But that is another tale.

"More revisions?"

Beyond than telling my story Horatio – now I beg you. Put this aright for me. You must find and protect this boy.

Horatio slumped in a chair. "No end to it. When will those flights of angels sing thee to thy rest?"

Nary a peep from that heavenly host. Horatio, I am condemned to wander gloomy halls until all is put aright – for my own sins, this time.

"Nothing is aright in Denmark since Fortinbras crowned himself emperor. Cruel taxes to pay for his conquests by land and sea, while people here go hungry and grow angrier by the day."

Rue the day he marched through our gates.

"I venture to say, my lord, how that came about."

I would reckon that treasonous were I king.

"If you were not a ghost, you could have me thrown in the dungeon."

If I were king Fortinbras, I would have any Hamlet's head that I saw on the block forthwith.

"Fortinbras now builds an empire in blood and, I fear, some new connivance with the Habsburgs, one day, with the Bourbon king of France the next, the Russian czar the next. He will stop at nothing now – already he plants his flag in Iceland, Norway, Denmark, Poland, Lithuania, he soon may risk all in a war with Gustavus Adolphus and the Swedes, while good Danish peasants starve to feed his armies."

...I see it now. My doubt caused this calamity, Horatio, I had one task – to avenge my father – and made a bloody stew of it.

"You could just as well say that I set off this chain of tragedy by confirming that your father's ghost was real that fateful night."

You did your duty as a true friend.

"A true friend would not indulge illusions."

Now, Horatio, you must be my remedy.

"I have no remedy for the world's ills, only to tell its stories. Let me be!"

Find my son, if he be of this world, and protect him. See that he claims his birthright, but burden him not with such murderous affairs as brought my end.

"One may not be possible without the other."

I put my faith in you, noble Horatio. Hamlet faded.

"You are the improbable, sir, charging me with the impossible!"

The ghost shimmered and fumbled about the room. *I must find my way out of this cursed castle.*

"My lord, with respect, doubt chains you, just as it did in life. Leave or stay, as you wish. You have a choice. We the living, do not."

Hamlet faded further into translucence. His medallion – a gold amulet inset with a raven engraved on black onyx, his black beret and his velvet boots were the last to fade from Horatio's view.

Horatio called after him: "I've enough of this castle and its ghosts."

A knock.

Enter servant.

"Sir, may I take your bags to the carriage?"

12. A BILL COMES DUE

Malthus van Schrum, the nosy, shuffling manager and part owner of the inn, caught up with Carlo in the alcove on his way out and bent to hand the little man a long sheet of paper covered with inked numerals in neat columns.

Carlo perused it. His face reddened. "Outrageous!"

"Sir? Is there some error?"

"The whole thing! Give this to your burghermaster. He invited us to this pile of offal."

"Pardon, sir, but the mayor only recommended the inn, that doesn't mean..."

"We're here under duress." Carlo brought down his silver handled, brass tipped cane sharply against the floor, threateningly close to the manager's slippered foot. The manager propelled himself back several paces.

Carlo didn't need the cane much for his sometimes aching, curvy back and muscular short legs, but it added to the scary persona of angry diabolical dwarf king he enjoyed affecting.

Carlo muttered to Rosa, loud enough for Van Schrum to overhear "...money grubbing, sausage-stuffing Dutchmen ..."

The manager forced a smile. "You and your troupe are welcome to continue your stay..."

"As if that would be our choice, were the bloody Spaniards not at the gates, and you Dutch profiteers hadn't taken our horses." Carlo held up the bill and ceremoniously tore it in half.

"We would like you to settle the balance due to this point sir, however...."

Carlo tore the bill again, into smaller and smaller pieces while staring up the manager. "You suppose that I will compensate you from my 'dwarf pot of gold,' eh?" He arched he eyebrows and caricatured a nasal dwarfish laugh.

The manager looked up and down the alcove. "Sir, I will have to take this up with the burghermaster."

Carlo hurled the ripped pieces of paper high over the manager's head. "*Ah*, it seems to be snowing. I'll have to go out and see to the wagon now."

"You and your clowns will regret this, H*err Karrrlo!"* The manager growled, squinting ominously, then picking pieces of paper out of his hair.

"Perhaps the burghermaster would like to hear that you are stealing silver and trying to extort gold in order to buy your freedom from the Spanish when they take the city."

"That is a foul lie, sir!"

"Is it?"

"We shall see who is the thief and the traitor, *Herr Karrrlo!"*

"You pathetic weasel. You dishonor our brave freedom fighters!" Carlo wagged a finger at Van Schrum. Then he turned on his heels, took Rosa's arm and stormed out the door with theatrical flourish.

Once outside, Carlo and Rosa burst out laughing when they set foot on the cobblestones. "Pot of gold!" Rosa howled.

Carlo slapped his belly. "Here's my pot!" Then he squatted and pointed behind him. "...and my gold!" It was then the heard the cannons – not the usual occasional back and forth firing from around the walls, but a steady roll of them, very loud, like rolling thunder. And the trumpets sounding – a wavering mournful sound like hunting hounds. Carlo waved his walking stick. "This is it, Rosa! No hiding now."

He set forth towards the city gates, stopping to bang his cane against the parked wagon's door and calling out for Isabella, Fortunio and Olivia, who emerged in various states of preparation for a show. It kept their spirits up to at least make ready and rehearse feebly with what strength they could muster. "Come, my dears, we go to meet our new masters or our maker."

"We go to fill our empty bellies or die." Isabella rubbed hers... "If the Sea Beggars bring promised relief."

"One more starving day and we would scarce be able to even move." Fortunate dragged his feet.

"Ye of little faith," said Olivia, holding her baby close. "We go to meet our liberators."

++++

The food line that soon formed stretched from the center of town all the way through the gates, across an improvised bridge over a canal where another had been burned. It snaked finally to a platform of flat bottomed supply boats lashed together from which sailors and marine troops unloaded barrels of salt herring, cured meats along with huge baskets of bread to be passed out to the famished populace.

The procession out of the long-closed city gates had quickly become a carnival of the near dying, delirious, savagely hungry and drunken joy, all talking, shouting, singing and making rude noises at once, some even donning grotesque carnival masks, caricature faces of asses, pigs, King Phillip II of Spain, rats...

"Don't wolf down the food when we get it, or you'll be sick," Isabella admonished as they inched forward finally clear of the outer wall. "You could even die."

"A supreme irony." Carlo rode high on Fortunio's shoulders – one of their comic routine normally, but Carlo insisted on a look at the panoply from the gates – flooded fields, Spanish fortifications smoldering in ruin, black smoke rising into an aching blue sky and on the brown water, long boats, barges, mighty ships at the rear, bristling cannons, their pine masts like forest trees, white sails far as Carlo could see to the west. Banners waved merrily in the blessed westerly winds that finally pushed the seawater inland.

A man in a weasel mask came slowly down the line pulling a cart with baskets of food that he handed out here and there. Seeing Olivia holding her baby, he stopped and passed her a long loaf of dark rye bread. Olivia thanked him. He lifted his mask and smiled.

"Pieter!" She blurted, before realizing herself.

He stared at her quizzically. "Yes...?"

Isabella, realizing the situation, interjected. "Have you seen her brother, Oliver?"

"Ah, Oliver. No, I have not, but..." He stared harder at Olivia.

"My brother has spoken of you often. I recognized the scar... the limp..." Her face flushed. "I mean..." She gestured at Fortunio. "This is my husband..."

"...Which one?" Pieter nodded up at Carlo, then at Fortunio.

"Her husband has two heads," Rosa said through a mouthful of the bread she had torn from Olivia's loaf.

Fortunio started laughing so hard that Carlo had to grab handfuls of his hair to keep from falling off his shoulders.

"Ouch!" Fortunio stomped in a circle, laughing and howling with Carlo hanging on to him like a wild horse.

Everyone started laughing and clapping. Life was returning to Leyden.

Others in the line hailed Pieter for bread.

"Well give Oliver my best..." Pieter moved on and held up a hand to the standees. "I carry relief only for the aged, infirm and those with children," he said and passed another loaf to an emaciated old woman before moving on.

When they had stopped laughing, Carlo remarked. "I hate to be rude to all our lovely hosts, but it is time, my dears, for us to bow off this stage. But how?"

By Umberto Tosi

PART THREE

By Umberto Tosi

++++

Lodewijk_de_Boisot, Admiral of the heroic, Dutch Sea Beggars. Portrait by Cornelis Visscher.

13. THE ADMIRAL

Olivia would have been jubilant but for the gnawing fear that replaced hunger in her belly. She stood by the side of the road, and held the bundle that was Ari close against the chill wind, rocking him gently in his sleepy bliss. She huddled against Isabella and Rosa among the stunned, emaciated survivors of Leiden's long siege, awaiting the grand ceremonial march of their heroic rescuers through opened-wide city gates.

Once his men had distributed food and essentials to the starving citizenry, Lodewijk van Boisot, Lord of Ruart, Admiral of Zeeland and of the Watergeuzen, liberator of Lillo and now, Leiden, disembarked from his command ship into a skiff that was rowed across the floodwaters to the gates of the city opened wide as lovers arms.

The great, early autumn storm - unseasonable in its force - had passed. Its tidal surge had given Boisot's flotilla a final push across flooded fields to rain fire upon the last of panicked, drowning Spanish mercenaries and break the siege at long last. The deadly night had given way to a fittingly glorious, gusty day with ecstatic blue sky and cottony towering clouds so radiant they hurt Olivia's eyes.

The townspeople cheered with hoarse, tired voices, beat drums and waved pennants at Boisot as he led eight hundred of his rough-cut rebel sea warriors up the wide street. Olivia noticed his face lined with fatigue, nevertheless resplendent in black boots, breeches, polished steel breastplate and gauntlets. He carried a plumed helmet under one arm and waved his sword high in salute to the crowd with the other.

Isabella nudged Rosa. "Wave! Yell! Let's get his attention!"

Olivia started to shout, but the weakness of her own voice disturbed her. She leaned against Isabella and shushed her. "Not the right time. We have to wait."

Isabella yelled half heartedly, then looked back at Olivia. After all they had endured, the unexpected blow fell the hardest, Isabella's eyes said.

"I know. He is your husband. I'm worried too. But they will be all right."

"He thinks God protects fools, and that is what he is. I don't know what trouble he has brought on us all this time."

Rosa pushed forward, parting the crowd and stepped into the path of the parade, but one of the town constables, out of nowhere, pulled her back. Rosa yelled at Boisot. "Liberate our men!"

Boisot gave her a momentary surprised look, but soldiered onward.

"Why have you imprisoned our players?" She referred to the sudden unexplained, midnight arrest of Carlo and Fortunio by two of Boisot's marines. "I demand justice!"

Isabella took Rosa's arm once the constable pushed her back to the side of the road. "You tried Rosa. But Olivia is right. We have to wait."

Olivia craned her neck at Boisot, who by this time had passed them. "I don't think he even knows about Carlo and Fortunio." Their arrest remained a mystery to the players, but Olivia suspected that it related somehow to Carlo's altercation with Van Schrumm the innkeeper – or perhaps another of Carlo's incautious theatrics, forgetting that, after all, they remained foreigners in this city.

"We have to find a way to appeal to the Admiral directly. Who knows what could happen? They could be hanged as spies." Isabella's voice broke. It was the first time in all their harrowing experiences together that she had seen Isabella so shaken.

Olivia, thinking upon their situation, had expected Boisot to present a pirate's visage. Instead, she had seen a kind face with gentle dark eyes, a soft smile, neatly trimmed, reddish beard, mustache and flowing hair. He nodded directly at the townspeople lining the streets to his left and right, high and low, almost shyly, as a might a long lost uncle showing up for dinner.

Near skeletal, smiling but hollow eyed Zeelanders, their magistrates, ministers, tradesmen, soldiers, women and children fell in behind Admiral Boisot and his men as they passed, wending their way to the Pieterskerk for thanksgiving service and ceremony.

Olivia, Isabella and Rosa chose not to follow. They stood for a moment in the street, trembling like windblown branches, then turned back towards the inn and their caravan wagon by the square. The storm had nearly stripped its lindens, elms and oaks of their fiery autumn leaves, the way plague and starvation had claimed so many thousands of Leiden defenders.

The icy storm, signaled an early, bitter winter to come, like her last one at Elsinore. Olivia mused. Olivia contemplated the last few tenacious, golden leaves that held yet to their branches – *much like myself, I feel now*. A vivid dream that she had two nights earlier revisited her suddenly. It had been the night the final battle, when the storm had been at its height, rocking the caravan, pelting its roof and sides while she slept fitfully within. In fact, she could not tell dream from reality at that point – whether her mother's ghost had visited her in waking state or had emerged from Morpheus.

Her mother, who believed in saintly apparitions, had held secretly to her Catholic faith. In Olivia's dream – if it was that – her mother, Lara, was reading to little Ophelia from one of her old books of Catholic hagiography. She looked up at "Olivia" and declared – in a burst of transcendental silver light – *"Fear not! Today is the feast of your guardian angel!"*

Admiral Boisot had proved a savior of sorts, although an unlikely angel – but then Olivia thought of Pieter.

Breaking off her reverie, she said: "I have an idea, Isabella. I need to find Pieter."

Olivia climbed inside the caravan wagon. She tried on her Oliver clothes again, for the first time since the final three months of her pregnancy. She had some trouble with the waistband, but that could be let out easily. She worried more about the blouse and tunic. Her breasts, though never large, had grown heavy with milk. She would have to nurse Ari well, wrap them tightly and pray they did not give her away when the time came.

14. BODIES IN WATER

It wasn't hard to find Pieter the next day and explain the situation. Fortunately, Pieter already seemed to be in the admiral's confidence. He apparently had been given a field promotion to sergeant acting as a liaison between Boisot's staff and the local garrison.

By next morning Oliver and Pieter climbed into a skiff and were rowed across the green brown floodwaters to a deeper channel where Boisot's command ship – a carrack bristling with cannon – rode at anchor.

Pieter explained that the admiral had set up an ad hoc tribunal on board, consisting of the mayor, a magistrate and himself, to review cases of misconduct – military and civilian – and sort out disputes among the citizenry.

"Why not at the town hall?" Oliver fidgeted and fought down the panicky thought that he might be under arrest somehow for espionage herself and soon exposed as Olivia in the process.

"The admiral prefers to stay aboard his vessel," Pieter answered, in a matter of fact voice, looking straight ahead at the ship as they drew near it.

Easier to hang prisoners off a yardarm out here away from the town, thought Oliver. Oliver had made the mistake of looking out over the floodwaters on the way over and seeing the bloated bodies of Spanish soldiers surrounding the burned out siege fortress whose still smoldering, blackened stone tower rose out of the floodwaters like a pillar of hell.

The smell of death – rotting vegetation and seawater – gagged Oliver as he climbed aboard the admiral's vessel. The roll and yaw of the ship in the wind gusts didn't help as he climbed a ladder and stepped aboard.

A first officer led Oliver and Pieter to the after deck and into the captain's navigation room where the mayor and an Estates General magistrate – both bilious green – sat at a thick polished oaken table on either side of Boisot himself, puffing calmly on a clay pipe. Boisot kept glancing at a bin stuffed with rolled-up sea maps on one side of the table, which Oliver took to mean he wanted to set sail out of this place soon as possible.

Various factotums of the mayor and the magistrate and officers crowded the low-ceilinged map cabin, illuminated by hot sunshine streaming from the round of windows aft. The air was sickly warm and smelled of sweat and tobacco. Though a good sailor on their passage from Denmark, Oliver fought to keep from gagging. Everyone in the room but Oliver seemed to be armed with pistols and sabers, like a pirate ship, he thought.

A bulbous nosed, stout bailiff, whom Oliver recognized from the Leiden town council, quickly reviewed "the matter of the Comici players." Two of them – Carlo and Fortunio – had been denounced as Habsburg spies by "the good innkeeper Malthus de Schrum.

After more preliminaries, the bailiff swore Oliver in. Oliver quickly asked to make a statement, and proceeded, struggling to maintain and even, masculine voice. "With respect, my lords, these two loyal colleagues of mine are innocent of all charges. They have proven their loyalty to your cause through the many months we all fought to hold the city."

The mayor cleared his throat and read more from a sheet of charges before him. "The good innkeeper Schrum has sworn that the one called Fortunio..." He pointed at the younger prisoner. "...did visit the Spanish lines in the dark of night many nights during the siege, and came back with many provisions ... and that the other one, the dwarf, did as well."

Carlo sat up, curled his lip and put a fist to his hip at the word "dwarf."

Oliver's neck felt clammy. Olivia's mind wandered to little Ari, wondering if Isabella had fed him yet from the bottle of her milk that she had left. She felt wetness oozing from her right nipple. Her heart raced. Surely it would become a flood that would soak through.

Spectators has begun talking amongst themselves. Boisot banged a wood block against the table talk and glared them back to silence.

"Beg pardon, my lord," Oliver objected, still raspy and struggling with modulation. "With great respect, we players have fought along side the defenders of this city all along. You, lord Mayor, have seen this. And we've given performance to raise spirits under terrible conditions all through the siege. Fortunio and I raided Spanish positions more than once, and brought back bloodied Spanish heads, along with enemy weapons and food."

"I will attest to that, my lord Admiral!" A familiar voice came from among the spectators at the back of the room. "I can vouch for this brave young man, and the rest of these players. They should be treated as heroes of Leiden, not traitors!" Pieter was on his feet. The onlookers stirred and Boisot silenced them again.

The admiral waved Pieter forward and spoke for the first time. "Pieter! Welcome."

Pieter stood up and bowed slightly to the admiral and the panel.

The admiral turned to the others on the tribunal. "This is our Pieter Orneck, a knight of Braban and a hero of Leiden and many battles past. He speaks with my personal blessing. Come forward!" This was the first Oliver ever heard of Pieter being titled or anything but a farm boy. Even the mayor looked surprised.

Later Oliver learned that Pieter had been a squire to Prince William the Silent himself while the prince had still been the Habsburg-appointed governor of Nassau duchy. Pieter followed William when the prince had turned against the Spanish crown and became leaders of the Dutch rebellion. Thenceforth, Pieter had fought alongside his prince against the Spanish, winning honors for himself until he was wounded seriously in combat. After his wounds healed, Prince William had dispatched him to Leiden as his special agent.

Pieter stepped to Oliver's side now, with only a trace of his limp, head high, and back as straight as he could hold it. He grasped Oliver's shoulder firmly with one hand in a gesture of comradeship.

Bradamante, the best known of female knights in chivalric literature, was the heroine of Lodovico Ariosto's much-read, fifteenth-century, epic poem "Orlando Furioso.

++++

15. BRADAMANTE'S SWORD

The admiral called a recess. He motioned for Oliver and Pieter to follow him back into his personal cabin.

"Shut the door. Sit, both of you." He gestured to a chair and his bunk and chose to lean against the door himself, looking down at them a while as he re-lit his white clay pipe and puffed. The sweet tobacco smell only added to Oliver's nausea.

"Tell me about your troupe." He looked at Oliver "How did you, a Danish lad of obvious breeding, come to be with these Venetian players?"

Oliver made up a roundabout story about being the third son of a tradesman, who had joined *I Comici* during their tour of Denmark to escape an arranged marriage and some trouble for rowdiness.

Boisot puffed and arched his eyebrows skeptically.

The more Oliver tried to make the story convincing, the more he tangled the words. *If I don't change the subject, I'll end up in irons myself.*

"... But, my lord, I am not here for myself, but to plead for our innocent players – Carlo and Fortunio"

The admiral raised a hand. "Enough with the 'lordships.' We are alone. You impress no one in this cabin. I am a sea beggar – a privateer and proud of it. No bowing and scraping to Phillip's fat papist geese."

Oliver furrowed his brow. "My lord? … I mean, sir? …I mean, admiral..."

Boisot laughed. "Do you know why we are called *Water Guezen* – Water Beggars?"

"I think so, yes sir." Oliver stammered and prayed for an exit and stifling sudden nervous giggles while a flight of geese honked across his imagination.

The Flemish word *geus* – goose – is a homonym of *gueux*, meaning "beggars" in French. Oliver knew the pun and that "goose" was a popular Flemish invective for the aristocracy. Oliver listened intently, as the admiral explained further, obviously relishing the retelling of what had become a seminal Dutch revolutionary tale.

"It started when four hundred Flemish nobles presented a petition for religious tolerance – *The Request* – to their Habsburg overlords in Brussels. It demanded an end the persecution of Protestants by the Inquisition, confiscation of property and other abuses.

"The villianous counselors of King Phillip II's regent, Margaret of Parma dismissed our *The Request* with contempt. Catherine had advised compromise, but the despot Spanish king overruled her from Madrid. His nobles mocked the petitioners as 'beggars' – *geuzen*, in Flemish – an appellation that rebels adopted with pride. We declared, one and all, that '*if we be geuzen, you be a flock honking, shitting gues.*' We have been 'Beggars' proudly, with a vengeance ever since, young man, as you have seen with our victory here in Leiden."

Oliver felt giddy. *Don't laugh, Oliver, the admiral will think I am mocking him and his cause.*

The admiral wrapped up his tale. Unrest boiled over, predictably, the petitioners were no longer able to restrain their followers. The Spanish lashed out. Philip put the bloody Iron Duke in charge of Flanders and sent an army north over the Spanish Road to smash the rebellion, only fueling it further. Oliver had heard all this before. He did notice that Boisot, painting his heroic panoply, left out the part about Calvinist mobs setting upon and killing Catholics in many townships and attacked churches, destroying art and sculptures that they deemed as graven images. In short, unrest became insurrection, and unremitting warfare. No end in sight.

What am I doing in the midst of these people? Oliver suddenly wanted to turn back into the Ophelia, the fair maiden of Elsinore in those sunnier days before it all went down – when they would let her be, as long as she stuck to her role, able to keep that richer, wilder world within to herself. But then, that dream was gone, as was Ophelia. She remembered Ari, ached to get back to him, and suddenly disliked the admiral for keeping her pinned there.

Boisot's voice cut into her thoughts. Lost in her thoughts she missed what he started to say/ It was something about their loyalties.

She straightened herself back into Oliver. "We are all of us players, lord … or … sir … admiral... loyal subjects to our art..."

Boisot laughed. "And fine players, too, I hear. I have just the roles for you."

Oliver, bewildered, half smiled. "You mean us to play a comedy for your men?"

"I mean you the play for our cause among the enemy."

Oliver blanched. "We have no training with arms, sir admiral."

"Perfect. What better than a bunch of players – Italian papists to boot? Well... except for you, 'Oliver' – whatever relatives of that dead Danish king call themselves these days.

Oliver rattled back, nearly losing himself: "My friends are Venetian, no papists. I have been told that the Republic of Venice has no love for the pope, sir.

"I see." He puffed some more. "And, you are not related to the Danish king, as I've heard?"

"Which king, my lord?"

"The one murdered by his nephew."

Oliver cleared his throat. "I favor neither the living tyrant, nor the dead one, my lord – who, with all respect, Admiral, murdered his own brother and usurped the Danish crown himself, if I may say."

"Assassination is the sport of kings," Boisot laughed. "You are a bold chap indeed. So, then, whom do you and your companions serve? Emperor Fortinbras? The doge of Venice?"

"Not the Spanish, my lord. We are but humble traveling players."

Pieter interjected. "They have given us great inspiration, lord admiral, such that would keep up our people's spirits up even in the darkest hours."

Boisot nodded and clamped his yellowish, battle-chipped teeth on the pipe stem.

Oliver took a breath, feeling slightly encouraged. Boisot leaning against the cabin door was making him feel claustrophobic at the same time. "My lord, I ask only that you release our two falsely accused, wholly innocent players – and allow us to be on our way."

Boisot grunted another laugh and said, more to himself than to them: "Nobody is wholly innocent, my lad." Boisot exhaled more smoke. "Where do you plan to go now, if I release these men and allow it?"

They had been stuck in Leiden for so long, they had ceased to make travel plans months ago, thankful only to survive each day.

"Lyon." Oliver blurted. "I have kin there." That seemed innocuous enough. Word was that the French and their Burgundian allies were staying out of the Flanders war for the moment, being busy with their own civil strife. But one never knew.

Boisot squinted. "The Spanish Road goes by Lyon. Did you know that?" By this Oliver – who had kept eyes and ears open – knew that Boisot meant the system of linked commercial roads going back to Roman times which the Spanish used to move and supply their armies from their lands in Lombardy where the Spanish massed mercenaries from Castille, Italy and other parts of Europe, even Ireland.

Following old trade routes, it traversed the Alps and followed the river valleys northward through Burgundy, Alsace finally into Flanders, a three week trek for a tercio of a thousand men – ten days by sea from northern Spain, but much more dangerous, given rough seas and Dutch and English privateers. Thus, the so-called Spanish Road had become the Habsburg lifeline to Philip's huge, expensive, ponderous mercenary army bleeding daily in Flanders.

"My companions' only wish is to work their way home to Italy, whether by land or sea."

Boisot puffed and looked them both up and down. "That can be arranged."

Oliver sat up. "A ship?"

Boisot gazed at Oliver for a long moment. Ophelia stirred within, responding to the sensuality in his soft brown eyes. Did he suspect? Finally, he spoke again. "I have a tour in mind." He looked back to Pieter. "Through Spanish Flanders, then you may go wherever you wish – sail from Antwerp or down the Spanish Road through your Lyon, and good luck to you."

It couldn't be that easy. There must be a price, Ophelia thought, remembering the court intrigues she had observed her father navigating all through her childhood.

"Will you release my fellow players, Carlo and Fortunio? Please?" Ophelia felt exhausted, but gathered herself back into the masculine role. The switch had always been so easy for her in the past, but not now.

"Pieter will accompany you."

Oliver looked at Pieter then back to Boisot with furrowed brow. "As a player...?"

"If you wish. He can be useful in many ways. Isn't that right, Pieter?"

Pieter nodded, and Oliver realized that the two men both had talked this over previously in secret.

Boisot continued. "You players go about your business and Pieter will go about the business of the Estates General on my behalf. Both will benefit."

And each could end up on a Spanish gibbet, or stake. Oliver blanched as Boisot's intentions became clear. What better cover for espionage and sabotage missions in Habsburg controlled lands than under the guise of a creaky troupe of Venetian players making their way home, tumbling and doing pratfalls along the way?" Oliver began to tremble visibly. Pieter caught his eye with a reassuring gaze. Oliver straightened and held it together lest all be lost right then and there.

"You will keep this meeting to yourselves." Boisot put the pipe in a tray. Oliver followed its thin plume, thinking.

Pieter answered for them both. "Yes, my lord. Of course!"

Oliver looked up. "My lord, with respect. We have no horses and lack supplies. We have no guarantee that the Spanish will allow us passage. I'm sure our chief players, Isabella and Carlo, would much prefer a ship directly home."

"Our ships are otherwise engaged," Boisot said. His voice hardened for the first time in their conversation.

"I am most heartily for your cause, sir...." Oliver paused, then thought better of talking further lest his voice betray the frustration, fear, even anger that he felt.

"But ...?" To Oliver's relief, Boisot shifted slightly away from the door.

"... but what about the Spanish authorities ... How far would we get through the rest of Flanders, much less along the road back to Italy?"

"Traders and couriers make constant use of these roads when the Spanish armies are not on the move. Your wagons will move freely with them."

"How long would will we be on this mission?" Oliver wanted to make clear that he got the point.

"Pieter will be your mission leader, otherwise proceed normally. Now, I must get on..." Boisot stepped back from the door at last.

Ophelia imagined Pieter passing encrypted messages to his superiors in invisible writing roundabout to the postal couriers and trusted traders passing in the opposite direction as themselves. She also imagined the horrors of Spanish punishment should they be caught.

She froze tat the thought of what might befall Ari. What price had she given in return for Carlo and Fortunio.

"And what of city gates and Spanish patrols?"

"You will carry documents bearing King Phillip's royal stamp, commissioning your troupe to perform for the soldiers and townspeople throughout his kingdom."

"Fake?"

"Genuine, straight from Madrid... through certain hands, with some alternations, of course..." Boisot grinned and raised a hand to further questioning.

"I will take up your fight, my lord admiral, as long as I am allowed to escort my sister, Olivia and her baby safely to Lyon where she might be welcomed into the bosom of her mother's family." Time, then, Ophelia thought, for Oliver to exit stage and disappear.

Boisot nodded. "Certainly.... Pieter will make all the arrangements for horses and money to get you on your way... Now, you may take your leave."

".... and our two incarcerated players?"

"They will be released to join you once all arrangements have been made..."

There would be no going back and no resting in place, only going forward. Olivia realized suddenly, that she had been recruited into battle and that she would now be a participant, not merely a spectator – like it or not – in warfare and the bloody games of monarchs and men. She had often imagined herself as a *"guerriera"* like Bradamante, the warrior woman made famous in the Italian chivalric romances she had read as a young girl. *Now, dear God help me, I have joined the fray. Bradamante be my guide.*

By Umberto Tosi

Christophe Plantin published the Antwerp Polygot Bible. He was one of the most influential printers and humanists of the late Renaissance. Plantin Press survives to this day.

16. PRINTING ON BOTH SIDES

"Such a lightness to it." Horatio held the small, cloth-covered book in his upturned palm.

"But a weight of worlds within." Christophe assessed his tall, angular visitor's response as he did all to came to him.

"Small enough to carry in my pouch." Horatio tucked it in and out of a pocket of his doublet. "Will my book be printed in this size?"

"All the fashion now. Books you may take everywhere."

"...and devour in secret..." Horatio riffled through the book's pages of low German text and woodcuts– a collection of writings by "H.N." – the initials of Hendrik Nicholis, the German mystic theologian and founder of the clandestine, Familia Caritatis – Family of Love – a fervent Utopian spiritual movement.

Christophe Plantin regarded Horatio with baleful, slightly drooping green eyes sailing on the sea of printed words churned out by the score of presses in his establishment. He was wiry with large hands, long of face, nose and ears – like a patient horse – accented by scruffy, roan mustache, stubbly beard and curly clipped hair. He had shaken Horatio's hand absentmindedly, but met his eyes upon the Dane's arrival – patently impressed by Plantin Press, with its towering, stepped gable brick facades, gardens and arched entry.

Horatio's mouth watered. A sweet pungency from the nearby docks engulfed and enraptured him – sugar, molasses, cinnamon, nutmeg mixed with the flatness of inks and paper.

Christophe sat on a stool next to a table littered with books, proofs, engravings and various papers. He gave Horatio time to peruse the book that he had given the Dane for the purpose of assessing reaction. "It could mean the stake or the rope if the Spanish caught you with that book."

Horatio looked up. "And you too, for printing them in the dark of night."

"A printer's life ... but I have my allies."

They talked low, just enough to hear each other over the clatter of dozens of presses on the floor outside of Christophe's small office. This was their first meeting in the flesh, after many months of correspondence, but Horatio felt a kinship. Horatio's informants had told him much about the fabled Antwerp publisher – official printer to the Hapsburg emperor Phillip II by day and by night, printer of revolutionary books for the Dutch rebels and heretical tracts by the Family of Love preaching spiritual compassion and the end of all official churches, Protestant and Catholic. "An acrobat's life, sir."

Horatio felt like a schoolboy standing in front of the great printer's desk.

"When do you plan to give me your manuscript, Horatio?"

Horatio cleared his throat. "I have brought you a manuscript. I need only complete the final pages while I am here in Antwerp." Horatio patted the leather pouch strapped from his shoulder, but he did not bring out the manuscript yet. He continued leafing through the Nicholis book. He read aloud from it, frowning. "... Christ reflects the love that unites us all..."

Horatio paused, his eyes scanning the pages of Nicholis' words *"... in peace eternal"* ... and so forth. Horatio looked up at Christophe, "This world seems quite the opposite of what your philosopher envisions. I see hate, tyranny, rancor, connivance, betrayal, and blood common among all people – of high and low birth – and now much sorrow in the lives of people enduring first plague, then injustice, and now war no longer fought in the fields, but in the streets of our cities. How do you persevere?

Christophe nodded. "I see no point in idealism, either, Horatio my friend. But what does despair gain us? I have tasted the bitter dregs of fear, doubt and hate and I find no other way to live truly, than with an open, loving spirit. It is for my own tranquility that I endeavor to love despite it all, not for heaven's sake."

Horatio considered Plantin's words in silence for a while. Then he handed the book back to Christophe. "Then, I shall do the same, noble sir Plantin, and share this product of my most earnest labors with you." With that, Horatio removed a large sheaf of papers tied in black ribbon from his pouch.

He laid his offering gingerly on the table beside his publisher at last. The title page read, in bold cursive, *"To Be, or Not to Be! – The Tragedy of Prince Hamlet."*

Christophe nodded in approval and looked up at Horatio wide eyed. *"En God zeide: Daar zij licht: en daar werd licht. –* And God said, let there be light, and there was light!" Christophe laughed to himself, and took Horatio's manuscript in hand. "I will read this and render you my thoughts swiftly."

"Thank you, my most noble printer! Together we make history today!"

"Somewhat so, Lord Horatio, but the lateness of your offering puts me in a spot – not unfamiliar to my kind."

"Yes, sir. I know. As you wrote me, my most powerful and influential readers await this book."

"The bloody tale of your Danish prince has raced ahead of you, whetting appetites all over Europe. It isn't every day that a king, queen and prince assassinate each other all at once."

"I would not put it that way, sir. There is much more to... as you will read..."

"...Already a passel of hasty epics about your Hamlet have preceded us while I awaited your opus, Horatio..."

"I know, sir, and I apologize..."

"... but none can claim to be that of someone like yourself, a noble witness who survived the massacre."

"... I would call it tragedy, not massacre, the heroic tale of a noble prince struggling within himself to put things aright."

"So be it, Horatio. This is why we need your book to tell the tale as you saw it."

"I have done my best, sir."

"I am deluged with requests – nay, demands – for your book. Emperor Phillip II himself, insists on a Spanish edition..."

"I am flattered...."

"Then, secretly, I have royal orders for editions in French, Italian and Dutch editions from Henri III, the pope, the doges of Venice and Genoa and William of Orange, all of whose assassins will have my head if I do not deliver."

"I will not fail you, my noble Christophe..."

"Never mind now, my Horatio. You have only proven yourself no different than the many writers whose wretched scrawls land on my desk."

"Am I to take that as a compliment, sir? You have a reputation for printing works by the greatest authors and poets of our age."

Christophe nodded diffidently as he tidied Horatio's manuscript. He handed Horatio back the new Nicolis book and waved him off. "Yes. Yes. Enough said. Return to your inn. This is my gift to you. Read Nicolis well – for he has a powerful following her in the low countries – and finish. Then I will send for you."

"Sir, one other thing."

"Yes. I know. I have heard the same as you. The Spanish may send troops into Antwerp soon..."

"And ...the king of Spain has declared bankruptcy to his Genoese creditors... "

"Yes. Phillip owes my firm still for our Polyglot Bible.

"I have heard that his mercenary soldiers are in a state of mutiny since the English queen seized the Spanish ship filled with gold Florins to pay them."

"So I've heard as well. But our governor holds his ground. He has reinforced the citadel and put his Walloons at the ready."

Horatio cursed under his breath. "I would have been well to sail straight to Genoa."

Christophe shook his head. "I doubt you could have done that without changing ships here or at another Flanders port. We are the center."

"For how long?"

"All the world needs Antwerp... trading, banking, praying, whoring ... French, Dutch, Walloons, Germans, Jews, East Indians, Venetians, Genoans, Lutherans, Anabaptists and Catholics, – all come here for one purpose, to prosper together."

"We shall see. I will take my leave now, and promise you the final pages by the end of this week when I sail again towards Italy."

Christophe shook Horatio's hand and waved him away with a half smile. "... Do not worry yourself, Horoatio. Antwerp will persevere, as have you, through the best and worst of days."

17. PAPIER-MÂCHÉ

"Nothing is the same for me."

"Nor for me, or for anyone," Isabella nodded towards townspeople passing on the street, taking advantage of a break in the late winter weather. Ophelia – again in the clothing and role of Oliver – helped Isabella, Carlo and Fortunio repair the carnival wagon, now back in their possession. They all felt a blithe serenity in getting to do ordinary tasks again, not connected with war and survival. They slapped on paints – white, yellows, reds and greens – with gusto, laughing like children who have been allowed to make a mess. The sun shone deceivingly bright through the bare trees, glistening off icy cobblestones and patches of snow.

Fortunio put a brush back into a pail of bloody crimson, and rubbed his hands together. "I won't ever be the same either now, with my fingers freezing off."

"Hurry. Get to work! We must take advantage of the sunshine." Isabella moved a stepladder from one side of the wagon to the other.

Rosa was minding baby Ari in their rooms at the inn, while Ophelia helped the troupe outside. She felt good to be participating again. And the sun and air cheered her. It was already mid-March. The troupe had played wildly through the city's lively, first carnival time since its liberation.

Now, Ophelia/Olivia welcomed the relative quiet of Lent, and noticing the first few tulips stems pushing up through the chill soil, freshly green in the garden across the square. Again, as Oliver, she had helped with planting the bulbs that fall while the city continued under Spanish siege – and act of faith, fulfilled by their first green shoots here and there, with red and yellow flowers peeking out of their buds.

True to his word, Boisot had freed Carlo and Fortunio, but busy with matters of war, provided the troupe no horses, provisions or permits to leave the city through the frigid months that followed. Still, it was a pleasant time. They played often for both the townspeople and the rebel fighters who stayed on in the city as well.

They performed through Advent, and again as part of the week-long carnival in February in which they acted on a portable stage wearing comic grotesque masks. They borrowed a team of donkeys to pull their wagon as a float in the parade of papier-mâché monsters and caricatures of King Phillip II and the Duke of Alva, and even their own dignitaries. Through it all, Ophelia felt that part of her had left the city already as the time for their departure approached.

"Bless these people, but I do not want to see another Easter with them." Isabella repeated often. She had been talking of little but returning home lately, to such an extent that Ophelia began to imagine Venice as a paradise of freedom, high culture opulence and feasting.

"...And much to vex a woman," Isabella admonished. "The Spanish – for all their faults – recognize a woman's dignity more than the Italians, even the Venetians, who make it neigh impossible for a woman to inherit property. Spanish women inherit and run estates, duchies, even may become queens – as with the English. Same for the French. And the Dutch... You have seen how women here in Holland run family businesses and households and manage the finances, and have the men slaving for them publicly, without fear of shaming from village louts."

Ophelia smirked. "Yes, but it's difficult to see these differences, and in any event, it's too late to dissuade me, my lady."

"You are one of us now, if you wish to stay, my dear – all the way home to Venice, as you like," Isabella said. "Though, what of your mother's family in Lyon?"

"Yes." Ophelia looked down. "Family. Little Ari needs to be with kin, I suppose. And myself too... Oh, I am in fits, Isabella. What welcome can I expect there, a shamed woman with a bastard child?"

"I shall write a story and we will put on a show for you there, in real life that will sway your relatives."

Ophelia kept painting as she talked. "But I barely know them...."

"They will know you by the time we're through....

"Fortunio cannot continue to pose as my 'husband,' if he mean to travel onward from Lyon with you and the other players."

"No, then. I have a better plot – you as the lost Danish princess, your Hamlet's widow... with his little, princely child. If the lords and ladies and merchants of Lyon are anything like all the other towns I've visited, they will be falling all over themselves to curry your royal favor."

"How... What would you...?"

"I have already written a play in which that happens. We will start presenting it as a true story – a secret wedding in a forest chapel before the prince met his tragic end."

"But then, why is this 'princess' not in Denmark?"

"Obviously, my dear, because of your child, heir to Hamlet's throne. You had to flee the wrath of that usurper Fortinbras."

Ophelia thought a while she dabbed bright yellow on the spokes of a carriage wheel.

"Your mother's kin should welcome you with open arms then and give protection to you and little Ari..."

"If they see profit in it, I'll wager. I remember my mother speaking of her brother-in-law as a particularly venal sort."

Carlo, all ears, commented from atop the carriage where he had been patching the roof. "I'd wager that the French crown would extend protection as well. King Henri is no friend of Fortinbras."

Ophelia stiffened. She put down her brush. "I smell more strife and death in this."

"Better than taking your chances with us as things have been going." Carlo stepped over to the ladder and sprang down, with surprising agility. "We could use whatever favor that your Burgundians and French can offer us at this point – if we are ever to get home in one piece."

Ophelia shuddered and shook her head. "I must go see how Ari is now. Excuse me." She took up a rag to wipe her hands of paint.

Isabella put a motherly hand on her arm. "One day at a time, dear. We're only talking. Let us move ahead and do our best, and see what opportunities present themselves. You always have a place with us... Don't worry."

"If we survive..." Ophelia laughed with some relief. "At this rate we may never escape from Leiden."

Their route and means of travel had remained uncertain for weeks now. At Carlo's urging, "Oliver" had inquired about a ship for Italy – or any Mediterranean port – even though she knew beforehand that Boisot had already mapped out their secret mission.

In a private moment after Boisot had dismissed them, Oliver had asked Pieter: "If you know more, tell me now, please."

"In due time," he had answered cryptically.

Oliver didn't like the sound of that, nor the sudden formality. Pieter's turnabout reminded Prince Hamlet's hurtfulness in those last days at Elsinore. "In due time, you'll need to be honest with us if you want our help."

Pieter gave no further response. "I have much to do. I must leave your company for now."

"When can I expect you to deliver our horses and the rest?"

"Soon..." He waved and left Oliver in the main square.

Ophelia – back with the troupe and in female guise as Olivia – nursed her baby and waited. No sight of Pieter for the ten days, but at least they had Carlo and Fortunio back, and possession of the wagon. Painting it seemed more an act of hope than a preparation for travel. They weren't going anywhere without the horses.

Then, without warning on the morning the players were outside painting, Pieter showed up on horseback, with two of their horses in tow. Ophelia was happy she had chosen to be Oliver that day, though she still had no idea how she would handle things should Pieter actually come with them on the road. Oliver waved and gave Pieter a boyish grin to signal that all was forgiven.

"Ah!" Carlo climbed down from the roof of the wagon and ambled out onto the street as Pieter dismounted. "Good man!" Carlo reached up and shook Pieter's hand, then walked behind him to lead the horses back to the stables behind the inn.

"Wait." Pieter kept hold of the reins. "There is more." He gestured down the road behind him, as two more riders came into view, leading four more horses hitched to another wagon, larger than that of the troupe, but black and with no windows.

"Paint this one too. Brightly. Same as yours." Pieter gestured to the conveyance. It looked much like a freight wagon seen commonly on well traveled roads, war or no war, good weather and bad.

Carlo scowled. "Please, good sir." Pieter tipped his cap.

Carlo put hands on hips and kept scowling. "Paint it yourself."

Oliver intervened. "I will help. It's no bother, Pieter." He gave a knowing look to Isabella and whispered, "Remember what I told you about him and Boisot."

Pieter dismounted and came near. "I will be happy to help." He picked up a rag and a paintbrush.

Warming for the first time in a week, he patted Oliver on the back. "I see you are back. Where is your sister, Olivia?"

"At the inn with little Ari."

"Getting to be a handful, that boy."

Oliver's face reddened. The Oliver-Olivia charade would be impossible to sustain once Pieter joined them on the road.

18. BLACK POWDER

"Where is Oliver?" Pieter looked up and down the street while he finished hitching a team of horses to the lead wagon in the troupe's now-brightly decked out caravan. *I Comici* would be back up to its full complement of three wagons for the trip. Pieter would lead the way in a canvas-topped trade wagon converted for the trip. Second, a pair of Boisot's marines dressed as players would drive four horses pulling the large, boxy freight wagon – now brightly decorated – heavy with some mystery cargo Pieter and his men had loaded. Carlo and Fortunio would drive the team pulling the troupe's original carnival wagon, which Pieter ordered at the rear of the procession.

Already seated on his perch, Carlo groused back at Pieter. "Oliver rode ahead to the next town last night to make arrangements for us."

"He didn't tell me." Pieter squinted in the bright morning sun as he checked the harnesses on the twitching, muscular dray animals. "On what horse?"

"We traded for one," Carlo shouted down from his perch, holding the reins of the last wagon, "a swift chestnut gelding. Oliver will be well ahead of us by now."

Olivia came out from the inn and held up little Ari to wave at the townspeople who had gathered to say farewell.

"Say bye bye, Ari!"

Ari burbled the words and waved happily.

Pieter stared at the two and remarked: "You and that golden child could pose for Titian."

"Ah, the Venetian master. You impress me, sir."

He tossed his head. "So, this peasant boy surprises you?"

Olivia's face reddened. "I know little of your origins, sir. I only meant that few of us..." She tried to amend her slip.

"Perhaps I misled your brother Oliver about my upbringing – which was humble, but not ignorant." He bowed slightly and caught her eyes.

She could see that he knew the game, but was willing to play it, in fact, with a hint of flirtation. Just the hint of a smile turned up her full lips and crinkled her eyes, holding his gaze.

"Now they tell us, Antwerp! Boisot and his Pieter have made puppets of us, no longer players." Carlo had fulminated at Isabella, after Pieter had delivered the news to them at the inn two nights earlier. "Our plan was straight for Paris, then Lyon, then down the Rhone by barge to Arles and a ship for home, all in a few weeks, with luck, but now that's in the pot."

Isabella smoothed his feathers and poured him a glass of Leiden beer. "I can deliver more of my plays to Plantin Press there. Christophe would be happy for a new play after the success of *Le Inammorati*. He would pay me well."

The prospect of money always gladdened Carlo. "I say we take a ship from there directly home then, and forget Paris."

Fortunio looked up from a book. "Boisot's Sea Beggars have the whole Flanders coast blocked. Forget it."

Carlo took a swag of his brew and wiped his mouth with his sleeve. "If these Dutch get us killed, it won't matter. Have you been able to find out what is in those barrels?"

Late at night, Fortunio climbed into the freight wagon after Pieter's guard fell asleep – aided by too much wine.

He discovered a dozen oaken barrels stacked inside. He had time for only a cursory inspection before he had heard Pieter's voice calling to the guard and had to slip away. "Stunk of herring, the one I got open, but the rest were sealed. It was dark in there."

"Why would they want us to carry herring?" Carlo had rolled his eyes. "If I have to eat anymore damned salted herring I'll grow fins!"

Fortunio thought for a moment. "There has to be something else in those barrels, maybe one or two with salt herring for cover, but the rest..."

Olivia had come into the common room with Ari bouncing in her arm. She put the baby down and stood him shakily on his feet, letting him stand erect while holding his mother's thumbs for support. "Look at that!" Her eyes brighten proudly.

"Fantastic!" Isabella bent to the child. "This young man will be walking before his first birthday."

"Black powder." Fortunio slapped a hand on the table in front of him. "The floor felt gritty. When I got back to my quarters, I noticed that my boots were coated in a grainy soot that I remember from my Venetian navy days, loading cannons. It has to be gunpowder! The barrels are loaded with gunpowder!"

They all looked at each other.

"We are to be a bomb on wheels! One lantern knocked over, and we go off like Neapolitan fireworks on New Years." Carlo swashed down the rest of his beer. "Pity. I hoping for casks of gold ducats – to pay Boisot's spies and rebels. Just one could buy us a ship to go home, and a villa of our own when we got there."

"Not if they cut our throats first," Olivia said, still walking her baby.

Fortunio glanced at the four walls of the room. "A barrel could bring down a garrison wall – and mow down a regiment, if nails are packed with the powder."

137

"I'm impressed with your military acumen, Fortunio." Carlo poured himself more beer from a pitcher. "Is it too late to tell this Pieter we've changed our minds?"

"...and have Boisot put you back in jail?" Isabella bent and picked up little Ari for some more bouncing. As Isabella did so, she looked the baby's mother in the eye. "Considering this danger, *you* should consider remaining here in Leiden with the child, Olivia, out of harm's way."

"I will not rot in this damp place another day. ... What is here for me? To become a nun or a whore?"

"You could keep being 'Oliver'."

"With a child, and without means?"

Fortunio interjected. "Perhaps our fears are exaggerated. What would be the point of a suicide mission? Pieter would not readily throw away his life, even if he held our own lives cheap."

Carlo arched an eyebrow. "Don't forget. He that he fights for a cause. I can think of a few instances..."

Isabella nodded. "Men are capable of anything in war."

The baby let go of Olivia's hands and slid down to the floor for a good crawl, sampling bits of fallen food here and there. "I will find out more from him." Olivia smiled.

"As man or woman?" Carlo smirked.

"I think, woman this time." Olivia answered. "It wouldn't be my first try at spying." She thought back to her painful attempt to discover Prince Hamlet's motives for her father and the queen. "This time, though, I hope to fare better."

19. BED AND BREDA

The residential palace of Stadtholder Orneck was the most sumptuous Olivia had ever seen, outshining those where she had grown up as Ophelia. The gold trimmed drapes, marble columns, tiled floors and arched ceilings did not impress Olivia as much as the library and the thousands of leather bound books lining its shelves floor to ceiling. "I could spend a year in this room reading in bliss," she sighed.

"What is it, child?" Sir Orneck cupped an ear and cocked his head. He reminded Olivia of a wrinkly, gray-whiskered old hound wearing the magnificent silks that would have been the envy of sultans.

Next to her, Isabella craned her neck at the scenes of Elysium painted with elaborate gold trim on the dome, decidedly Italian rather than Dutch. "I feel that I am back in Venice," she said.

"I feel..." Olivia's voice tailed off. She did not want to confess that she felt quite at home in the Orneck mansion, having grown up in the summer and winter palaces of Denmark. It would have sounded patronizing.

She sighed, suddenly feeling the exhaustion from the long journey on which Pieter had led the troupe, snaking through the towns of Holland and Zeeland, performing each night, while he and his cohorts delivered gunpowder, arms and messages to rebels in the dead of night.

"Tomaso Vincidor designed it all, inside and out." Old Orneck's stentorian voice echoed off the dome as he swept a hand around at everything.

"Ah. The great Bolognese master! Exquisite, sir!" Carlo bellowed back.

Deaf as a melon, and too vain to use a horn. Carlo made a surreptitious survey of Lord Orneck – whom he saw at the perfect incarnation of one of the wealthy, bumbling, half-deaf old lords that he often played for laughs on stage.

Vincidor had been a protégé of Raphael who had spent his last years in Breda helping the wealthy lords and burghers of Brabant outdo each other in grandeur.

"We are honored by your most gracious hospitality, my lord." Olivia curtsied Orneck when they got back to the banquet room where they would dine later.

"You're most welcome. It is small thanks for the great service you players have been doing for us, not the least of which is bringing my nephew Pieter back home, however curious your mode of transportation."

Orneck led them into another large room, a hall where the troupe would perform after their celebratory. The hall had a raised stage framed by gilded Corinthian columns at one end. The walls were hung with exquisite Flemish tapestries, in the Burgundian style, interwoven with gold and silver threads and colors more brilliant than Ophelia had ever seen, even in Elsinore. The tapestries depicted fantastically detailed battle scenes, including a new one that Lord Orneck described as depicting the siege of Haarlem in all its gore.

Fortunio muttered, shuddering, "Not exactly conducive to comedy, these scenes."

Pieter – whom Ophelia now knew as no peasant boy, but rather as a scion of the House of Orneck – approached them. "I see uncle is giving you the grand tour. You must think us ostentatious."

"On the contrary. I never knew that my lord, Pieter, possessed such rarefied refinement..." Olivia smirked in the way Pieter already could read, then whispered aside, out of Orneck's range, "... for a simple *farm* boy."

Pieter narrowed his eyes, showing no sign of their secret intimacy, or the merriment of their previous night. He and Olivia had become lovers over the past weeks, though carefully discreet.

The players had been hailed as "The Heroes of Leiden" when their caravan arrived in Breda, greeted by a delegation and escorted – not to the usual inn or camp spot, but to be guests at the Orneck stadthaus, given separate room with comforts laid out.

The stately Duchy of Brabant *residentzstaad* – still nominally part of the Habsburg domain – contrasted with the solid pragmatism of Leiden and the other towns of the newly formed, States General that the troupe had played.

Pieter had set their exhausting itinerary, lingering in each town and village, presumably to throw off Spanish agents and Walloon Catholic sympathizers. Carlo had raised no more objections. Pieter and his companions seemed both the troupe's guardians and their keepers. *I Comici* performed dutifully in each town, relieving the grimness of wartime with Isabella's irreverent sexual farces played with the carnival spirit of delicious grotesqueness and always ending love's triumph, weddings, setting things right for their young protagonists in overcoming overbearing elders and venal schemers. "Would that life imitated art," Isabella would say, flourishing her inky quill over a last page.

Pieter said nothing further about the missing "Oliver" when he failed to appear in the next town, or the next, or the next. "Oliver was called back to Denmark on some family business." Carlo lamely read a fake dispatch. Pieter just nodded, then gave Olivia a conspiratorial smile. She and Pieter began talking together freely after that, and seemed to take up where his friendship with Oliver had left off – and warmed more with each town they visited.

As it turned out, there was no need for an awkward confession about her gender ruse. Pieter had seen through her clever guise as soon as "Oliver" had exited stage. That made it easier for her to reveal her true self – not as Olivia, but as Ophelia. She told him about life at Elsinore, though sketchily about her growing up with Prince Hamlet and their experiences together. She did not lie outright, but saw that Pieter already had assumed that Prince Hamlet was the father of her child. But moreover, he assumed that she and the prince had been married secretly before his untimely death. She said nothing to change that impression. Lest he grow jealous, she did confess to her "marriage" with Fortunio being faked, though continued the pretense in public, at least until they arrived in Breda.

He took it all in, and asked no further explanations. "Our worlds have been torn asunder and we both have had to shape new ones, and new lives in this war torn time. I understand."

Pieter announced that they would stay a while in Breda – take rest from the rigors of the road. What he meant was that he would wait to meet with Prince William himself – at the Orange-Nassau prince's own palace, which was not far from that of Orneck. When they got to Breda, William ordered Pieter to suspend his mission, while the prince would be negotiating a truce with the new Spanish governor general Luis de Requesens.

++++

Everything seemed to slow down and grow sumptuous. Olivia was given her own bedchamber, with an antechamber and nurse to help care for baby Ari. Pieter wasted no time sneaking up to Olivia's bedchamber on the first night, taking advantage of their unaccustomed privacy.

They had, by now, explored each other often during opportune moments in the course of their travels. Though one would have thought she knew him well, the depth of his passion and tenderness in the plush, private setting of this palace bedroom suite surprised her. It dawned on Ophelia that she had not known such intimate, poetic love from a man before, only in her readings and dreams. She and Pieter were like two different persons together in their deeper intimacy – a shift from the roguishness of their original friendship in Leiden, as "two young men," – a "poor lame soldier" and a commedia player. But she realized now that their friendship had enriched their intimacy. She remembered a similar transition from childhood friendship to young passion between her and Prince Hamlet, but one that didn't go so well.

Now they felt part of one another, more than surreptitious lovers on the fly. She had grown bold with him naked in silk sheets, surprising herself. He was a true warrior, not like her Hamlet, muscular and scarred, serene in his powerful body, but affectionate, just as she had imagined him during her walks as Oliver along with the battlements of Leiden with him.

"I fear that our Prince William – being a noble man of high ideals – will trust these Spanish too much." Pensive, after he and Olivia had expended their passions among twisted silken sheets, Pieter stared from their canopied bed into the glowing embers of the room's white marble fireplace sculpted with cherubs. "Our prince believes that he can reason with the devil."

Olivia leaned against his bare shoulder and ran a hand over his chest, feeling its scars and soft furriness. "Nothing ventured, as they say..."

He leaned to kiss her again, sleepily. "This will be good for you and the child – a haven to rest and play while we let those who would change history have their day."

143

"You sound impatient, Pieter, nonetheless."

"If I am called upon to resume my mission, you and little Ari should stay here, and go no farther with us."

"You would leave me by the road? Here? I know none of these people..."

"I will arrange it. They will provide protection and shelter you as an honored guest."

"Not without you...."

"Oh, yes. I already gained the consent of Lady Charlotte d'Bourbon, Princess of Orange, the consort of William the Silent."

"You didn't ask me..." Olivia sat up, away from him.

"It would not be possible, in the first place, without the princess' approval."

"Still, you should have … I am not to be traded off like a cow."

"You take me wrong, Olivia."

"You put me in an awkward place. How can I refuse such an invitation from the princess?"

"... She has other things to worry about... She would only think you a reckless fool..."

"... Now you call me a fool?"

"I didn't mean it that way."

"I don't see how this city is any safer from the Spanish butchers than was Leiden, or Haarlem, or any other town. I'd as soon take my chances on the road as a player, thank you."

"At least speak with the princess. She has agreed to see you privately. You've become quite a heroine in everyone's eyes here..."

Olivia smiled in the darkness next to him, still feeling his warmth, breathing him in, but still miffed. "No need to patronize me, Pieter. I've grown up with queens and kings and princesses, and found them of all sorts... not always remarkable."

She noticed Pieter flinch, his face come overcome momentarily with surprise in the yellow light of the fire. She took a breath, realizing she had disclosed more than she would have intended.

He composed himself quickly. "If you mean kings and queens on stage, our Princess Charlotte is more heroine than any portrayed in your plays, poems and romances."

Olivia remained quiet for a moment. Collecting her thoughts. Maybe it would be good for him to wonder about her secrets for a change.

"The princess is a bold woman who has braved terrible hardships."

"She is French?"

"Yes. Locked away in a nunnery at age 13 by a tyrannical father."

"Get thee to a nunnery."

"What?"

"Nothing. Just a saying, I remember. Please go on, sir."

"She became an abbess, but escaped with the help of the Huguenots, and fled to Heidelberg where she met our prince."

"Truly a romance to challenge my pen..."

"I tell you all this in confidence, my dear Olivia.

"You're a very fine gossip for a man, Pieter." She thought she could see his face redden. "She is a Catholic then?"

"Most certainly not. She had long favored the protestant cause and converted."

"Where I come from, a prince marrying a convert would raise some bushy clerical eyebrows."

"Here as well, but the Union of Utrecht will be a republic where all may live and work together in peace, and do today within our lands – Lutheran, Catholic, Anabaptist, Moriscos, Jews."

"And enrich yourselves well overseas..."

"...and why not?"

145

"My mother was secretly a Roman Catholic. I have never told anyone." Olivia looked into the fireplace now too.

Pieter hesitated. "Olivia. I want to ask you..." He stopped.

"Ask me what?"

"About what I had mentioned before..."

"But never said, outright, Pieter."

Pieter went silent again.

Olivia resumed." I am told Lady Charlotte is Prince William's third wife."

"That is correct."

"I thought he was married to Lady Anne."

"Annulled. She was mad, so they say." Pieter lowered his voice.

"Did he send Princess Anne to the block?" Olivia drew it out, running a finger across her throat. "...Like that English king..."

"Henry. But no. She was put into the care of nuns."

"There it is again. Get thee to a nunnery."

"You keep saying that."

"I was mad once too. Perhaps I am still."

"Mad as a fox." He glanced towards the drapes. No light yet. "I must return to my quarters soon, my dear, lest we make a scandal ourselves.

"And my Fortunio returns from his night with the town boys..."

"No more of this ruse with Fortunio, Olivia." Pieter turned and looked straight into her eyes in a way that made her catch her breath. "We must marry."

"Must?" She searched his face. "That is not a reason."

"For love, not fakery -- in a sanctified way, in our church. So that you and Ari can have my family's protection." He cupped her face softly in both of his long fingered hands.

Olivia stared back at him, silent for a while. Finally she responded. "Pieter. You honor me. But what of my child?"

"Prince William and Princess Charlotte already know the truth."

"What truth?"

"... of Ari's father, and your secret marriage to Prince Hamlet."

Olivia froze. "Why? What have you been saying?"

"I've known since Boisot told me."

Oliva gasped.

"Boisot has eyes everywhere. He knew how you came to be with the players, and that your marriage to Fortunio was fake."

Olivia took a breath and furrowed her brow. "I feel like a fool."

"Don't fret. He told no one but me, and that was only because I would have to be traveling with you on our mission."

"And you let me *'confess'* all to you? Did I make you laugh?"

"Of course not. I was glad."

"Glad?"

"That you chose not to deceive me. Glad that my dear friend 'Oliver' had turned out to be a beautiful woman, and lover, and still my friend. And glad that you were not spoken for, not really."

"You *are* a rogue, Pieter."

"And now with the advent of this new book by that Horatio fellow, it will be harder for you to keep your secrets."

"What book?"

"The Tragedy of Hamlet. It names you Hamlet's betrothed, but does not dwell on you."

Olivia grimaced at the memory of Horatio. "I don't know whether to be offended or relieved at his slighting me."

"Boisot wrote me about the book. He assumes that there had been a marriage as well."

"Nice of the admiral to defend my honor."

"In any event, the admiral has greater problems with which to cope."

"I fear that you propose marriage to me now only as a means to keep me penned in your uncle's palace out of harms way, while you go off and get yourself killed."

"I would return. Safe."

"I have known but one love in my life before you, Pieter, and he came to a very bad end."

"We all come to an end, dear Olivia, with only faith in God's kingdom come if we can muster it."

"... and why not follow your heart while it still beats?" Olivia completed the lines from one of Isabella's romantic comedies that they had performed in Ghent.

"Our noble Prince William has by example, espoused his true love in Charlotte – and she is much loved by the populace as well. She has become his right hand in affairs of state..."

"Now I am intrigued." Olivia reached over and squeezed his arm and kissed his shoulder, hoping to lead him back to mirth. "I will be honored to meet your princess."

He seemed cheered, but with a quaver. Still puzzled by her earlier remark, she reckoned. "Good. Tomorrow."

"I will thank her for such a generous offer. And I thank you for yours, my dear Pieter. But I'm still going to leave with my friends when the time comes. I will not take advantage of you."

"We will see about that." He pulled her gently to him.

20. BY THE BOOK

Carlo pulled a small, black leather-covered book from his shoulder bag and opened it on the stone bench he straddled amid the flowers of Orneck palace gardens. Finches, linnets and sedge warblers chattered from the trees and hedges. The air hung sweet in the midsummer afternoon, smelling faintly of roses. Isabella and Olivia sat on a straw linen blanket shaded by a motherly, turquoise-leafed, ash.

"Get this." Carlo read aloud. "'... 'I saw myself this kingly ghost – Hamlet's father – who called upon our sweet prince to set aside his kindly spirit to avenge a murder most foul.'"

Olivia set down the daisy she had been twirling with her fingers, rose and walked to Carlo's bench. "What have you here?"

"Toad's tripe!" Carlo slammed the book closed and held it up so she could read the gold embossed title on the cover,

"Hamlet's tale... as told by his old school chum, Horatio Orlando Virgilius." Carlo smirked and gave his beard a pull.

"*Horatio*. I had wondered if he survived. I see that he has done well for himself, however." Olivia ran a fingers over the book cover, feeling the gold-embossed letters of Horatio's name.

Isabella called over to Carlo. "Does the book mention us?"

"By name. The author tells all about how Prince Hamlet cornered King Claudius into admitting guilt by having our troupe play a version of 'The Murder of Gonzago.' ... As if we, a motley collection of clowns could shake a king and cause hell to break loose."

Isabella shifted forward from the trunk of the ash where she had been resting her back. "Better that the author put blame on a band of Venetian players, than upon himself or his prince, or worse yet, his present king."

"From what I hear, Fortinbras is an ambitious despot of the worst kind." Carlo shifted around and let his short legs swing off the bench. "Take a look, if you like." He proffered the book to Olivia and patted the seat next to him."

"May I?" She sat and took the slim volume, gingerly turning pages, reading passages here and there.

"Ghost, my *arse!*" Carlo flipped a chubby hand at the book.

Isabella, still lounging on the blanket, raised her eyebrows in her connubial warning way, meaning he should button his lip.

Carlo pressed on, looking straight back at his wife. "You know it, too, Isabella – quite well – what was proposed secretly to us in Calais ... by a secret agent of that prince who called himself Fortinbras of Norway, then fighting in Poland?"

"Carlo! *You* remember! We thought the man likely an impostor, devil up to no good."

Carlo, talking loudly, as he always did after a flagon of beer, threw up his hands. "All right, then my love..."

Olivia closed the book, raised a hand at Isabella and turned to Carlo. "No. What? Carlo, please go on – tell me."

Carlo beamed, vindicated. "This happened shortly before we boarded a ship for Denmark. This agent of prince Fortinbras offered me a hundred gold florins if I would have our giant, Nunco play a certain prank on King Claudius and Prince Hamlet."

Isabella kept shaking her head, but Carlo proceeded, looking back at Olivia.

150

"This was real, Olivia! Fortinbras' agent showed me a bag of the gold coins!"

Isabella fumed. "Did he give you any coins? No. This is but another of your tall tales, Carlo. The dwarf paid her no mind.

"When we got to Denmark, I was to have Nunco whiten his face with chalk and parade the parapets of Elsinore suited in stage armor all whitened in chalk dust, like a ghost of old King Hamlet '*when he the ambitious Norway combated.*'

Isabella glared. "Don't believe him, Olivia."

"Fortinbras' man even showed me a script. He promised us another hundred florins after our prankish ghost walk was done. That is, if we had not been thrown in a dungeon by then."

Olivia reopened the book and riffled the pages. "I saw that Horatio's book does mention a ghost? Is that what Horatio says drove our prince mad?"

Carlo shook his head. "Horatio makes the ghost real."

Olivia looked puzzled. "And it was a prank, gone wrong?"

Carlo, seeing he was going too far now, put a hand on Olivia's arm. "Who knows? What I do know is that your Prince Hamlet likely had gone mad already, with all due respect, Olivia.

"Did you accept Fortinbras' offer?"

"By Zeus, no! Impersonating a king, even a dead one, is a hanging offense. I refused. I feared the offer was a trap, and even if not, it would have been too risky. We didn't even know whether we would be invited to play inside Elsinore at that time – only in Arhaus and perhaps Copenhagen."

Isabella interjected: "The whole Denmark trip – your idea, Carlo –- proved disastrous in any case, so..."

Olivia held up a hand. "And Nunco? I don't remember you having any giant with your troupe at Elsinore."

"The big lout went off on a drunk and never showed up when we left. He was like that...He's probably still in some Paris tavern...We miss him. His mock rampages on stage made our patrons laugh and soil their pants at the same time."

"You don't think...?" Olivia laid the book down on her lap and gazed across the garden.

Carlo took back the book gently and opened it again.

"Tell me, Olivia, is this Horatio a reliable fellow? I recall him from when we played for King Claudius, but he and I never spoke."

Olivia nodded her head and answered in a faraway voice. "A noble gentleman and scholar, as I recall. I only wish he had talked sense into our prince instead of abetting his madness." Olivia's voice hardened.

Isabella came over and looked at Horatio's book. "Do you suppose that our Nunco took the gold for himself, and did as Fortinbras's agent asked?"

"A bloody foul joke that turned out to be." Carlo shrugged. "... but damn effective – if it got Fortinbras the Danish throne that he and his father before him, had so coveted."

"It would not have mattered in the end. My lord Hamlet did not act upon ghostly words alone. He caught his uncle with your 'Mousetrap' and showed him up as the murderer that he was. Would that it were otherwise and we had all gone on in blessed ignorance."

Isabella saw the glint of tears on Olivia's cheeks, and gave Carlo another reproving look. "Did you *have* to talk about that book and drag up all that sorrow for our dear Olivia? Did you forget who she was and all that she has suffered?"

++++

Princess Charlotte de Bourbon, French noblewoman, poet, scholar, former nun, protestant convert and beloved third wife of Prince William the Silent, 1579, portrait to Daniël van den Queborn

21. CHARLOTTE

Prince William the Silent's palace overlooked a pond inside the walls of the citadel and looked even grander than that of Staadtholder Orneck, built with the riches Dutch traders hauled in from the East and West Indies. So far, Olivia had seen nothing of the legendary prince – only his portrait, by Anthonis Mor, which stared down at her intensely from a wall. It showed Prince William as a young man, looking fierce in black and gold armor plate and ornate helmet, holding a sword. The painting made her shiver every time she crossed the grand hall. "One of our Utrecht masters," Princess Charlotte told her. "Such incredible lighting, and character. I expect this man to leap out from the frame, a youth in whom I see a much fiercer man that my husband, though we have seen so much war."

Olivia studied the painting up close, remembering a portrait of Hamlet's father as a fierce, armored warrior that had hung in the banquet room of Elsinore until King Claudius had it removed. In King Hamlet's case the warrior pose rang true. The late Danish king had relished battle much more than his court and family and the boring details of ruling Denmark.

Seeming to read Olivia's thoughts, Charlotte commented: "My lord William is a man of gentle sensibility, but he has never shirked from this war thrust upon all of us by Phillip of Spain and his Iron Duke. We had peace when Catherine of Parma ruled as Flanders' governor general."

As a personal guest of Princess Charlotte, Olivia enjoyed her own suite, with her own maid on call, and a nanny to help with Ari, who now toddled about the suite merrily pulling on curtains and banging goblets against the chairs and picking up words in Dutch as quickly as he d had Italian from Isabella.

It felt like the happier, old days in Elsinore, but more ostentatious, with Italian marble tiles, bas reliefs from mythology, brilliant tapestries of bucolic scenes and gilded arched ceilings, warmed by red velvet drapes.

"I miss Isabella and the fluttery thrill of playing characters on stage," Olivia wrote in her journal. *"But I don't miss the bumps of wagon travel – worrying that we will run out of money and food to eat, or worse, be ambushed by highwaymen. I am growing lazy. A maid comes and empties the chamber pots, takes my clothes to launder, helps me bathe and makes my bed. I am becoming Queen of Sheba, but best not get used to it."*

Olivia's window opened onto a balcony overlooking private gardens. And books. All the books she could read from a vast library– including translations of classic Greek writings more numerous than Hamlet's royal collection.

Still, she missed Isabella, Carlo and Fortunio who remained at Orneck's palace along with Pieter, now her betrothed and therefore requiring her for propriety not sleep under the same roof as he.

Olivia wrote on in her journal: *"I am treated as visiting royalty. Princess Charlotte herself engages me in brilliant dialogs. The princess has an unquenchable a thirst for knowledge and ideas, just as do I.*

She calls me her trusted friend and companion. And I feel the same for her, though always mindful of her regal position. We observe formalities in front of visitors and servants. But in private, we chatter about all and sundry ideas, idle and profound."

Charlotte's hospitality to her new protégé expanded quickly to include Olivia's free use of the grounds and admission to the princess' private courtyard where she took instructions and practiced military arts – archery, use of firearms, daggers and swords and self defense alongside the princess – both in masculine garb suited for combat exercises.

"Women of our new republic must be prepared to defend themselves, like the warrior women saints of old Christendom – and as Plato wrote in his Republic where women share all rights and duties with men. They would learn the same martial arts as men to defend their state, he stated, though few of our male scholars cite this in their lectures." Charlotte took on the fierce look of her husband's portrait –- talking freely to Olivia now, without formalities of royalty and rank.

Olivia nodded graciously. "Yes. Well spoken my lady. Thank you." Olivia didn't need Charlotte's or Plato's advice to understand the necessity of knowing how to use sword, pistol and bow. She had learned this during her semi-feral girlhood in the Denmark countryside.

More recently, she had experienced her fill of mortal conflict directly since landing in Flanders. She always concealed a dagger on her, whether dressed as woman or man, and sometimes carried a pistol as well. She had to be careful about this whenever she roamed outdoors near in Charlotte's quarters, lest she be discovered and mistaken for an assassin. According to the princess, there were many sent at them by the Spanish.

In personal matters, Olivia had held back with Charlotte at first, cautious with her words. The princess' serious demeanor – long-faced, with a prominent but well shaped nose, dark hair pulled back tightly, her good-Dutch-woman black skirt – under which she showed great with child – blouse and cloak set off by a high ruffled white collar that made her skin look even paler.

Her seeming severity put Olivia off at first, but Charlotte's large dark eyes drew her with knowing compassion and playfulness.

The princess soon dispelled whatever reservations her young visitor may have held. Charlotte showed her a romance novella dedicated to her by the poet Moderata Fonte. As Olivia leafed through it, Charlotte asked her, if she wanted to be called Ophelia again.

"No, my lady. I laid Ophelia to rest in Denmark. I am as newly born as my son...."

"...and often feel like a stranger in your own life?"

Olivia nodded silently.

"That sensation overcomes me often, even now, amidst all this happiness."

Olivia told Charlotte everything after that, and in turn took heart from the princess' tales of incarceration by nunnery all through the best years of her youth – a place of some peace, but of forcible indoctrination and rigid rules and alienation from her mother's reformist teachings and enduring love. "My lowest point was when I received word of my mother's illness and was denied permission to leave the convent to be with her those last hours and see her buried."

Olivia listened, partook but missed the freer life of the road as well, despite the indulgences of a princess. She wondered if this grand palace would become her gilded cage.

22. THE CROWS

Olivia realized that she felt safe for the first time since Elsinore and serene for the first time since Hamlet had returned there from Wittenberg with Horatio, filled with sorrow and rage over his father's death. Charlotte took special care to see that the servants provided Olivia all she wanted, and that the two had time to enjoy each other's company when the princess was not busy with the many affairs of state entrusted her by Prince William.

The Prince had sent Pieter on a mission to which she was not privy. Pieter had slipped out of Breda one night quietly, in the same three-wagon caravan – including the big one Olivia guessed contained arms, gunpowder and gold to supply insurgent bands – posing again as an actor along with a pair of his ruffians.

For cover, Pieter again took Isabella, Carlo and Fortunio, and a few new young players they had recruited from the town – conscripted for the rebel cause, just as she had once been. Olivia feared for her love and as much for her fellow players and felt guilty as if she had willfully abandoned her adopted family for a better, richer surrogate in Charlotte.

Olivia didn't like the separation from her friends. But she savored the security and bounty that Charlotte's protection afforded her. Here amid finery and sweet scented gardens, she could see Ari grow, and enjoy the company of this sisterly princess who she could see wielded real power with grace. And she began to like having time to herself, reading, walking with her baby in the garden, sketching again, as she had done in her youth, writing poems.

Nothing lasts forever. The fringes eroded first. Charlotte became less available as the birth of the princess' child drew close.

Each morning, the princess continued to grant audiences to various nobles, town and country folk to hear their petitions and complaints. She napped, then spent afternoon writing letters to her husband and answering claims, then would dine with Olivia, but retire early.

Then, for days running, the princess did not leave her chambers at all. Servants and doctors came and went, not allowing Olivia in Charlotte's quarters. "Her highness is indisposed"

Then came word of plague in an outlying village. Soldiers blocked the roads into Breda from the palace and the citadel as a precaution.

Olivia fretted and grew restless in turns. She had something she wanted to confide to the princess, and now she was cut off. The situation reminded Olivia all too vividly of the breached birth that had killed her mother, Lara.

Olivia's own time of the month had come and gone with no result, and then she began the feel the familiar swelling of her breasts and queasiness. The mushroom potion she had taken to prevent such occurrences, she knew was not foolproof. There were other remedies, but she would need to find them here in what few forests existed in this watery, cultivated land, and even so, she did not yet know what her decision would be, given the consequences of being with child again in this awkward, perhaps dangerous moment.

By midweek after her discovery, the rainy spring gloom of the region gave way to an exceptionally bright day. Olivia summoned Greta, the personal maid assigned her. "I need some air. I want to get out and picnic in the country. Dress Ari," Greta, a cherubic sandy haired, buxom girl had replaced Olivia's regular helper, Marta. "...And have Jan bring the plain cart to the west servant's entrance for just you and I and little Ari. I don't want any fuss."

Jan was the old master of the stables, husband of Marta, who often let Olivia come down to feed and sometimes exercise the horses. Olivia ordered the black four-wheeled, hooded cart – like those used by Mennonite farmers in the area, instead of one of Princess Charlotte's ornate carriages that would have drawn attention outside the gates.

Greta asked if she should alert one of the palace guards to accompany them.

"No guardsmen." No one to spy on me, she thought. "No need for a procession. I want to enjoy this beautiful day on my own. We will not stray far from the citadel and be back before sunset."

"What of the plague, ma'am?"

"We will take the back road only to the prince's private lands, not to Breda."

"... Yes, ma'am," said the new nanny, who finished dressing little Ari – already giggling with excitement, and had donned picnic clothes herself.

"Fine," said Olivia. "Have the cook to prepare a picnic basket for Ari, Greta and me and have it put in the cart."

A stable boy – not Jan – hitched a chestnut mare to the requested cart and led it on foot to the servants' entrance where Olivia – now in her male attire – awaited with Greta holding little Ari, who squirmed to get at the horse. Olivia had petted and fed carrots to this mare a few days earlier in the stables.

"Oh! Sir?" The stable boy stopped short, looking quizzically at Olivia, who appeared to him as a young man.

"I'm Oliver," she said to the boy, and took the reins. "I'll drive the cart. You may return to your stables."

Greta giggled as "Oliver" helped her and the baby onto the bench seat of the cart, then mounted, reins in hand, and set the mare to pull them at a steady walk, along the back drive and onto the main farm road.

A little more than an hour from the palace, outside the city, they came to a side road that led to a forest glen and small lake that the Greta told her about, having grown up in a nearby village, she said.

The glen was as beautiful as Greta promised, a world of emerald summer green, with a dancing stream, even a small waterfall. They found a pier and some benches. All three of them sat and enjoyed a meal of dark rye bread, sausages and Holland cheese, with the sweet plums and milk for little Ari. Olivia gave Ari some of the honey, fig and walnut mortar she brought in a parchment pouch, saving some that she would need with the rue and other herbs she would seek in the woods.

Olivia gathered up the food and put it back in the cart while Greta watched Ari play with some flowers and stones smoothed by the nearby stream.

Olivia hugged the boy and kissed him on both cheeks. "You play with Greta. Mama needs to do an errand and be right back."

She looked at Greta. "Watch Ari, please, while I gather some spring flowers and leaves for my collection."

"Yes, ma'am." Greta nodded and curtsied, holding Ari by one hand.

It didn't take long for Olivia to find a stand of rue, herbs and the roots and dark waxy berries she sought – just like ones that Emma, the midwife from a village near Elsinore, had shown her and she had seen in an illustrated Plantin Press botany book as a girl.

She packed all she had gathered into a pouch and started back to the cart. She realized that she had wandered a ways from their picnic spot. As she got closer, she thought she heard cries. She hoped it had only been the cawing of crows, but broke into a run towards the carriage, crackling branches and stumbling along the way, shouting to Greta and Ari.

23. THE GAME OF WARS

"War once was a noble pursuit of kings leading their knights in holy cause, Tullio. The monarch who commanded the most knights pledged to him would be the victor. By those standards our great king Phillip would be victorious by now against these Dutch outlaws."

Tullio settled in for another rant by his red-sashed superior, who waxed poetic on the glory of battle just like all those men who profit from war in the safety of their palaces.

"Today, Tullio, war has become a soulless clash of overpaid, complaining mercenary thugs and the rabble incited by heretics."

Cardinal Abaga Oneglia Spinola sipped Ligurian red from a gilded goblet – a fine vintage from his villa overlooking the Genoa harbor where Spain sent soldiers by galley ship to start the long march north over the Alps to Flanders. The ruddy Cardinal, his high cheeks flushed with wine, his gray eyes in a chronic acquisitive bulge, indelicate hands grasping his goblet like a hammer – regarded his trembling factotum, Fra Tullio –bony, pale in brown Dominican robes – like a kestrel hovering over a twitchy mouse. A Judas mouse, never eaten, Tullio's job was to lead juicier prey into the cardinal's talons.

It was just past midnight – a time when the cardinal liked to issue his instructions for the following day. Orange and pink candlelight illuminated the walls and crimson velvet drapes of the cardinal's apartment office overlooking the somnolent river Senne, a few paces from the Brussels' Ducal Palace from where Habsburg glory and misrule of Flanders emanated.

"I confess, Tullio. I fear that those lickspittle advisors in Madrid have misled King Phillip, blessed be him. Fools! The king's lackeys called our Fernando back to Madrid just because of a few setbacks."

Tullio shuffled a folder of papers. "Your eminence. You wanted to see the reports?"

The cardinal waved a hand almost smacking his underling. "In a moment, Tullio." He sipped more wine. "The fools should be redoubling their support for him."

Tullio nodded. "So true, your eminence."

"...a true commander who led his men in the field and showed the enemy no mercy. Another six months, and he would have beaten these vile Dutch blasphemers back to hell where they belong!"

The cardinal gestured towards the oil portrait of Fernando Álvarez de Toledo y Pimentel, third Grand Duke of Alva – the Iron Duke – by Titian that hung on the cardinal's office wall, for the time being. Titian had painted the Iron Duke wearing the same gold-leafed, glistening black armor as worn by William of Orange in the portrait by Anthonis Mor, no doubt influenced by the master. Spinola had met Mor and Titian when Cardinal Antoine Perrenot de Granvelle – a grand patron of the arts – had been secretary of state for Catherine of Parma, who at that time had been appointed regent of Flanders by the Spanish crown.

Granvelle had overridden Catherine's moderate approach to dealing with rising Protestantism, with bloody results that had led to open revolt and her succession by the bloody Iron Duke.

Spinola succeeded Granvelle after the latter withdrew to his home in Burgundy. Spinola, if anything, believed in even harsher repression of the Protestant gentry than Granvelle, but – being well versed in his Machiavelli – approached things in a more politic way, masking his intentions and picking only those fights he could win.

163

He resented that the Titian painting would soon be shipped back to Madrid, once his remaining staff received word that the duke had arrived there. "He could have made it a donation." By that Tullio knew the cardinal meant himself, not the papal empire. He wanted to add the Titian to his collection of Italian and Dutch masterpieces.

Spinola wasn't happy about the pope sending him to Flanders – so far from Rome, and so troubled a place. But he vowed to make his presence matter and demonstrate his usefulness to both the Holy See and the Spanish crown.

Rome was all for burning Dutch heretics, but for that moment, preferred that Phillip II press his Mediterranean war against the Ottoman Turks – with eyes to enrich Vatican coffers from Egypt and Constantinople – instead of squandering Spanish forces and fortunes on pacifying Flanders.

On cue, Tullio interjected the cardinal's favorite point of harangue. "And paying Spain's debt." He kept the cardinal's books and knew well the extent of the Habsburg crown's massive indebtedness to Genoa bankers – including the cardinal's branch of the Spinolas – who had been financing Phillip II's ships, overseas and Flanders adventures. The mighty bankers of Genoa, including the Spinolas, had been burned by two successive Habsburg defaults. The Spanish crown was bankrupt, and its promissory notes no longer honored by suppliers. Worse yet, no one knew when the crown would be able to pay the arrears it owed to tens of thousands of soldiers it maintained in Flanders.

Madrid's paper money was no longer being honored, and gold shipments had been delayed, or lost, as when Queen Elizabeth's English seized and impounded a vessel loaded in gold florins destined for the Flanders army. The troops – mercenaries units from Spain, Germany and Italy were growing more restive by the day.

Some decisive gain was needed quickly to restore confidence. In Spinola's dour opinion, the present commander was not up to the task. "King Phillip expects us to clean up us royal messes. But at the same time, his majesty sends this weak-chinned Luis de Requesens to play peacemaker. It's too late!" He snarled. He relished his snarl, tough seldom displayed it in public.

This was Tullio's chance to warn the Cardinal again of the tense military situation in Antwerp, that he tried hard to ignore. "I hear news that the garrison there – and perhaps even here in Brussels – will mutiny if the soldiers are not paid soon. The crown is many months arrears, likewise with contractors supplying victuals. Their main baker has cut off credit and declared bankruptcy. That means no bread. Soon they will have a citadel seething with thousands of half starved, armed men

The cardinal said nothing at first. "This is a problem for the high command. As clergy, we care for these men's souls, not the bellies." His mouth twitched into a half smile as he sipped more wine.

Tullio said nothing. He knew that his cardinal was not averse to seeing the high command up to its neck in offal. It meant that Madrid would find more gold and squander more riches and send more hapless soldiers into the bloody swamp of this endless war with the stubborn Dutch. All the more gain for the Spinolas and the church.

"Best we keep ourselves away from Antwerp, for the present. Eh, Tullio?"

Tullio nodded without looking up from the week's intelligence summaries. "Next item, your eminence – following up on Elsinore assassinations."

"Is that what we are calling those murders now. I thought it was a family feud."

"That, too, your eminence. In any event, our agents report that the players – the dramatic troupe – whose performance, they say may have precipitated the crisis, has been touring Flanders under the protection of the traitor Prince William himself."

"Ach... those players! Troublemakers! Why do we tolerate them?" Back in northern Italy, when the cardinal had been archbishop of Milan, he had pressed to have secular theater banned and actors denounced as heretics in all the duchies and city states loyal to Rome.

"Yes your eminence – the Comici players – the same ones who helped Fortinbras take the Danish crown? "

"... And brought trouble for us..."

Tullio looked up, warming to his ability to rile up the cardinal and bask in his ire. "Prince William's protection of these players signals his growing closeness to Fortinbras."

The cardinal widened his eyes and smacked down his goblet, sending up drops of wine. "Of course! The players helped rid him of his the Danish king and opened the gates of Elsinore to his army of Norwegians and Poles!"

"True, your eminence. They say King Fortinbras looks to make himself as powerful a Nordic potentate as Gustavus Adolphus."

"We will be besieged – Dutch, English, Germans, Swedes and now Danes, if we do not act wisely. Already, Fortinbras has raised the levies to let our cargo ships through the Danish straits from Baltic to the North Seas. Think of it, Tullio. Shiploads of metals, timber, grain could will be choked off, if our weak-chinned, drooling Luis de Requesens y Zúñiga doesn't do something soon."

Tullio smirked to himself, having gained momentary acknowledgement from the cardinal – conversing, for an instant, under an illusion of equality. "... and next, who knows? He'll make a pact with the Turks just like the Bourbon French and their unholy Ottoman alliance."

Tullio knew any reference to the Bourbons was sure to fire up his superior's wrath – particularly anything to do with the late Francis I who had sacked Rome and secured a "sacrilegious alliance" with Sulieman that continued to endure, much to the ire of the pope and the Spanish Habsburg king.

"And the Bourbons call themselves Catholic! Tullio, we are surrounded by traitors and infidels out to destroy Holy Christendom!" The cardinal pounded his table and knocked over one of the candlesticks, which Tullio quickly righted and relit with a taper. "This overweening Fortinbras could have us by the throat, unless someone puts him in his place."

"Yes, your eminence." Tullio slumped back into subservience. "But the comic players that you inquired about... They say that Fortinbras wants them to return to Denmark... He says, to receive his 'special thanks.'" Tullio put a hand up to his throat and hissed a strangling sound.

The cardinal enjoyed these little jests in private moments, he knew. "... if we can believe the lies of that Danish emissary... Horatio ... something... The one stuck in Antwerp."

The cardinal grinned. "I read this Horatio's book – a honeyed paean to Hamlet – his 'sweet prince.' He should have entitled it: "Sodomites in Love'."

"They say the book is very popular."

"The public loves reading exaggerated pulp about palace intrigues, sin and the murder of kings and queens."

Tullio came in on cue. "And printers like Christophe Plantin enrich themselves." The cardinal hated Plantin for refusing to publish the cardinal's book justifying the Iron Duke's 'Council of Troubles' – known among the populace as "The Court of Blood" – and denying that it presided over summary executions of thousands of Protestants and their suspected sympathizers – wiping out whole towns in some cases.

"Damn these printers, spreading heresy and sedition. Hang them all..." The cardinal smiled to himself. "Tullio, you know, if our soldiers mutiny in Antwerp – running amok as they have in other towns – who knows what may happen to this Horatio and his precious printers.

"We have some key officers in our direct pay, there, your eminence. Shall I...?"

The cardinal held up a hand. "We must proceed with caution. This Christophe Plantin has powerful allies in Madrid. His is King Phillip's official printer, as well as for the our church in Iberia."

The cardinal had gotten nowhere trying to convince King Phillip to drop Plantin as official publisher for both sacred and secular books throughout the Habsburg Empire.

Cardinal Spinola wrote to Phillip's advisors in Madrid, to no avail, that "... we know from our agents that this rogue, Christophe Plantin, prints tracts, pamphlets and books that spread the lies of our enemies."

"We must take matters into our own hands, Tullio. Where are these players?"

"Yes, your eminence. You'll see from this week's reports that our agents put them in Breda, residence of the traitorous William of Orange.

"Bless our devious friars, nuns and deacons, Tullio.

The cardinal thought for a while. "... All the while our prissy new governor general Requesens holds peace talks with the William and his generals, when he should have the turncoat assassinated."

Tullio nodded ascent. "Perhaps a poison, your eminence?"

"What if these players were killed by a band of brigands who just happened by? That would shake up matters?"

"The report says the troupe left William's palace to play the Braban townships – moving in our direction, by luck."

"The idea has appeal, Tullio. But I am more interested in this woman your report names as Ophelia, with them."

"You'll see a woman named Ophelia mentioned a report from our man inside Plantin Press."

"This 'Ophelia' - was she in Antwerp?"

"No. They say she is still in Breda at William's palace, with her young son."

"A son?"

"Yes, your eminence. A small boy, about the right age to have been conceived in Denmark before this Prince Hamlet's bloody demise."

"Our agent at Plantin Press overheard Horatio telling Plantin that his Prince Hamlet had briefly courted a nymph named Ophelia. In fact, our agent says he heard that she and the prince had grown up together in Denmark. The agent heard Horatio saying that Ophelia had escaped Hamlet's royal family massacre at Elsinore. And note this, your eminence: Horation added that this Ophelia could have been carrying the prince's child at the time!"

"So that is why Fortinbras wants so much to know about her."

"This Horatio told Plantin that he would not include this speculation in his book for fear of besmirching his prince's reputation, according to our man, also for fear of endangering the life of mother and child..."

"He plays many sides as well, this Horatio."

"He remains in Antwerp. Shall I have him pay us a visit?"

"Not at the moment. But we have a play here, Tullio, one that will catch us a king ourselves."

Tullio sat up. "Shall I fetch a quill and paper?"

"Listen first, Tullio, then you will encrypt the appropriate orders to those who will help us carry this out..."

"First, the players must never be returned to Fortinbras. We will have them dispatched here. Secondly, we must take this child of Ophelia into our protection ... a convent for safekeeping... And let this King Fortinbras know, quietly, that we have a pretender to his throne in our hands."

Tullio listened intently so as not to miss a word.

"... With that we will gain leverage... This Fortinbras already sends his emissary to Genoa – and for only one reason."

"For an alliance, your eminence?"

"For money, you dunce! Everyone wants a helping of Spanish gold, *el dorado* – like pigs who come running for slop. Fortinbras is already in debt to the Fugger bank in Augsburg and needs still more ducats to keep building his warships for the Baltic and North Seas. Plus, he's using up the timber his merchants would be selling to Genoa to build Spanish ships, so he's turning to our banks for help."

Tullio laughed. "The tail wags the imperial dogs. First the Medici, then the Fuggers, now the Spinolas and the Dorias have their hands in every king's purse."

"Kings win or lose, but bankers always profit, Tullio... But first things, first.: We bait the Fortinbras' hook with this baby prince that has come our way."

"And our new Governor Requesens?"

"He need not know, for now." Spinola thought a while.

"And the girl, Ophelia...? Was that her name?"

"She would only complicate matters. She is a heretic. Have her eliminated, but quietly, no showy ecclesiastical trials..."

"Yes, your eminence." Tullio's hands itched for his quill. The cardinal's satrap liked nothing better than clarity of purpose in carrying out his cardinal's intentions.

"Wait." The cardinal thought a while longer. "Tullio, I have had an epiphany. I think we have hit upon our grand solution here!"

Tullio put down his quill and gazed expectantly at his master.

The cardinal beamed. "I dreamed of a fire-breathing serpent last night. As it rose up, I did not cower. I drew my sword and severed its head. The blood spurted orange as it collapsed and died. Now I realize this was revelation!"

Tullio tilted his head. "Your eminence?"

"Cut the head from the serpent, Tullio. Now I realize the solution. These rebels have us chasing our tails. When we lay siege to one of their towns, they hunker down, tie up our forces while their rebels attack us elsewhere. It is not the old fashioned warfare of fixed lines and battles anymore. It is like an outbreak of boils afflicting the Spanish body everywhere."

Tullio nodded. "I see your point, your eminence."

"But instead of fighting town-by-town, what if we sever the heads of those turncoat princes that lead this rebellion?"

171

"That would be fine, your eminence, but what about their armies and castles?"

"That's just it, Tullio. We don't need to fight their whole armies and navies. We only need to hand pick a small number loyal good friars and friends and pay them handsomely to walk among them, unsuspected, and assassinate each and every one of those haughty Protestant bastard leaders, from Prince William on down."

Tullio could not restrain himself from clapping his hands together in glee.

"We already have the agents in place, Tullio. Why limit ourselves to eliminating only those paltry players and that errant Ophelia, when we have it in our power to deal a death blow to the whole Estates General rebellion?"

Tullio rubbed his hands together and picked up his quill again. "I will set right to work, your eminence, and make up a list of candidates for your mission!"

"Good fellow, Tullio. Now leave us so that I may finish my wine and read for a while. This has been a good night, Tullio."

"Yes, your eminence, thank you, of course." Tullio gathered up his papers, knelt to kiss the cardinal's ring and withdrew.

24. BLOOD MOON

Olivia or Oliver ... I am Ophelia nevermore.

I am no one but myself.

I have blood on my hands – the blood of a man, not a rabbit...

But I have my son, alive, safe, unscathed and innocent yet.

He plays inside this walled, overgrown garden of a now abandoned, crumbling convent, disbanded no doubt, by the Anabaptists. I can tell by all the broken statuary and damaged bas reliefs ... Haunted, perhaps, but a good place to hide for now... '

I see it all over and over, like a play rehearsing in my mind, not real. Yet the blood spatters and turns dark on my tunic. My dagger needs to be wifped of its dried blood. How easily I did thrust my blade upwards into the exposed softness under his chin, just as I had often in practice on mannequins in the armory courtyard, the same except for the shock of hot gushing blood.

All the while, my little Ari screamed from the stream, not in horror, for he had not a good view, but in delight to be splashing in the shallow edges of the pond.

I was more afraid of plunging into the stream to fetch him than I had been of our would-be assassin, though he had already murdered poor Greta. God rest her soul. I was such a fool to have gone off that way with my baby without guards.

Fool. Fool! But there is no going back now. I don't know who dispatched this assassin. The Spanish now talk of truce – but they are lying pigs. This township is rife with Catholic sympathizers.

Was this part of a larger assault -- a siege of Breda? Or was my attacker simply a fear-maddened villager fleeing the plague? I have had my fill of sieges! As a girl reading chivalric fiction, I dreamed of adventures. Now I only yearn meadows and rabbits.

Little Ari, none the worse for his soaking, nurses at my breast in the dark, his eyes closed in bliss. I ache everywhere and wonder if I broke any bones in my death struggle with our attacker.

Poor Greta lies gashed, already dead in the glen when I rushed onto the scene. I dared not remove her, nor the brigand's lifeless body – a wiry man with black, curly hair under his peasant's cap, but no more a peasant than I, judging from his armaments. Had he been a country bandit, he surely would have had accomplices who likely would have set me upon. But he was alone. And, on what errand? Robbery? Assassination? Madness?

It is said that armed, battle-maddened deserters from the Spanish tercios wander this countryside looking for booty with which to return to their homes in the German states, Piedmont, Milan, Burgundy and Spain looting and butchering whoever crosses their path. But the one I slew looked too healthy and finely attired – in leathers and breastplate – to be a simple soldier.

I huddle inside this Mennonite cart. I listen to owls and gusty winds rustling the newly leafed trees. The sounds calm me. Above us, gossamer clouds blur a pregnant gibbous moon rising over the empty convent's campanile.

The mad prince in mourning black, his doublet torn, hair gone feral, leaps from dream twilight out of the shadows along the convent wall and grasps both my wrists.

So, my fair Ophelia. I see that you have gotten thyself to a nunnery after all.

I stare into Prince Hamlet's all-too-familiar, green eyes – serene now, not afire with animal rage as they had been when I saw him last, an age ago, it seems.

"Is this another paroxysm of love for me, Lord Hamlet, as my father so foolishly told me once? God rest his soul."

I cannot linger, neither should you! His visage wavered like a reflection in moving water. *Get thy child far away from here, with urgent haste, Ophelia!*

I catch myself and pull back from sleep. I must keep vigilant. The air smells of wet new grass and dung, which tells me that a dairy farmer will likely herd his cows here for grazing by morning. Someone will find the bodies in the glen tomorrow as well.

By morning, I need to take Ari away from here, but first I must rest. This place feels safe for now. Gather my strength. Get Ari fed and to sleep. Then I mash stinking rue leafs and petals into what is left of the fig and walnut mortar.

I recall the passage on "stinking rue" from Flavinius' botany volume: "Rue provokes urine and women's courses. The leaves and seed thereof taken with figs and walnuts, is called Mithridates' counter-poison against the plague, and causes all venomous things to become harmless as well."

I gag the mixture down, trying to savor the honey and figs and ignore the pungency of the herb. I did not have rue the first time, with Hamlet, but I do not rue it now. Still, my Ari and I will surely die from this adversity unless I am agile and fortunate, blessed even. No walls and no heroes and princes can protect us. Ari has only me.

I will resume our flight before this gibbous moon sets, but I have little choice but to slip back into the palace at dawn, I would hope little noticed, and there, gather my things and my wits.

The mare waits patiently in her traces. I watered and fed her the last apple from our basket while I consumed what remained of the bread and wine, taking them as sacraments after my baptism in blood.

I tremble. I feel a warm, sticky wetness down below. I am bleeding. I double over with sudden, agonizing cramps. I recall the blows and kicks from my would-be assassin now. Nature – and my attacker – could well be doing what I had intended, but without the help of rue.

I may have lost Pieter's child – if it had been meant to be – but I have saved my Ari's young life. And I have triumphed over adversity and my attacker, just as did the women warriors of my youthful chivalric epics.

Yet I feel no glory, only a bleak emptiness. Are soldiers all this way in war? No choice but to go forward, tending my baby. I hang to life. At sunup I will make my way cautiously back to Charlotte's palace and pray that the attack on Ari and myself was not part of some larger invasion.

When – if – Isabella, Carlo and Fortunio return, I will leave with them as quickly as I can convince them to depart from this danger all around – with Pieter or without.

I have my own mission, to protect Ari's life – not his. I have my family – my only family now, save phantom hopes of finding kin in Lyon.

I am not of Pieter's family nor am I a soldier for king or cause, church or state. One by one, their chimeras consume them - Prince Hamlet, now Pieter, the Spanish, the Dutch, the dukes, kings, queens, princes vie and kill each other from day to day until one-by-one they exit stage, forgotten soon with their illusions of glory and vengeance, leaving their women to mourn.

Ari pulls on my blouse. He wants to nurse again. By small miracle, I feel the fullness in my breast, and my nipples wetting on cue – as if nothing had happened. As little Ari suckles, his eyelids blink slowly towards sleep. He reaches up and plays with the gold raven amulet on its chain, as he does often. "Yes, little Ari. Your father gave that to me, once long ago. Someday soon, it will be yours."

Ari drifts at last into sweet sleep, and I too, finally, let Morpheus take me in his arms, to sleep, to dream…

25. PERILOUS BIRTH

... I gather rosemary, pansies, rue and daggers from vines and branches. I sing, oh, nonnie, nonnie. ...

Someone's coming. The cart is no good. I have unhitched the horse for the night.

I run, legs heavy. I scoop up Ari.

His eyes open. He laughs. He stares up at me wondering and I clutch him and run for a gate in the garden wall.

A blood moon casts shadows of two men in hooded cloaks behind us, gaining. "Halt!" One shouts. They catch up to me, and grab my shoulders.

I let Ari slide to the ground. "Run! Run, Ari!" I shout as they try to wrestle me against the convent wall. I yell, "Let me go! I surrender."

They relax momentarily and that is when I slash out with my dagger, catching one across the throat before I plunge it into the other's belly, tugging upwards until he falls. Blood everywhere. Ari giggles.

Their hoods fall away and I see their faces in the rose light. They are my father and my brother, Laertes.

Prince Hamlet runs towards me, picks up Ari and holds him close. He whispers, but I can't hear every word:

Why wouldst thou be a breeder of sinners?

I find the words to hurl back this time: "Why wouldn't thou have become a deceiver, my lord"

If thou wouldst marry, then marry a fool.

"I was the fool, believing you ever loved me."

I did deny it to you, but never to myself.

"You see, my lord, I have gotten myself to a nunnery. And, you see? This nunnery is as empty as were your words."

The ghost shimmers like a hanging teardrop. *Forgive me, fair Ophelia. What a fool and peasant slave am I. And now we have a child, Aricin, son of kings, our love's issue.*

"No, my lord. Now I deny you this child. He is not yours. He did not come into this world to carry forth your line, nor to fulfill yours or your father's destiny. He is not for crowning, and not for sacrifice"

But he must -- to set things aright, just as I was called to do.

"Never!" I draw a rapier and try to run the ghost through, to no avail.

The shade of Hamlet darkens, takes hold of Ari and lifts him high. The boy giggles. I fear he will smash the child against the flagstones, but he wraps Ari into his black cloak and disappears. I am screaming, slashing the air with my rapier...

I wake up in cold sweat, shivering. I throw open my own cloak and find Ari still sleeping there like an angel. I see the thin blue of first light to the east. It is time. I slip quietly from the cart and harness the horse again, slapping the reins to urge it on, back toward Charlotte's palace, safe haven, at least for the moment, while I gather my wits.

++++

Nobody wondered why Olivia slept for days, waking only to nurse Ari feebly. It doesn't matter. Her milk has been giving out. The nanny already had him drinking cows milk from a cup. The boy was getting bigger now, a laughing, solid, running boy, full of mischief, yet charmer enough to endear himself and get away with most everything. Marta returned and took up weaning him to palace fare, of which there was abundance. No one asked poor Greta. They assumed that she had gone back to her village like others among the fearful staff. Servants gossip, but don't ask questions.

The servants were grateful to be in the palace where they felt safe from marauding bands and from the plague in town. Although Olivia recovered her strength, she kept to her quarters. Marta brought her food, along with the latest gossip about what was going on around them.

Marta looked pale when she told Olivia that Princess Charlotte had been in difficult labor for the past day and night. Once again, Olivia relived memories of her mother's death in childbirth. Finally came news that Charlotte had given birth to a baby boy, but was in a weakened condition.

Olivia asked when she might see Charlotte and the new baby, but days passed without an answer. Then, Marta stopped coming to Olivia's chambers. Various servants brought Olivia and Ari food and whatever they needed, but did not answer her questions. After four days of this, Olivia ventured out of her quarters down to the kitchen to find Marta or someone else who might give her news.

There was Marta chopping turnips and onions. "Oh, yes, Miss Olivia. I've had to help here," Marta said. She put down her knife, wiped both hands on her apron and walked out of the kitchen into a corridor followed by Olivia.

Marta resumed in hushed terms. "We're not to talk about this, but everyone's been very busy preparing for the evacuation."

Olivia looked incredulous. "Evacuation?"

"Beg pardon, miss, but I thought you knew that Princess Charlotte and the baby will leave Breda on the orders of Prince William?"

"This is all new to me."

"The majordomo said I was to help pack you and Ari for departure too as soon as I finished today in the kitchen."

"Departure for where?"

"That is being held secret, miss. I've heard that they think the Spanish may attack Breda and this palace now that the peace talks have failed."

"Nobody told me that either – about the talks. What of Pieter, and my friends?"

"Your betrothed, miss?"

"And Isabella, Carlo and the rest of the Comici troupe left , perhaps with Lord Pieter, for Brussels or somewhere – oh God, weeks ago now."

Marta looked up and down the hallway. "Sorry, miss, you'll have to ask the princess or her people about that. I must return to my duties."

"Yes, you go, Marta. Thank you." Olivia took Marta's hand momentarily before letting her return to her kitchen chores.

26. KILLING THE MESSENGERS

"We strike at their weakest point, over and over, and they are on the run at last!" Pieter's pale face looked flushed with sun and victory upon his return, ebullient with the havoc he had brought upon the enemy, relieved at the truce having failed. "The offer amounted to nothing more than buying time for the Spanish to reinforce their garrisons." William had given Pieter a field promotion to major after he and his squad had destroyed a key Spanish bridge over a Rhine tributary using the barrels of black powder they had smuggled behind Spanish lines in the players' caravan wagon.

Olivia waited for a chance to tell Pieter that she no longer wanted to be his wife, but he was so full of himself that first day, she never had the chance. She turned to Isabella. "I want only to get myself and Ari to Lyon, out of this cursed country, away from this war, and I hope, to find my mother's family and some serenity."

Prince William had put Pieter in charge of the evacuation, using the prince's quarters as a command center, now that both he and Princess Charlotte had withdrawn. That meant Pieter would be spending practically all of his waking hours at the palace where Olivia still remained – betrothal propriety be damned.

In the ensuing organized chaos of preparation, however, they found little time to meet in private despite their proximity. That suited Olivia, while she considered her alternatives, and what to say to him.

Isabella's return, meanwhile, lifted Olivia's spirits. The actress and playwright embraced her young protégée immediately. "I worried so much about you," Olivia told her between hugs. Then she related the terrible events of the past week to Isabella.

"Yes. I agree. All of us, not just you, must break free of Pieter and this war, even though I know your fondness for him is deep."

"I must put all my attention on Ari now. I don't think my assailant acted alone. Whoever sent him knows I am here and will try again."

Carlo walked from the wagons into the palace library where Isabella and Olivia had been talking quietly. "When we were in Leiden, we only agreed to help Pieter until we got him and those supplies to Antwerp, for whatever purposes they had. We seemed to have gone everywhere but Antwerp so far." Antwerp still had an open harbor where the players could possibly find a ship for Italy.

Isabella objected. "Olivia needs to go to Lyon, Carlo."

"We have to get home, Isabella, and through Antwerp is the best way."

"… To drown at sea. You know I am averse … I agree to go to Antwerp, but to perform and for me to submit my new romance to Plantin Press."

Carlo was not happy but agreed. "We'll decide once we get there. Olivia may find some other transportation."

"She is one of us now, Carlo."

Carlo nodded. "I know."

++++

"Voltemand and Cornelius!" Olivia took a few minutes to recognize the late King Claudius' former emissaries, who were standing awkwardly by the back entrance to Prince William's palace in the plain white cotton blouses and black woolen garments of local tradesmen.

Voltemand tried to slouch when he saw Olivia, but still had the look of a fierce blond Viking warrior, towering over his rotund, curl27.y haired Italianate partner. Cornelius blanched, then broke a half-surprised, half terrified grin at seeing this ghost from the past, Ophelia. She put a finger to her lips to hush them before they pronounced her name. "Olivia," she said and walked up to them. "You remember me, the queen's chambermaid from Elsinore?"

Cornelius, stuttered, and did a stiff, half bow. Voltemand stared and said nothing. The duo had arrived with a wagon load of newly wrought wheels for the carriages being made ready for those who would be departing the palace soon. Cornelius moved closer to Olivia and whispered, "My lady, please, we beg your discretion as to our identity as well."

Olivia nodded. She had already surmised their predicament, having to flee Denmark as well as herself. They had been the ambassadors to Old Norway, after all, who had delivered the complaints that caused Fortinbras' late, then ailing uncle, to chastise him for his recruitment of the rogue army that eventually helped put Fortinbras the younger on the Danish throne after the Elsinore murders. One of Fortinbras' first orders after taking power at Elsinore had been for the heads of these two.

"Find an excuse, please, to stay a little while," Olivia implored them privately after they had unloaded their cargo in the carriage house. "We could well find common cause and be of mutual assistance to each other."

Cornelius shook his head and started to back away, but Voltemand placed a huge paw on his shoulder to restrain him. "Yes, my lady. Of course," he said.

What with all the servants rushing about preparing for the evacuation of the prince and princess, Olivia led the two of them to an emptied storeroom near her quarters. "I am assuming that you two gentlemen have no desire to stay here in Breda for long."

Cornelius nodded his head vehemently. "We are bound for France, where they are no friends of Fortinbras. We plan to join Reynaldo in Paris. He has a tavern there."

Olivia could hardly contain herself Reynaldo! She had always called him Uncle Reynaldo, the ever-cheerful secretary to her father, who always remembered to bring back gifts for her and Laertes from his travels for the Lord Chamberlain. Now she recalled that not long before his murder, her father had dispatched Reynaldo to check on Laertes in Paris and report back. "I may have a way for you to get across Flanders to France, if you can help us as well, with that wagon and horses. But first you must meet someone. Please wait here." With that, Olivia went to fetch Isabella and Carlo.

At that moment, a courier arrived at the palace gates with a dispatch for Prince William, "urgent, from Admiral Boisot." The sergeant at the gate reached out. "Give it to me and I'll see that the prince gets it."

"The admiral has ordered that I deliver it only to his highness in person."

The sergeant huffed, and sent a corporal to inquire with his superiors.

Neither was aware that the prince had already departed the palace secretly for the new rebel headquarters in a covered carriage at dawn.

"Take the messenger to Lord Pieter," the prince's majordomo told the corporal. "His lordship is in command here now, until further notice."

Two guards escorted the courier to a reception hall where Pieter held court. The courier, a small, compact man with ferret eyes peering from under a helmet did not remove, bowed ceremoniously.

"State your business, sir." Pieter did not bother with introductions. "You have a dispatch for me to read?"

"Your highness, I carry a critical, secret message from the admiral that I have been order to communicate to you only in private, of the utmost urgency."

"Yes, yes." Pieter shrugged and didn't bother to correct this errant fool. *Why not let this rude, self-important messenger think he's talking to Prince William? The imbecile obviously wouldn't know a prince from a whore master if he passed him on a road.* Pieter waved the two guards out of the room and bade the messenger to approach the prince's throne where he sat. "Come forward, then."

The courier walked slowly up close to Pieter. He reached into a leather bag he carried on one shoulder and before Pieter could react, pulled a cocked pistol and fired once, point blank.

The g27.uards rushed into the room as Pieter toppled over one side of the throne, his head a mass of blood. The courier took a second, cocked flintlock pistol from the pouch and fired it as well, felling one of the guards and causing the other to jump back. The assassin then bolted out the door and down a hallway, sword drawn – too late to avoid two other guards. Pistols drawn, they shot him through the heart – though Pieter, were he alive, would have commanded them to take the assassin alive for questioning. A valet, panicked, ran into the kitchen and shouted: "Oh my God, *the prince* has been murdered!" The palace erupted in pandemonium.

Hearing the noise, Voltemand and Cornelius rushed out of the storeroom where they had been waiting for Ophelia. They ran right into the arms of a squad of guards, and were arrested on the spot.

"We've got two more of the plotters," the sergeant of the guards announced to no one in particular. They bound the hapless, terrified Voltemand and Cornelius to high backed chairs and locked them in an alcove off the library. They posted a guard at the door, awaiting further instructions.

"I saw Olivia letting those two traitors into the palace through the kitchen!" One of the butlers told the sergeant, shaking.

"I never trusted that whore. She and those Venetian players are in league with the pope!" The sergeant spat to his men. "Bring me that witch too. We'll get to the bottom of this plot and have all their heads."

27. FLIGHT INTO FLANDERS

"Attention, you there! Soldier! You are relieved. Report to the sergeant major at the main gate immediately."

The corporal guarding the alcove door snapped off a salute to the lanky, pale young officer and marched off down a hallway. The corporal dared not question the order, nor take much notice of the officer's black silks and burnished steel-armor being grander than that of his immediate superiors.

Voltemand and Cornelius struggled against their bonds in terror when the officer came through the alcove door with his sword drawn. It took them a few moments before they recognized the officer cutting them free as Ophelia.

"Commander Oliver Punchbowl at your service, gentlemen," Ophelia saluted. The two managed weak laughs. "You like the costume? One of our finest. But no time to gawk. Follow me!"

With that, Oliver strode out, and marched down the hallway in the opposite direction from where the guard had gone. He led them through a series of twists and turns, staircases, doors and passageways and out of the palace through a side door to where the Comici player's carnival wagon stood on a service road, hitched to a team of horses.

Oliver waved to a black bearded dwarf in similar black silken finery and a velvet slouch hat who sat atop the wagon's buckboard, holding the reins. "Get inside!" Oliver pointed the two men to steps leading to a door at the back of the wagon. They barely got inside when the wagon lurched ahead.

Inside, two women – one olive skinned, voluptuous and sharp eyed as Cleopatra's cat, seated in a high-backed chair holding a small boy, asleep.

The other women, comely, with classic features, looked them over with mirthful serenity as if already writing them into one of her plays. Cornelius recognized her.

Cornelius' eyes lit up. "Ah ha! Now I remember!"

"And we remember you, noble Cornelius and Voltemand, from Elsinore in happier days..."

Cornelius caught his breath, wheezing from their run. "You are the ones that Lord Polonius so described as ..."

Rosa cut in and burlesqued the late lamented lord chamberlain's nasal tenor.

"...*The best actors in the world, either for tragedy, comedy, history, pastoral, pastoral-comical, historical-pastoral, tragical-historical, tragical-comical-historical-pastoral, scene indivisible, or poem unlimited...*"

The pair laughed nervously, eying Ophelia, still in military costume.

Ophelia took a moment, then laughed herself. "It's all right. Rosa does my father to perfection. He was ever the *lord high exaggerator.*"

The wagon swayed to a stop. Oliver pushed Voltemand and Cornelius behind a curtain that partitioned the wagon's interior. Both of them paled when they noticed Fortunio in a pirate's costume, with saber and pistol tucked in his black sash, sitting on a barrel behind the curtain. Fortunio put a hand up to silence them and motioned each of them to climb into two other empty wooden barrels.

The barrels smelled inside of gunpowder and herring. They perspired profusely and took only short breaths. They heard soldiers outside talking to Carlo, then checking everyone inside the wagon. Finally the wagon moved forward again.

It seemed an eternity before Fortunio let the ashen-faced, queasy pair out of the barrels. They regained their balance and staggered back through the wagon's cloth partition to confront the others.

Ophelia removed her infantry officer breastplate, helmet and cloak and looked more like herself again. "They made a fuss, but the guards at the west gate know and let us through without much problem."

"Thanks to your gold coins, gentlemen," Rosa laughed. "At least a bagful. We'll keep the rest, for your safe passage, fellows."

Cornelius fished in his pockets. "Where did you..."

"Your wagon," said Fortunio. "I got to it before the soldiers and brought over what I could find, including some of your clothes and of course, the gold... You didn't hide it very well, gentlemen, if you'll excuse my saying."

Miraculously, the baby boy stayed asleep in Rosa's ample arms.

Ophelia, still looking boyish in black pantaloons, boots and soldier's blouse sat on a stool next to a dresser. "You'll get used to them."

"What have you conspired?" Voltemand found his voice at last – speaking measured baritone, sounding unperturbed in contrast to his associate.

Ophelia responded, with equal calm. "None of us have much choice but to be out of this region. Being an Italian troupe will get us through Spanish controlled territory to Antwerp, a most cosmopolitan city, where you will be able to book passage on a ship for the French coast, and I, perhaps with you."

It was only after they had Breda well behind them and stopped for the night at a small village to the west that Ophelia left the wagon, again, in her familiar male attire as Oliver.

Walking swiftly, her head down, she found a shaded, secluded place under the copse of oaks where they had tied the horses. There, she leaned behind a massive tree trunk. She didn't want to let go. But she slid to the ground and began to sob uncontrollably, letting the full shock of Pieter's horribly mistaken assassination hit her. Though she had planned to part with him, she felt inconsolable loss in this moment. Pieter died a prince, in William's place, she realized. Two princes I have loved, and each has met a bloody end.

By Umberto Tosi

PART FOUR

By Umberto Tosi

28. IRRECONCILABLE PRINCES

When Ophelia was a child, she let herself believe in sprites, faeries, sea and wood nymphs, elves and even dragons. She would cast magical beings liberally into her verses and draw them in her journals.

When she was eight, she would recite the ancient Greek poet Hesiod's *Theogony of Neralds* to a captive audience consisting of her little brother, their respective rag dolls and puppets, and sometimes their clucking nanny.

"*Proto, Eukrante, Amphitrite, and Sao ... Eudora, Thetis ... Kymothoe, Speio, Thoe*, and lovely *Halia, ...*" Ophelia pantomimed as she recited.

"*... Pasithea, Erato,* and *Eunike* of the rosy arms...*" She would grin proudly between breaths. "*...Nesaia, Aktaia, and Protomedeia ... Doris, Panope,* and beautiful *Galatea ...*" On Ophelia would go, in full girlish voice, until little Laertes would cover his ears and yell at her to stop.

Even as a child, however, Ophelia chose not to believe in ghosts. The dead, she continued to feel through adulthood, "ought move on, past grieving, and let us be until we join them."

Her disbelief had not, however, barred dead Hamlet from intruding often on her dreams. The dreams varied. On some nights, he would appear in his maddened, cruel and ignoble incarnation and lash out at her much in the way he did during their last days at Elsinor. On other nights, the graceful, witty, noble and scholarly Hamlet with whom she had grown up would light her dreams. On still other nights, both Hamlets appeared – her sweet prince metamorphosing into the bitter, back and forth.

Often, when she wakened from such nightmares, the maelstrom of confusion, compassion, sorrow and anger that she felt at Elsinore would come back to her, as she had expressed so poignantly then.

++++

"Oh, what a noble mind is here o'erthrown
The courtier's, soldier's, scholar's, eye, tongue,
sword,
Th' expectancy and rose of the fair state,
The glass of fashion and the mould of form,
Th' observed of all observers, quite, quite down!
And I, of ladies most deject and wretched,
That sucked the honey of his music vows,
Now see that noble and most sovereign reason
Like sweet bells jangled, out of tune and harsh;
That unmatched form and feature of blown youth
Blasted with ecstasy. Oh, woe is me,
T' have seen what I have seen, see what I see!"

++++

Once again she let herself be caught up the memory of that day when she had approached Lord Hamlet to give him back his letters and gifts – even the raven amulet – and make an end to all that had transpired between them.

Her words that day, remembered and dreamed, were always the same, scripted as in one of the dramas in which she now played, but real at that moment.

"My lord, I have remembrances of yours
That I have longèd to redeliver.
I pray you now receive them."

To which he had so callously denied ever giving her gifts, writing her letters or ever having cared for her, then adding demeaning taunts, telling her, in so many words, that she was a painted whore who should never marry and should get herself to a nunnery post haste.

That, again! Even now, years later, Ophelia clenched her jaw remembering his dissociated rants, disheveled, attempting to give the lie to everything they had known, at the same time, his wild eyes telling her of his despair in denying their truth in vain.

But Ophelia bore witness of all – the bitter and the sweet – of them. Her memories remained intact in her consciousness, not to be erased or scratched out even by the cruelest of tongues.

29. SAND CASTLES

They had frolicked through the castle rooms, hallways and out in the fields almost from the day each learned how to walk – she, young Hamlet and later, her brother Laertes, cheerful, iracsible children growing up together embraced by walls of protective privilege.

In those fleeting days of her youth, they were a constant trio – or sometimes, gang of five with the mischievous Rosencranz and the dreamy Guildenstern who were allowed to summer with them off and on. They would tease about which of them would play king, queen and prince of Sonia Castle. They vowed allegiance to Sonia, their kingdom of dreams forever, it seemed during those timeless northern summer day, playing on the vast sand banks by the Wadden Sea near the Old Viking town of Ribe. Ophelia's brother Laertes, still with his happy baby cheeks at eight years of age, played architect with sticks and buckets of wet sand laced with seaweed and dune grasses. Hamlet, the young, impatient prince, directed them to add towers, spires, turrets, windmills and the toy cannons he brought with them on the cart from the Ribe.

Ophelia and her brother constructed inner and outer walls and a moat, fashioned of driftwood, sea shells and fish bones, thatched with grasses and wild flowers.

They had built another Sonia the summer before that one, but this was the masterpiece, never to be matched. It survived two incoming tides, standing tall, reflected by the water around it as they observed from the dunes until the tide went out again. They wove tales about themselves in that castle – king, queen and first knight, ruling a wonderland, fighting off dragons and invaders.

The next day's tide – higher from a waxing moon – did its work. All that was left of Sonia, their magic castle, were piles of muddy sand – all but their memories where its pennants had fluttered.

With hardly a soul about on the vast seashore, the king's guards could relax and play dice near the royal carriages higher up the beach road where the prince had ordered them to halt. To the occasional fishermen mending their nets on the beach, they were three lads adventuring. Ophelia dressed herself in her brother's play clothes, enjoying the freedom of it – wolf pups frolicking, sons of nobility summering near the seashore, whom the locals gave wide berth.

Prince Hamlet's father, King Hamlet ordered the women and children to be taken there – less than three days leisurely travel by river and canal across the Jutland Peninsula – for protection as his wars with Norwegian and Polish armies grew more dangerous.

Ophelia's father first stayed in Elsinore with the kin, but visited Ribe often to counsel Queen Gertrude and see to her comfort. Polonius spent little time with Ophelia and Laertes on these visits, leaving their care to the servants. He remained as oblivious to his daughter's boyish attire, as he did to her studiousness.

The girl had always been her late mother's daughter, Laertes his son. Not too early to think on the advantages presenting the maiden's hand suitably to a prince, if the opportunity presented itself. Queen Gertrude hinted as much to Polonius one day as they observed the young prince and Ophelia, slipping back into the summer palace from the stables, trying to stay unnoticed. Polonius savored, but dared not lean too heavily upon the queen's subtle encouragement. Dare he think of a royal union?

This could require some maneuvering, he thought. Before departing again for Elsinore, he would tell Laertes that he should be the "man of the family" in his father's absence and watch over his elder sister Ophelia, "for young girls can be weak minded and subject to their emotions." But Laertes proved no match for his sister, nor the prince himself as the prime instigator of their mischief.

After that first summer, Hamlet's father and Queen Gertrude expanded their royal Ribe residence into a grander palace, where the queen could stay, safely away from war and plague, in greater comfort during King Hamlet's campaigns. Her majesty enjoyed her summer soujourns by the Jutland Sea so much that she continued to return there, with her son the prince, with Ophelia and Laertes as well born playmates.

The children matured each season, becoming adolescents as they roamed the shores and woods more widely each summer, while the queen enjoyed the palace and its gardens and more and more frequent visits from the king's brother, Claudius, sent to see to her provisions and comfort.

Ophelia sprouted like a sunflower reaching towards the light, a feral child at heart. For two summers she stood a head above both her brother and Hamlet. They didn't mind much because she rode, always in boy's attire, as one of the boys and called herself," Oliver." The local merchants, trandesmen, peasants and clergy got used to seeing them as a threesome of brash lads from the summer palace, riding about on swift horses provided from the royal stables.

Laertes "the man" expressed misgivings when young prince Hamlet ordered his personal man-of-arms to instruct "Oliver" in the arts of archery, fencing and even the use of arquebus and musket, though firearms were more the weapons of foot soldiers than their betters.

The threesome rode into the vast wooded royal lands beyond the dunes and rye fields to hunt. "Oliver" learned to bag deer and small game as expertly as the prince. She picked milk wort flowers, known as Freya's hair, and wove them into her headband.

The locals gawked covertly, but never dared to stare or comment.

"Peasants, not many generations from fierce, unchristian tribes, the Jutes in these parts. They know their place now, and grateful for it," Ophelia's brother, trying to sound grown up, commented.

Hamlet, haughtier in his childhood, gazed at a horse-drawn cart in the distance, carrying peasants to a field. "Yes. Laertes. Were it not for my father, these wretches would starve under the yoke of Fortinbras and Norway's taxes. But be not deceived. These humble peasants and fisherman once were Viking warriors and would have our heads mounted on pikes in a minute, given the chance, Laertes.

"Let us be Vikings riding to Valhalla!" Ophelia broke the serious mood and let out a whoop. "Onward. A race!" She spurred her horse to a gallop. The others followed. "To that oak!" She pointed to a massive tree ahead by the road that towered over its neighbors. Hamlet and Laertes followed at full gallop. They knew that oak well, having carved symbols and their initials on it.

An abandoned woodcutter's stone cottage, deep in the forest became their headquarters. The former residents had died in the last plague, ten years earlier. They picked wild berries, gathered nuts, herbs and mushrooms, and hunted and roasted rabbit and game birds, even a wild pig.

Here amid the hills and tall trees, they could hear wolves sing in the distance, owls sounding their pipes, frogs incessant creaking chirps from the ponds. Above them bats swooped insects under a myriad of stars that drew Ophelia to lie flat on a grassy place and stare upwards, her imagination traveling to heavens and other worlds.

30. FREYA'S CHILD

When darkness closed in and the summer air cooled, they lit a fire and told each other stories before the cottage's flaming hearth. Prince Hamlet packed in some of his more prized books for them to read aloud – most from Venice, Antwerp and London. Some were ancient, hand copied with exquisite illuminations, some in Latin, others Greek and still others, very old, hand copied in Runic letters – forbidden by church and state – "except for princes," he smirked.

Ophelia devoured the ancient myths like a starved puppy. She memorized verses from the prince's rare, illuminated copies of the *Poetic Edda* and *Prose Edda* – collections of the poetry and stories of the ancient Norse gods and goddesses compiled, according to the prince, by a thirteenth century Icelandic poet and scholar, Snorri , about whom she resented having never been taught by her church sanctioned instructors.

Ophelia soon could recite Edda verses aloud, playacting the roles. The prince applauded and joined in, less so, her brother, who played along. She collected gods and goddesses and read romances about valiant *guerieras* – female knights like Bradamante – by Aristo and his imitators with the same single-mindedness as she collected flowers, leaves and shells and incorporated them with her poems into the secret journals she kept by candlelight.

Ophelia consumed the stories of Freya, the Norse goddess of love, life, war and death, protector of women, children and wild creatures. She made herself a cloak of feathers that she had gathered in the fields, though not all from falcons like the cloak of Freya.

Young Ophelia donned beads of local stones and imaged herself wearing Freya's magic golden necklace, leading fallen heroes to Valhalla with her flying chariot pulled by giant cats. Ophelia took to calling her white mare, Hildisvíni, sometimes, after Freya's magic boar, into which the goddess transformed her human lover, Otta, whenever it suited her.

Ophelia and Hamlet and, reluctantly, Laertes – invented games around the myths. Hamlet would pretend to be Thor, disguised as a bride infiltrating Loki's wedding to steal back his magic hammer.

Laertes balked at even pretending to be Freya's brother Freyr. "You play dangerous games with our prince." he admonished her privately. But their games continued. The young prince himself continued to play Thor and Odin, or knight, general or king, as suited his moods.

On Fridays, Ophelia would declare it "my day. I am the queen Freya for whom this day is named." Prince Hamlet bowed ceremoniously, while Laertes muttered about sacrilege.

These idylls would end – not to be spoken of again, however.

One warm, damp August day towards the end of their last Wadden Sea summer, the three of them rode farther south along the Jutland shoreline and cut deeper into the woods than they ever had before. The prince was in one of his moods – darker than ever. On his thirteenth birthday, just passed, he had proclaimed his intention to join his father on the battlefield in Poland.

Queen Gertrude would have none of it. The prince waved a birthday letter he had received from his father the king.

The prince interpreted the letter as a summons to battle. Queen Gertrude said otherwise. "Your father says only that you must be a man now, soon fit to lead our kingdom in war or peace if called upon."

"Perhaps the king has a premonition, God forbid," whispered Polonius to his own son, Laertes, at the prince's birthday dinner table. Ophelia tried to look demure and said nothing.

The prince's uncle Claudius, visiting the summer palace again, rose and made a birthday toast. "Long live the king! Hail to his son, the prince. May God protect them, and help our king return victorious over Norway before young Hamlet is called to battle."

Polonius raised his goblet, and whispered again to his own son, "and may our good king make an end to these wars while his subjects still have a penny left."

Ophelia kept her eyes on the queen, and noted the telltale glances between her and Claudius. Prince Hamlet downed a grownup goblet of wine and again declared himself battle ready. "In good time, my son." Claudius put a hand on the young man's arm. "You will be a glorious commander one day." Claudius took the letter and made a fuss of perusing it one more time. "Though, not today. I know my dear brother, our king. If he were summoning you, he would have written it directly, and would have sent me and the summer palace guard specific instructions for your transport."

Prince Hamlet scowled and took the letter back. "I am not your son, sir!"

"Of course not, son."

Gertrude raised her eyebrows for Claudius to say no more, and the dinner continued in silence.

31. MUSHROOMS AND HARES

Hamlet called out Laertes and Ophelia at dawn, with a saddled horse for each, plus two pack horses that looked to be loaded with provisions.

Once they distanced a bit from the summer palace, out of the earshot of gossipy servants and insolent guards, the prince informed them that he intended to ride south, into the German states and on to join his father's army in Poland. "You may accompany me, or not, as you like."

"It would be my delight and honor." Ophelia spoke with exaggerated courtliness over the sound of the horses. "And I thank my lord for having provided us such fine steeds." She brought her favorite white mare along side the prince. "And, my lords, what of our Rosencranz and Guildenstern?"

She glanced forward and back in mock concern. She already knew the answer to her question. The funny, tongue-wagging pair's parents – though friends of Ophelia's father – had already taken their two boys back to Elsinore with the courtiers and servants sent to ready the castle for fall and winter, now that their all-too-brief summer breathed its last sultry days. Ophelia smirked and caught Hamlet's faint smile, acknowledging that she and her brother got to remain among the privileged few at Prince Hamlet's insistence.

Laertes trotted his horse up to their side. "My lord, with respect, please reconsider. There will be naught but trouble in this. My father and your uncle will learn of this. They will have you taken back and blame me for it all."

"It is my choice, Laertes, and mine alone. Go back now if you will not second it."

Laertes waved a hand at Ophelia and started pulling his roan stallion around. Ophelia looked straight ahead and urged her mare into a canter with the prince.

"Don't worry, my brother, I have my longbow. You will be safe," she shouted back at Laertes, who reddened with anger, but turned again to follow.

They had reached the wide, flat beach of their childhood now. A morning low tide left an expanse of glistening wet sand on which gave the horses firm footing. The prince prodded his black stallion into an exuberant gallop. Ophelia fell back alongside her brother and the pack horses watching Hamlet.

"Fear not, brother. Our prince will change his mind 'ere long. We will be home for dinner unbloodied."

"And if he doesn't?"

"Then you have your sword and I my longbow!"

"I am not laughing. Our father and Claudius will send a party after us and we'll be the scapegoats for the prince's misbehavior."

"We are in the hands of the gods and our prince."

Ophelia sat up in her saddle, cutting a fine figure in male attire, imagining battle and the carnage of canons with more curiosity than apprehension.

The three rode in silence for a while. They skirted the beaches where they had once splashed and built their sand castles, and for miles beyond, past boats and fisherman mending nets, who stared at them with wonder, some whistling, others bowing with mock ceremony. The morning mist grew thicker as they made their way, until a thick fog enveloped them. Still the prince led them on, holding to the seashore until it turned too rocky for them to pass.

They found an opening in the dunes and followed a narrow trail soon losing sight of the shoreline. The trail curved into tall reeds, and then along what appeared to be a fog-shrouded bog. By now they had no idea where they were or what direction they traveled.

They followed the winding path for a while, keeping clear of the bogs, taking the fork that led them to higher ground whenever the trail spit. After a while they moved into brush, then through a thickening forest of oaks, elms and birches, and out onto a small meadow, as far as they could tell in the fog, which clung to them and the land as if a permanent condition.

Hamlet halted them by a stony, rapid creek flanked with white birches, reeds, grasses and vines. He dismounted. "Good spot to water our horses." Ophelia and Laertes followed suit, letting the horses drink.

Ophelia hitched her horse to a branch, took her bow and stole quietly upstream along the bank, slipping between the trees. Before long she bagged a brace of partridges and a brown hare, each with one sure shot. Silently, she retrieved her arrow and tied her catch with leather cords slung over her back.

Not hearing Laertes or Hamlet call, she took her time getting back to the horses. She picked asters, goldenrod and purple salvia for her hat. She came upon a dark thicket, moist from summer rains, covered in dead leaves, debris and small animal droppings. She closed her eyes briefly, imagining herself blind, and able to maneuver by the keen, practiced sense of smell – the somber wetness of decomposing leaves and pine needles and wet straw, the sweetness of cedar, lavender, wild iris, a touch of salt from the nearby seashore, her own leather boots along a well worn, narrow pathway leading deeper into the woods.

Pulling aside a branch, she felt for what she expected to find – a shy cluster of bell shaped, golden-capped mushrooms with purple gills, and slender wavy stalks, looking like sea creatures. She knew these well from an illustrated volume on herbs, potions and medicines that her mother had kept.

These, it said, were good for "seeing" and – ground into a broth or tea, as a love potion. She examined each carefully, not to confuse them with death caps or deadly saprobics. She had picked such poisonous fungi at other times, dried and put each in well marked vials as well – adding to her collection. She appreciated the deadly beauty of them – and had learned the uses of many toxic fungi and plants that could be fatal or curative depending upon their preparation and application.

Not far from the gold-caps she spotted the familiar spiky leaves and deceivingly pretty yellow blossoms of henbane – similar to nightshade, and even more toxic in misuse. Extract from the flowers, leaves and stems of henbane – like nightshade, mandrake and datura – could be used for relieving pain, with stronger effect than the bark of willow– but only extremely small doses, a drop or two diluted in wine or water. Ophelia knew that even a small vial of henbane extract could be lethal if ingested – not only by mouth; poured into the ear, for example.

Queen Gertrude, Hamlet's mother, had shown great interest in Ophelia's collection of pressed flowers, seeds and plant cuttings. Her majesty was particularly fascinated by the henbane in particular – "so lovely and so lethal," she would laugh. The queen privately asked Ophelia to transplant a wild henbane plant into a flower pot "for the royal garden. We take delight in its delicate yellow blossoms," said the Queen.

Cultivating nostrums for the queen provided Ophelia cover for her explorations. She was well aware of the witchcraft trials and burnings by the hundreds sanctioned by Protestant ministers as zealous as any papal Inquisitors – particularly of peasant women and other commoners in Jutland, with its ancient Norse history.

She had learned much about herbs and potions from Lena, an old woman who lived in a forest cottage outside of Ribe and was frequently called to the summer palace for her curative skills when someone was sick. Ophelia rode to her cottage frequently, and got the queen to provide special papers appointing the old woman as a purveyor to the court – affording her, likewise, with protection from local witch-hunts.

After Ophelia's mother died, the queen had taken the sorrowful girl under her wing, encouraging her learning of poetry, music and courtly manners. This meant more time with Prince Hamlet as the two grew up, a situation that pleased Polonius greatly.

Whenever she could, Ophelia also continued to collect herbs and flowers that she pressed, dried and drew in her chap books of poetry. She also continued learn the many non-decorative uses of plants – the medicinal and the magical.

After she had picked what plants and mushrooms she wanted and put them into small leather bags, Ophelia made her way back through the trees to the horses, soundlessly, as if stalking them from downwind, practicing her hunting skills. She startled Laertes by seeming to materialize out of the air before he could call her.

Laertes helped tie her catch on of the pack saddles. He hailed the prince and pointed out the partridges and hare. "Look, my prince! The cook will make us a feast of this game tonight!" He tried to look hopeful.

The prince regarded him with apparent contempt, then smiled at Ophelia and mounted his horse. Ophelia tugged her brother's sleeve and muttered so Hamlet could not hear her. "Don't bait our prince, my brother, while his mind is set. He will think on the folly of this gambit and change it soon enough."

"Folly? Then why must we follow?"

"He is the prince and we are his army." She put a hand to the dagger sheathed on her belt.

They rode upstream along the creek for a while, then crossed a broad meadow, from where they picked up another trail that led downhill through a gentle ravine to another broad beach. The fog thinned, but the air weighed heavy with summer heat. Ophelia could smell impending rain, as a bank of purplish gunpowder clouds moved in from the sea.

32. CASTAWAYS

The farther they rode, the freer Ophelia felt from all of the intricate pretenses of palace life. No more fair maiden, dutiful lady in training. And as long as the crown prince led their adventure, her brother would have to hold his tongue, including remarks about her boyish attire. "Father will hear of this, Ophelia," Laertes had groused, taking in her black leather pants, doublet and cap, longbow across her back, silver dagger sheathed in her wide belt.

"Not if you don't tell him, my brother."

"Beware, my dear sister. Our prince will dally with you, but one day soon, be called to his royal destiny, leaving behind his inferiors."

"I am not his or anyone's inferior."

"Hold back, Ophelia. He may take pleasure in our company today - as father says, youth will be youth. Ruin your reputation and your chances."

"Thank you, my brother. Your advice would mean more if you did not play the bad boy so well yourself." Their old brother-sister argument reared its head.

"You see already how he is obsessed with princely matters – of duty, war, gaining the approval of his father..."

"We are at his side. His father is far away."

"You must consider, good sister, that a young woman must think of her reputation."

"...and why not so for boys?" Ophelia pulled her cap down low and spurred her horse. "Don't worry, brother, I am no violet easily plucked."

She mounted and let her horse have its head for a while, breaking into an easy gallop, feeling the mist on her face.

She breathed worlds of possibilities and tasted freedom, beholden to none, far from the circumspect existence of a noble young ladies, no thoughts of marriage or children or piety. The three were in their element – in the leathers of huntsmen, with their daggers, swords and bows – pelts hanging from their saddles. Ophelia most of all.

They continued south, the vast tidal planes of the Jutland Peninsula's western shore to their right, bogs, fields, woods and low hills to their left. They kept to what trails they could find, past a fishing village, then into coastal highlands again. The horses were tiring.

They followed a twisting trail for a long while down a gentle valley to a stream following into an inlet they had never seen.

There, at the mouth of an estuary, silhouetted against late afternoon sun and a sparkling North Sea, they came upon the eerie wreck of a ship – a galleon, English or Spanish – Hamlet judged from its four masts of which only a main mast and mizzen remained intact – and the tapering gourd-like shape of its hull, with algae covered cracks in its planking. Tarnished brass cannon muzzles peeked from some of the open ports on two decks.

Hamlet trotted his horse closer to it – "a pirate ship." Ophelia could tell that he said this half in jest. "If these be pirates, lay on!" Hamlet drew his sword and poked it into the lower cannon ports of the hull, as if skewering a large fish. No one responded.

"Show yourselves, you sea dogs." Hamlet had been on seagoing ships, not just canal barges, and liked to impress them with his invented knowledge of buccaneers he'd never seen.

Laertes, still astride his roan, drew sword as well, and waved about with mock growling. Ophelia pulled an arrow from her quiver and notched it in her longbow. A man appeared on what was left of the galleon's forecastle.

213

"Ahoy, *niños!*" The man raised his hands and grinned too widely for his gaunt narrow face. "I surrender!" He had a black beard that came to a perfect point. Dark, glistening curls framed a cinnamon face, with coal eyes. He looked like an obscure saint painted on wooden Slavic ikons that Ophelia had seen at Elsinore, booty from Poland.

He wore a ragged, brown, habit, hood back. He picked up a bulging cloth sack in one bony hand and held it for them to see. "*Ayuda me, por favor, muchachos.*" He pointed aft where a tall ladder stood askew and half fallen against the hull.

Ophelia lowered her bow, walked her steed to the side of the beached vessel, leaned out from her saddle and put the ladder straight against a deck rail with one hand.

"*Muchas gracias!* ... You saved me, *Indios!*" He kept talking rapidly and tried a melange of Dutch and low German peppered with Castillian and Italian that Hamlet, Ophelia and Laertes tried to follow.

The three, swords still at the ready, watched Padre Beppo climb down the ladder talking as he went. When he reached ground he bowed and made a priestly blessing motion and mumbled in Latin at each of them in turn. They giggled. He looked more diminutive and childlike on the sand now than he had when looming from the forecastle.

He introduced himself as "Father Beppo." Short for Giuseppe, born in Genoa, it turned out, not Spain. A Roman Catholic priest, he said, though he seemed a simple friar.

Seeing no threat, they each dismounted. Ophelia made the introductions: "Pleased to meet you. I am *Freya*. My brother, *Freyr*." She nodded towards Laertes, who scowled and shook his head. She paused a beat. Fra Beppo smiled, guilelessly. "And this Crown Prince ... *Thor*."

She could hardly contain a laugh. Hamlet grimaced and raised a fist in salute. Lightning crackled above, followed by a thunder clap that made them jump and startled the horses.

"Perfect timing," Ophelia muttered to her brother.

Ophelia stood the tallest of the three playmates that summer – as girls often do outgrow boys at their age. Padre Beppo stood slightly shorter than herself or her brother, who had grown quickly in the last year. She was able to see the top Fra Beppo's head as they walked, hurrying to get out of the oncoming rain. They stumbled along, best they could in Spanish, mixed with Italian and a few words of Dutch. She saw that he had left his tonsure grow nearly over, and calculated how long he must have been at sea.

"Bless you, *muchachos*, you relieve my long wait for Francisco and our men return, *Dios* willing." He crossed himself again and pointed out to sea.

"*Pescando*," he said twice – fishing – and made a fish sign on the sand. "Ask me, I tell you they fish… for *esperanza*, but catch nothing. We have had little to eat these last days but insects, a few wild berries and grass that made us vomit, if you will excuse me."

"We have provisions to share, good father, and I have herbs and mushrooms for that dyspepsia" Ophelia noticed a beached longboat beyond the ship, and skid marks in the sand from another one put to sea.

The sky darkened more, and the rain started, baby drops at first, then rolling thunder and a downpour.

Father Beppo crossed himself. "I pray our comrades return safely." He led the three hurriedly to his camp upstream – a lodge that Ophelia recognized an old Viking long house that Father Beppo and his men apparently had repaired with ship's planking, spars and tar, plus a few huts fashioned of same.

Another, very thin, tall, half starved looking man with a large black mustache, accompanied by a pair of nanny goats greeted and led them inside the largest hut – a makeshift church with an improvised plank altar, and an incongruously ornate silver chalice, obviously Roman Catholic. The other side of the hut contained a few benches and tables, apparently for meeting or eating, of which there seemed to be little – a few hard biscuits, some dried meat and fish.

Ophelia went back out into the rain to stable the horses under an improvised lean-to behind the main hut. She collected some of their provisions along with the rabbits and partridge she had killed that day. The prince nodded his approval when she returned inside. Father Beppo and his pallid cohort thanked her profusely. He quickly stoked the smoldering coals that had been banked in the fire pit.

Ophelia noticed that they had made a crude chimney of river stones, that worked just well enough so that incoming rain didn't put out the fire. The taller man with the beard appeared to be their chief cook. His hands trembled as the man eyed Ophelia's bounty of food with the hollow eyes of a starved man. He quickly dressed Ophelia's game and put bird and rabbit pieces on a skewer for roasting.

Thunder crashed outside and they heard rain pelting the roof of the hut, which leaked here and there.

Ophelia put a loaf of coarse bread from her bags on a table while the priest and his colleague tended to the fire. Father Beppo put a kettle of water atop coals on one side of the fire pit. After it began to steam, Ophelia found some tin goblets, put a few of her cache of wild, long-stemmed golden mushrooms in each one, and ladled hot water over them.

"We will let these steep and enjoy them soon, padre. It will give your body and your dreams strength."

The priest went to an oaken cask that sat on a table behind the altar. He filled three cups with a clear liquid from an oaken cask, one for each guest, then filled one for himself and his helper.

"A toast!" He raised his cup. "To our honored guests – Freya, her brother Freyr and Thor" The three had to keep from laughing so as not to choke, as they sipped from their cups.

Hamlet coughed and wiped his eyes after the first swallow. "What...?

The monk and that tall man looked at each other and laughed. "Acqua vitae! The sacred wine of Christ, – a dark blood brandy from cherries. One of the few treasures – thanks to the good Lord – that we saved from our shipwreck." He pointed to the cask.

"Let me try that … if you please." Ophelia put out her hand and took a cup of the liquid, which – in her usual way of doing Hamlet one better, she downed all at once.

"Ah. Yes!!" She pounded the cup down on the altar and they both laughed. Laertes took a turn, trying not to flinch.

The "sacramental" spirits immediately took greater effect than the beer they had been allowed at home.

After they consumed their fill of game, bread and dried apples, Ophelia served them the mushroom tea. At first there was no effect, as the continued to converse. But subtly, everything slowed down, then seemed to turn liquid – not right a way, but in the manner of a vivid dream in which the ordinary becomes extraordinary.

33. THE RAVEN'S HEAD

Inside, they all sat at a table, keeping dry while the rain pounded outside, they drank more acqua vitae and tried their best to talk more. Padre Beppo, stepped outside the hut every so often to see if the rest of the men were returning. Ophelia found more metal cups and made a mushroom tea for each of them.

Father Beppo sipped some of it, relaxed and began to relate how he had come founder on this shore in the galleon with these few surviving men...

The tall, gaunt crewman finished off his tea, ate the mushrooms at the bottom of the cup, then left the main hut in search of "music."

Father Beppo sat on an empty keg. He laughed absently; his gaze drifted far away. "Forgive his behavior. My wretched companions believe they have landed in the New World."

"The world is new to everyone, every day." Ophelia clasped her hands. "Please, good father, tell us all about your adventure on the high seas!"

Laertes, again, scowled. The Prince, meanwhile, strolled about the makeshift church, examining everything while the priest talked.

Father Beppo's started his tale: "I never intended to sail the ocean, or fight for the King of Spain, or for any mortal, monarch or paymaster. In truth, I joined the clergy to keep from being conscripted. But fate – and all yes, blessedly, our Lord found me."

He talked slowly, obviously enthralled at having fresh listeners. Fra Bappo had been assigned as chaplain to one of the Spanish galleons escorting one of King Phillip's supply ships from Spain to the king's forces in restive Flanders. The seas turned rough when they reached the English Channel.

Fra Beppo's ship and its escorts had to fight off English privateers all the way along the northern French and Zeeland coasts. Fra Beppo said Mass for the crew each morning and led prayers between sea battles, if necessary. After each engagement he would comfort the wounded and give last rites to the dying.

After a months at sea, the sailors grew weak, their Spanish marine musketeers died, one by one, from wounds and dysentery. Fresh water and supplies dwindled. A Dutch Sea Begger blockade made resupply from Antwerp difficult. The Dutch privateers would hit and run, rather than try to board the more heavily armed Spanish ships. In one engagement, a Dutch incendiary and cannon salvo damaged Father Beppo's ship badly, leaving it listing and barely able to sail.

Their captain, mortally injured, ordered the ship to sail northward rather than risk threading through the English Channel patrolled by Queen Elizabeth's privateers in England's then sputtering, undeclared war with Spain. He hoped sail up through the North Sea, taking advantage of favorable currents, round Scotland, and then head south to resupply and repair in Ireland, then on to the Atlantic and find the north Iberian shore. Shades of a greater Spanish sea disaster to come, Ophelia could not have known at the time.

But a second storm soon blew their damaged galleon still further off course and separated it from its escorts. They drifted for days trying to make headway with their remaining, usable sails, compass lost and skies overcast. Water and provisions scant, they devoured all the flour, what salted herring was left, what paltry fish they could catch, even roasted ship rats.

Nearly all of those who had survived the Dutch barrage perished subsequently at sea, including the captain and his remaining officers.

Only Fra Beppo and a handful of crewmen survived – all of them poor and ignorant Mediterranean peasants and fishermen who had been conscripted with promises of gold and glory. They turned to their priest as captain and leader.

In their parched delirious the surviving crewmen convinced themselves that they had been swept westward to toward the Americas, where they would land and find gold, women and abundance. Father Beppo knew better, but did not deny them this sustaining dream.

Finally they sighted land. They beached the barely maneuverable galleon trying to sail into the estuary. The survivors kissed the ground and thanked God for having guided them safely to the New World. They made camp, and three of them set off immediately to find "Eldorado" and the Fountain of Youth. "They never returned."

The young prince tilted his head as he did when a fanciful thought rattled into his mind. "Good friar, excuse me, how would you know? We three could be those retches returned to you young and with coin." He rattled the ducats he carried in a small leather purse, and smirked.

Fra Beppo shrugged. "You are a bright lad, but you think too much. True gold is not found in the Edorado of the soul – in simplicity."

"Then bless the simpletons of this world, for they are legion." Hamlet glanced at Laertes and Ophelia conspiratorially, for they had spoken often with contempt about their elders.

Fra Beppo didn't take the bait. "I prayed to wean them from dreams of Eldorado to dreams of God's real paradise of love," Fra Beppo proceeded slowly like a child trying to fit pieces of a wooden puzzle together. "Someday, long from now, you will come to remember this tale, when you face dragons of your own."

"I will slay them." Hamlet made a swoosh with his finger.

"The war's horrors opened my eyes and let this humble friar glimpse the eternal, far light of God's grace to be found everywhere. Our Lord Jesus sees no Catholics or protestants or Turks, only sinners and sufferers – those who can believe in love, and those whose passion is punishment and damnation of others and thereby themselves."

The rain softened to a light drizzle. Father Beppo ran outside and back down to the estuary when they heard the other men return in their longboat, unscathed by the storm. Ophelia was surprised they were only two – one stocky, from Genoa, the other wiry, from Sardinia. They were wet and looked exhausted, and had only a scant catch of North Sea cod to show for their troubles.

They roasted the fish along with Ophelia's sinewy hare and partridge devoured the cheeses and dark bread from Ophelia's supplies, along with the wild berries she had picked. She steeped more of the mushroom broth in tin cups for them while they downed aqua vitae. Cheered, feeling their stomachs full for the first time in many weeks, the men chattered about repairing the ship and sailing further along the coast of this "New World" to find their fortunes. Father Beppo said nothing.

After they finished their repast, the tall one returned, a battered viola and horsehair bow in hand. He sat on a sea trunk, hunched over his instrument and, to Ophelia's surprise, began playing one lilting Neapolitan ballad after another. The crewmen sang the mournful love songs with him, and made Ophelia tearful.

Ophelia realized she was feeling the familiar effects of the mushroom tea – as she and Hamlet had a few secret times before. She felt her skin glowing from beneath her clothing. The ramshackle hut took on the aspect of a magnificent cathedral, its twigged roof became flying buttresses, its dim interior transformed into soaring, peaked arches. Colors of leaves and twigs, smells of soil and damp straw became revelations. Bird calls, leaves rustling, twigs scratching against the hut blended into a madrigal with the sailors' raspy voices rolled up into a crescendo of rain then hail. Lightening flashed through the chinks in the hut, thunder rolled and pounded above them, wind whistled and cough.

Every sight, sound, smell, feeling and word lost its name. None were separate from the others, yet all were distinct to her – that state of bliss that she would try in vain to express fully in her songs and poetry that needed neither explanation or faith to experience.

Ophelia saw Father Beppo with the head of a raven, bathed in silvery light, with a bear skin cape and a necklace of bones.

Hamlet stood up, teetered, then steadied himself. Lightening flashed around him, in black furs – Thor – not a brutish war god, but a luminescent, hero, seeking the way forward.

Hamlet put a hand out to Ophelia, and they danced a slow pavane around the dirt floor of the hut. In the shadows, they kissed brazenly.

When the couple spun back into the light of the fire, Prince Hamlet stopped, sank to one knee in mock ceremony and asked for "my Freya's" hand in marriage.

Laertes came close and groused. "Please! My lord, think on this." He gave his sister a stern look. "This is a mockery."

She pushed her brother to one side and took Hamlet's hand. "Yes, my lord. In love and honor, I pledge myself to thee with all my heart and soul." She curtsied. The prince kissed her hand.

Laertes downed more of the sacramental spirits and sulked.

Father Beppo exclaimed: *"Splendido!"* The diminutive priest whispered to his bearded companion. "I had best perform the rites of marriage, lest these young, firery lovers live in sin 'ere long."

Thus a pretend wedding – all mock pomp and ceremony – became something ritualistically real. Ophelia unrolled her feather cape from a saddle bag and donned it. Hamlet stood tall in his black leather doublet.

Solemnly, Father Beppo recited a passage of Paul's First Epistle to the Corinthians from his tattered bible, in a bastardized Latin.

"Love suffers long and is kind; love does not envy; love does not parade itself, is not puffed up; does not behave rudely, does not seek its own, is not provoked, thinks no evil; does not rejoice in iniquity, but rejoices in the truth; bears all things, believes all things, hopes all things, endures all things. Love never fails."

Ophelia and Prince Hamlet exchanged vows whose weight they could not measure, but gave to each other with naïve faith. Padre Beppo chanted over them in Latin, and pronounced them man and wife.

Out of nowhere, it seemed, Father Beppo, produced two large, coin-shaped golden amulets inset with a raven engraved on black onyx – Old Norse symbols that Ophelia knew well, but wondered how such came to be in the possession of this friar. Each medallion was hung on a gold chain.

He gave one to Hamlet and told him to put it on his bride, speaking words in a tongue that Ophelia did not recognize. Then he did the same for Ophelia. The prince and his bride danced to the bearded man's fiddle until nearly dawn. They fell asleep on a fur blanket in Father Beppo's tiny hut, which he offered them as nuptial cottage, retiring himself in the church.

They awoke – still as chaste as the day they were born – to a late morning sun. The rain had ended.

The night went until dawn, when they fell asleep. The details melted like butter in the morning sun.

All through that night of half-sleep, Ophelia had seen visions of bears, elk and snowy egrets. She had run with Freya's sacred boar. Wolves escorting them, howling with yellow eyes. Owls whistled and myriads of cicadas rustled from the trees. Lara, Ophelia's mother, rose from her grave as a sylph in a royal blue silk shift, her fiery hair flowing and aglow. She beckoned her daughter through flames in an ancient Jute language Ophelia somehow understood, but whose content she would not remember,

"Fly away, my little sparrow, while you can," her mother sang. Ophelia tried to take wing, but felt too heavy. Her mother ascended as a blue white star, through the hut's chimney hole and into the constellations of stars.

Ophelia felt herself lighten and rise now too, upwards, upwards, weightless, rising and rising, following her mother's light into the night sky. Lightning, hail, winds and torrential rain raged all around without touching her. Ophelia then rose ever upwards through the flashing peacock Aurora Borealis, the same as she had observed often from the ramparts of Elsinore as a child when her mother had scooped her up from bed to see the northern sky aglow, just the two of them.

And she heard her mother say: "*Mind thyself, my daughter. Live. Be not afraid of the water, plunge forth, join with currents and let the river's power be yours.*"

Ophelia could see the northern lights in each thing she touched, and from every face of those in the hut, of her family, of the court where she had grown up, and of humanity, it seemed. Father Beppo levitated, and revealed his wizardry.

Then, the sky blackened and she envisioned her father, ascending from now, but from a grave, gray-faced dead, a wound pierced his chest like that of Jesus. She saw her brother Laertes ghost as well. And Lord Hamlet, his handsome face distorted and blue from poison, came forth, covered in animal skins, and asked her to lead to Valhalla.

In disjointed dreams, they ran into the rain, naked and dancing to a different music, into the water where clouds parted to a giant moon, yellow as wheat, so close.

They floated in visions to the vanishing point, until she awakened, dazed, faintly euphoric, on the hut floor, still in her hunting attire, not clear how she got there or for how long she had slept, if at all.

When she exited the hut, blinking in the morning sun, she saw that Prince Hamlet and her brother had already saddled and loaded the horses. She guessed that her brother had, at last, brought Lord Hamlet "to his senses."

Focusing her eyes, Ophelia drew in a breath when she saw what had happened to Fra Beppo. Hamlet and Laertes obviously had overcome the groggy priest and crewmen, taken them prisoner and bound them together to a long rope tied to one of the pack horses.

"What have you done, my lord?" Ophelia called out.

"Come, nymph!" Hamlet shouted to her.

She shook her head. "Not until you release this priest!"

"He and his men are prisoners of war I will present to my father." Hamlet sat tall in his saddle, then said to her, more softly. "Don't worry, fair Ophelia, they will not be harmed."

"I pray not," Ophelia answered, straightened up and made for her own horse.

Laertes shouted. "We have word of a great victory."

It was then Ophelia noticed Bernardo, of the queen's guard, at attention off to one side Hamlet, flanked by a squad of arquebusiers with their musket loaders, and four cavalry men, pikes at the ready, helmet guards down over their faces like Apocalypse horsemen themselves.

34. PRESSING THE LILY

Hamlet did not look at Ophelia all the way back. By main roads, their trip home was hatefully swift. Laertes pulled his horse next to Ophelia's and bid her to lag out of earshot. "His highness the prince informs me that you are not to speak of last night – not a word of your mock wedding."

"Mock?" Ophelia bit her lip.

"I warned you not to indulge the prince's games, my sister."

Ophelia went to her quarters after they arrived. The servants were accustomed to seeing her in her male attire after such outings. She did not change out of them this time. Avoiding thought – she sorted the flowers, herbs, mushrooms and stones she had collected.

Hamlet entered. "Do not weep, my Freya!"

"I rue, but I do not weep, my prince." She turned her head away. "Even a prince should knock before entering a lady's chamber."

"You are more comrade than lady, my Ophelia."

"Then why shun me?"

"I am called to my duty. I must do right by my king!"

"And right by yourself?"

"The day will come, when all is aright, a prince becomes a king and marries."

"Only, not now, my lord? Right?" She turned back and stared into his steely eyes, searching. "Do not toy with me, sir!" She clenched her teeth.

He kissed her mouth. "By my honor..."

She pushed him back. By your honor, my lord? Truly? Am I to hear this as a promise?"

"Not given lightly..." He stepped towards her.

"A cock, or a king's promise?"

227

He smirked and moved to kiss her again. This time she returned his kiss. They lingered in each others' arms.

She heard voices and footsteps approaching from the corridor. "My father and brother. You must go."

Hamlet climbed out her balcony and down a vine. He knew the way.

A knock. Enter Polonius and Laertes. "How be'st thou my daughter?"

"I be now a viola."

"Da gamba? Then play on!"

"The violet of many colors, you call pansy."

Laertes raised an eyebrow. "Plucked or unplucked."

"Pansies are for knowing."

Polonius looked puzzled, then raised a finger and cleared his throat. "Consider the pansies of the field, how they grow: they neither toil nor spin..."

"That's lilies, father." Ophelia grinned.

"My point exactly!" Polonius looked his daughter up and down. "...and yet I say to you that even Solomon in all his glory was not arrayed like one of these" He pointed at Ophelia's doublet, then her cap. "Nor one of these!"

"Father. I ..."

"Why is my daughter arrayed like a coarse weed and not the lily I raised you to be?"

Ophelia made an exaggerated curtsy. "Oh father, forgive me. Your fair maiden will find her fair raiments forthwith!"

"You shame me, daughter! Now, make haste. We leave for Elsinore to feast and celebrate our king's great triumph."

"And count the spoils." Ophelia stepped back. "No, father and no, dear brother, allow me to tend my own wardrobe."

++++

King Hamlet had returned to Elsinore in triumph, the Norwegians defeated, their king, Fortinbras the Elder, slain by King Hamlet himself in a battlefield duel – ending with disputed Norwegian territories ceded to Denmark. King Hamlet's terms of surrender put the slain king's brother on the Norwegian throne and forced the king's hot-headed son, Crown Prince Fortinbras, into Polish exile, where he blustered about revenge, but commanded no forces for the moment.

The younger Fortinbras, unlike Prince Hamlet, was a single-minded, obsessive sort, with adequate wealth to raise a new army of mercenaries, given time, but for the present, peace prevailed. No one could have predicted that Prince Fortinbras would come marching into Elsinore one day, unopposed – all it's leaders slain by their own hands.

King Hamlet released Fra Beppo and the marooned crewmen quickly, and gave them the option of staying or returning home. Under the new peace, he said, Denmark, though Protestant, had no direct quarrel with Madrid or Rome at the present.

The Danish tribes – many descended, not that long ago, from its wild Jutes and Frieslanders, beat their drums all through the remaining days of that Nordic summer. Denmark was more a melancholy land. From that point onward, Ophelia saw little of the prince, who "set aside childish things" and kept to father's side constantly attending affairs of state and presiding over ceremonies.

35. GETTING TO NUNNERY

Hamlet teased Ophelia about their "nuptial" after that, but only when they found themselves alone – which became less and less often.

"Get thee to a nunnery." Ophelia shot back at him. It had been their favorite, blasphemous tease. She said it first one day, flirtatiously on soft grass under an generous oak while her brother stalked the woods for a stag. Hamlet – they had reached that age – took her to him. Their bodies knew what to do, pressing, intertwining, sliding and moving together. They trembled at the newness of their intimacy and awareness of each other.

They kissed, clumsily at first, then languidly, again, one way and another, until he ran his hands where she wanted them to be, but not just yet. "Get thee to a nunnery" – meaning go to a whorehouse. I'm not your harlot.

Such lascivious word play from her saucy mouth, made his blood rush. He kissed the lobe of her ear softly, and whispered – giggling so he could hardly say it: "Only...if thou gets thyself to a nunnery with me." That put them both in sin, whore and whoremonger.

Ophelia and young Hamlet knew well their naughty, forbidden literature, and let its erotic puns and visions inform their secret language. Orgiastic nuns and fornicating friars ran amok through *The Land of Cockaigne,* the satirical, carnivalesque medieval text that depicted a sensual topsy-turvy paradise where monks beat their abbots, houses were tiled with pies, boiled eggs ran around in tights on tiny legs, roast chickens flew into the yawning mouths of idlers. There it rained cheeses and boots grew on trees.

amlet had sneaked a copy to Ophelia from the the royal library – providing fodder for *double entendres* that they exchanged, and that made her feel deceptively special to the prince.

She was to dream often of that irreverent fleshy world later, reading more of the poetry, and uproarious novels of Rabelais, seeing paintings by Hieronymus Bosch and Pieter Bruegel the Elder in Antwerp, all of which she would have missed had her life ended in the stream outside of Elsinore.

"Yes, my prince. I shall get me to a nunnery and await thy apparition." Ophelia struck a beatific pose – hands in prayer, playfully blocking his further advances. She rose. They heard the snapping of branches. She saw her brother coming out from the trees, as she brushed leaves and twigs off herself, hoping he had not seen anything. The prince, already up, strode towards Laertes as if he had just arrived himself.

The "nunnery" persisted as their private jest. "Get thee to a nunnery..." then with variations and twists...

Hamlet: "Get thee to a nunnery."

Ophelia: "How now, Abélard?" – in reference to the storied, forbidden, twelfth century romance between monk and nun, poet philosophers Héloïse and Abélard. Each took the cloth after Héloïse's irate uncle had Abélard castrated for impregnating his niece. The two, nevertheless, carried on a lifelong, poetic correspondence – abbey to abbey.

Hamlet: "Get thine uncle to a nunnery."

Ophelia had often mused over the legendary child born of Héloïse and Abélard, whom they named, oddly, Astrolabe, seemingly after a nautical navigation device, not a saint.

Scouring her books, Ophelia could find very little about the child that Abélard's family took in after the parents became monk and nun.

Ophelia, being that kind of whimsical child, wrote a fantasy romance about little orphan Astrolabe growing up as a son of scandal abandoned by his penitent parents. In Ophelia's romance, Astrolabe learned the secret of levitation from a wizard and visited the stars, then returned to declared that they were firery gods did not favor lovers. She showed the romance to Hamlet, who thought it comical – commented sardonically that her Astrolabe reminded him of himself.

Ophelia had felt most alive those summers. Now, they seemed desiccated as the pressed flowers she collected – to be sketched, admired, then put aside.

As time wore on, Ophelia and Laertes hardly saw less and less of the prince during the months after the king's return. The prince nodded only perfunctory goodbyes to Ophelia when he left Elsionore to study at the university in Wittenberg.

Laertes was to go to Paris to study. Ophelia was expected to marry a groom to be chosen for her. Ophelia's father kept a tighter rein on his daughter. Polonius arranged for the ladies of the court to instruct Ophelia in ladylike ways.

Ophelia complied, but continued to write her fantasies, which now included imagining Freya slaying each and every courtier with her magic bow.

Then everything turned ugly. King Hamlet died mysteriously, while napping in his royal garden – said of "sudden convulsions" and buried in haste.

The king's brother Claudius petitioned the supreme council to ascent the Danish throne immediately after King Hamlet's death – "for the stability of kingdom" – bypassing the young Prince Hamlet.

And, as is widely known, Claudius married his brother's wife, Queen Gertrude with unseemly haste that smacked of something more than custom and a way of legitimizing his rule.

Claudius, people had to admit, showed himself a skillful ruler, avoiding further wars and keeping Denmark's advantage over its former enemies.

Prince Hamlet returned from Wittenberg, changed, serious, heavy with Lutheran, if not true belief – and with him, a new friend, Horatio – distant from Ophelia at first.

How could her prince have become so callous towards her overnight, after all they had known together? Was this the way of princes – as her brother had warned – to discard her like last year's castoff clothing, like a plaything?

Did I invent all those adventures and a love that never existed? "I hate him!" She clenched her jaws and banished him from her mind, just as he seemed to have done to her. Her prince of summers, now in his winter of eternal discontent. His smiling wit and his kind eyes would return to her mind and break her heart again. Eventually, Ophelia had to put away her childhood dreams in order to endure – doing as told with the other young ladies in the castle, whom she had always disdained for their enforced innocence – and self-satisfied ignorance, she labeled it. She felt walled up by custom and duty, playing the fair maiden – with Freya gone away to Valhalla.

36. ELSINORE'S SHADOWS

During the long winters at Elsinore, Ophelia had spent more of her time alone, reading and writing her journals and poetry.

She made a game of observing people coming, going, plotting, gossiping, enduring life in the gloom of Elsinore castle, a place so unlike her imagined Sonia.

She learned much about affairs of state, spying on her father, Polonius, who had risen to lord chamberlain. She perceived the machinations of adults more shrewdly than did the young prince, whose attention focused upon philosophies rather than practicalities. Ophelia, like her mother, loved books. But unlike her mother, she took to observing the real life intrigues of court as well.

Edging beyond her station, she watched and listened, unnoticed, playing in the shadows, as her father plied the royal chambers and council rooms, conversing with Hamlet's father about war and peace, taxes and land, arms, harvests, plagues, peasants and soldiers. She told little of what she knew to her brother or father, who would be quick to scold.

Her mother preferred poetry and popular romances cranked out by Venetian publishers whose handy sized books had become all the rage among ladies of the court, along with those from Antwerp, Lyon and Augsburg. Ophelia memorized many of the poems, particularly those of her mother's favorite, by Louise Labé, published in Lara's home city of Lyon. The poet, a great aunt of her mother, had inscribed a copy of her book to Lara. The introduction, which Ophelia read over many time, started out as follows:

"It is time for women to apply themselves to the sciences and other disciplines. And if a woman reaches to point of putting her ideas in writing, she must take great pains to accomplish with and never be shy of accepting the glory."

Even after his victory over the Norwegians, Hamlet's father while he still lived, could not rest easy in his castle for long before going off battle. He had to quash raiders, incursions and petty rebellions, punctuated by treacherous truces made by tired kings only to be broken by ambitious upstart. Danes fought Swedes, Russians, Estonians and Poles – even Bohemians. Lutheran attacked Roman Catholic and vice versa, with France and the German princely states pushing at the gates.

Denmark controlled the narrow straits between the North and Baltic seas, and thus vital trade in foodstuffs, metals and goods. To support his army, King Hamlet could only raise the levies through the straits so high without incurring the anger of surrounding states. But Denmark's landed gentry and wealthy merchants resisted higher taxes and fees as well. Queen Gertrude grew tired of austerity and crisis. The days of abundance and serenity that he had promised after vanquishing the Norwegians faded quickly amid new troubles preoccupying the king.

Denmark, actually, had seen little peace since the end of old Queen Margaret's reign and the dissolution of her Kalmar Union of Scandinavian States. It was every duchy and township for itself, with more cannons, grenades and muskets replacing archers and lancers – and ever more mercenaries to drain treasuries and savage the lands and friend and foe alike.

Ophelia took all this in with a dispassionate eye. The wars seemed a far off game in her mind – played with her brother's wooden soldiers.

235

The blood and terror of battle seemed far removed from Elsinore's cool corridors where she, her brother and Hamlet played hide and seek.

Unlike the other girls, as a child, Ophelia had imagined herself in black leathers, bow in hand, riding her white mare in pursuit of an elk, never in a bridal gown offered up to the most advantageous pasty faced suitor that her father could find.

Hamlet's moods continued to intensify following his homecoming to the point where Ophelia felt fearful around him for the first time in her life. The gentle prince she befriended and loved in her blossoming had turned into a brooding, mercurial lout, obsessed about his father's untimely death, his mother's presumed sins and those of all women.

"Shall I wear pants again and not a dress, my lord?" She called it after him as he walked by her in a passageway to the grand hall, his head down, muttering to himself. "If you prefer me as a boy, then..." He kept walking and made no sign of having heard her jibe. Just as well, for she regretted it immediately.

Her brother and father then warned her away from this very prince now – too late, she neglected to tell them, for they had been already close in all but the final acts of love. She wanted him, but he pushed her away with rough words that seemed to protest too much. Then, worst of all, her father and the queen, nudged her to close to him again– for their own purposes, not for love. They urged her to betray his feelings to her, and most terribly, weak, she complied and despised them all for it.

Those dreamy summer days on the beach with him had been swept away as surely as the tides rolled in over their sand castles.

Ophelia, perforce, no longer acted out those old dreams. She no longer had access to the royal stables armory. They forbade her the hunt, and she hid away her bow and arrows lest they take them away as well.

But she hunted and rode as Freya at night when she closed her eyes and returned to her castle Sonia – taking refuge, as she had done over the years since her mother's death. She had nowhere to turn, it seemed, nothing but lonely days in Elsinore, made bearable only by dwelling in the volumes of poetry and romances that her mother had left to her.

Out of habit, now, rather than as memento, she wore the raven amulet every day on a fine gold chain. Hamlet had not worn his – as least as far as she could see – since his return from Wittenberg. When they talked, which was rare now, he never looked at her directly, much less seeing that she still wore this memento of their adventure, their Valhalla marriage.

Ophelia could not reconcile the embittered, sarcastic, volatile, misogynist who returned to Elsinore with the graceful, bright, adventurous young prince she had always known. He toyed with her like a cat with a mouse – drawing her in, then assailing her with insinuations and obscene innuendos.

She tried to stay clear of him, but then her father encouraged her to help understand "the prince's madness." She grew to hate them both in the process.

Truth was, she disliked her father – his prattling, posturing and platitudes. She knew such disloyalty was a sin for a fair maiden, but she did not regard any of her family life as fair in any sense of that word. He had treated their mother – a secret Catholic and therefore a threat – as a pariah in private, while fussing over her at court ceremonies. She raged more than she sobbed at her father's assassination. Madness, the king, queen and courtiers call it, and waited for her storm to pass while she choked on guilt and anger more than sorrow.

My father dies cowering behind a tapestry, as he lived, spying and conniving with his betters. The king is to blame, as is the prince. My brother raises a mob to storm the castle – venting blind rage. Damn them all!

37. TRANSPORTED

Olivia carries all Ophelia's memories – numbering so many more that those told about Elsinore and her melancholy Dane. None of the many tales of Hamlet's tragedy tell of the prince's last night with Ophelia. Just prior to his departure for England, Hamlet entered Ophelia's bedchamber silently. It was late the night that he had confronted Claudius by having the players "catch the conscience of the King" with the "Mousetrap" scene that he had devised from *The Murder of Gonzago*. That night, Elsinore reeked with the king's murderous, guilty rage.

Ophelia had gone to bed, but lay in the darkness, illuminated only by one dim candle, and stared up at the red velvet canopy of her bed as if it were about to rain blood.

She did not hear the prince enter. He cupped a hand to her mouth. When she calmed, he spoke rapidly, but not of love. She strained to understand what he blurted and choked. "I have him now."

He questioned her about what her father had known of King Claudius' plans. "My father told me nothing of the royal doings," she responded in a hoarse whisper. He tried to hold her while she hammered against him in futile rage.

"Forgive me, for I never meant harm against your father. I took the poor foolish man for Claudius waiting to kill me from behind a curtain."

"You cannot make it right. Not my father, nor your own father. Murders most foul. You can't make any of it right!" She glared at him, her face aglow in the firelight of her hearth, like a chastising angel.

He stared back. Calmer now: "I see that thou hast not lost thy senses, but that thou art enraged – mad only in the same sense as I at my uncle's infamy."

239

Ophelia sat up and slapped the prince solidly across his face – more than a girlish smack. His lip bled. His eyes watered from the blow. His ears rang. No one – not even his father, his mother or his nanny had ever struck this proud prince. He stared at her stunned – both of them blinking with tears.

Just as suddenly, they embraced. They kissed as if dying and coming back to life. There was no castle, no king, no murders, nor doubts nor danger or fathers' vengeance, no time, nothing but their young, wanton bodies, themselves, no longer in the reality of Elsinore. They lay together on a bearskin in a meadow of the coastal forest by the Wadden Sea once again.

His clothing and his hands felt rough through her nightgown. She pulled loose his doublet and tore at his shirt, passion mixed in anger overflowing. She had never felt him full unclothed, but her hands and mouth knew his body, as he did hers.

They coupled until dawn, consumed in passionate blissful, loving encounter – fully this time. Intimate in unashamed flesh as they had once been in mind and spirit – a perfect moment before oblivion while the executioner waited, it seemed to Ophelia in retrospect, but one that gave birth to new life.

For those moonlit hours it seemed to Ophelia as if they had been transported to Castle Sonia looking out on silver tide pools, cobalt and orange ocean and sunset sky. She knew in that moment what had happened. The palpable internal feelings of being with child – the fullness, the nausea – did not surprise her when they showed up many weeks later, as the players' caravan swayed along the rutted roads taking her away from Elsinore, down the Jutland Peninsula to the seaport where a ship would carry them all to the Netherlands after her untimely "death."

Even in its splotchy, misshapen newborn state, Ophelia could see Hamlet's features in the face of her child. From a wee babe, growing into his delights each day, Ari remained, to be sure, a prince, though, Ophelia had vowed, a prince only of dreams, of Sonia, not of nations, not of Elsinore, but of Sonia, of imagination and knowledge, she prayed. The baby was theirs – not of Ophelia and Hamlet, but of Freya and Thor – unconstrained by castle walls.

"In thy orisons, nymph, be all my sins remembered." He had whispered again, afterwards when the prince slipped from her bed into the moonless night, the last she ever saw of him.

By Umberto Tosi

PART FIVE

St. Michael's Abbey, Antwerp, 1570, by Michael Stich. Below: Antwerp illustrated map.

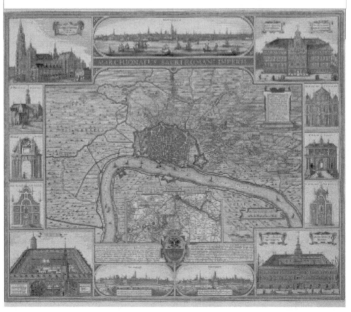

38. ANTWERP

Baby Ari rides a stick horse, with a head of painted leather and a mane of real horse hair. He waves a thin stick – either as riding crop or sword. I breathe easier seeing my little man at play again, after days of fever that we feared was the small pox. We have news of plague in northern Italy. Isabella tells Carlo to stop complaining about being stuck in Antwerp – always at it, those two.

The river glistens silvery purple this time of morning, busy with ships and boats, wide, generous at this point as it nears the open sea. Antwerp's red and gray buildings and streets stop at its edge, with open arms to the bounty it brings, but like me with no desire to cross. I have had my fill of rivers and sea, though I am tempted more than ever to give up my plans for Lyon, and sail straight to Italy with my companions.

I see Ari's father in him more every day. Behind baby giggles, his gray green wolf eyes regard me from terrain we both knew well.

My sweet and bitter prince haunts me through those eyes, and hardens my resolve to steer my boy far away from where his father fell. Little Ari full of mischief circles Isabella, Rosa and I, galloping in little pony jumps as we watch Carlo haggle once again with a ship owner on the wharf where we have brought the lead carnival wagon that would have to be taken on board if a deal for passage is made.

I am hoping nothing comes of this negotiation like all the others. I don't want to tell Isabella yes or no about sailing to Italy.

I want to put off deciding. As long as I don't decide, I feel it will be all right; nothing will change, but of course, it changes constantly like the river, forever flowing. Maybe I will go with them after all. I don't want to choose between my friends and my kin in Lyon, especially since my kin exist only in my hopes at this point.

I smell the river Scheldt, heavy from its winding trip through forests, fields and farms – rich with soil – and I smell a trace of salt from the North Sea not far downstream. Great wooden ships nestle in their slips along the breakwater where we stand. They rise and fall, breathing, sleeping, dreaming of vast open seas. Their bared masts yaw and pitch ever so gently in a brisk autumn breeze announcing winter's approach – not a good season to set sail, but commerce and greed tolerate no restraints.

Men sweat and stoop, loading and unloading barrels, casks, boxes, bundles, crates from ships, off and onto to carts, horses snort and stamp, the lucky ones munching from feedbags.

Always horses and carts – thousands of them clatter in all directions through the pulsing streets of this city. All manner, class, age, temper of people rush about their affairs in every description, intent on their crisscrossing purposes.

We arrived in August for the start of "Land's Jewels" and fall festivals, a windfall for Isabella and Carlo to put on their most ambitious productions amid the celebrations in a city crowded with carefree visitors out to spend their money and forget war, toil and pestilence. We found ourselves in pageants with hundreds of decorated chariots, marching bands, and costumed celebrants.

We've been three months here now, dithering and performing in Antwerp, a city of brick, granite and aspirations, livelier and grander I could have imagined, smelling of horse dung, herring, damp stones, ink and ideas. People scurry and labor and do so many things exquisitely well.

As a child, I discovered wonders only in nature, outside of town's and castle's walls. But, here I have seen works wrought by human hands that dazzle my eyes, arouse my senses, feed my spirit and roil my mind.

This is not home. I have no home. But it is a town in which I feel at home – whose walls embrace more than they keep out, and one that tugs on me as well.

I can see the great, white, lacy cathedral spire piercing this morning's misty sky, the landmark from where I can position myself from any avenue within the city walls. "The journey is not yet over when one can discern the church and steeple," say the Dutch. My mission remains incomplete, and for me, not even yet defined.

The Cathedral of Our Lady, *Onze-Lieve-Vrouwekathedraal* – I visit this sacred space and addend its services to bathe myself in its heavenly Italian, French and German music more stirring and wondrous than anything I have ever heard – choral polyphony that soars to fill the Gothic arched space.

I am conscious of being a protestant interloper treading on Catholic soil, under papist Habsburg rule – uneasy to be sure.

The Spanish overlords of this city have hanged and burned the protestant likes of me – devout or not – in this very cathedral square not so long ago when the King Phillip and the pope had had their Inquisition off leash.

247

For now, the ever-present papist clergy of priests, monks and nuns mingle but do not define or direct. I can't tell a Walloon from Calvinist, a Catholic from a Lutheran from a Jew. Silver and gold seem to flow through everyone's veins instead of blood.

Frenchmen, Spaniards, Portuguese, English, Jews, Moriscos, dark-eyed, jewel cutters from India – all in Antwerp dance to drum of commerce, no matter their skin or faith. Iron mongers, goldsmiths,bankers, artists, printers, engravers, merchants, weavers, traders, craftsmen, musicians, rhetoricians – the rich porridge of burghers bubbles over with confident prosperity. Merchants, tradesmen, farmers and artists come from near and far to do business here.

I explored the city as Oliver every chance I got. I sketched and took notes and sipped beer in the taverns. I sauntered into the Bourse, an imposing edifice crowded with bankers, merchants and swindlers bidding on the cargoes of thousands of ships and wagons. Lace from Spain. Glass from Venice. Ceramics from China. Sugar, molasses and stone icons from the New World. Tin of England. Spices from Java and Goa. It is said that "in Antwerp, one can buy a great painting or hire an assassin on the same day, any day of the week."

I discovered the Antwerp of gamblers too, high and low. Workmen, peasants, clerks, nobles and tradesmen partake in every conventional game of chance – dice, wheels, cards, the city-sponsored lottery. But the real gamblers of Antwerp are the mercantile traders and bankers who wager up and down on the prices of everything that moves in and out of their port city every day.

I am fascinated by the human drama, and by the artists of Flanders whose insights illuminate human behavior beyond the old biblical iconography – the greed and profligacy unimagined by the common people, their kings and clergy of yore.

My host – the widow Cöck, owner of the Antwerp's greatest printing establishment – seeing my interest – gave me a book of Jan van der Heyden etchings from drawings by Pieter Bruegel the Elder, whose fame by these means had already reached Denmark when I was a child. I remember my mother having this volume. I carry my new copy about and savor its pages like rare wine, my eyes drinking in each phantasmal rendering. Roaming Antwerp, I understand the drama of life in these drawings now – the metaphors, not just the fantasies.

I see reality in Bruegel's images of preoccupied, grasping men wading in search of coins through their wrecked merchant scales and broken gaming boards. The drawing, *Elck and Nemo* – "Everyone and Nobody" – speaks to me as I roam the city, as a young man – like so many others, unnoticed.

At the mercantile exchange, among the men bumping and bidding against each other, I see the grotesque images of *Battle of the Moneybags and Strongboxes* – another of the dream-like etchings, that one bearing the Latin inscription *"Always, each man is seeking for himself alone ... No light will help him in this lonely place."*

Such is the world into which I have brought my Ari – a world where the seven cardinal vices out shout the seven virtues, as far as I can see. One day, after a visit to the Bourse, I gazed for a long time at an engraving of the Flemish master Bruegel's *Big Fish Eat Little Fish.* In it, a father tells his child, amid a macabre scene of devouring greed, "Look, son. I have long known that the big fish eat the small." It is an old Latin proverb. Must I tell by innocent Ari the same one day – as cautionary wisdom?

Sweaty traders – fat and thin, princes and pretenders – crammed the exchanges. The widow Cŏck's eldest son, Jan, is among them. I try to avoid him on the street, just as I have done in her home, where he occupies a suite on the upper floor.

Jan's stringy blond beard did not disguise his weak chin, nor does it add the character that his ferret eyes lacked. I felt those eyes groping me from afar whenever his mother wasn't present.

I had taken great care to be discreet with my gender switches, no longer being on stage with my *commedia* players. I could confide in the widow, but did not trust her son. I was careful to remain suitably feminine in his presence, and slip away as Oliver only when he was out of sight.

Nevertheless, there he was one day, as I walked down a narrow street near the Bourse. He crossed the street and walked straight at me, looking intensely at my face.

"Well, who have we here?" He squinted and smirked.

I tried to evade him, but it was no use.

"Don't be concerned, *sir,*" he hissed. "Or should I say, 'my lady?' Your secret is safe with me." He bowed and bid me to walk beside him. "I can be your guide and companion … miss Oliv..."

"The name is Oliver, sir!" I smacked down his shoulders with both hands hard enough to show him I meant business.

We walked a ways and talked. I did not want to offend him – and thereby his mother, whose hospitality and friendship I valued.

He proved harmless enough, but love stricken and eager to impress me. He took me into the exchange and a round of rancid taverns, spending ducats freely – gold from his mother, no doubt.

I am practiced enough with my male identity to have no problems with his tavern friends. After a few moments they wouldn't have noticed if I showed them my tits, they were so consumed with cards and dice and bragging about their supposed market killings and sexual conquests. I wondered how these sallow city princes would have done on the walls of Leiden under Spanish musket fire.

No one seemed to notice a storm on the horizon that looked plain to me, perhaps because of my recent education in war.

I heard merchants complaining that business has gone poorly since the Spanish monarchy declared bankruptcy and reneged on the promissory notes it gave out to supply its army. But I see little sign of this.

There is talk of a mutiny by unpaid soldiers garrisoned in the citadel, a fortress that sprouts like a giant mushroom next to the west wall of the city. Clouds gather. But the city life goes on. The Spanish have as much trouble with their mercenaries as they do with Prince William's rebels.

++++

"Where's Ari?" Isabella pokes me out of my contemplation.

I look about me with immediate panic. My boy, nearing age three now, can dart as quickly as a wild hare. He has quickness of mind as well – full of mirth and mischief. I know that I spoil the little prince. He knows well how to unravel me.

I realized too late, that my reverie there on the docks had compromised my vigilance. I looked up the down the wharf for him. "Oh my God! There he is!" I spotted little Ari now, racing along the edge of the breakwater on his stick horse, laughing with high pitched glee.

I ran hiked my skirt and ran after him. He looked back, enjoying the game, and ran faster on his little legs, making the stick horse bob up and down in a pretend gallop right along the edge of the stone breakwater. One misstep and he would fall into the dark, swift river.

Just ahead, the wall ended at a slip where a ship was moored. I feared Ari will run right off of it and tumble between the wall and the ship's massive, moving hull. Isabella ran alongside me. Carlo broke off from the ship captain, pivoted and angled to cut Ari off – all of us shouting at the boy.

Just then, a rangy, red haired gentleman leapt from the ship's deck onto the breakwater and scooped Ari into his arms. I nearly crashed into the man to get my baby – my heart thumping so that I fear it will leap from my body.

"Oh thank God ! … and thank you sir!" I took Ari from him and into my arms. Only then did I look directly into the man's face and blanch with recognition. "Horatio?"

Before he could reciprocate my greeting, I turned away and headed back to the caravan wagon apace. I couldn't be sure it was Horatio, and I didn't want to find out. But I could think of nothing but the encounter all the next day, wondering...

++++

SPAERT HEERE, V VOLCK.

Volcxken Diercx, aka, "Vola," co-founded Antwerp's "Aux Quatre Vents," Four Winds Press, largest in northern Europe, in 1548 with husband Hieronymus Cŏck, and ran it for thirty years after his death in 1570.

39. VOLA

Again! I thought I had glimpsed Horatio in the audience when we performed at the guild hall three nights ago. But he gave no sign of recognizing me. Thank the muses for masks and makeup. It was another of our racy, mistaken identity, romantic farces with lots of tumbling and slapstick.

We invited Volcxken Diercx – the widow Cöck. She loves our farces, though stone faced when it comes to her business. Carlo, with a sharp ear and quick tongue, dubbed her "Vola" – and that is what I began calling her myself, with great affection.

Carlo liked to flirt with her subtly. "*Vola* means 'flying' in my native Italian. You fly far above mere mortals, my lady!" Sometimes he calls her "*Vogel*" – bird, or "*Zangvogel,*" songbird in Dutch, for her love of madrigal. Isabella, who holds Vola in high esteem as well, didn't seem to mind.

Isabella told me much about "Vola" and how she and her late husband, the etcher and engraver Hieronymus Cöck, had established their great printing house, the largest in northern Europe. *"At the Sign of the Four Winds"*, printed and published works writers from Italy and Flanders and engravings of works by the greatest artists of the age – Rafael, Titian, Albrecht Durer, Hieronymus Bosch and Bruegel the Elder.

Vola has been our host these past months. Her steadfastness calms me.

I arrived in Antwerp shaken. Even now, I cannot go out without looking behind me constantly. I feel eyes on my back, real or not. Our gracious widow dispenses wisdom and shares the great books in her collection with me.

And what a collection, surpassing that in the Orneck library in Breda. Books from all over the world, printed in a dozen tongues.

Books everywhere in her mansion. Every day, I inhale them. I touch and taste their paper and ink. I hear their words in my head. I wondered if Vola could possibly have read them all.

Vola had rooms filled with volume of every size and description. They lined shelves that cover her walls. In every room, I saw books on tables, on chairs, on the floors, opened, closed, bookmarked, often with notes written on scrolls of paper stuffed into them or lying nearby.

I have come to appreciate the artistry of her illustrated volumes – in the hundreds – with their drawings and poetry. I come to know the faces of famous artists and thinkers etched on those pages. I pore over illustrated maps that contain and configure land and sea over which I have traveled. She accepts the world's dangers, undeterred, stoic, surrounding herself with artists, writers, greatness and small dogs that she pampers and feeds tidbits from the table. It is an act of prosperity. She didn't have to tell me that she came up from poverty – but not ignorance. Her father was a tailor who read.

She encourages me to wear my flowers – my garlands, wrist bands and blossoms in my hair, and does not think me mad for it. She knows that flowers calm me. I pick them from the garden in the back of her town house near the university – planted with exotics from Asia and the New World as well as local weeds. Now I wear the fall flowers – marigolds, dahlias, bronze fennel, golden chrysanthemums. People on the street stare, but they shrug me off being with my players.

When her husband Hieronymus was young, she traveled Europe with him in search of the finest writing and art to publish. The couple stayed at Isabella's family *palazzo* off the Grand Canal in Venice for many weeks. Isabella was but a maiden at the time, and learned much from their visitors from Flanders. Hieronymus and his wife had just started their printing enterprise in Antwerp with very little means. They had traveled to Venice from Antwerp to meet famous Italian artists, writers and mapmakers and publish their works in the north.

Lady V sees my soul. I am taken with this queen of art and commerce, even more so than I was with dear princess Charlotte. She flaxen haired, with distant, sea-blue eyes and moist, expressive lips often pursed with subtle wit. She is a tiny woman, comfortable in her matronly body, with sturdy hands that bespeak authority. Her clothes are fine, but simple. She works and entertains – with the diligence of the Dutch and the graciousness of the French.

Her mansion occupies four floors of a building next to the Four Winds printing house in the heart of Antwerp near the river, with porticoes and private gardens at the rear. After we had been there a few weeks, she began inviting me to her modest private quarters to converse on some nights after Ari was asleep and when we were not performing. She looks nothing like my mother, but I know my mother would have become fond of her quickly too. Before long, I told Vola everything of my past lives – old and new, in confidence. She listened intently. Afterwards, she encouraged me to put my vision, adventures and loves into writing, poetry and drawings. "You are blessed," she told me.

"I have not thought of putting it that way, my lady." I felt my face flush.

"We ladies in ink must stay close," she tells me.

I laugh. "I like that. 'Ladies in Ink.'

She surprises me by offering to publish a book of my poems and sketches from our time in Leiden, calling it, *Turning Tide*. Later, I detected a sliver of envy mixed with prideful congratulations from Isabella, whose new plays were being printed by rival Plantin.

"You will always be the mother of my inventions, Isabella," I reassured her.

"... and you, Ophelia, are my most wondrous protégé."

I felt myself pulled in all directions as the time approaches when the troupe would sail for Italy. I knew that Isabella – despite trying to sound tolerant of whatever I would decide – wanted me to come with her and the players. Part of me wanted neither Venice nor Lyon, but longed to stay where I was, in Antwerp, with my child, surrounded by Vola's books. I had become fond of this watery city – a place I could imagine myself living free – not as a princess in a sand castle, not in gloomy Elsinore, nor in a besieged, desperate war ravaged town as was Leiden.

40. 'MAKING THINGS ARIGHT'

What did I tell you? Hamlet sat, looking pensive, atop a barrel, fiddling with his raven medallion, his black velvet cape fluttering in the afternoon breeze.

"Begone!" Horatio gave the air a shove.

"Sir?" Marcellus looked over at Horatio from where he had been tying off a sail flap.

"Not you, Marcellus!" Horatio waved him back.

"If you say so, sir." Marcellus looked about the empty deck of the caravel that had brought them to Antwerp. Their crew had long since abandoned them in the delay. He shook his head and went back to his task.

"Fine! I admit the lady did resemble Ophelia. It proves nothing."

Oh! Listen to yourself, Horatio. 'Resemble?' Is that why your eyes went wide as walnuts? Hamlet let go of his medallion and floated along the deck.

"Stop hovering! I hate when you do that!"

Marcellus dropped the line he had been making tight. "Beg pardon, sir. I am nearly finished now."

"Not you, Marcellus, Excuse my interruption."

"Sir Horatio, please, speak on, and I will attend."

"I am practicing a speech. You may ignore me and go about your business Marcellus, thank you."

Marcellus tied one last knot. "Done." He rubbed his hands together and regarded his handiwork. "Sir. Should I gather us a crew now?"

"Soon. Horatio. First I must meet with our Englishman once more for maps and documents."

"Lord Bunzel?"

"Shh." Horatio looked about.

"Then it is done?"

Horatio lowered his voice. "Thank the gods, the Sea Beggars and English Sea Dogs will grant us passage, at last, through the blockage."

Just after Horatio sailed into Antwerp, The Sea Beggars, with English help, had closed off most of the Flanders coastline except to commerce they deemed essential, or profitable to those traders they favored. Horatio had thought the blockaders would honor his Danish flag and diplomatic status. But then he found himself in the middle of a row when Fortinbras jacked up his levies on Dutch and English shipping through the Danish straits to and from Baltic granaries, and pressed Queen Elizabeth for payment of an old debt owed his predecessor.

At first, Horatio was happy to stay a while in Antwerp, with all its culture – and be able to keep an eye on the printing of his book. But the months dragged on and here it was practically the Feast of All Saints and winter would come soon, adding to the dangers of sailing.

But with fall, came an opportunity. The herring season would afford them cover. Hundreds of Dutch fishing ships would take sea out of ports from Amsterdam to Antwerp as North Sea waters turned cold bringing with them a bounty of herring, salmon and cod that would be caught and packed in salt barrels for weeks. The blockaders allowed merchant ships to transport tons of these salted fish far and wide – to German, English, French, and Mediterranean ports – further enriching Dutch traders and their own cause.

Hamlet swooped between them and undid the sail that Marcellus had tied, letting it billow loosely. Marcellus jumped to catch a corner of it and wrestle it down.

The prince hovered close to Horatio's face. *You'll be sailing nowhere for now, my Horatio!*

Horatio glowered. "What would you have now, my lord? I told your story, as I pledged. More than that, I cannot do."

"As you wish, sir. But I am no lord." Marcellus pulled the sailcloth back into place and began tying it again.

"Pay me no mind, Marcellus. I am out of sorts." Horatio made for the gangway and disembarked. "Continue your tasks, my good man. I will return soon."

++++

Horatio made his way down the wharf — accompanied by the unseen Hamlet — as Marcellus stood up, scratched his head, then continued working.

Hamlet kept pace easily with Horatio's lanky deliberate strides. *There is no sense in trying to avoid me, noble friend.*

"If that *was* Ophelia, why didn't you appear to her?"

I do find myself wandering her dreams, but awake, alas, she chooses to see me not.

"I can understand why. I advise you to try again, my lord, so that you can tell her all that you wish, without my intervention."

Horatio, do you think it's easy for a spirit to walk right into the minds of the living?

"You seem to slip in and out of my head with ease, my lord."

I have but one message: You must get Ophelia and my son away from this place!

"*Your* son, now. Then you are certain?"

I think you are the one convinced now, Horatio. You should speak to Ophelia now. You just saved her boy's life, no doubt. She will trust you.

"Only because you pushed me out onto the sea wall at the precise moment the little lad came running by."

I was only giving your cue to enter stage. Now you must speak your lines to her yourself.

"I am a dunce. I know. The boy's eyes startled me. It was as though my noble prince Hamlet gazed into my soul – from out of a gibbering baby – blue with silver flecks floating like stray leaves – while the imp kicked and rained blows on my head with barbed stick, and screamed for his hobby horse that at my feet from where he had run into me."

Not three years old and already a valiant horseman. Hamlet puffed out his ghostly chest.

"Before I could think, two women ran up. The younger of the two pulled the boy from my arms and spun around – but I got a look at her face, and the garland of flowers round her neck, as Ophelia would wear."

As when she went mad.

"Perhaps I am mad. I cannot say. A dwarf tugged hard my cloak suddenly, pulling me off balance. It was the little king – the wee actor who had made us laugh in royal robes at Elsinore, along with his player queen, whom I now recognized as the elder of the two women on the wharf."

Did the two women give sign that they recognized you? I didn't get a good look.

"No, but the dwarf did. He started hectoring me about my book! He squawked that I got him and his players all wrong."

Hardly...

"He lied outright. The dwarf – Carlo – claims that he never played '*the Murder of Gonzago,*' as you had told him that night. He goes about babbling that they did only a farce – '*The Cuckold*' – at Elsinore, and made King Claudius laugh so hard he peed his royal leggings, and had to be escorted out of the hall."

An amusing idea, but not revealing.

"The devil even quoted obscenities from this so-called comedy of his."

I would have boxed his ears, if I could.

"I should have... It was a ruse to distract me. He ran off in the mid-sentence, hooting, tumbling and whistling. By then, the two women vanished with the baby. And you disappeared as well, but I am quite used to that."

Did you give chase?

"No. The bells sounded midday – time confer with my Englishman."

You mean, pay him his gold. Do not be too trusting. Recall that Claudius' English friend would have had my head but for quick thinking.

"I will keep my wits about me, noble friend. I only wish that you had as well."

I need no reminder of the souls weighing upon me, Horatio – Ophelia's foolish father, her fuming brother, my own mother, whose untimely deaths were my unintended doing, casualties of unmindful and unfocused enterprise.

"You take too much upon yourself, my ghostly prince. Victims of fate, not your hand, my prince. Think upon the original crime of your uncle, setting tragedy in relentless motion. Fate affects us all."

Still, I feel I am condemned to roam this mortal coil, dragging the chains of my fate until I make things aright.

"Or I make them aright for you, my prince. – a task that seems to grow more uncertain with time. "

41. HANGMAN AND LOVER

Antwerp Citadel, Spanish Infantry Garrison 2, Barracks 6, Tercio 16:

28 October 1576:

My dear Rosalie,

Forgive me for my long neglect in writing to you. Know that I post you this missive with a heart full of love and – regrettably – dread of what transpires here in Flanders.

With father gone and mother ailing, I turn to you, my eldest sister, to take what measures you deem necessary for the family's good once you have read what I have to say.

Forgive the grave tone of my letter, sister. I know you are strong, but what I am about to relate may grieve you nonetheless.

First of all, let this letter – with its notarized list – serve as will and testament leaving you, our mother and your children what gold and worldly goods I have been able to send home to Lombardy and gather for myself during these two years in Flanders.

Secondly, allow me explain how this has become an urgent necessity.

The soldiers of our company have not been paid in months. Somehow, the captain, his officers and their staffs seem to carry comfortably, having billeted themselves in Antwerp's finest houses.

Like the other common soldiers, I have been forced to borrow from the company fund – that is, from the captain, at high interest, for all essentials – clothing, billeting, bread and gunpowder, for which they charge each soldier, be he lancer or musketeer.

The higher-ups encourage the soldiers to loot in lieu of army pay, and the officers take a cut of everything stolen as well. This sickens me, my devout sister.

You know that our mother and father did not raise us to murder and steal from our brothers and sisters. I take what of value that I can find in desperation, but not by dishonorable means.

My comrades illusions of returning home with riches dwindle as they sell off their booty now, ironically to sharp-eyed Antwerp merchants – Catholic and Protestant – for a fraction of its worth.

A galleon bound for Antwerp from Madrid, carrying gold florins intended for our back pay, has been captured by Queen Elizabeth's English privateers. So I overheard the captain say. The garrison is sure to rise up once the soldiers hear of this. After that, I fear for the lives of all in this city.

Our garrison citadel is like a cask of Greek fire ready to light. The captain had Ugo, our company's hangman, execute three more deserters on Tuesday last in haste before the Feast of All Saints. Ugo disappeared the next day. He either deserted himself – which is unlikely – or was dumped in the river Scheldt with his throat cut by one of our own. Now the captain has taken it into his drunken head to name me his new hangman – a sentence of death should the men mutiny as they have in two other garrison cities. The mutineers will kill the captain first, then his lieutenant and guards, then myself,

Forgive this indelicate bluntness, dear sister. We have always cherished each other in honesty, and though you may be disturbed by what I tell you here, it is best that I give you my truth without milk and honey.

The captain laughed as he had his sergeant handed me the executioner's mantle, noose and ax. "You are Death himself – my one-eyed giant. Your ugly face will scare order into these bastards into obedience!"

I spit three times at the thought. I am no cowardly hangman. I am a soldier. The Spanish recruiters promised glory. I have witnessed only dishonor, dissolution, cruelty and greed.

There is no honor in strangling a condemned wretch – though they call it mercy from the fire. There is no glory in pillaging, no greatness in most of what passes for life in our garrison. Why could they have not appointed me a halberdier, or even the company barber. A week ago, I allowed a condemned prisoner to escape in secret – saying that he had thrown himself into the river and drowned. For that I could be hanged myself, or worse, if the captain knew. I dare not confess this even to our gentle chaplain, Fra Beppo.

We are barely soldiers anymore. There is a sense of doom among the men.

Because I am able to read and write in several tongues – like yourself, thanks to our learned father – my comrades come to me more frequently every day to help them compose their last testaments and write what they believe will be farewell letters loved ones at home.

Amidst all this despair, I have found a good woman, who, by miracle, loves me as much as I her. She is printer's daughter, educated. She reads me poetry. Some might call her plain, but to me, she is beautiful and I cannot fathom why she has given me her heart.

Her father has cast her out for consorting with me – a Catholic by birth, and worse yet, a soldier in the hated Habsburg garrison. Her name is Anna. She is chaste – free of the pox that afflicts half the regiment. I have told her much about you, sister. She bakes delicious torts. I know you will embrace her when, God willing, we return to Lombardy.

Our chaplain, Father Giuseppe – called Beppo – married us a week ago in a village church outside the city walls. I cannot keep a wife where I am barracked and I am will not leave her to the streets, so I have deserted now myself. We have nowhere to go.

I have fought long and bloody battles – too many to count. I have killed many men and seen my comrades hacked in twain and burned by pitch – suffering agonies of body and soul.

I no longer believe we are defenders of the Catholic faith against heresy and the devil, as the Spanish generals and their bishops tell us. I do not believe we fight for right. Nor do I believe – after all I've seen – that all of the empire's horses and men can ever crush this Dutch rebellion.

Do not repeat these treasonous thoughts, my sister, for your own sake. But do understand that only in truth may I keep what honor remains.

In conclusion, my beloved sister, I pray that this letter is not my final goodbye. I leave you with what hope I can muster at this point, and promise to send further word whenever possible, until that blessed day when I may tread our vineyard road, find our humble family home and embrace you once again. May the Blessed Virgin and all the saints keep you well and safe. – *Your devoted brother, Bruno.*

42. BEHIND THE CURTAIN

"Congratulations. A fine show, Lady Ophelia." Horatio kept a respectful distance, as he would approaching a small bird.

"Thank you sir. But I am Olivia." Her face flushed under her heavy white powder. Dots of perspiration glistened on her temples where golden wisps of her hair ventured out from under the silver helmet of her warrior's costume. Her heart pounded but she gave him no sign of it, only a stage smile, nodded back to him just as she had her applauding audience minutes ago.

They had just performed the last of the new comedies published by Isabella. The troupe had drawn from the local guild of players to fill out the parts, just as they had in other cities only too happy to play host to such *I Comici.*

Horatio leaned toward her, craning his slender neck. She was taller than most. He was taller. They stood out among the milling players and well-wishers. She pulled back, and smiled to a couple edging toward them.

The man grinned flirtatiously at her. The wife scowled, then forced a smile and pulled her man away towards Fortunio and Rosa standing restlessly in the reception line. Here in the elaborate formal neo-Grecian interior of Christophe Plantin's riverside mansion, the players had to observe more the niceties of playing a manor house as opposed to the rough and tumble of street theater – but the money was good.

"Please, may we I speak a moment with you in private?" Horatio's earnest look reminded her of the courtliness of Elsinore, where good manners mattered even when blood didn't.

She recalled that this young man — now more mature — had at least been respectful with her, although she had given him little but perfunctory greetings and cold stares. She had resented the affection Hamlet had given to him after the two had arrived from Wittenberg University. She didn't know what vexed her more after the prince returned, Hamlet's caustic melancholy, or that Horatio was the only person to whom the prince would speak civilly.

Now she saw Horatio, not as a courtier or a student, but as a traveler in Antwerp like herself. That put them on a more equal footing. And both had suffered crushing losses, she reckoned – with no wish to stir up memories on her part. "I cannot divine what you would possibly want of me, Horatio, but I want nothing of you, sir."

Horatio gave her only a slight nod back. Their eyes belied their words, gazing at each other, adrift in shared memories of Elsinore. His pulse quickened with that familiar, forbidden attraction, pulling him into the riddle of her flowers.

They found an open balcony off the great hall. They stood for a long moment in the chill early November night air, stars wheeling above, a near-full moon silvery on the river. They could see the lanterns of boats bobbing along the docks. "That is my ship." Horatio spoke first. He pointed to a set of masts barely visible in a slip upstream. "Day after tomorrow we sail for Genoa. The Sea Beggars guarantee safe passage, under cover of the fishing fleet, flying a Dutch merchant flag until we reach the English channel, then our Danish banner."

"*Bon voyage*, then, sir." Olivia tried to sound sincere.

Suddenly, she wanted to get back to her quarters at Vola's home, where a maid was watching Ari, and hold him, sleepy eyed in her arms.

"I beg that you come aboard with us – for sake of yourself and your son. I guarantee your safety and your child's as well."

"We are both quite content right here in Antwerp. You needn't concern yourself, sir."

"I have concern for us all, Lady Ophelia, given recent news."

"Please, sir. Call me Olivia."

"Lady Olivia, then. I have received the gravest information."

"Sir Horatio, I think your book has already told me all I needed to know from you.. You are quite the storyteller." Olivia tacked away, keeping a cool distance between them on the small balcony.."

"Thank you, Lady *Opheel*..., I mean... Olivia."

"You are quite welcome. Now, I must take my leave before my fellow players miss me." Her voice chilled. She heeled about.

She was miffed. She wanted to question Carlo and Isabella about this new sailing plan and why they had not told her of it.

Olivia had her own plans.

Two days earlier, in male attire as Oliver, she had been driving the widow Volcxken's surrey along a row of guild houses near the wall of the citadel. She was looking for the house of guild players to pick up two actors who were to rehearse with them that day. She had slowed the horse to look at street signs when she saw a man in a black cape round a corner into an alley. Something familiar about his sure gait made her catch her breath. She left the surrey, tied the horse to a post quickly and followed down the alley. She was sure it was Hamlet again, but not in a dream this time, unless she slept now.

She followed the curve of the alley onto another street, where she emerged, blinking in the morning sunlight, and bumped into a friar – not Hamlet, but a face as familiar.

The hair of his friar's tonsure had gone all white, and he had plumped up from the marooned Franciscan monk that she and Hamlet had met so many years ago in Jutland – *Father Beppo*. The little priest seemed even shorter than she remembered him. It took a moment for him to recognize her. Then he blanched and threw open his arms.

"Ophelia, my child," he shouted, causing passers by to look at them. Then he lowered his voice. "What heaven sent you?"

"More like, from what *hell* have I arrived?" She squinted, smiling.

He nodded to her gold chain with its carved onyx raven amulet. "I see that you still wear it – the sign of your marriage that I gave to each of you."

Olivia blushed and fell silent for a moment, wondering if she should tell the monk that she had seen the ghose of Prince Hamlet wearing the same amulet in her dreams.

Fra Beppo broke the silence and informed her that he had to take his leave because the captain of the citadel garrison would arrive soon with his entourage to see the bishop, for reasons unclear. But Fra Bappo gave Olivia the name of a church where they could meet privately the next day – not at the cathedral, but at St. Michael's Abbey, a Dominican canon sanctuary of priests.

++++

The abbey was a city within the city, surrounded by a high wall which contained its gardens and buildings, crowned by a splendid baroque church. Olivia – today Oliver – gained entry dressed as a young man in black – taken for a seminary student.

The church's soaring, vaulted nave was nearly empty when she arrived the next day. A few steps out a side door and along a flagstone path, she spied a rough, wooden tower built against the side of the vestry, with steps leading up to a platform that jutted parallel to the vestry's eaves. Oliver caught sight of father Beppo's gray Franciscan vestments moving its top platform – different from Dominican brown – and pigeons, many pigeons cooing enthusiastically. Oliver climbed a wooden ladder to the monk. "Father Beppo!"

He peeked out over the railing of the platform, and waved, reminding Olivia of that first time she saw him on the deck of that beached galleon in Jutland.

"Saint Francis preaching to the birds." She grinned, put her palms together and bowed when she reached the platform. "If I were an artist I would paint you as such."

"You do me too much honor, my child." He attached a silk band to the leg of a plump, gray-green bird, and placed the feathered creature – its strong wings fluttering – back into its coop.

"Witness the *Wings of Saint Francis*," he declared, "my carrier pigeons. These are from Genoa." He pointed to one side of joined cages, then to the other. "And these other birds will wing their way to Lyon, unerringly, to where I venture a guess, you – my Danish dove – are destined to fly yourself."

"I owe my life to such brave birds, used to communicate with our rescuers all through the siege of Leiden."

"You survived the siege of Leiden? You have become a heroine, my Ophelia."

"I had little choice but to survive."

"My Franciscan pigeons fly for love and faith, not war. The Spanish have their own winged messengers at the citadel, but do not know about my birds. The Dominicans allow me to keep them here."

"Of what use, father?"

"Errands of mercy. I am garrison chaplain. I provide the soldiers a means to send messages home – away from prying official eyes – secure as secrets from the confessional."

"How fine a mission, father."

"I see that you have tales to tell as well, my child."

They climbed down and found a bench under a linden tree in the garden.

They sat in silence for a while, taking in the scent of a field of lavender behind the church. Then began the back and forth of relating respective stories of how they came to cross paths at this juncture.

His tale was straightforward enough – departing from Elsinore after the royal tragedy, fearing Fortinbras, the luck of catching a ship for Antwerp where he made contact and volunteered to be a chaplain to the citadel, not a ship, remembering his experiences with the ill fated galleon.

She told him all about her rescue and flight from Denmark with the players and ... hesitating at first – about the birth of her child in Leiden, fathered by the now fallen prince, and finally, her hopes of reuniting with her Aunt Clara in Lyon.

He was not surprised to find her alive, only at encountering her in Antwerp. He told her that he had ministered her "burial" at Queen Gertrude's request.

"But you are a papist. How would the queen have let you..."

"Oh. You did not know. I converted for a time, to the Lutheran creed – and under Danish, as well as papal law, I retained my priestly consecration, no matter what, unless excommunicated. It served me well until I managed my escape southwards. Only the intervention of your father, by the way, saved me from prison otherwise as a Spanish spy."

Olivia felt a rush of tears at the mention of her father after so long. The power of her sudden grief surprised her. She daubed her eyes with the back of one hand. "Beg your pardon, father."

He was quiet a while longer. Then brightened. "A pilgrimage," he said. "I have papal commission to lead a pilgrimage to Rome." Father Beppo had no papal permission, only forged documents he hoped would get him out of the Antwerp garrison before any uprising. It might prove useful to invite a few more "pilgrims" along.

"We will travel south, skirting Brussels, probably into the Duchy of Luxembourg and Franche Comte through Metz, following the Moselle, and other waterways where we can. I have maps of the Spanish Road and trade routes. As a pilgrimage the Holy Roman authorities will let us pass, as will the Bourbons once we enter those lands under French protection."

He paused for her to take this in. "Continuing south, we will reach Gray from where travel by barge, for a reasonable fee, down *La Rivière Saône* past Dijon –- beautiful country, vinyards, our abbeys, few soldiers – to la belle *Rivière Rhône* and your Lyon within a fortnight. You may stay there, or continue with us southwards down the *Rhône* to the port of Arles, then sail for Italy."

"You make it sound so perfect – like a summer in the country," She mused a while, considering darker images."But Ophelia is officially a dead woman. As you say, you *buried* my remains.... but how?"

"Stones made the coffin heavy with grief in your absence, thank the Lord."

"My brother. Did he believe....?"

"Yes, I'm sorry to say, Laertes was there, and your Hamlet and they fought. But I could do nothing. The queen made me vow to tell no one else, and I feared for my own life as well. "

273

"Poor Laertes. My brother is gone now too – truly, and at the hand of Prince Hamlet, his once noble friend, whom I did love also, in death himself. And my father, my poor, dear, foolish father."

"A prince's noble intentions gone wrong. You, yourself would have likely perished in that slaughter, and been inside that coffin instead of stones we buried, perhaps, had you stayed at Elsinore. Then where would your little prince be?"

"Please, do not call Ari that. He will be no prince, if I can help it."

"The danger? There is no escaping peril in this life."

"... and the sickness.... of regal pride and bloodletting. Better that he become a player, or a musician, artist and artisan or a scholar, a merchant, tradesman, a doctor or a smith. Better yet a master printer. He loves to play with the books that I read to him and delights in the drawings."

"Or a he could become a fisherman..."

"Not of your kind, priest, forgive my bluntness."

Father Beppo smiled... "I am not worthy of being called fisher of men. ... nor can I lead you to a promised land, only southwards for your own purposes."

"That will suffice for me, good father. And I will be able to provide my own horses and a wagon," She referred to one a team and carriage that Isabella and Carlo had promised to leave behind with her when they sailed – given that Horatio's ship would accommodate only one caravan.

Father Beppo brightened at this unexpected bonus. "Will you bring any of the others with you?"

"Only my son. But I am hesitant. I must bid those who have been my friends and protectors a reluctant goodbye before we leave. I might not be able to do this, father. I don't want to disappoint you." Olivia's voice turned tearful. He patted her hand. I will await you at the cathedral at dawn, but we must be on our way after that."

'Oliver' turned to leave.

"One more thing, my lady."

"What is that, father?"

"I have something I must give you."

Olivia looked him over and frowned.

"Not here. I have something I found at Elsinore and have brought all this way with me, not wanting to leave it there, yet not knowing if I would ever see you again."

"It is?"

"You will see. I will have it for you when we meet next."

"I need nothing from Elsinore, father." Olivia bit her lip and stopped herself from asking more.

"You will want this I am sure – if not for yourself, then for Ari, and most importantly for you both when you arrive in Lyon."

Olivia shook her head, turned and walked away, her mind racing, her breath short, jumping at shadows until she reached her quarters at Vola's house.

43. BOOK OF DREAMS

I climb stairs endlessly in a shambled, strange palace that I know, yet cannot identify. I stumble on one of the risers and see that it has crumbled, at this point. A hundred doors at each landing and Ari has run through one of them. I hear him laughing and squealing. Walls are missing and floorboards rotting and I imagine him falling through a hole in the floor before I can find him.

The brass balustrade bends away, and dangles out from the staircase, which narrows at this point, projecting in spirals high over a marble floor I can barely see below, in the dim orange light. I stand, back to the wall, queasy – vertigo calling me to jump to my death. I gag on heavy fumes – the gritty, nauseating smoke of burning buildings, of things – furniture, painted walls, paper, oils, roof timbers, fabric, charred food and carcasses. I hear dogs baying and yelping, donkeys and goats braying, cows moaning and horses' equine terror.

Orange fire licks its way up the draperies towards me on the staircase. The books! I think of Vola's precious library aflame, and all those words flying away in cinders. Every thought, phrase, poem, notion, every artist's curving lines contain universes aflame.

++++

I woke up clammy and shivering, my hair matted and damp on my pillow. I ran to Ari's crib, relieved to seem him angelic in his sleep. I opened the drapes. Out our third floor window, I saw the glow of a fiery ball on the western horizon, in the direction of the garrison citadel.

Then I heard a distant boom, then two, then three in a row, then a barrage coming from the west, strong enough to rattle our windows. I know the sound of Spanish mortars, having heard them daily during the siege of Leiden.

I will be 'Oliver' today. I washed and dressed Ari.

"Go bye bye?" He points out a window. *"Horsie!"* He fetched his stick horse from under a chair and leaped about the bedchamber, then down the back stairs to the kitchen, causing me to hold my breath.

Vola, already up, was baking bread. It calms her. She tried to laugh at Ari's antics, but her face looked heavy with worry.

"This all happened before," Vola told me as I followed Ari into the kitchen. She did not explain right away. Instead, she took her tea and biscuits, and went about her morning routine, looking over newly arrived books while the comforting smell of baking bread halted the pervading odors of fear, fire and gunpowder from outside the house.

"When I was a child. The Anabaptists rose up and took the city, proclaiming the end of idolatry and corruption, and an era of sharing and love, except that bands of them roamed the streets, set fire to houses, hanged supposed idolaters, looted and burned down their houses.

"Then the army arrived and killed them all, in battle and mass executions. Madness reigned – only for a fortnight, but left death and black embers in its wake – man's intolerance worse than any plague. I was but a girl of eight, and survived only by blind fate. My brother and two sisters perished in a fire and my mother went mad."

I know of that kind of madness, I told her. "Why must human beings be so beastly?"

"You slander the beasts." She answered. "This is the heart of man. Women know it more than men and poets know it most deeply."

277

"I have known enough of men. I will never have another," I told her.

"Then it's off to a *nunnery* with you?" She knew enough of my story to tease me with this expression.

"I chose a cloister of my own making, Vola. I am done with kings and assassins."

The cannon fire grew louder and closer. "Time for you to go, Ophelia. Take your child and sail away with your players. I will an apprentice take you to the wharf by horse cart as soon as you can get your things."

++++

Engraving from "Wrath" by Pieter Bruegel the Elder, published by Volcxken Diercx.

44. TO BE, OR BEGONE

Ari liked to play with books – open them, leaf pages for illustrations and stare at them, speaking in his three-year-old's secret language. Olivia imagined these coos and mishmash of syllables to be a tongue spoken in the timeless land were babies live before birth. He loved the engraving and would point at this and that; turn the book round and round to regard an image from all angles.

Vola let Olivia have books of animal drawings and fairy tales for Ari to enjoy. But this morning, as Olivia finished washing and dressing, Ari chose his mother's favorite book of drawings – the one Vola gave her when she first arrived in Antwerp. Olivia rushed over to him to take it away. He yelled and gripped it tight. Afraid of tearing the pages, she let go and tried to coax it away.

She hoped his hands were clean as he fondled the center pages, with its most precious rendering – *The Seven Cardinal Sins*, after Pieter Bruegel the Elder by Pieter van der Heyden overflowing with images of debauchery and deadly vices drawing in unblinking detail, yet humanist compassion.

She stepped back, musing on this image – of boy and art – a picture of innocence and vice, and saw it as a tableaux – or a painting. A sight, she thought, that I would have never seen had Fortunio let me drown back in Denmark.

"Not for baby," Olivia finally said, but Ari gripped the book all the harder as if to show it to her.

"SALIGIA" she whispered to herself, a nervous habit from childhood – the capital letters floated in her head. She had memorized the Latin mnemonic from her mother's secret Catholic catechism: *superbia, avaritia, luxuria, invidia, gula, ira, acedia* – pride, avarice, envy, lust, anger and sloth – those.

She used to whisper the acronym over and over – as a secret epithet at conniving courtiers rather than as a penitent cautionary prayer to herself.

Now the SALIGIA seemed prophetic. She had seen each and every cardinal sin in excess.

And now Antwerp, the city that had seemed a civilized sanctuary since Olivia and the other players had arrived.

This, like all calamities, could have been seen coming, but for complacency. *The crown would let anything terrible happen to this jewel of its northern possessions?* Carlo had reassured Olivia when she brought up Horatio's warning. "This city is Spain's gold mine. Madrid collects more in taxes on Antwerp trade than it does from all the gold and silver it takes from the Americas, I am told." Then Carlo changed his story overnight, agreeing to sail with Horatio.

Olivia confronted him on this right after Horatio reveal the arrangement to her. "Why would you trust Horatio with all of our fates, Carlo. You know he is an emissary of Fortinbras."

"Fortinbras has no quarrel with us, only King Claudius and he is, as you know, long dead."

"But what about Ari?"

"I hardly think one so powerful as Emperor Fortinbras would bother himself with the child of a player in Flanders."

Olivia fumed. "You obliviousness astounds me, sir. You and Isabella promised me in Breda that you would go south by land, and take me as far as Lyon."

"But Horatio offered us free passage straight to Genoa – in ten short days – and in return asks only that Fortunio help crew his vessel. He's even providing victuals."

"Anything to save a ducat, Carlo," Isabella had chimed in.

"I am tired of this cold damp Flanders. I long for our Italian sun, our wine, our oranges and music."

281

Olivia had slumped at Carlo's declaration. "I see the impossibility of agreement, Carlo. I am sad to tell you that I must go my own way henceforth."

"As you wish, my fair Olivia. You have become a fine player. We will miss you." Just like that. He waxed eloquent as if reciting lines of a high romance. But life was not stage. There would be no cues, prompts, curtains or applause where she was going. Olivia would be on her own now.

++++

Her determination evaporated quickly, nonetheless. She regretted her decision. She thought she saw the ghost of Hamlet in her uncharacteristic indecisiveness, and did in fact glimpse a male figure in black disturbing her drapes unseen.

All the following day, she imagined everything that could go wrong traveling overland with Fra Beppo to Lyon.

The burnt odor from morning grew stronger by the minute – not the charcoal of smelters, or the friendly smoke of fireplaces and cooking pits, but the stifling smell of things going terriby wrong. She stepped into Vola's courtyard from the kitchen and saw the smoke – a bilious black mass billowing into blue skies. Curious, she walked around to the front of the house for better view.

She saw about a dozen soldiers gathering up the street. She dodged back into the shadows of Vola's arched doorway. The soldiers were not in rank – more like a mob. They wore the red sashes of the Spanish *tercios* – armed with muskets, pistols, lances and swords. She peeked out, carefully. A pair of the renegade soldiers appeared to be breaking down the doors of one of the guild halls. His comrades shouted a people's windows.

Without warning, a team of dray horses pulling a wagon passed in front of the doorway where Olivia stood and turned into the alley to Vola's delivery bay. Olivia recognized the wagon's colors and comic decorations. She looked up to see the driver – "Fortunio!"

"Isabella told me to bring you the wagon. It's the least we can do. She knew, in the end, that you would decide to go your own way. She wanted to help you."

Olivia followed the wagon, and saw that Fortunio had hitched a swift chestnut horse behind it. She caught up with Fortunio as he climbed off the wagon in Vola's courtyard.

She threw her arms about him. "Oh, Fortunio. I have changed my mind so many times. I want to come with all of you now – to Italy or anywhere."

Fortunio patted her shoulder. "You don't know what danger we might face at sea, Olivia – pirates, Spanish warships, storms. You are best off traveling by land – with that priest. Ari will be safer."

"If we can get out of Antwerp now. There is some terrible disturbance with the soldiers..."

"I know. Mutineers took over the citadel and killed all the officers. They fired cannon and mortars into the heart of the city. Now they've seized the town hall and killed half the council.

"They are looting the treasury and the guilds. They've been lighting fires everywhere. They are robbing and killing citizens and burning down their houses block by block. It is a hell on the west side of the city and all along the wharf."

"What about Isabella, Rosa, Carlo?..."

"They are safely aboard. Horatio has paid a mercenary guard to cordon off the pier where he is docked. But they won't hold out long. He will sail within the hour. I must return to the ship, quickly on the steed that I brought.

"Then, I will get Ari and ride back to the ship with you now..."

Fortunio shook his head. "No, my dear Oliva. It is far too dangerous now for you to get through with the baby."

"What about you, Fortunio?"

"I can take cathedral way and ride – at full gallop – around to the eastern end of the dock where Horatio and Marcellus are hoisting sails as we speak."

Olivia weighed her options. Alone, she would have joined him, but with Ari it was a different story. "Then, please tell Isabella, Rosa and Carlo that I will miss them greatly..."

"And me?"

"Of course, *you* most of all my dear Fortunio, my brave rescuer! I owe you my life."

"There are provisions in the wagon for a fortnight's travel – dried fruit, wine, cured meats, bread, confections – and the last barrel of Pieter's 'salted herring," if you know what I mean. I did not have time to unload it ...You know its contents. Be careful." He arched his eyebrows, referring, as Olivia knew, to the black powder.

"I will, but..."

"No time to waste, you must take Ari and drive the wagon out of the city by the southern gate immediately, before the mutineers spread out from town hall, where they are occupied at the moment. Take Vola with you, but do not tarry!"

Ophelia looked back and forth, as if expecting mutineers to crash into the courtyard at that moment. She hugged Fortunio one last time before he walked to the back to the Comici wagon and mounted the stallion he had brought.

"There is a letter inside. It will give you directions to where to deliver along safe routes. People will help you on your way."

"Farewell..."

"We will write to you care of the printer Jean I de Toures – Isabella's publisher of Lyon, and tell you where when we get to Italy. I imagine we will dock in Genoa first and perform there before proceeding to Venice. Perhaps one day you can join us again there."

"You can come play in Lyon. Isabella told me she has played there in the past..."

Fortunio smiled wistfully. "Someday, perhaps, my water lily."

45. THE ONE-EYED KING

One-eye says the soldiers always hated the townspeople with all their finery, feasting while lowly peasant privates and corporals eat hard bread and chafe in sweaty barracks between sieges in which these same Flanders folk try to kill them.

When it comes to warfare, only what is unsaid makes any real sense. But one-eye doesn't hate us. He is the only soldier among us – a deserter from the deserters, our lone guard. He sits on a emptied cast of wine with a pale, Dutch woman who keeps her eyes cast down under a bonnet that hides most of her fair face and wispy blond hair. Both sit awkwardly, apart from the rest of the group.

I don't know if it is day or night in these damp catacombs beneath the cathedral. I remember the bright blustery day back in June that I climbed the thousand stairs to top of this magnificent church. I emerged from the stairwell into blinding light.

I felt dizzy looking out over the city, river and green countryside. I knew what it was to fly above brick and stone buildings with red and orange tile rooftops, to swoop over the maze streets, and spy upon the people and their horses oblivious and busy as ants, embraced by stone walls, above the squat citadel with its cannons and guards. I was one with gliding gulls, crows and flitting songbirds serene and free.

Would that I could have this kind of life and not my own, I thought, hearing their wild caws – or the merriment of the wedding procession I saw wending towards the church to the beating of drums and blare of horns far below me.

Processions, always processions in Antwerp and every activity, it seems accompanied by musicians, even the shouts of the stock exchange and every proper and improper ceremony.

Now only drums beat with cannon and musket fire and screams of those dragged off by soldiery rabid with pent up lust, avarice and anger. Now we hide beneath the city with its rats.

Up there, I could see the wharf's red brick pavement littered with crates, bales and barrels men and horses hauled to and from moored ships. Green fields beckoned from the tree-lined opposite shore of the river and beyond, a bank of fog rested over the North Sea waiting to swallow mariners, indifferent to the upheaval of now.

No more proper Walloons and Dutchmen setting fine examples of civilization, art, commerce and good governance. Having grown up where prideful kings and bishops ruled in the absolute down to the village square, I had been pleasantly surprised to discover that Guicciardini's description of Antwerp's happy governing medium was true – led by a diversely representative chamber that "balances princely and popular power." But this day has given Guicciardini the lie. The balance is undone and madness darkens the skies with black and yellow smoke of a city on fire over which gulls still soar, strangely silent.

More refugees arrive with news of the continuing chaos. Rampaging soldiers of the "black silk" regiment set all of the houses along the river aflame after they filled their pouches with loot and beheaded residents, man, woman and child. Those hidden inside will roast as the soldiers march on in search of more booty. The church seems safe for now, after the priests offered up gilded, jewel encrusted treasures to a contingent in return for protection that we can only hope will hold.

Father Beppo leads a haggard group of townspeople in listless prayer. Few of them are regular parishioners. There are Protestants with Catholics – Dutch with Walloon – a smattering of the usual Antwerp foreigners – English, French, Portuguese, Spanish, an Augsburg watchmaker and his family.

I notice that Father Beppo carries a large leather shoulder pouch that he keeps tight to himself with one arm. I wonder if it contains that something that he promised me from Elsinore. I want it less now than when he first told me of it. I want nothing of all this bloodshed, past or present, only safe haven for Ari, a home, family, for which now, Lyon seems only a distant hope.

It has been three days since the start of the rebellion. I ladle a cup of water for Ari from the cistern. Our provisions run low. Money is of no use for now. Ari has tired himself out crying and kicking for food.

I am sorry now that I weaned him so young. He lays his head against my chest and falls asleep after sipping the water. I sip some water. It is dusky and does not wash away the metallic taste of unrelenting apprehension that I share with this motley congregation.

So far, I understand, the marauders have respected the sanctity of the church – at least to the extent of not putting it the the torch – though they stripped the vestry of gold platters, silver goblets, marble statuary and silken accouterments.

Ari, Vola and I are fortunate to be here. I failed to get away with Ari in the wagon soon enough after Fortunio rode off for the docks. Soldiers showed up on our street sooner than I had imagined. I only hoped that Fortunio had made it to the waterfront, and that they had sailed safely out of the maelstrom.

A self-appointed leader of the mutineers appeared at Vola's door soon thereafter and demanded a ransom in exchange for our lives. Vola gave him box of gold coins and jewels in exchange for a promise to keep her, Olivia,

Ari and the servants safe, along with her house and printing presses. She promised him that her "wealthy husband" would pay them even more gold when he returned from a business trip to Brussels. She did not tell him that she is a widow.

The mutineer sergeant painted a cross on Vola's door and posted guards in front of the house. But the next day, he and his men were gone. Soldiers from another regiment – these wearing blue sashes, showed up, drunk and surly. They broke into Vola's house and tore it apart in search of loot. They beat, then beheaded the cook and his helper, and raped two of Vola's maids before cutting their throats – all in a day's work for these veterans of sieges and massacres.

I thought we would be next, but Vola had an escape plan. I was still dressed as Oliver, but I doubted that would keep us safe in flight, with little Ari in tow. Like Job in my old Geneva Bible, however, "*I have escaped with the skinne of my tethe*" to this catacomb that may yet prove to be our tomb.

Vola led Ari and I down deep into her wine and root cellar as the soldiers ransacked the house. She rolled back an old wooden cabinet to reveal a door that opened to a passageway.

We could hear soldiers shouting to each other and stomping around the floors above.

"Books, books, books! Nothing but cursed books!"

Most of them could not read. I heard one yell: "Set them on fire! Books burn hot!"

Vola pulled us along. "Make haste!"

"What about my dray horses?" I was thinking about the players' team and wagon. I also remembered the barrel packed with gunpowder.

"Don't worry." Vola reassured me. "Lars and a few of my apprentices unloaded your wagon and took your horses to safe place last night." Lars was her master engraver – a stubby man with a graying, reddish beard, squinting parrot eyes and quick little hands.

"Why? ..."

"We only unloaded things we thought my slow you down," Vola said quickly. "The chests of props and costumes,… and the costumes... that oaken barrel. Lars said it took three men to lift it."

"What is the 'other place' where he took my horses?"

"A stable … very safe. Don't worry, my friends will care well for your horses... I'll explain later."

Luckily I had strapped my linen bag of coins – which I carried for emergencies – under my shirt that morning.

My eyes watered. Invisible stinging fumes infiltrated my nostrils and tasted bitter – like meat fallen off a spit onto hot coals. Vola shut and secured the secret door behind us. I lifted Ari into my arms – kicking because he wanted to walk – and stepped after her into darkness, guided only by the rustle of her skirt and scrape of her soft leather boots, and the heady scent of her lilac water. "When do we reach the River Styx," I whispered.

"You'll hear Cerberus bark three times," Vola growled softly.

"Dark humor goes over well underground. I'll have to remember that."

I'm not sure if Vola guffawed or grunted.

I stumbled on a stone riser. Just then, we heard powerful booms echo through the tunnel from above. It sounded like rolling thunder – violent and very close. It made the ground and tunnel walls shake. I felt dust rain upon us, caking my eyelashes.

Ari cried and I hugged him closer. "It's okay little man, its just a thunder storm."

I feel Vola close by me. "A storm of men."

"I am sorry, my dear lady. If that is what I think it was, I'm afraid your house is now a ruin."

I tell her abut Pieter's barrel of gunpowder. "It must have exploded in the fire."

Vola listened, but kept us moving down the tunnel. When Olivia finished, Vola continued to trudge I silence, then said: "Then I pray that your 'gift' took as many of those damned Spanish bastards straight to hell along with my house!"

"What about your books, your printing house?"

"Books can be replaced, and my main printing house lies some paces down the street, near Plantin, well guarded. We have an arrangement."

Vola waved us onward, touching one side of the tunnel wall to guide herself. "This way," she whispered, and soon they climbed a short flight of stone steps and found ourselves beneath the cathedral.

Vola and her late husband Hieronymus had this underground passageway dug many years earlier. A publisher could not be too careful, given the risks of persecution and uprisings. The passageway connected to a tunnel that ran along their street past the cathedral, which had a side passage of its own.

Few things surprise me anymore. I saw Father Beppo among those gathering in the catacomb, his pilgrimage plans – if they ever were real – obviously postponed. I locked eyes with him momentarily, but neither of us made outward sign of recognition. I heard cooing, incongruously serene, and there atop a tomb – perhaps of a saint – I saw a two small, wire and wooden crates, each holding a pair of Father Beppo's prize messengers.

My eyes must have been sunken and glassy from too much torchlight and not enough food. Vola threaded through the people seated and sprawled around the cavernous vaulted underground sanctuary.

Her face had lost its quiet cheer and regrouped -- pinched and purposeful, her pale aqua eyes glistening either in sorrow or rage, or both. I know she was searching the survivors for her son. Jan had been out all the previous night and had not returned when the uprising commenced. Her other son, Samuel, had gone to Florence, with wife and child in Brussels, and a daughter, Marise likewise was away with her spouse in London, secretly.

Vola caught my eye in the torchlight illumining the cavernous sanctuary. She took my hand, then gazed lovingly for a moment at Ari. Her gaze made me feel faint – like it was some magic blessing.

Vola announced to me in low tones: "Time to leave this tomb." I raised my eyebrows. She didn't wait for my question, just slipped back through the crowd. I followed with Ari. A few of the others, who had noticed our passage, followed us as well.

We exited through an oaken door, descended a short flight of broken stone stairs and threaded through another passageway. Again, blackness swallowed us. I held onto an edge of Vola's cape collar. *She seems to know where she is going.*

Finally we stumbled onto what seemed to be another set of stone stairs. I almost dropped Ari, who by this time was crying again. Poor baby I tried to shush him, terrified of his giving us away.

Vola strode up the stairs, without hesitation, and I followed.

We emerged through a hatch into bright sunlight. Blinking, I made out a garden, surrounded by tall hedges – no, by the walls of a building. At first I think it must be in the cathedral's curia.

Then I recognized the tall windows and red brick step gables, the peaceful, manicured flower beds of lingering fall acacias, dahlia's and roses – how the Dutch love their flowers.

It was Christophe Plantin's printing establishment. I felt reassured by its steadfastness, standing through it all. Everything was eerily quiet. Looking up, past the roof of Plantin's five story building, I spotted an ominous tower of grimy smoke rising to into the clouds some distance away.

I noticed Lars for the first time. We circled the courtyard to a large stable door. Lars rolled back the door of a stall. I nearly jumped for joy when I was my dray horses and the caravan wagon.

Lars gets the rig out with help from One-Eye.

Suddenly, there was Christophe himself. I recalled him from when I had accompanied Isabella proudly delivering him a manuscript. My stomach churned. Did Isabella, Carlo, Fortunio and Rosa sail in time to escape the mutiny? Why did I abandon my little family – who saved my life, taught me so much, sustained and sheltered Ari and I for so long?

I didn't want them to go off with Horatio, but now I prayed that they did so and were far out at sea by now. Palantin greeted Vola warmly. They were long time competitors, but old friends as well.

Christophe turned out to have been one of the fortunate ones who has survived the calamity. The soldiers murdered thousands all over the city, he told us.

His structure – a five story quadrangle with its center garden – proved easy to defend. He was ready for trouble, I learned after he led Vola and I, with Ari, into his second floor office.

He had hired a platoon of irregular Walloon lancers and musketeers to guard print building on all sides – paying them generously in gold ducats.

His building also was set apart from the rows along the riverfront, saving it from the flames. Seeing Plantin's guards, the mutineers moved on to easier pickings.

Vola nodded at his arrangements.

293

"I did not worry when I didn't see you taking shelter in the Our Lady's catacombs. I knew you had no need for your tunnel, and felt confident that you had devised a way to ward off the devil. "Vola laughed joyously for the first time since the trouble had begun, and drank down the flagon of beer that Christophe had offered her, along with one for me, and a small cup for Ari.

"I'm glad to see you alive and kicking, my esteemed lady. Especially kicking!" He gave her a slight bow. Of the two friendly competitors, hers was the greater printing house – though now it would need much repair. "How will you fare?"

"I have printers aplenty hidden away, my friend. You are not the only one who was prepared, only the better."

"I expect these drunken marauders will clear out soon with their booty, before the governor general sends in reinforcements. Those that stay will bargain for their freedom, as the rebellious garrison did at Bruxelles."

Vola looked down, her shoulders slumped. "Our beloved Antwerp will never be the same, I fear." She looked out of Christophe's window at his garden, neat and greens as if there no human tragedy had occurred.

"After this," Vola goes on, "there will not be a man, woman or child – Catholic or Protestant, rich or poor, saint or sinner – in all of Flanders, who will stand with the Habsburg tyrant.

All now will join Prince William's cause, even the doubters and profiteers – the holy men, scholars, thieves, merchants, fishermen, choirmasters, farmers, assassins, highwaymen, nuns, nonces and nobles. Not street or road or billet will be safe for the Spanish, night or day."

46. SANCTUARY

Olivia, Ari, Vola and Lars remained under Plantin's protection another three days, praying that his provisions would hold out. Like Vola, he had sent his 150 printers, engravers, apprentices and helpers home the day before hostilities broke out, urging them to leave Antwerp if they could, and in some cases, giving them help in doing so. But a few dozen of them remained – along with Vola's people – and took shelter at his establishment. Other stragglers showed up as well, after Olivia, including Father Beppo, miraculously still in possession of his two pigeon crates. He had found his way through the tunnel, followed by one-eye and his Dutch maiden, a half dozen men and women including the cathedral's deacon. Each had that hollow-eyed look great suffering that Olivia recognized from having seen victims of Spanish terror who Boisot's Sea Beggars had rescued and brought to Leiden after the liberation.

Anna – one-eye's bride – told Olivia the terrible details. A score of renegade mercenaries had broken into the cathedral's catacombs just after Olivia and Vola had gotten away. The soldiers demanded gold and valuables from everyone. The soldiers were drunk, enraged and disheveled remnants of the force of mutineers who had been sacking the city for three days.

They had apparently stripped away everything of value they could find on the streets and were on one last round of looting before fleeing the city with the rest of their comrades, hoping to get home with their booty. Two tercios of regular army were said to be marching on Antwerp from Brussels to quell the rebellion.

When their quarry hesitated – more from the torpor of their underground confinement than out of reluctance to hand over their meager belongings – the mutineers attacked. Better to slaughter the whole bunch and take what they wanted than to waste time in a standoff. The one-eyed sergeant from Lombardy – Bruno, as Olivia learned was his name – drew his halberd and fought back along with several of the other men. Bruno cut a half dozen of them down. But the soldiers outnumbered them. They drove the terrified refugees back, firing pistols and muskets.

Bruno, his lady and a handful of survivors – including Fra Beppo, clinging to his bird cages – their backs to the wall – escaped through the oaken door into the next chamber and barricaded it. They listened through the door as the soldiers took whatever they could find off those they had killed and finally left. They dared not venture back into the catacomb and the rest of the church. Father Beppo, carrying their remaining torch, discovered the tunnel that eventually lead them to Plantin Press.

Fra Beppo approached Olivia after things settled down and asked to speak to her alone. She noticed that he still carried the leather pouch, but did not inquire about it.

She excused herself from the priest for a moment to leave Ari with Anna, who by this time, had become something of a friend. "I will be at the stables and return within the half hour. Thank you."

Anna smiled and took Ari, and began to play in that way familiar to big sisters used to tending younger siblings. The one-eyed giant even managed a grin. Olivia had gotten over her initial fear of Bruno, seeing the kindness in his eye and the gentleness of his way with Anna.

Olivia and Fra Beppo then walked to the shed that housed her team and wagon.

"Methinks it is time we began our pilgrimage." He gave her his most beatific smile, as if nothing had happened but a slight delay in travel plans. He eyed the wagon.

"I don't know, father. I may stay here to help my friend Vola and ..."

"Pardon me, my lady, but I doubt it would be wise for you to remain in Antwerp when the cardinals agents arrive here along with the regiments from Brussels."

"Brussels?"

"Let me put it bluntly. The cardinal wants you and your little prince gone."

Olivia flashed on the attack in the forest outside of Breda.

The priest could see her blanch. "I am not a favorite of the cardinal myself, but I do have friends elsewhere. You will be safe with me."

"And in return?"

He waved a hand at the horses and over to the wagon. Travel accommodations, my dear. It seems my own transport and horses were appropriated by my former regiment faithful."

Olivia regarded him a long while. He said nothing more to convince her – a good sign.

"The governor general will blame the Protestants for this mutiny. He will report to King Phillip that disloyal elements in Antwerp fomented the uprising to help William and his Beggars."

"From what I understand, father, the mutineers have indeed helped the rebels. They have turned everyone here against the crown."

"The governor general will have to cover his backside. There will be a purge. The Inquisition will do its terrible work, arresting, torturing and burning any and all suspects, guilty or innocent, to satisfy the king."

"I have seen their terrible work."

"You come from Protestant Denmark – that is enough right there to get you arrested on suspicion of heresy and treason."

"And you, father?"

"I follow our Saint Francis … That is all. Be as the birds" He nodded to his pigeon crates. "Finding grace in how God made you, one with this world and the next. The pigeon does not pine to be a lark, or a cat, or a fish."

Olivia swayed, weak-kneed, then recovered herself. "Ari," she said. "For Ari's sake, then. I will take you only as far as Lyon – and only on condition you tell no one of my story."

"My lips are as sealed as if leaving the confessional, my child. The Franciscan abbey at Lyon will be more than adequate, thank you, and you will find having a priest along very useful."

"I am counting on that, father." Olivia was about to leave when Fra Beppo unshouldered his pouch. "It is time that I gave you this." He smiled, head slightly bowed, holding the pouch out to her until she took it.

"Thank you, father."

"This will be our secret," Father Beppo said.

"Like our other secret," Olivia touched her raven pendant.

"Better," he said and took his leave.

The Sack of Antwerp, aka, "The Spanish Fury" in all its horror in this engraving by Hans Colaert.

++++

47. A MOTHER'S GIFTS

The following morning, sun glared between the drawn drapes of the tall glass window the second floor office in Christophe's building where Olivia and Ari had slept. Olivia blinked, blinded in the direct glare, like the finger of God beckoning her to rise.

She and Ari had been given a cot in one of Christophe's counting offices, along with Anna and some of the other women. Olivia thought of Fra Beppo's leather pouch the moment she she sat up and touched her stocking feet to dark wood floor. She had peeked inside of it, but could find no privacy to examine its contents.

Too many people here, but the wagon would have to do. She found a basin of water, washed off and dressed herself and Ari quickly.

She took him and the pouch downstairs with her. A cook had prepared a morning gruel with milk and raisins that she fed to Ari.

Vola joined them shortly from another part of the building, followed by Christophe. It dawned on Olivia, seeing their exchange of warm glances, that there was something more than friendship and business rivalry between the handsome Christophe and the still comely, wise widow.

The wagon had been rolled into the courtyard, but the horses were not yet hitched. Ari jumped up its three wooden steps and entered it with delight.

"Bye bye! Please!"

"Soon." Olivia found some scraps of paper for little Ari and pieces of charcoal with which to draw. He had taken to drawing with a passion lately and shown some talent at it, Ophelia thought, though wary of being a doting mother. In any case, it would keep the child occupied, albeit ending up with charcoal blackened fingers and smudges on his round face.

She flipped open the wagon's shutters. She spread the contents of the pouch out on a table – a white oak baroque affair that the players had used often as a prop. She gazed over everything and caught her breath, then broke into tears. "Oh, mother! Mother dear."

She saw drawings, poems, journal pages in her mother's graceful, familiar script – pages and pages. Olivia ran the flat of her hands over them feeling the images and words, smelling the faint lilac water scent of her mother that the papers still emanated. She pulled a chair up the table, and sat, tears blurring her vision too much to read anything. She swept up an armful of pages and held them close to her breast. Her tears turned to sobs – longing for her mother overwhelmed her along with a deep throated sorrow, not for herself, but for all those she had loved and were now gone.

"Mama sad?" Little Ari put down his charcoal and came close. He hugged her shoulders, leaving black smudges on her collar. She turned and brought him into her arms, crushing the papers and kissing his round cheeks, neck and forehead. He giggled. "That tickle, mama!"

She let him go and drew a breath to contain herself and started going over the pages, one by one. "Bless you, father Beppo. You don't know what a gift this is," she whispered to herself.

Olivia felt a presence behind her.

Ari yelled. "Beeepo! Beeepo!" He ran to the doorway where Fra Beppo stood and pulled on the wooden beads of his rosary belt.

"How long have you been standing there?" Olivia got up, pulled Ari away and redirected the boy to his drawing.

"I only just arrived, my lady. Forgive me if I startled you."

"I was examining what you gave me. Thank you, good father. It means so much to me."

"Please. I only did my duty. When Queen Gertrude – God rest her soul – gave me these papers, she said only that I should deliver them to your mother's sister in Lyon, if I should have the opportunity – or unless I encountered you first. That we doubted would happen"

"... You didn't know..."

"I did believe. Miracles happen. The queen told me of your survival. I said prayers over your empty coffin."

"You are good at keeping secrets, father."

"Practice from the confessional, my child."

"But then there was so much else to mourn...."

"You cannot dream of how glad I am that you kept these mementos." Olivia waved towards the papers on the table. "I had nothing of my dear mother."

"You have your mother's spirit. Queen Gertrude said you had a lot of your mother in you..."

Olivia blushed and looked down. "Then I should leave you with these memories, my child." Father Beppo bowed his head."

"Yes, thank you again, father. I'm sure my aunt Clara will treasure these as much as I when we reach Lyon."

"God willing."

"Yes ... then." Olivia made a little curtsy.

"One more thing."

"Yes?"

"I think you should have this as well." He reached into this wide sleeve and pulled out a rolled parchment tied with gold ribbon.

"Oh." Olivia leaned forward to take it from him. "Something more of my mother's – or perhaps father?"

"A document from long ago, notarized here in Antwerp after I become aware of your presence."

302

Olivia furrowed her brow as she slipped off the ribbon and unrolled the parchment flat on the table. She saw it was some sort of document, inked in cursive Latin, with a formal, crimson wax, Roman church seal at the bottom. She squinted and held it up closer to the light from the window. "I confess I am not practiced in reading sacred or ancient texts, father."

"*Contractum matrimonium inter sanctum...*" She scanned to the bottom and saw her name, "*Ophelia filia domini Polonius Corambis...*" and that of Hamlet – "*Regia Celsitudinis VICULUS princeps Daniae.*" and finally, that of Father Beppo as: "*Giuseppe Visarti Pater, Pater sancte, sacri ordinis Sancti Francisci.*" The date was ten years earlier, obviously from that day in Jutland when she was but twelve years old and Hamlet was twelve.'

Olivia felt tears welling up again, these bitter. She proffered the marriage contract back to the priest. He held his hands up. "I think you will need this, my child, where you are going."

"Take it, please, before I tear it to shreds!"

"No! Think, of your child. When you get to Lyon ..."

"I will be just fine, there. I'll say I was married to one of our players – Fortunio Zanetti, from a fine Venetian family. That has been my story."

"It will never hold, in Lyon. Your people will like know many of the high families of Venice, as they would those of Florence, Milan, Genoa and Burgundy."

Olivia looked down. She let the parchment drop to her side. Father Beppo picked it up gingerly, dusted it off and rolled it back up. He took the ribbon off Olivia's table and retied it round the scroll.

"You will gain respect and status, my child. This document – with my word to back it – proves your son a crown prince, no less, heir to a throne, and you its Regent Queen.

"I have no wish for such trappings – or the knives that come with them."

"As you wish, my child. But think upon it, and do not throw away what may insure your survival – and more, when the time comes."

He grasped her wrist and put the scroll back in her hand gently, curling her fingers around it.

She looked over Ari, who had made large circles and zig zags in charcoal on the paper and all over the floor of the wagon. She nodded and took the scroll, holding with both hands, looking up into Fra Beppo's eyes tearfully.

"God be with you, my fair princess."

"Best that you stay with me, Father, on this journey and let God be where He chooses."

"Sonia." Olivia took a breath.

Fra Beppo tilted his head.

Olivia shook hers and looked past him, far north seeing the waves, glassy green swells of the Jutland shore, the fishing boats drawn up on the sand, the dunes in frothy swirls, the castle – Sonia – of her dreams, the place of peace where she always could find refuge. She tried to picture Lyon, but kept seeing Castle Sonia on the summer beach of her childhood memories.

Ophelia Rising

PART SIX

48. POETIC EXECUTION

Jean Paul Ducat wrote the most lyrical poetry when not gambling, but still drunk. There he was, a dandy in a pheasant-plumed, green velvet cap, dismounting from a chestnut horse most likely appropriated amid the chaos on the streets of Antwerp.

Olivia was not impressed. "Do you wish to be remembered as a wastrel or a bard?" She sat upon the buck board of the wagon, reins in hand ready to urge on her twitching team. Yet she could use another hand. Father Beppo gathered belongings while One Eye hefted baggage and supplies onto the rear of the wagon. Anna scurried after little Ari running about the Plantin rose bushes.

"I'll be lucky to be remembered at all, as with any of us, my dear Olivia."

"Why write then?"

"Because I must."

Olivia nodded. She unfolded a scrap of paper torn from a book and, again, read a fragment of his verses printed on it. "These are exquisite."

"My muse thanks you."

"And you are a fool."

"But will you take me with your merry band."

"Not so merry, but if Vola asks, then I must." She looked down at the torn page again, where a note in Vola's hand appeared below the printed verses.

"You have a horse. Why not go on your own?"

"I have my reasons."

"You must be a fugitive."

"Only a fellow pilgrim."

"And clever. Who would look for a renegade, heretic poet among simple, Franciscan pilgrims."

"I am nothing but a simple rhymer – as simple as you, my lady."

"None of that." Olivia smirked, hoping he didn't notice her blush. She could see how this rogue seduced unwary ladies, with his good teeth and dashing black curls, the wide shoulders – a young bull, this one – and wide-eyed, tawny, clean-shaved, deceivingly boyish face, except for the scar just below one of his high, wide set cheekbones. Flirting came as easy to him as sleep to a cat in the sunshine. And he could rhyme. Pity for such a fine specimen to be strangle on the gibbet.

"You know, sir, that one of us – the one-eyed giant – was a hangman?"

"Another bird in flight, I presume."

"For Vola's sake, you may accompany us, but only as far as Lyon, and only if you be a helping traveler."

The rogue poet bowed. "I thank you!" He made to hitch his horse to the back of the wagon. Returning, he climbed up next of Olivia without being asked.

"You my guardian eagle," he doffed his cap.

"Deuteronomy – Like an eagle that stirs up its nest,

That hovers over its young, you spread your wings so that we fledglings may rest on your pinions."

"There will be little rest for anyone on this journey, including blasphemous French poets." Having a native French speaker could prove useful, Olivia mused.

One-Eye, Anna and Olivia had painted over the wagon's gaudy theatrical decorations with a solemn gray, given them by one of Christophe's servants. Just before dawn the following day, they rumbled across Antwerp's southern moat bridge onto the the road to Brussels, which Olivia planned to skirt. No more Habsburg cities for her.

Privately, Anna noted that her new friend, Olivia, did not flinch at the shambling visage of her giant one-eyed inamorata. "You show no sign of the disdain I have seen from other high-born ladies, miss Olivia."

"I have seen enough to know handsome is as handsome does, my dear Anna … and I am no lady."

The mutiny had run its course, leaving much of Antwerp razed and thousands of its townspeople slaughtered. Breaking ranks, crazed mutineers departed – ahead of the Spanish relief force marching on the city – and made haste for their various homelands with as much booty as they could haul – sometimes in trains of wagons. Survivors rallied best they could. All night, bands of Dutch men and some women survivors, joined by others from nearby towns moved silently through the smoky streets, wearing hoods, dispatching straggling soldiers with hatchets and knives, stripping the bodies of gold and weapons.

The blustery, rainy chill of impending winter followed them southwards as our "pilgrims" made their way. Comradeship of travel and survival quickly overcame the awkwardness of strangers thrown together by fate. They pooled what each had brought for the journey– cinnamon pouches, books, pieces of Indian dyed textiles – to barter for food and shelter and horse feed where they could. The good father also accepted alms from generous farmers and townspeople along the route, as customary for pilgrims – more for appearances than need, but Olivia welcomed it. She had spent hardly a coin or two from her full pouch.

They were a fine sight. Olivia almost laughed out loud seeing her wagon, piled with bags and Father Beppo's pigeon crates tied onto the roof.

They stopped only at those abbeys that Fra Beppo thought trustworthy – meaning none affiliated with bishops connected directly with the Habsburg crown and the Vatican curia.

Muddy roads made for labored, sloppy progress. It took a fortnight rather than five days to make their way south through the duchy of Luxembourg, through the Moselle valley.

For the most part, they following the trade road One Eye remembered from his march to Flanders with tercios of the Spanish army, but avoiding garrisons. After Luxembourg City they followed the Moselle upstream and after several days, passed into the lower Dosages range with its woodsy summits of pine and cedar, little rushes and water falls, ruins of Roman fortresses and rolling vineyards. It would have seemed lovely but for the dangers.

Travelers – mostly traders – had begun to thin out with a cold November ending, but farmers still hauled their harvests of grapes, squashes and rye in massive carts to various trading stops and town shops. It seemed inevitable they would be accosted by robbers on a deserted stretch of roadway through the Dosage forests.

Thank God for One-Eye, murmured Father Beppo in unholy observation after Bruno dispatched four of the highway men single handed while Oliver and the Etienne fought off the other dozen or so, swinging swords and firing pistols to keep them at bay.

The rogue poet, it turned out, could fight as well as he could rhyme. Oliver managed to send a grim smile his way.

The poet's skill at arms almost made up for the annoyance of his constant flirting. With half their number fallen, the robbers retreated into the forests. One-Eye observed that the thieves got more than they bargained for in setting upon these pilgrims. No doubt they have been stripping army deserters of their loot successfully these past weeks.

"Well now profits will be up among the robbers with half dozen fewer of them sharing in their ill gotten gains," Jean Paul observed.

Peace at last! Olivia breathed, as they rolled into Forecourt *sir la Saône,* a sweet village hugging the banks of its welcoming river. There, Fra Beppo knew the local abbot and said he could arrange for them to hire a barge to take them a three-or-four-day's journey downstream, south into Burgundy to where *la Saône* joined *la Rhône* at Lyon. The sun shone like a blessing, glinting off the peaceful river flowing swiftly towards Olivia's promised destination.

I can be Ophelia again! Home, she thought, a sunny one, not Elsinore, not Antwerp or Leiden. She pictured her aunt Clara with wide open arms, kissing her and picking up little Ari and …

At that point she remembered the marriage contract given her by Father Beppo, and all its complications – more necessary than ever she had contemplated, yet presenting an opportunity for herself and her son to plant their feet on welcoming soil at least – a story that was, after all true – her marriage to her aberrant prince – that the old priest could verify and secure her a place again at last. But there would be no going back from its implication – declaring her, after all, a princess by holy matrimony recognized her in Burgundy, and she raised a protestant.

"Be careful," the poet told her, almost reading her mind as she looked out from the river's quay to the spires of the town's simple church. "Rome is even more powerful now then ever in this sleepy Burgoyne countryside."

"How would you know?"

"I read. I listen."

"So do I, sir."

"Then you should have gotten word of the St. Bartholomew's Day massacre."

"So many massacres these days. I know if it, the wholesale of Huguenots, four years ago. They say that the massacre dashed the Dutch hopes of French help in their rebellion."

"Worse that that for us, my lady. It made a ruin of Lyon with all the murder of its thriving French Protestants. If you are Danish..."

"My family there are Catholics... at least they were when my mother grew up. Now, who knows?"

The poet touched her arm and whispered in her ear – a subtly intimate gesture that she did not resist. "Be careful, beautiful lady. Even suspicion can get one killed – especially by the envious who are ever quick to denounce their neighbors, rivals and even presumed friends these days."

Olivia thought of her unfinished play, *Daughter of Kenosha.* She had been penning new lines, following the continued intrusion of a certain prince in her troubled dreams of late.

++++

Olivia, Friar Joseph and Ghost Prince on a road somewhere outside the village of Forecourt sir la Saône

OLIVIA

Why do you men invoke Our Lord when being most cruel?

FRIAR

Blessed are those who hunger and thirst after righteousness.

OLIVIA

Then they are righteous in their cruelty?

FRIAR

Self righteous. They cannot hunger and thirst after that which they falsely believe they possess already. Therefore they are unblessed.

GHOST PRINCE

I know that thirst, good friar.

OLIVIA (to the ghost)

A thirst that kills.

FRIAR (continues his sermonette)

Pride comes not from heaven. Divine evocation makes a poor, porous cloth to cover the evils of man.

313

GHOST PRINCE
My cause was righteous, yet I felled her innocent father and brother …
FRIAR
Rage renders actions ill no matter how just the cause. Pray for grace.
GHOST PRINCE
None forthcoming.
OLIVIA
Princes do as they like.
GHOST PRINCE
But the heart pays dearly. Forgive me, fair woman.
OLIVIA
Get thee to an abbey, my lord, and allow me my rage.
FRIAR (regarding her)
Rage atop rage will curdle mother's milk and make you a Medea.
OLIVIA
If denying him ownership of my child makes me Medea, so be it.
GHOST PRINCE
Ownership exists not in my ghostly realm. I plead only to make things aright.
OLIVIA
In my realm, nothing needs righting, my lord.
FRIAR
The more you spurn your prince the greater will be his efforts to woo you.
OLIVIA
He is no longer "'my prince." And I am no longer a maid for wooing, or plying. …

++++

Olivia went over the lines again in her mind, while the rogue poet's unsubtle supplications melted – indecipherable as butter in the hot sun. This doesn't work, she muttered to herself, and poet frowned. Such writing, made public, could get me hanged for heresy.

"Why don't you change your name, poet, and confound your enemies and pursuers by fading into the crowd?"

"Then I could not publish my poetry, for it would give me away."

"Then sing."

"I am a bard without song."

"Why must you write?"

"Because I must."

"Then I must be true to what I am as well."

"I see what you are, *Olivia or Oliver*, as you choose, but by any name, a rose."

Olivia turned away, not showing him her subtle smile. "I am not for wooing."

++++

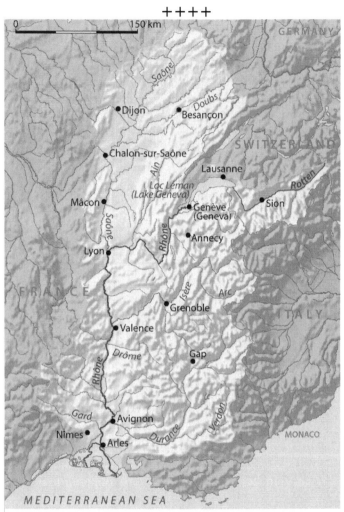

Ophelia's route: The Saône flows into the Rhone at Lyon - major commercial channels to the Mediterranean from Roman times through the renaissance.

49. AT THE LION'S GATE

Wrestling a clumsy wagon and clomping team off a barge onto a cobblestone quay was not the way Ophelia had pictured her grand entrance to Lyon. No fanfares. Nobody among the bustling, noisy workmen loading and unloading boats up the down the quay even looked at her – or rather, *him*, being Oliver today, out of caution, attired unobtrusively – as perhaps a young gentleman, or tradesman's apprentice, oddly, with a small boy in toe. God rest his mother – taken by the cholera – Oliver might tell anyone who inquired, hence their black vestments.

Three days days of drifting serenely down the Saône under mercifully fair skies had given Olivia time to take stock. The river nudged the barge along gently – nothing like being at sea. She felt its current carrying her past vineyards, orchards, farmhouses, granaries, country churches, battlements, green hills like folds of an unmade bed, thick with trees, backed by crags and snow capped peaks in the distance.

What would she find? Who would know her? She had been only a child when she last saw her Aunt Clara. All she had to go by was one of her mother's etchings showing an adolescent Clara posed as a wood nymph. Certainly Clara would not recognize her niece now – and how to explain her sudden return from the dead, with little Ari on her hip?

"She will think me a fraud, a fallen woman with bastard child come to take advantage," Ophelia had told Father Beppo whom she came upon staring up a myriad stars from the stern of the barge moored to a village landing on the second night south from *Fouchécourt sur la Saône*.

He patted her hand. "I have considered that problem, my child." He handed her an envelope from his robes – a little man of surprises. She examined it by the dim light of the barge's lanterns and noticed a red wax seal similar to the one on the marriage certificate he had given her.

"Take this missive to the prioress of abbey of St. Francis when we reach Lyon. It verifies your identity as daughter of the Danish lord chamberlain Polonius and his spouse, Lara de Santille of Lyon. In it, I also give written testament to I know of your history, including my presiding over the sacred union with your Danish prince."

Get thee to a nunnery. Ophelia slept fitfully that night – as she had every night of this journey. The ghost prince showed up again. She refused to call him Lord Hamlet, even in her dreams. Back in Elsinore again, or the ruins of it, she walked the hallways, but could not escape him. She came into a cobwebbed room, empty but for the prince half seated on the arm of a dilapidated throne, brooding. He extended his hand, and she handed him Father Beppo's envelope. He examined it closely on both side then handed it back.

Open it.

"It will break the seal!"

Then seal it back with a candle. Use your raven amulet for a signet. Nobody ever checks.

Ophelia tried to leave the room but Hamlet appeared before her at every turn.

It *pays to open people's mail. Take my word for it.*

The prince waved a hand at Frederick Rosencrantz and Knud Gyldensterne, who stood behind the throne, each with his own severed head under one arm.

That would have been my fate had I not intercepted my uncle's letter to the English king ordering my death.

Guildenstern put his head back on and interjected. *How were we to know what was in King Claudius' letter? You didn't have to forge a new letter to have the English king chop our heads off in your place!"* Rosencrantz did same.

Hamlet's ghost glared at them. *Some friends you two turned out to be. You and Guildenstern didst make love to this employment. You got what you deserved for meddling royal affairs. Neither of you weigh upon my conscience.*

Ophelia felt the old anger rising bitter in her throat. "But what of me? Does not the murder of my father and brother weigh at all upon your princely conscience?"

Hamlet doffed his cap. *Ah! Welcome to the fray. At last you have found your tongue, fair Ophelia.*

"... and my sword." Ophelia – Oliver – drew a pistol, but Hamlet disappeared, as did the decapitated duo.

She rushed toward the door, then noticed a form moving behind heavy black velvet drapes. She drew a sword and stabbed at it. A body tumbled out, impaled and bleeding. "Father!"

Polonius gazed up at his daughter with hurt and puzzlement in his eyes. *The letter. Read the letter,* her father gasped, dying.

Ophelia awakened to the noise of the barge-men's morning duties.

Then it hit Ophelia that Father Beppo and her other companions would no longer be at her side in Lyon. They would be traveling onward from Lyon, down the Rhone to Arles and the Mediterranean, and thence by ship to the nearby Italian coast and Rome's port of Ostia.

Ophelia watched as her companions unloaded their personal belongings from her wagon, leaving her own. The bargeman loaded more cargo, then bid all who wished to continue down river to get back aboard. Father Beppo took the birdcages off the wagon last, very lovingly. He let Ari feed them, to the boy's delight, unaware that would be the last time. The friar, One-Eyed Bruno, Anna and the rogue poet exchanged embraces and tearful goodbyes with Ophelia and little Ari.

She watched the barge slip away, downstream, her new found friends waving as the bargeman maneuvered his craft from bank out toward the curly borderline where the glacier blue water of the Saône sidled with the silt-laden chocolaty Rhône as they became one, southwards.

She felt a void open, deeper and wider than she had ever experienced. She realized that for the first time in her life, she stood truly alone – Ari's only protector, and no one else for her – no mother or father, no Isabella, no Charlotte, no Vola, no one. Her mind raced. She did not even know if Isabella, Carlo, Rosa and Fortunio escaped from Antwerp alive.

Sunlight played on the wide flowing water, calling her back to it, as did that rushing brook at Elsinore, to drown, to sleep.... She held Ari's hand tightly almost as if he were her mooring.

"Bye bye, beepo!" Little Ari waved and repeated his sing-song farewells like a pretend game – hide and seek. Any minute now, the funny little friar would pop up – out of the water or from behind one of the barrels or crates on the dock.

Out in midstream, she saw Father Beppo's diminutive form throw his arms up. A gray pigeon, wings pumping, rose swiftly into the sky and disappeared to the south. The sight gave her goose flesh. She wondered about his reasons.

"Bye bye, pidgy!" little Ari waved at the pigeon and pulled at her hand. She held him tight.

Ophelia/Oliver followed Fra Beppo's directions, driving the team along the quay, past the *Cathédrale Saint-Jean-Baptiste de Lyon* watching from across a bridge on the opposite bank of the river, skirting houses, squares and buildings marching up the hillside that was Lyon, overlooked by the Gothic spires of *Eglise Saint Nizier.* The closer she got to her destination the slower she let the horses walk.

The road took her beyond the city walls, where the buildings gave way to orchards, fields, vineyards, manors and peasant huts. Those few souls Oliver encountered on the road paid her scant attention – which he found reassuring.

Soon he saw what he thought must be the abbey of St. Francis. The horses labored up a grade, then pulled the wagon around a bend leading into a cozy valley. Oliver could see the two, baroque chapel bell towers nested among the groves of trees in all directions. In the orchards, crews of men on ladders appeared to be harvesting leaves into large wicker baskets – assisted by flocks of grim looking, purposeful children who scurried about carrying the baskets to an from freight wagons – one child holding each handle. He saw none of the abbey's friars.

Oliver reined in the horses onto a little side road before anyone could notice, and stopped the wagon under a massive ficus tree on the edge of the orchard.

If Ophelia were to present herself to the prioress with Father Beppo's documents, she would need to change out of her male attire. But Oliver did not do so right away.

Oliver climbed off the wagon and let Ari down under the cool shade. He watered the horses from stream that meandered through the orchard a few paces from the ficus. He gave Ari water from it, and quenched his own thirst. Then he took out some bread, apples and perennial salted herring for them to eat.

"What do de people doing?" Ari pointed in the direction of the working crews whose voices – shouts back and forth – drifted unintelligibly to where they had camped.

"Picking fruit or some such, I don't know, Ari."

"Leeeeaves."

"What?"

"The mans picking leaves." Ari pointed towards where they had seen the crews.

"Yes. Smart boy!" Ari's mother gave him a kiss on the forehead. "Now eat your apple." Oliver took his knife from its scabbard and sliced up the apple – plump, its skin a rose mottled with gold, like the leaves turning. Oliver had picked several of them the day earlier, ashore at a town where the barge had docked for the evening. Its fragrance – like summer lingering into fall – mixed with the flinty pungency of the orchard soil and the faintly metallic scent of the nearby brook cascading over its stone bed mixing with a touch of lavender from a nearby field they had passed before reaching this spot. Ari took a bite of apple section, then dropped it to search for interesting rocks and bugs to look at.

Seated on one of the thick roots of the ficus, Oliver broke the seal and opened Fra Beppo's envelope.

Inside, he found three straw-colored sheets of fine, high-linen paper. Two sheets were covered in elegant. Black-inked Latin script. The third piece of paper looked blank. Oliver took time reading the Latin. Fra Beppo had addressed the first letter to the prioress, Sister Veronica Noele, and the second to the abbot, Father Rene Combray, covering both sides of the page.

To Oliver's relief, all seemed according to plan at first glance. The letters asked the abbot and abbess to help Ophelia reunite with her family, and invoked the name of the order. Father Beppo described Ophelia's history discreetly, mentioned ties to family in Lyon, her child being of her late husband... Prince Hamlet of Denmark.

Oliver stopped and drew a breath, starting to feel ashamed of having been suspicious of Father Beppo. The letter went on to describe to the fate of Prince Hamlet in favorable terms. Fra Beppo wrote that he had presided over Ophelia's "true, Catholic marriage" to the prince, and vouched for the child – "Prince Aricin" being of that issue. This – and the many omissions in that story – made Oliver uncomfortable, although accepting of Father Beppo's reasons nonetheless.

One reference, however, did stick in Oliver's craw. Fra Beppo claimed the Ophelia had been baptized a Roman Catholic as a small child in Lyon Cathedral when her mother Lara had been visiting with her family in Burgundy. Ophelia had no recollection of this, nor had she ever seen any reference to it in her mother's journals. Ophelia – as Olivia or Oliver or herself – had little desire – even if practical at the moment – to have herself and her son affiliated so closely and publicly with the Roman church, which she had seen so often as agent of bloody persecutions.

Oliver shook his head, replaced the two letters in Fra Beppo's envelope and inspected the third, blank piece of paper. He knew well about innocent looking blank sheets from Pieter, crisscrossing Flanders, trading coded messages with agents written in lemon juice or milk, then dried carefully, rendering the writing invisible. But why would Father Beppo want to send secret, coded, invisible messages to anyone at the abbey, unless it were for ill purpose?

323

He held the blank sheet up to the sun – as was the standard way to check – and drew a breath at recognizing the telltale, faintly glowing script that began to appear. The writing looked to be encoded with a cypher that Oliver could not comprehend, but the meaning of its secrecy seemed all to clear. Oliver looked up at the Ari, still playing under the tree.

"We were correct to proceed with caution, my precious child. And now we must become even more vigilant." It did no occur to Oliver that Father Beppo may have had anything but evil intent, despite their many shared experiences, nor that the Franciscan priest may have written the coded message to protect Ophelia in some way – or even that the message may have been about something unrelated to her entirely. She had seen too much to walk wide-eyed down such a shadowed path – not in these times.

++++

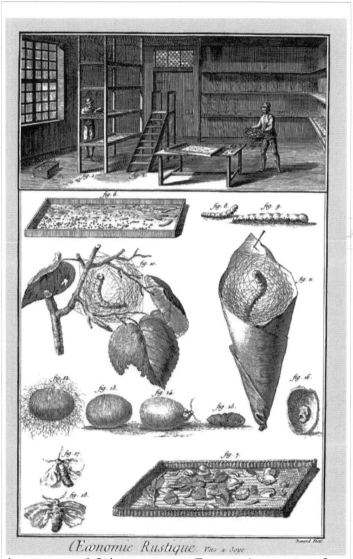

Lyon was 16th-century Europe's center for sericultuure and silk weaving.

50. SILKEN TRACKS

"Look, mama!..." Little Ari interrupted his mother's musing with the wave of a branch he had found. It was bare save for a few last, golden autumn oak leaves.

"Yes. Good boy, Ari."

He danced about, waving the branch in the air, then stopped to gaze closely at some tiny, gauzy white egg-shaped beads embedded in silky threads that looked like spider webs between the veins of its dead leaves.

Oliver recognized the silky beads instantly, from etching in an illustrated book on sericulture in Vola's study. She remembered white translucent cocoons clinging to *mulberry* leaves! Of silkworms, of course! The workmen must have been harvesting silkworms.

The silkworms called to mind shimmering silken dresses worn by Ophelia's mother – her ornately dyed scarves, vests and skirt, the decorative tapestries, spreads and drapes of their private quarters in Elsinore – all of which Lara had shipped from Lyon – woven and embossed in exquisite, detailed floral, fruit and geometric patterns – pomegranates, peonies, oranges, roses, crests and feathers evoking the East from where the ancient art of silk spinning had come and taken hold in Italy and Lyon.

Oliver realized that the three-story yellow block houses she had passed on road that led to the orchard must of have been *magnaneries* where they boiled the precious silken threads from cocoons and began the spinning and weaving.

A shadow flitted from behind the wagon. Oliver rose, knife still drawn. Silent and quick as a cat, he rounded the wagon from the opposite side and stopped short.

A girl, thin, with frazzled black hair, her olive skin buffed with dust – no more than ten – her cotton shift gray with dust, no shoes, rose from a crouch and stared at the tall, golden haired young gentleman with dark, defiant eyes. The girl gripped a stone the size of a pomegranate in one bony hand.

Oliver stopped. "It's okay. I'm not going to hurt you, girl. Put down the stone." Oliver glanced back to check Ari. The girl backed away very slowly.

Suddenly Ari appeared behind the girl, coming from her end of the wagon.

"Ari, stop. Go back to the tree."

The girl half turned. Her shoulders relaxed, eyes widened and a slight grin flitted across her face.

Ari stopped in his tracks and stared up at her, head cocked, chewing on a chunk of dark bread. The girl fixed her gaze on the bread. Before Oliver could stop him, held bread up the girl.

"For you," Ari smiled, bright eyed. "You like bread? I like bread. I feed bread to Beepo's pidgies"

The girl glanced to Oliver, back to the bread, back to Oliver, who nodded approval.

The girl dropped the rock, took the piece from Ari's hand, not roughly, but with some haste, and bit off a chunk of apple.

Cautiously, Oliver coaxed Ari away from the girl to her side.

The girl finished off the bread. Oliver gave her more bread, some water, raisins and some of the salt herring, which the waif took, smelled, tasted, made a face, but likewise wolfed down.

"What is your name?"

The girl continued to eat. By this time Oliver had got her to come around and sit on the step of the wagon. She said nothing, but regarded Oliver with feral cat eyes.

"Where do you live?" Oliver tried to look casual as she gathered up her belongings and put them one-by-one into the wagon.

"Are you lost? Where are your mother and father? Mam-ma. Pap-pa." Oliver made a cradling gesture in case the girl was deaf or did not understand her French.

Oliver fetched Ari, who had resumed playing with the silkworms.

"Francesca," finally, the girl said.

"Oliver...and Ari" Oliver pointed to himself and then at Ari. "We must leave here now. You can go home."

Francesca shook her head vehemently. Then she pointed back and forth to herself and the wagon.

"You need a ride? I am going *that* way." Without thinking, Oliver made a decision on the spot. He pointed back up the road from where he and Ari had come.

The girl nodded and smiled, and Oliver noticed that she was rather pretty under all that grime.

"Well, you have to tell me where you want to go."

Francesca spilled out a torrent of words that Oliver strained to understand. Oliver realized that the girl was speaking the local Occitan vernacular, – *lenga d'òc* – the native tongue that Ophelia's mother spoke on occasion, and that now Ophelia had all but forgotten. It sounded to Oliver like a melange of French and Italianate tongues, with guttural lisp and confounded her as much as had Isabella's and Carlo's Venetian – but only at first.

Oliver put Ari up on the wagon driver seat, climbed up himself and pointed the girl to the back. "There's a seat at the rear. You can ride there and get off wherever you need. I'll be walking the horses very slowly. You'll be very safe." Oliver smiled.

The girl shook her head and pointed up to where Oliver and Ari sat. Oliver shrugged. Without waiting, the girl climbed up and squeezed herself onto the bench with them. Ari laughed, and Oliver flapped the reins to get the horses moving.

"What will I do with you?" Oliver asked, looking straight ahead, meaning herself as much as their new passenger.

Francesca opened up, her young voice modulated by approaching womanhood and childhood hardship. Words. Words. Words, from which Oliver managed a gist. Francesca the orphan, luckily born in wedlock – at least faked – of peasant parents, mother dead in childbirth, father felled in the anti-protestant rampages. Lucky, said the priests, who baptized her and the nuns who taught her rudiments of catechism and reading and put her to work in the tending silkworms and minding the boiling and spinning, twelve hours a day, six days a week, the orphan quarters growing colder as winter approached again until she fled, fearful of the croup, seeking she knew not what.

This could be Ari, thought Ophelia. Without me. An orphan, as I myself am an orphan. Oliver reached over and hugged Francesca's thin shoulders. The girl gave her a big toothed smile, the first since their encounter.

As the wagon trundled along, Oliver again mulled over the contents of Father Beppo's letters – and worried most about secrets those encrypted, invisibly inked words contained.

They came over a low rise leading to a narrow wooden bridge over the creek. Oliver looked up and realized that this was not the way that they had come from the city earlier.

The ruins of a Roman aqueduct skirted a rise parallel to the road, then crossed the stream. Though, she had seen a few by now on her down-river voyage, ruins of the ancient empire still captured her imagination – these grand arches especially. She could see the faint ghosts of Roman legions, the poets, senators, philosophers, slaves that had traveled this road to the once magnificent, imperial city of Lugdunum, predecessor of Lyon.

What grand, ancient dreams lay in ruins here – where battle-scarred legionnaires claimed their reward of land in this western province granted Roman senator Lucius Munatius Plancus, the city's fabulously wealthy founder?

The clatter of horses ahead snapped Oliver out of this musing. He reined in the horses to avoid a carriage coming from the opposite direction, coming to a stop, horse to horse.

The carriage was white, like the horses, with gold trimmed high wheels, open to the sun here in the south of France where winter's chill came late. Two women, well dressed in colorful silk, rode together, looking like twin poppies with red parasols – in the Chinese style – covering their heads. The carriage's liveried driver scowled at Oliver. "You there, back off!"

Oliver tugged the reins and coaxed the team backwards, but the wagon moved only a few paces then its front wheels turned awkwardly, wedging it against one rail of the bridge.

"Fool! Look before you cross a bridge!" The carriage driver flicked his whip at Oliver's horses. A footman came around from the back of the carriage and took Oliver's horses by the bit.

Oliver flicked a whip back at him. "Hey. Hands off my horses." The footman – a broomstick of a man in ill fitting livery – knitted his bushy eyebrows. "Make way for the Marquesa!" He hollered and shook his fist at Oliver.

A fine carriage, but nothing near as fine as the queen's carriages in which Ophelia had ridden often with her father. "Pretentious bumpkins!" Oliver let the words slip out without thinking.

Francesca giggled. Ari stood up on the seat, squealed and pointed a wee finger at the footman and shouted: "Make way for the king!"

One of the women started to laugh, and stood up in her carriage. "What is going on here, Ciccio?" She hectored her driver. Her laugh bubbled, full throated, her voice, a dark wine. She let her parasol down, revealing finely coiffed hair, but the sun's glare made it difficult for Oliver see her face, only that she was a young woman.

Oliver wrestled Ari safely back to a sitting position on the wagon seat. Francesca put an arm around the boy to keep him still as Oliver stood up, doffing feathered cap.

"Beg your pardon, madame. Terribly sorry. A moment's more indulgence, Ma'am and I will have this wagon out of your way."

The woman laughed again. "Oh, my. What refined speech! Silk farmers sending their sons to *le Collège de Sorbonne* these days?"

"Beg pardon, my lady, I am a traveler, new to Lyon."

"Yes. Apparently. And the children? Are they your servants?" She pursed her lips sarcastically.

"Oui, madam," Francesca spoke up. "I am nanny, to my master's son, madam," she declared in her Occitian."

"A likely story," the woman laughed and raised an eyebrow.

Oliver urged the horses forward slightly then back, trying to free the wagon and back off the span.

"Fools!" The woman shouted at her two servants. "Back our own carriage off the bridge and let this young man pass, or we will be here all day."

The carriage driver and footman jumped to the task. Soon the carriage was backed off to a wide spot at the foot of the bridge with enough room for Oliver to drive his team and wagon slowly past.

"Thank you so very much my lady." Oliver doffed a cap again rolling by the carriage. "Again, I apologize, kind lady." At this point Oliver got a good look at this gracious lady, and blanched.

It could not be. Oliver nearly dropped the reins recognizing the woman's face – a striking likeness to the portrait that Ophelia carried with her.

"Aunt Clara," Oliver blurted.

"What?" The woman, who already had resumed her seat, let her parasol fall back again and looked at her companion, an older woman with reddish hair. "Clara? What is that boy saying?"

"Beg pardon, my lady. I'm afraid I confused you with someone..."

"If you mean my mother, the Countess Clara. I am Sylvia, her daughter and only child."

"Baroness of Savoy and Delacroix," the footman added quickly ... and show respect, lad!"

Oliver had halted his wagon, stood up, doffed his cap and bowed again. "I meant no offense, my lady... I simply came looking for..."

"What is your business with my late mother..."

"As a child, I knew her sister, Lara, in Denmark, and daughter, Ophelia. We were playmates... My father was one of the king's generals – alas, perished in battle not long before the royal family's untimely end – after which I felt compelled to leave Elsinore.

"I know of this tragic tale." She looked down and for the first time Oliver saw her beaming face cloud. "Perhaps you can come to our palace and shed more light on what happened there – to my cousin, Ophelia and the others. I read the new book by Horatio, whatever-his-name-is... but it all about the prince for the most part."

"Yes. I have some of your late aunt's effects – drawings, poetry, that I had hoped to give your mother. How was she taken?"

"She was taken a year ago by the smallpox, God rest her soul."

The Baroness Sylvia looked back up to Oliver on the wagon and noticed that this fine featured young man lower lip was trembling and his eyes glistening.

"You knew her."

"In a manner of speaking, my lady," Oliver said, voice breaking. "Begging your pardon, I must be off now..."

"To where, young man?"

Oliver slumped and nodded. "The river I suppose."

"I'll have none of it. Your child looks hungry and your 'nanny' looks starved. You're not so plump yourself, young man."

Oliver shrugged and shook his head. "We will be fine," my lady.

Francesca poked his ribs with her elbow.

Clara called out. "We will have none of that. Turn your wagon around there – at the clearing – and follow us to our *maison* – as our guest. You arrived just in time for winter carnival! You must stay and join our celebrations!"

++++

Republic of Genoa, 1493 woodcut by Nuremberg engravers Michel Wolgemut and Wilhelm Pleydenwurf

51. GENOA RULES

Horatio made quick to present himself to the Prospero Centurione Fattinanti, Doge of the Most Serene Republic of Genoa, protectorate of the Habsburg Empire, duly elected by the city state's ruling families. Horatio asked no directions. He consulted an illustrated map given him by his publisher Christophe before having sailed from Antwerp. Putting on no airs, and accompanied only by his aide Marcellus, he reached the magnificent, white marble, Romanesque *Palazzo Ducale* on foot, several blocks up a hill – like everything in this perched city – from the port where his ship moored and his passengers – including Isabella and Carlo's commedia troupe – were still disembarking.

Without ado, palace guards examined his documents, granted him and Marcellus admission and escorted them up a wide marble staircase, flanked with paintings and gilded trappings.

The doge's secretary, Enzo Palmieri, sat at gilded, white oak desk giving instructions to a visibly quaking assistant. Enzo dismissed the aide when the Danish pair entered. Palmieri received Horatio's papers almost offhandedly, without rising from his chair. He bid the pair to seat themselves on two plush, red velvet winged chairs across the desk from him.

Stiff with mock indignation, Horatio coolly demanded to present his papers to the doge personally.

Palmieri glanced over the documents. "Apologies, Signore *Ambassador.* Doge Prospero is indisposed, but he has conferred upon me, his humble servant, all necessary authority to see to your installation and comfort."

Horatio raised an eyebrow at Marcellus. Both were familiar with this man's reputation. Doges came and went – elected by the council for two years – but Enzo Palmieri remained – behind the scenes – as the most influential personage in Genoa, balancing the old and new generations of rival merchant princes led by Gianandrea Doria.

He was, among other functions, chief secretary and steward to the council as well as the doge – and chief counsel to the Doria family. Genoa's fixer-in-chief, chef-*artiste*, poet of some note, chess master of moving kings, queens, bishops and knights. Quietly, he counseled, and channeled money and arranged treaties, secret deals, military campaigns, festivals and executions – private and public.

His influence spread well beyond the Ligurian borders. He had a network of spies and informants in and outside the duchy. The pope, probably as insurance, had made Palmieri a Count Palantine. Celebrated women of letters, along with wealthy wives and widows in several kingdoms were rumored to have invited him to their beds on many occasions –- for his wit and sway, not his looks. The joke was that he made love to Spanish, French, Italian and Turkish mistresses to maintain Europe's balance of power.

Face-to-face, Horatio could see the advantages of Palmieri's deceptively mild looks. The powerful would trust this butterball face – cherubic lips, the halo-fringed pate of a favorite uncle. The too-clever would dismiss him; fools would ignore him; enemies underestimate him consistently.

Palmieri signed and countersigned several documents swiftly and return two to Horatio.

"These grant you and your aide full diplomatic status. I look forward to a fruitful relationship between our two governments."

"Likewise, my king sends his best wishes for peaceful productive relations to your doge and his republic."

Palmieri cleared his throat. "Not that's out of the way." He sat back in his tall, leather-backed chair. He looked Horatio over and nodded. "So, you are the famous diplomatic- author – a titan of letters and statecraft, not unlike our Machiavelli in Florence."

"Hardly, sir."

"Don't be modest. I read your book. Quite an opus. History writ large in the blood of kings."

"A humble attempt to set the story of my noble prince aright."

"A tragedy of Greek proportions."

"Has Plantin's Italian translation already reached Genoa?"

"Yes, you'll be glad to hear, but I read it already in French. An extraordinary tale well told, your excellency."

"I am flattered, sir."

"... and you piqued my curiosity. I would like to put some questions to you."

"You make that sound ominous." Horatio smiled.

Palmieri laughed. "Don't worry. We never go beyond thumbscrews for authors here in Genoa."

"Very civilized, signor Palmieri."

"Of course, your excellency. There will be ample time for literary discourse. In the meantime, my people will help you and your aide get settled – and your entourage."

"Oh, you mean the *I Comici* players who sailed with me from Antwerp?"

"Ah, the players of '*Mousetrap*' fame who felled the King of Denmark. Of course."

"I would not go so far as to assert that, sir. But you are quite schooled about my humble writings, sir."

Palmieri nodded. "Not officially members of your Danish delegation."

"No, but ..."

"Of course, we offer them our hospitality as well, and will see they are accommodated."

"Thank you, senor Palmieri."

"We hope that your fine Venetian players will perform as well in our grand festivities to come."

"Ah. And those are?"

"The wedding feast in April following Holy Week and spring festival three months hence. Senor ambassador, you have arrived in time for the grandest celebrations in the history of the republic!"

"I cannot speak for the players, Signor Palmieri, but I believe they will be sailing onward to Venice well before the wedding you describe."

Palmieri smiled. "Surely you can persuade them to extend their stay. I would hate to have them detained myself, but the doge has, in fact, a keen interest in hearing more about their travels through the troubled north."

Horatio maintained his composure, though consciously resting a palm on the pommel of his sword. "I'll do what I can, sir. This news is rather sudden."

Palmieri raised an eyebrow. "The Spinola family and the Doge did send special invitations to your King Fortinbras months ago. I am surprised you are unaware of it."

Horatio flushed. "No... but we encountered trouble in Antwerp, then we were at sea..."

Palmieri gave Horatio his official tight-lipped smile again. "It was sent directly to Denmark by ship. Genoa's carrier pigeon network does not extend that far."

"And, if I may ask, did your doge receive a response from King Fortinbras?"

Palmieri nodded. His eyes narrowed – a falcon with prey in sight. "Very graciously. His message conveyed regrets that the king cannot attend in person, but would be sure to send his representative." Palmieri paused. "... I presume that meant yourself, senor ambassador."

Horatio's hesitation told Palmieri that this was all news to Denmark's new ambassador.

"Yes. Absolutely. Thank you, senor Palmieri. Yes! We will be honored to represent our king at the wedding."

"Splendid" Palmieri took a clove-scented envelope from his desk and handed it to Horatio. "You'll find your official invitation to the wedding and all the festivities here."

"Most generous. Thank you." Not wanting to expose his lack of information further, Horatio did not ask for details about the wedding in question. It would be easy to find out all that he needed from the old Danish minister – left from King Claudius reign.

Even more, Horatio wanted to ask about Ophelia, not the wedding, but that might not be wise. Plus there was a good chance that Palmieri knew as little as he about whether Ophelia escaped from Antwerp alive – much less knew of her existence. He knows that this would be the first thing the Isabella and Carlo would ask when he saw them after this meeting.

The house provided for the Danish mission was comfortable – a sandstone and marble affair a few blocks from Genoa's cathedral San Lorenzo. Well situated and appointed, but – to Horatio's liking – not ostentatious.

Horatio made haste to find out about the wedding. What he found out confirmed much of what he knew about Genoa.

No expense was to be spared to celebrate of the wedding of the Marchesa Bernardetta Spinola to her cousin, Giorgio Grimaldi Doria, representing the merger of Genoa's richest and powerful families. These two houses of merchant bankers, military leaders, peers and prelates were first among the fabulously wealthy consortia that ruled the republic – Balbi, Grimaldi, Pallavicini, Tesso and Serra – that sat the Grand Council.

Their power – the power of the purse as well as the sword – extended well beyond their maritime republic. Charles IV and his successor Phillip II had put their Habsburg empire deeply in debt to the banks of these families, financing the building of Spain's armadas and trade fleets and wars, the most costly of which had become Spain's bloody, prolonged attempt to suppress the Dutch revolt and restore Roman Catholic hegemony in Northern Europe.

The Marchesa was a stunning beauty, almond eyes, auburn hair. Titian had been commission to paint her in a luminous, silver-white satin wedding dress with magnificent ruffles and enough jewelry to buy a Spanish galleon.

The citywide celebration would demonstrate the power and opulence of the Genoese maritime duchy to allies and foes alike – Spain, France, Holy Roman imperialists, the Papal States, the surviving Italian city states, England and even the Suleiman's Ottoman Turks. Ambassadors were dispatched – under special truce – from duchies and kingdoms far and wide, including Genoa's long time rival Venice. The pope granted the populace special dispensation from fasting and other dietary restrictions for the celebrations, and the nobility allowed peasants extra days off.

Horatio pondered what to report back to his king diplomatically, given that Fortinbras – or his conniving courtiers – had kept him in the dark while he was in Antwerp. Most of all, he fretted about Ophelia. He had thought about her incessantly during their sea voyage from Antwerp, along the Atlantic, through the strait of Gibraltar and into the Mediterranean. Ophelia – or Olivia, as she called herself now – had *chosen* to stay behind of her own free will.

He had invited her, pleaded, and given her ample opportunity to sail away from Antwerp and its dangers with them. Why should he worry now? Yet he did. Did she remain in Antwerp through the mutiny? Had she traveled somehow to Lyon and her mother's family, or did she cross that river to where Prince Hamlet waited, never to return? What would he say to her, and she to him if he ever saw her again?

++++

The Spanish Road: These were the trade routes that Madrid used to supply its armies in Flanders during the Eighty Years War.

52. THAT STARS ARE FIRE

"So, Senor Palmieri thinks you a Machiavelli" Marcellus spun and made a mock bow.

"He is more Machiavelli than I will ever be." Horatio didn't look up from a satchel of papers he was sorting.

"I think he meant to flatter your skill as a writer and statesman, rather than as a schemer, sir."

"I never aspired to be any of those, Marcellus."

Marcellus helped Horatio sort through boxes of papers and belongings from the ship, still swaying with sea motion as he moved about the marble floor. "Some are born great, some achieve greatness and some have greatness thrust upon them. Sir."

"So I have heard say – a line from a comedy, I believe. But no, Marcellus, my thirst has always been for knowledge not greatness, and my calling was to natural philosophy and mathematics, or so I studied at Wittenberg University."

"... Did our lord Hamlet study natural philosophy as well, when you knew him at Wittenberg, or perhaps statecraft?"

"No. My lord studied statecraft and war as befitting a prince, but in truth, his calling was contemplative – to poetics.

"Is is true that, as a student, you once stole Tycho Brahe's gold nose and put it on a bust of Frederick the Wise at Wittenberg?"

"It was the prince who, let us say, *borrowed* Lord Tycho's nose – copper by the way; Tycho only wore the gold one for formal affairs. And we attached it to a marble bust of the dean, not the King Frederick's."

"You and the prince must have made a pair. How did you get the nose away from the man – known for bad temper?"

"The astronomer feasted and drank himself into a stupor every night – at least when clouds obscured his view of the stars. Our prince knew Tycho and his family well, the astronomer being a lord of noble birth from the richest family in Denmark. Did you know that Tycho's uncle once saved Hamlet's grandfather from drowning?"

"A man of action as well as thought, your Tycho. The nose. I heard say he lost his own dueling..."

"... with a friend, in fact, over a mathematical dispute. The friend proved a better swordsman than our Tycho, the prince told me."

"But not a better friend, I take it."

"Oh, but these two made their peace and became fast friends again."

"Your Tycho sounds more like a pirate than an astronomer."

"Lord Brahe is a star pirate... a fearless raider of the heavens far above the seas."

"What says your lord astronomer about the much-discussed new star that he is supposed to have discovered in 1572, confounding scholars – as you recall, we both saw that star, shining brightly that dark night the ghost of King Hamlet first appeared on the battlements of Elsinore."

"In Cassiopeia. The stars did not align in our prince's favor then..." Horatio thought a while, sorting through more papers.

"May the stars favor this mission of ours, then, sir."

"Our learned astronomer Tycho, though, is no astrologer. He took measure of the Cassiopeia phenomenon – "*Stella Nova*," he entitled it. Plantin gave me a copy right from his presses in Antwerp, which I have read, but cannot say I fully comprehend as yet."

Marcellus continued his sorting. He found a small, carved mahogany chest near the bottom of one of the boxes he was unpacking. The gold clasp on the chest bore the Danish royal emblem. He opened the chest and saw a sheaf of yellowed envelopes bundled with a tooled leather strap. He passed the sheaf to Horatio. "Sir. What shall I do with these?"

Horatio reached over and snatched the wooden chest as well as the envelopes from Marcellus. "Thank you, Marcellus. I will take care of these."

Marcellus had time to notice the name that the top envelope bore, inked in graceful cursive: "Ophelia."

Horatio took the chest to a desk in a room they had arranged as his office. Marcellus followed him into the office with a box of papers, trying for a peek at the letters.

"That will be enough, Marcellus. Let the servants finish with the unpacking."

"Yes, sir Horatio."

Horatio looked levelly at him. "I suppose you are wondering ..."

"I do not speculate, sir."

"I had meant to give those letters to Ophelia if she had reached our ship, for they are, by rights, hers – confiscated by her father, Polonius, I'm afraid, before his untimely end."

Marcellus nodded. "I understand, sir."

"I did not mention these in my book out of respect, of course."

"Of course, sir."

"But I confess to having read them..."

"Curiosity, sir..."

"They may have contained other vital information."

"I'm sure, sir."

"Marcellus, do you 'doubt that the stars are fire.'?"

"I know not the substance of stars, sir. Some say they are the lights of angels."

"Are you, sir, taken with the heretical philosophy of that raving Italian monk, Giordano Bruno, of infinite universes and stars as suns with earths and planets...?"

"Best we speak softly of Bruno here in Genoa, where the Inquisition has many ears."

"They say the mystic monk speaks in England.."

"My prince and I heard him speak at Wittenberg before he was cast out by the Lutheran church – of *conincidentia oppositorum*, the coincidence of contraries essential to all phenomena..."

"And our noble prince Hamlet... writing that stars are fire... What did he say of Bruno?"

"Very little, Marcellus. We had other pursuits then in our university youth. But our brass-nosed Tycho Brahe did also say that 'stars are fire,' but that they are neither fixed in their sphere, nor carried by angels – as tradition has dictated. Lord Brahe's words affected Prince Hamlet strongly – perhaps because Tycho is a Dane and a powerful lord at that.

"We heard him lecture so at Wittenberg. He denied the church and scholarly doctrine of the stars being part of an immutable sphere rotating around the earth, placed there by God. The stars move, in their own ways, like the planets, like the earth, the heavens too. Perhaps he has escaped church censure because he tells of his theories in mathematical equations, in parallaxes, degrees and paradoxes. If new *stelle novae* – new stars – are a reality – then other stars may also come and go, dance together, live and die like men, he said."

Marcellus laughed. ".. and give birth like our mothers?"

Horatio nodded. "Yes. And give birth. As Holy Mother gave birth to Our Lord, Marcellus."

Chastened, Marcellus bowed his head momentarily. "Amen."

"Nothing of this world is eternal, Marcellus, perhaps not even the stars."

"But lovers still pledge their undying love," sir.

Marcellus tried to steer the conversation towards lighter skies, but Horatio's face turned more pensive.

"... as did once our Prince Hamlet, Marcellus." Horatio turned the packet of letters over in his hand. "'Never wonder if I love you,' he wrote in these letters to the fair Ophelia. I tell you this in confidence, my loyal friend."

"Would that our prince were here with us now, my esteemed Horatio to see the wonders of our voyage and this fair maritime city."

Horatio sat himself in a chair behind the desk, looking down at its marble top pensively. "Our prince may not be so far away as you think, Marcellus."

"You mean, like our Ophelia, seeming to be risen?"

"No, Marcellus. I saw our prince felled with my own eyes."

"Whoever she is, this Ophelia does more than doubt Lord Hamlet's love. She denies it."

"She doth protest too much, I believe." Horatio continued to stare at the desk.

Marcellus nodded, and turned away to other business. "Perhaps it is you, Horatio, who protests too much," he mumbled to himself.

++++

Lord Tycho Brahe

53. UNEASY HEADS

"Watch your head!"

"Oh yes. Uneasy lies the head .. and so forth..."

"No, I mean the archway. The passageway narrows from here... not built for lanky Norsemen ...three steps down now, then to the left ..."

They talked in whispers as they treaded softly.

Horatio suppressed a cough. His eyes watered from Marcellus's torch, their only light along the windowless back corridor between the Spinola palace upper level living quarters and its armory, where soldiers slept at this hour. From there, he could cross the luxuriant gardens and, with luck, find the unguarded back gate on this moonless night.

"We're close now." Marcellus hissed. "Shh!"

"What's that?" Horatio nearly ran him down where he stopped suddenly in a crouch.

"Guards. Still up and about ... must have brought in a couple of girls back from the celebrations. Marcellus extinguished the torch with a leather rag and set it down on the stone floor. They sat in darkness blacker than Horatio had ever experienced. He could hear voices faintly, a couple of women – one shrill, the other rounded – and one man, probably a soldier.

Marcellus patted Horatio's arm in the darkness. "Don't worry," he whispered. "Wait. The soldier and his bawds will soon succumb to their wine."

Horatio settled his back against the darkened corridor's cool tiled wall. The silence reminded him of Elsinore, cold and dark since Fortinbras had his own, grander castle built from which to rule his expanding empire.

The new king – the man of action that Hamlet had so praised – had declared a New Kalmar Union – under his "mighty Christian forces marching with Viking ferocity" – cross in one hand and sword in the other.

Although he still called himself king of Denmark, Emperor Fortinbras had incorporated Danish lands into a Norwegian-controlled duchy. Using whatever pretext that suited him, Fortinbras took Iceland back, then moved his mercenary army eastward into southern Sweden, then overran the Baltic States and conquered half of Poland – with its wheat fields – torching its villages and leaving its Catholic townspeople to starve.

Horatio continued to play the dutiful diplomat despite his misgivings. Since his arrival, he had negotiated a trade agreement between Denmark and the Duchy of Genoa – despite ongoing Catholic and Protestant wars. Profit trumped religion for these crafty Genovese merchants, as it had for those in Antwerp. They knew that, regardless of holy alliance, kings – north and south – had to borrow money constantly to maintain their armies and keep one jump ahead of beheading at the hands of their enemies.

Regardless of his continued displays of loyalty, however, Fortinbras – through his latest missives – had put Horatio into more and more dangerous and compromising positions – including espionage. Marcellus, who had traveled more wisely as an agent of the late King Claudius, proved invaluable.

Horatio sensed the ground moving under him. Fortinbras didn't trust him. The king anticipated a Danish revolt and had no doubts about which side Horatio would take when the time came.

I know too much, Horatio told himself, *and cannot undo what I know.*

Were Prince Hamlet still alive, he would have urged his friend Horatio to take precautions and go his own way while he had the chance.

"Horatio is not a pipe for fortune's finger, to sound what stops she please," the prince once said of him.

Marcellus tugged Horatio's sleeve and whispered. "The revelers have quieted. I will crawl forward for a look. Wait and listen. Count a decent interval and if you hear nothing, it means I am in the armory and it is safe to follow, sir."

"Yes. Go." He gave Marcellus's arm a pat.

In his doublet, Horatio carried plans for new, faster, fully rigged galleons being built for Spain – at enormous expense – in the Genoa shipyard owned by the Spinola family. "The Spanish squander all their gold on warships," Genoa's chief councilor had told Horatio, showing him the yards. "Genoa profits."

Emperor Fortinbras would have little use for the galleon diagrams. His navy did not venture often beyond the North Sea and preferred speedier corsairs and galleys. But Horatio had learned through the English envoy Lord Walsingham – Queen Elizabeth's chief agent – that the English would pay generously for such charts – perhaps in the booty they seized from Spanish galleons. Better yet for Fortinbras, delivering the Genoese master shipbuilding plans to Queen Elizabeth could cement new alliance with England.

Horatio heard Marcellus take a breath before moving off in the darkness. "Wish me good fortune, sir."

"That I do, my loyal friend," Horatio said. "And a true Roman, at my side."

As he waited in the pitch blackness. Horatio kept thinking of Ophelia. He wondered again if she had survived the sacking of Antwerp. He thought he had seen her – or her ghost – the day earlier, right here on a street outside the Grimaldi Palace, but that could not be.

"Psst!" Marcellus returned. "All is clear. Where were you? Did you fall asleep? Come, follow me. Make haste. Our coach awaits beyond the garden."

54. SALAMI THEATER

"A travesty!" Horatio accosted Carlo back stage in one of the Doria palace chambers the commedia players used for dressing rooms.

"*Commedia*, my friend, com-me-dia. That is our calling, not history!"

"Butchery!" Horatio had lost that famous composure that had seen him through so much worse than a bad play, but he was beyond caring.

"To think our lord chamberlain once called your troupe the 'best players in the world'!"

"That pompous piddle, Polonius?"

"Show some respect for the dead, you knave!"

"You fabricate a legend about your Prince Hamlet and call it a history. And now you mock us? Don't forget, Isabella and I were there, at Elsinore too when a lot the story happened."

" ...and remember how your *'Mousetrap'* precipitated the final tragedy, just as I wrote it."

"*The Mousetrap* was your agitated Prince Hamlet's idea. I thought it stank, frankly, and it had a ridiculous ending." Carlo relished his moments of mockery. "Who would believe that an assassin could pour poison into a king's ear without waking him from his nap? Ha!" Carlo brushed off his full-body sausage costume and straightened his mustard yellow cap.

The dwarf had been so much more civil during their ten days at sea, *when I could have thrown him overboard*, Horatio thought. "You defile the memory of a noble prince..."

"...More to the point, your trashy narrative."

"That's ripe, coming from a buffoon like you!"

"... You plagiarized one of the oldest stories around. I've played it myself."

"My book speaks truth, every word!"

353

"You filched your plot from the *Saga of King Hrolf Kraki*."

"I designed no 'plot' in telling Lord Hamlet's tale. Mock me, but not my prince."

"My job, sir, is to mock everyone!"

They had argued this on the ship coming to Genoa from Antwerp, but not as vociferously.

Carlo shrugged. "Try to understand, my friend Horatio. We're sick of having to play "the Mousetrap" on demand of prurient peers everywhere we go. We meant you no disrespect with our parody. It is our way of pushing back."

"Nonetheless, Carlo, I demand you play this farce no more, or I will see you and your whole caravan of clowns imprisoned." Horatio rattled a playbill in front of him – embarrassed at having allowed his temper to flare. "*La Tragedia del Prociutto.* 'The tragedy of ham?' Is that supposed to be funny?"

Carlo cupped one ear. "What's that? Ah ha! Me thinks I heard thunderclaps of laughter... How now?"

"You Italians go wild for anything about food – an hour of talking and tumbling salamis, sausages, hams, cheeses and talking pastries, and every fool in the audience cheers 'bravo, barvo!'"

"... They cheered me, and I'm no ham." Horatio recognized Rosa's voice. Horatio turned and nearly bumped into her, doing turns in green tights, beaming from giant, purple-and-yellow pansy mask as she had done in their farce. "You see. I am a flower not food." She bowed, almost hitting his face with a petal.

Carlo stood up on his chair. "Your fair Ophelia – or Olivia as we called her – made this costume."

Horatio took a breath, feeling an unwelcome lump in his throat.

"Pansies are for thoughts," Rosa recited. "Olivia played this part when we did 'Prociutto' in Antwerp.

Horatio stepped in front of the door, blocking them both. "There will be no next show!" He raised the playbill in the air.

"*Au contraire, mon ami!* We have Councilor Secretary Palmieri's official sanction." Isabella came up behind Horatio at the door. Carlo waved a letter from his dressing table drawer.

Horatio backed into the hallway. Carlo and Isabella let him brush by and smiled. She took his arm and spoke levelly to him. "Be hopeful, Horatio. I think you mourn your Ophelia prematurely. Our Olivia is nothing if not resourceful."

Horatio let his shoulders sag. "And her little boy – my prince's likeness, you know?"

"She will have protected him. She is no shrinking violet. I have seen her swift with sword and pistol when called upon."

"Not the Ophelia I knew ..."

"There is much you did not know. I hope she will be able to explain to you someday – and rejoin us."

Horatio saw a figure in black in the shadows down the hallway behind Isabella – unmistakably the shimmering shade of his prince, nodding ghostly approval.

"You seem to have at least one supporter, my lady Isabella."

Isabella smiled. "Thank you sir. Think on it."

Horatio did not explain further.

He bid goodbye to Isabella, but not Carlo, and walked down the hall, then down a flight of marble stairs that descended into foyer, which lead outside onto the cobbled street.

Now the ghost of Hamlet appeared at his side, hectoring him about the boy once more.

Courtiers took little notice of the lanky, copper haired man talking to himself.

Pay those clowns no mind, Horatio.

"In one farcical evening clowns undo all my work."

355

Once told, a story cannot be untold. Take satisfaction in that you have reported me and my cause aright, Horatio.

"Only between the covers of a book can causes be set aright. Here in life, causes more often go astray., my lord."

It is my son who is astray, Horatio. You must find him before he is taken by those with evil intentions.

"Easier said than done, my lord. I thought ghosts could fly and see beyond us on this mortal plane."

Not that I can reckon, Horatio. I have yet to visit the moon, planets or stars, heaven or – thanks to God – hell.

My death so far has been a pedestrian affair. Rather boring, in fact. But after Elsinore, boring suits me.

"Do not prod me toward the impossible, please, my lord. You of all people know where that leads."

As a spirit I cannot show you what is beyond your ken, only what you already know, but do not yet acknowledge. The answer resides in you, my friend.

++++

Martyrdom of San Lorenzo, patron saint of Genoa, detail, by Titian, c. 1560.

55. ROASTING SAN LORENZO

"With respect, Signor Palmieri," Horatio covered his wine cup to keep the servant from refilling it. "I would expect your church fathers to take offense at roasting of a pig for San Lorenzo." Horatio said this deadpan. "Wasn't your city's patron saint himself roasted by the Romans?"

"Joyfully. When he was done on one side, he told his torturers to turn him over. That is why San Lorenzo is also patron saint of cooks."

Enzo Palmieri had seen to it that Horatio had the seat next to his own at a main tables of this betrothal feast in the great hall of the ducal palace. This was not out of good will. Genoa's patron, Habsburg Spain had eyes on Denmark for the time being. King Phillip II wanted to keep the unpredictable Fortinbras out of Spain's fight with the Dutch rebels and their undeclared English allies, despite Denmark's protestantism.

Horatio didn't know whether he was guest or prisoner. Two of Palmieri henchmen stood next to each of the doors to the dining hall. Three days earlier, Palmieri's men had seized Horatio in an alley not far from the palace, and taken him to a dungeon many flights of stone stairs underground locked him in a solitary cell without explanation.

No one spoke to him, not even the guard who shoved flagons of warm beer and a wooden bowl of gray porridge through a slot regularly, and collected his slop bucket. He could hear prisoners shouting, and periodically, the screams, apparently from someone being interrogated somewhere not far from his cell.

On the third day, Palmieri showed up at his cell, in formal silks, and released Horatio as inexplicably as he had been arrested. "You have been invited to dinner, sir."

"What is the meaning of this?" Horatio, rose to as full a height as his chains would allow, his muscles aching. "I demand to see the doge! This is an outrage to the Greater Danish Kingdom!"

Palmieri nodded, waiting for Horatio to finish. "Your diplomatic protection does not cover espionage, I'm afraid, sir."

"I am no spy."

Palmieri coughed politely. "We shall see about that, sir. But you could well avoid the gallows or worse tonight, if you follow me."

He ordered his guards to unchain Horatio, give him a basin of water to clean himself up, and provided him a suit of fresh clothes – his own, apparently taken from the Horatio's bedchamber in the Danish legation.

Palmieri's guards marched him out, again, blindfolded until they arrived at a private entrance to the Doria palace. Inside, when they removed his blindfold, Horatio blinked in the brightly lit dining hall with its mosaic-domed ceiling, illuminated by dozens of ornate candelabras and torches, where other guests were beginning to arrive.

With no explanations yet asked or given, Palmieri had seated Horatio at his own table close to those of the bride's and groom's families. Horatio saw Genoa's leading lights all around them – the bishop and his retinue, a hundred honored guests from the leading houses of Europe. This was not for ordinary citizens or peasants – prominent artists, yes, but craftsmen no.

The annual San Lorenzo pageant rolled up into a lavish, banquet celebrating the royal couple's engagement and doubling the splendor. It was well underway, the decade's most lavish, capping off ten days of city festivities that would go on another week.

"The patron saint of cooks forgives everything but bad cuisine." Palmieri laughed.

Horatio was feeling the wine, a velvety red from Tuscany. "Your cook roasts pigs with the zeal of a Grand Inquisitor,"

"We Genovese are known for cuisine, not auto da fe. This is not Spain. No Grand Inquisitor here – for the moment." Palmieri grinned.

"Then I may breathe easy. No roasting of heretics in your duchy – even Lutheran ones?"

"Especially not Danish emissaries."

"My emperor is at war, once again with the Catholic princes of Poland. That may not please your friends, Signor Palmieri."

"We are under the Holy Roman Emperor's protection, not his yoke."

"You prefer the rack, I hear. Is that how you come to know so much about the Danish boy?"

Palmieri ignored the question. "... your friend Marcellus too."

"Marcellus knows nothing about matters of state, sir. " Horatio kept pace, waiting for his moment. "The Virgin Queen favors the rope and the block... as does our king."

"... and your ancient Greeks, the Brazen Bull."

Horatio sipped his wine, determined not to be unnerved by Palmieri's game of veiled intimidation. "... Yes, a macabre bronze sculpture inside which a condemned wretch was roasted over coals.

Palmieri waved over a servant carrying a tray of steaming *fiandoncelli* – fried pastries stuffed with raisins, bone marrow, cheese, egg yolks and cinnamon. "You know the history, then, commissioned for Phalaris, despot of Sicily's ancient Magna Graecia. How are you with despots there in Denmark. I hear terrible things?"

"I would not count our Fortinbras so cruel."

"What of the rebellion against this accidental king from Norway, and his holy wars of expansion?"

"False rumor, sir."

"Then, may I discount that rumor about wealthy Danish nobles of the *Rigsraad*, 'Council of the Realm' reaching out to Holy Roman Emperor Rudolf of Prague to check the tyrant Fortinbras in return their material help against the Turks?"

"No Dane would want to exchange a Norwegian despot for a Holy Roman one – a mystic crackpot, with all due respect as well."

Palmieri paused. "Oh, if you look deeper, you might judge that emperor and his learned court with more care." He turned to chat with the contessa next to him for a while. Then he turned back to Horatio. "It would seem to me that your rebellious Danish lords would welcome a prince of their own around whom to rally, with money and goodwill from our side."

"I doubt it sir."

"Not even a verified, legitimate heir of your Prince Hamlet to take up the succession?"

Horatio steeled himself against showing surprise at anything Palmieri said, even this.

"There is a story. I know, Signor Palmieri, but only that. I looked well into this rumor in writing my book, and I can testify to it being just that – a mythic, marriage and a mythic child. I was a confidante of Prince Hamlet, and I can tell you there was no such nuptial."

Palmieri smiled to himself. "If you come to my chambers after this dinner, Sir, I would be pleased to show you otherwise. I have reliable testimony of the very priest who performed the ceremony, a Franciscan father."

"... of Prince Hamlet... to Ophelia? A childhood prank, sir." Horatio fought to steer Palmieri away from the truth that he himself was only just learning in full.

"Just come and I will explain."

The chatter in the dining hall rose and fell with successive courses being served. Musicians played continuously from a balcony that skirted the elegant, walnut paneled hall, hung with magnificent tapestries and lit with brilliant silver chandeliers hanging from its arched ceiling.

56. THE BRAZEN BULL

Servants took away their plates and brought more along with platters of partridge, milk veal sausages, fried sweetbreads, German-style capons baked with sweet wine and mace, raisin stuffed rolls.

"Imagine how such a vessel would confine a prisoner while the tyrant's men stoked a fire beneath it and roasted him to a crisp inside. The bull's neck was fitted with tuned pipes that transformed the wretch's screams into bovine braying."

"A cruel despot. Phalarus phallus."

"... but magnanimous. The tyrant gave the Brazen Bull's inventor the honor of being its first roastee..."

"A cautionary tale for men of our station. Be careful what you propose to your king."

"Rather like our singers, wouldn't you say?" Palmieri waved a hand at the singers in the loft – half dozen voices weaving polyphonic harmonies with violas and flutes.

Horatio smiled, keeping politely neutral.

"I see that those famous Lutheran professors at your Wittenberg University taught you well, sir."

"They specialized in the sins of others, sir. Our own, not so much...But I did not study theology, I made astronomy and natural philosophy my field of learning."

"Then you will be able, perhaps, to tell me if the stars are right for our endeavor."

"Not really, sir. I did not favor astrology myself. I studied the planets and stars for themselves, asking their secrets not trying to divine ours from them."

"Ah, well, then, Horatio, we must forge our own fate..."

More food, more music, more toasts from the main table now – to the newly betrothed their families, Genoa, the alliance with Spain, Holy Roman Emperor Rudolf II, the Papa Clemens Octavus and with effluent rhetoric, Genoa's own San Lorenzo in whose name may the newlyweds and their issue be blessed.

The courses progressed from soups to game to fish – sweet pastry tarts stuffed with spleens of bass, mullet and pike simmered in orange juice, raisins and cinnamon. Trout tails sautéed in lemon. Lobster tails in cream sauces, eels baked in marzipan – every platter arranged artistically, with swirls of nuts and garnish.

Every plate, platter, dish, silver goblet and cup had been designed – along with table settings and the multicolored attire of the servers – under the supervision of Palmieri himself.

Coolly, he kept watch on everything as he talked with Horatio and, to his right, occasionally with the Countess Eleana Risetti, scholar of mathematics, Horatio learned, and the wife of Sandro Risetti, one of the wealthiest bankers of Florence – second only to the Medici. He had stayed home with gout, and sent along their plump shy son as escort whom Palmieri sat at a faraway table to him leeway with the lovely Eleana. The countess kept darting her green eyes at Horatio invitingly as she conversed with Palmieri.

Dancers appeared in outlandish, brilliant feathered costumes, the women like snowy egrets, the men in black, like crows. They swirled, dipped, circled to the music, and some took flight by means of wires attached to the rafters.

A few guests oo-ed and ah-ed, but most kept talking and eating, giving scant attention to the spectacle. He started to regret assailing Carlo that way, and almost hoped that the commedia players, would appear at this banquet to lighten his mood.

Enzo Palmieri brought up the issue again. "Think about what I say, Horatio. There are some among us who would prefer that your little Danish prince be eliminated along with all attendant complications. Your own King Fortinbras, the first among them."

"I've had no indication that he is even aware of any child pretender to his throne."

"So, you admit that the little prince indeed, does exist?"

"I said, 'if,' signor."

"Horatio, I know one thing. You must help us bring your little Danish prince under our protection. If not, he – and his mother – face mortal danger from all sides."

"You overestimate my powers, signor Palmieri."

"Do not dance around, Horatio. Dancing is for the betrothed at this feast..."

"If – again, if – I were to locate this boy, how could I trust you to keep him safe?"

"Oh. Sir. We would never harm a child – and a prince of Denmark. It would set a bad precedent. And what would then be our card to play in this game? You hold the key, Horatio."

Horatio half-turned to face Palmieri. "Neither of us wants an international incident on so happy an occasion, signore. You cannot ask me to go against my crown. That would be treason. I must insist in the name of King Fortinbras."

Palmieri raised his hands. "No need for posturing, Horatio. I do not doubt your honor." Palmieri then continued in a low voice. "In reality, I know that there is no love lost between you and your king these weary days, Signor Horatio. Therefore let us refrain from threats."

"No threat is meant, sir. Simply a matter of state."

"A matter of bargaining, I would put it more precisely."

"What is it that you want?"

365

"Niccolo Machiavelli – your hero..." Palmieri smirked. "... told his Florentine prince that the enterprising are simply those who understand that there is little difference between obstacle and opportunity and are able to turn both to their advantage."

"I seek no advantage, sir, simply justice."

"Well spoken, Signor Horatio. Now, let's get onto the truth. You want to usurp this despot, Fortinbras. You and the Danish gentry welcomed him once, but feel his oppression now."

"Don't presume, Signor Palmieri."

"I never presume. I know. I see common interest."

"Your Catholic friends would be wrong to presume that Danes can be brought back into the Roman fold so easily."

Palmieri smiled. "This is about military power, trade and money. Religion has little to do with it, my Horatio. With Denmark, the Spanish and Austrian Habsburg emperors gain control over the strategic passages between the Baltic and North Seas."

"I doubt that my fellow Danes would take to being like Genoa – a pawn of Spain."

Palmieri squinted and finished chewing a mouthful of batter-fried eel. "A marriage of convenience only. They fight all the wars while we grow richer by the day."

"What does Denmark stand to gain?"

"Freedom from Fortinbras' yoke."

"Trade one tyranny for another?"

"Look at us. Genoa does as it likes. It would be the same for Denmark."

"Tell William of Orange and the Netherlanders that – almost eighty years fighting bloody Spanish rule."

"...Needless... If Phillip had listened to his governor, the Duchess of Parma..."

"My point, exactly sir. The Spanish have gold, arms, men and the Inquisition, so why should they act reasonably?"

"Because the Dutch 'Geuzen' have ground down the Habsburg's to the point of bankruptcy. Already Phillip toys with default. Our bankers are not happy."

"You invite me to a dangerous game, Palmieri."

"No game. I only pass on word from others with greater power than myself, not of this little duchy."

"Who are...?"

"...Friends who may well serve your own purposes, Horatio."

"You mistake me. Even if this boy prince does exist and I could find the fair Ophelia, I would have little say in these matters."

"You have power of influence, sir. You can tell your Danes that they will have arms and money to free themselves again, overthrow this tyrant for a new king."

"Your Phillip of Spain and Flanders, I suppose?"

"No! A true Dane. The rightful heir to your throne. He is the son denied his kingdom, the issue of your Crown Prince Hamlet."

".... if at all, sir, not a legitimate heir."

"Necessity begets legitimacy."

"How so?"

"What if I told you that we have the contract of your royal prince's marriage to this boy's mother, signed by a priest, that long preceded the birth of Ophelia's child?"

"A Roman Catholic priest?"

"Unlike the English, the Church of Denmark never formally broke off relations with the Roman Church and never received any anathematization by the Holy See. The Danes never have been at war with the Catholic powers to the south."

"And I am to trust that a neutral Denmark and not a conquered one would serve their purposes?"

"... under proper supervision."

"And that supervision would be myself?"

"If you cooperate, otherwise ..."

Horatio looked away, "Do not presume upon my honor, sir!"

"Brutus was an honorable man. See where that got him. You have the weaker hand in this game."

"Not a game, sir."

"Uneasy lies the head that counsels the head that wears the crown."

"What is your meaning, sir?"

"You cannot deny that your Fortinbras faces a rebellion, on which you must soon choose sides."

"Rebellions are common as fleas in the northland."

"...that even you, Horatio, the tyrant's chief chancellor, privately encourage."

More drummers joined the lutes and pipes and violas, and played a gigue now, signaling time for the dance. The groom-to-be led his future bride to a wide circular floor of highly polished, exquisitely inlaid hardwoods that adjoined the dining area.

The first dance, following tradition, was a lavolta, an animated dance for couples. The honored fiancees looked appropriately joyful in their elegant finery – though he stood comically shorter than she, but maintaining a haughty impression as they performed the Volta's ornate, mannered steps and jumps, arm-in-arm, letting her dress spin high, to the male onlookers' delight. The orchestra shifted respectfully to a pavane as the newlyweds' respective parents, followed those at the first and second tables took to the floor, then a branles circle dance.

This would go long into the night. Palmieri, signaled by an aide, stood and excused himself to the guests on both sides of his chair. Horatio rose and Palmieri took his hand firmly, gazing straight into his eyes. "You will be wise, Horatio, to take this offer."

"Or else?"

"There is always the alternative."

"Why am I not surprised?"

"You know very well that there are others – agents of the English, or Cardinal Spinola, or your own Fortinbras – who would pay handsomely for the boy and his mother to disappear." Palmieri arched an eyebrow, his bare head illuminated by the torches. "King Phillip's more moderate advisors prefer the first alternative of sponsoring the boy's succession against Fortinbras."

Horatio muttered to himself. "Seems I have no alternative." He bent to Palmieri's ear. "I will comply to your terms. You have my word. Assuming, of course, that I can find the boy – and his mother. Our arrangement must include safe passage for her too."

"Excellent, Sir Horatio. I will see to all of that."

Horatio thought otherwise, but best to play along. He had no idea where to find Ophelia or her son at that moment. "You have convinced me, Signor Palmieri. When do we commence?"

Palmieri whispered to him. "For now, you remain our guest, but with better accommodations, I assure you. I will arrange the rest."

"The boy's father was my truest, most beloved friend and a noble prince. My loyalty is to his memory, nothing else."

Palmieri nodded and gave Horatio's hand a firmer squeeze before letting go and turning away.

Two of Palmieri's guards stepped up. One took Horatio's arm. "Come with us, sir."

Horatio pulled his arm away and followed them. To his relief they led him down up a marble staircase to the great entryway of the palazzo and saluted him as he walked back out into the street, a free man again.

Back in his ambassadorial quarters, Horatio lay awake on his bed the rest of the night and rose exhausted at first light.

57. A PLAN UNDONE

"I wish I had news." Father Beppo whispered to Horatio. They walked, heads bowed, two hooded Franciscan priests – one genuine, the other hastily disguised – up a narrow street curving from the docks towards the *piazza del duomo* San Lorenzo.

"But you did say she reached Lyon safely." Horatio took a breath and nodded to himself.

"But she did not arrive the the abbey where they would have taken care of her."

"Perhaps she went straight to her aunt..."

"The aunt died some time ago. No reports of her approaching the De Santille manor, at least not from my contacts."

"How do you know all this."

"The wings of St. Francis."

"Pigeons?"

"Yes."

"Does it matter?"

Horatio stopped and faced Beppo. "You should have stayed with her until she got to the abbey in Lyon, instead of leaving her at the dock."

"I am known too well in Lyon. In any case, I arranged everything. I gave her an encoded message to the prioress as well as the abbot – both allies – with all the details. They would have kept her and the boy safe – made sure she was guarded, discreetly."

Horatio shook his head. "Don't misunderstand me. I'm grateful to you for helping her escape the hell of Antwerp, in any event ..."

"Fret not, sir Horatio. One way or another, I'll get word, and she will turn up safely."

Horatio bent to glare directly into the placid eyes of the diminutive priest. "Take heed, good reverend. I am not the only one searching for Ophelia and the child. But I venture that I am the only one who can and will keep them from mortal danger."

"Come back to complain more?" Carlo laid the folio he was reading down on the table where he sat feet dangling over a precarious stool.

Horatio cocked his head to peek at the folio's title. "Another Hamlet story?"

"A new play-in-progress by an English bard."

"Anyone of note?"

"No, just another traveling thespian who asked me to read his work. They all seem to have plays in their purses. I only agreed to look at it because of your book."

"Well, if you please, set it aside. I have something to tell you. I need your help."

58. TANGLED SILKS

Ari giggled as he watched Sylvia twirl her scarlet parasol in the carriage that Oliver followed with the wagon. Oliver guessed it was on purpose. The baroness stopped, then sped up the spinning whenever Ari's giggles waned, evoking a new burst of laughter and squeals. Then she tossed her hair and winked at Ari.

Oliver began to regret the disguise, yearning to reveal herself as Ophelia to this delightful cousin, but holding back, nevertheless, out of uncertainty.

After a pleasant ride through the rolling countryside, Sylvia's carriage led them through the gates of the baroness' estate, dominated by a palace in the Italian style on a hillside overlooking the Saône, amid orchards and vineyards.

Inside, Oliver, Francesca and the baby were greeted by the servants and shown to quarters for freshening up – large bed chamber for Oliver, and a smaller, adjoining chamber for Francesca and Ari. All of this left Oliver puzzled.

It came clearer when Sylvia introduced Oliver to her husband, the aged baron later that evening in a sumptuous sitting room. "This is Oliver ..." She paused.

"Oliver ... Corambus..." Oliver bowed.

Sylvia's eyes widened. "You are some relation to my aunt?"

"My father was cousin to Polonius – the lamented Lord High Chamberlain of Denmark" Oliver added hastily.

Sylvia beamed. "Then you are a cousin to our lamented Ophelia as well!"

"Distant..." Oliver blushed.

"And to me as well," Sylvia beamed again.

"Not by blood," Oliver smiled back. "But family ties, nonetheless."

More questions followed. Oliver managed to piece together what he hoped would be a credible history for the years since leaving Elsinore – performing with the Comici players, writing verses, a few published.

Sylvia seized upon the book hungrily and asked Oliver to recite some of the poems.

"Later perhaps," Oliver reddened.

"You should submit your work to l'Atelier du Griffon, our famous Lyonnaise publishing house. We are well acquainted with the Sébastien Gryphe family – printers of world famous authors – Rabelais and Erasmus, and many biblical and ancient Greek translations.

"Thank, you, cousin Sylvia...yes. Perhaps.

Sylvia blushed. "I'm being such a pest. You need time to rest and get comfortable after your long travels. I will take my leave for now."

Oliver rejoined Francesca and Ari and each settled in for a much needed rest. Awake and refreshed in the late afternoon, Oliver surveyed the situation. He now looked the part that Sylvia had given him – having washed off the dust of travel and changed into a fine young prince's attire from the wagon's costume trunk – black silk shirt and pants, leather doublet, frilled linen collar. *So-ooo dashing,* Ophelia whispered to the reflection of Oliver in the bedchamber's full length gold veined mirror. *You can take the player out of the play, but not the play out of the player.*

"Splendid!" The baron, a wizened dried apricot of a man festooned in the latest silks tapped his ebony walking stick on the marble floor and seated himself on a red velvet cushioned, ash wood chair whose high back had been carved with the Lyonnaise crest. "Young, Oliver, I am pleased that my dear wife has discovered you."

"Likewise, I'm sure." Oliver smiled and caught cousin Sylvia's flirtatious eye, not unpleasantly. *I am as tangled in the webbing of my lies as the silkworm in his leafy cocoon.*

"You have arrived in time for our Advent festivities – and after Advent and the new year, should you continue to grace us here, you will have the pleasure of meeting the personage who will be our most distinguished guest here as well – Cardinal Spinola – a nuncio of the pope." The baron paused. "...not that you are not very special to us yourself, being kin."

Oliver blanched. Inappropriate words filled his mouth like foul tasting food one could neither swallow nor spit out at a banquet. *The pope who gave blasphemous thanks for the St. Bartholomew's massacre and his current favorite, bloody red cardinal.* Oliver gritted his teeth, a worm entombed in his own silk threads.

Sylvia rescued all from the awkward silence. "You'll enjoy our festival, Oliver. Perhaps you could lend your fine wagon as a float in tomorrow's procession."

The baron snorted at Sylvia. "My dear. You know that sort of thing is for the tradespeople. Not us. Antics of the Abbeys of Misrule. Tiresome."

"Oh, but it's all in great fun."

"Only to give license to common trash to mock their betters. Your guest should stay clear of carnivals."

Sylvia pouted. "Our cousin Oliver is a fine player and poet."

Oliver shook his head. "You flatter me, my lady." Oliver said.

Sylvia brightened, then turned to Oliver. "Come with me and I'll have the majordomo show you around our home and estate. We have many works you will enjoy seeing..."

"Yes, thank you." Oliver bowed to the baron. "And thank you, my lord, for this hospitality on behalf of my son and I. We look forward to those events you have described." *Like a hanging*, thought Oliver.

59. COSTUMES AND CAMELS

For the next week, each morning, after the first meal, Oliver walked the rose garden with Ari and Francesca. Oliver kept Ari and the orphan girl close, and liked what he observed, gradually feeling more confidence in the arrangement.

Francesca – scrubbed, fed and in finer clothes – seemed transformed from the waif that had appeared at Oliver's wagon. The girl seemed capable and fit naturally into her role of nanny – gentle but vigilant with Ari, all "Yes, my lord," with Oliver to the point of mutual smirks when no one was looking. Francesca knew Oliver's secret, and was quick to convey her trustworthiness with it – evoking, in fact, the orphan girl's rapt admiration. She proved a bright girl.

Oliver liked how she relished reading storybooks to Ari. Closing a book one evening after Ari fell asleep under Oliver's watchful eye, Francesca looked into the eyes of her new patron, then back to the book. "I can imagine what stories you could tell one day, my lord, beyond the tales in these books."

"Dangerous things, these books." Oliver looked at Francesca and tapped a volume. "... voyages to worlds you cannot imagine, and where there are those who will forbid you to go, my child."

++++

Christmas passed, full of cheer and many cakes, as did the entrance of a new year without Oliver revealing his true identity. Much as the urge to do so grew strong, the freedom and pleasantness is young-squire's life at the baron's estate counter-balanced it.

"Let me join you in the carnival, cousin." Sylvia found Oliver one morning in the players' wagon trying on masks from the costume trunk. Francesca was playing with Ari in a garden next to the stables where the wagon had been stowed.

"I don't know if I want to take part myself, cousin."

"Oh, but you must."

"Your baron may not like it."

"Oh, he's all smoke and no fire." Sylvia put a hand on Oliver's arm and looked pleadingly into his eyes. "I will be very discreet."

"It is pretty much an all male pageant, except for the wives beating husbands, riding donkeys."

Oliver laughed. "Well deserved, I venture."

"I can dress a as a boy – and wear a mask." She pulled pants, blouses and vests from trunk and each sized each up to her body as she talked briskly. "I love these outfits.."

Silvia rummaged more and came up with blue silk knee-length pantaloons, an ornate jacket and fierce turban, which she popped onto her head. "Ah! Don't I make a splendid Turkish grenadier?"

Oliver fidgeted, glancing this way and that. "Oh, absolutely, cousin... but..."

"Of course!" She fished an extravagant black winged mustache and sinister pointed beard from a small drawer in the trunk and put the set to her face, making growling noises. "Where is my scimitar?" She took up a broomstick and waved it at Oliver, holding the beard to her face with her other hand. "All we need is some glue, cousin."

Oliver put his hands up. "I surrender, cousin. I am convinced, now please stop before someone comes in."

"I envy you getting to be someone different each night on stage. How dull to be stuck in one role."

"Even the role of a baroness with all at your beck and call? I think many would envy you, cousin."

"What is it like, being someone else?"

"Players think nothing of it, their stock and trade – with pride sometimes, with trepidation too – of being pelted with rotten eggs and fruit or worse."

"I dream of it – of being truly my secret self in costume, rather than in what is my lot in life, high or low." Sylvia stroked her fake beard as if pondering, and then laughed.

"It is said that only in telling stories can we step into the shoes of others as ourselves – or so I have read." Oliver chose his words carefully.

"In any case, carnival is pure enjoyment full of life. Wait until you take part – as we must, not as mere spectators, cousin!"

"Oh, it's all right. I don't have need. I have enjoyed my share of festivals, cousin Sylvia."

"Ah, but not in Lyon. People come from far and wide in grotesque masks and get ups – sea monsters, dragons, giants, trolls, lizards, foxes, rabbits, knights and knaves. They say ours is the most extravagant in creation – floats, dancers, drummers, masks of every description, mock courts."

"I remember something like this from my childhood in Copenhagen..." Oliver did not want to mention Leiden, Breda or Antwerp.

"Oh, this one is grand. Each of the guilds marches as its own abbey of misrule and performs elaborate ceremonies, with mock princes, abbots, abbesses, captains, admirals, counts, princesses, judges, patriarchs, men dressed as women and sometimes vice versa – presided over by the Queen of Misrule. Our Lyonnaise players guild forms its own Theater of Errors, cast by misfits, and a mock regency. I have taken the liberty of getting you invited."

"I've play many a 'theater of errors' – but not intentionally." Oliver laughed, trying to back slowly away from where Sylvia seemed to be going.

Sylvia patted Oliver's arm. "It's all arranged, then cousin..."

Oliver nodded, unsure.

Sylvia dropped the broomstick, mustache and beard, and embraced Oliver, who patted her shoulders awkwardly, feeling affection nonetheless. "Oh, Oliver! You have brought light into my life, my noble cousin, for which I hold you dear to my heart."

Ari climbed into the wagon at that moment, followed by Francesca, who held back when Ari ran to them arms out. "Mama!" He shouted. "I saw camel! He had a hump."

"Must have wandered out from the Baron's menagerie," said Sylvia, picking up Ari. "I am your cousin... my dear Ari .. Would that I were mother to such a fine boy," she added, looking over to Oliver and winking.

Oliver flushed. *Does Sylvia suspect?* Oliver stepped to Sylvia and took up the child. "I have had to be mother as well as father these past months. Such a lovely thing for Ari to be with you as well as Francesca now – a family again at last."

Sylvia stepped to Oliver, and kissed both his and Ari's cheeks. "It is I who am grateful..." Oliver handed the boy to Francesca at that point.

"With your permission, my lord," Francesca said with labored French diction. "I will take Ari to chapel for prayers."

Oliver nodded. "Thank you, Francesca. I will meet you at the house."

Sylvia piped up. "Yes. We've already been to our morning prayers."

Oliver looked quizzically at her. She winked and squeezed his arm as Francesca made her exit from the wagon into the garden with Ari.

60. TAKING THE RED

Too many questions. Cardinal Abaga Oneglia Spinola consumed every elaborate course and every word spoken at the baron's table with a gourmand's insatiable appetite. Especially, he wanted to know about the baroness' young cousin from the north, seated too far down from him for direct inquiry, but not too far for the cardinal to take note of the lad's nervous glances. The cardinal grilled the baroness instead, but found her responses vague and vexing. The lady wanted to talk art and fashion, prying for details about court painters and their models.

Later, in his guest quarters – taking up a wing of the baron's palace – the cardinal had Tullio re-read an intercepted message decoded from a priest in Genoa, who signed himself "Fra Beppo. The intercepted message had been intended for the abbot of the Franciscan monastery just outside of Lyon.

Satisfied, the cardinal sat back in a plush chair. "The little bird has flown into our net, Tullio." The cardinal looked up from his desk at his secretary, sitting patiently nearby, quill and tablet in hand. "Good things come to those who wait. Now we have work to do."

Tullio got little sleep that night, writing, then encoding messages dictated by the cardinal – to Genoa, Madrid and Rome. Finished, at first light, he made his way downstairs, holding a small lantern, to the rear courtyard of the Baron's palace, messages tucked into a brown linen pouch under one arm.

He roused three of the cardinal's papal couriers quartered above the stables, gave them the cardinal's encoded messages to dispatch to their respective recipients.

Snuffing out his lantern and quick stepping back across the stable yard, Tullio nearly collided with two shrouded young men walking just ahead of him at an angle. The taller of the two, towards him, a short sword drawn. "Who goes there? ..."

"Please, sir. It is I..."

The taller one sheathed his sword when he caught sight of Tullio's stricken face in the predawn light.

Tullio froze in terror as he stared up into the face of a bear, amber eyes glinting. He heard a muffled laugh. The tall one pulled the bear-head off and revealed a face. "Oliver. Sir. I beg your pardon." Then Tullio noted that the bear's companion was a fox that appeared to be upstanding on its hind legs – but didn't remove its mask. The companion looked away. Oliver looked straight at Tullio.

"Out for morning prayers, friar?"

"Something along those lines, sir. And you?"

"Just returning from the hunt," Oliver put a thumb behind him.

"Are you hunters or prey?" Tullio rose up slightly from his habitual stoop, his gray eyes leering up into Oliver's cheerful, tired face, surveying it rather than making connection.

"A bit of both, I would guess. More of a revel – with this fair city's celebrants of Shrove Tuesday, ready now for the rigors of Lent."

Tullio crossed himself. "Praise be."

Oliver's companion tittered, "... the Lord be with you and your cardinal."

Tullio recognized the mellow, throaty voice of his hostess, the baroness, but gave no sign of it. "Then a good day to you both."

By Umberto Tosi

PART SEVEN

By Umberto Tosi

61. CLOISTERED

The convent of St. George... Ophelia awakened... bells, a gruel of groats, various unidentifiable victuals, a fortunate addition of dried fruits and a sliver of salted cod. A plentiful morning... And flowers... Thank you, Sister Ludmilla. Nothing made sense. Why was she in this nunnery – like a bad dream, an incarnation of Prince Hamlet's mocking words echoing over the years from Elsinore.

Ophelia had to orient herself first. Then, by degrees, begin to understand the nuances of her predicament – who were her enemies, what were their purposes and why had they confined her to this particular nunnery so far from all that she knew – and nowhere else?

It seemed that they did not know how to treat her – incarcerated in contradictions. Ophelia was held in a limbo in which she was considered both princess and prisoner – a ward of the monarch, a pawn in an international power play, a bargaining chip? Was she errant player caught in the papal vise, or the queen mother of Denmark's rightful boy-king, or a usurper and saboteur, fornicator and witch?

It became obvious to Ophelia that the cloister of St. George – inside the walls of Prague Castle at the heart of the Holy Roman Empire, was no ordinary nunnery. The empire's noble families sent their girls there for the best education. The Benedictine nuns of St. George had build a great tradition of learning and philosophy. The abbesses were members of royal families, with autonomy from the archbishop and direct ties to Rome.

"It's my name day and the feast of our patron saint, Ludmilla of Bohemia." The pale nun's face seemed ever aglow with beatitude. Or, thought Ophelia, did Ludmilla as a plain, pudgy child headed towards nunnery, develop an uncanny talent for staging – of finding the perfect lighting for angelic poses?

Ophelia challenged her fevered mind to draw the contours and shadows of the good sister – no angles to her face or form, round everywhere, wide set eyes, dark and wondering, reminding Ophelia of the ceramic dolls from the East seen in Antwerp's markets.

"You *are* my Saint Ludmilla," Ophelia rasped, disturbed by the weakness of her seldom used voice.

"Heavens no, my lady! I am a humble servant of Our Lord and no more." A country girl, she did not add, but Ophelia sensed it, yet one who somehow could read, because Sister Ludmilla had been reading poetry aloud to her by candlelight whenever the guards slept or were off somewhere. Perhaps Ophelia had dreamed that part.

The girl knew her plants and flowers, and brought armfuls to Ophelia's cell, seeing how the presence of them calmed her ward. More than that, Ophelia recognized certain herbs – left intentionally or not – swallowed their leaves and sucked bitter juice from their stems, as she did in pique or for remedies as a child too long ago to remember now. Had she ever been the pampered maiden of Elsinore castle that Prince Hamlet was said to favor?

She dreamed of her castle by the sea, Sonya, more magnificent and phantasmal each Night after night,in her troubled sleep, she floated over Sonia's ramparts, hooded and caped in dark silk, calling for *Ari. Ari. Ari.*

It was like the nightmare she used to have when Ari was a baby, of losing him, or his running off into a vast battlefield, or being stolen while she, like a fool, wasn't looking.

This was different. The nightmare didn't evaporate on awakening. The pain of it cut deeper than any that her keepers could inflict upon her – psychic or physical.

Ophelia liked Ludmilla. The only one. She took pleasure studying the face and form – the angles – of this angel of mercy and had begun to sketch her, once Mother Superior deemed Ophelia trustworthy of handling a lump of charcoal and loosely tied bundle of scrap paper, stained from the Vltava's spring flood.

Before anything else – before the beginning, when the Ophelia moth emerged from its cocoon, blinking, damp, unsure of its shape – Sister Ludmilla had shifted from dutiful caretaker, to an ally and liberator – at least in getting Ophelia freed from the painful twilight of linen bindings. Sister Ludmilla persuaded Mother Superior – and through her, the iron monsignor – that the prescribed treatments of cold water soakings that squeezed her like a ripe lemon in her bindings, salt and oil purgatives making her wretch in both directions "expelling the devil" - deep thudding about the body with thinly padded, wooden bats that rendered her weak and bone sore without a marks.

Rough treatment subsided, however, as Sister Ludmilla coached Ophelia into meditative quietude, and persuade her holy keepers that their regimen had driven Satan's madness out of her, and rendered their charge harmless enough to unbind and allow about her cell.

Still, she could not stop the tremors. Ophelia shivered less from the dampness than from the incongruous, lascivious shame and vulnerability of feeling her rough-woven, swill-gray prisoner's shift scratching night and day against her frail nakedness.

And the gruel – real food at last, extra portions stolen in by Sister Ludmilla, even an apple, a turnip, a onion tearfully consumed – and the nips of strong wine from a leather flask for strength, making her thinned body giddy, but able to endure being dragged stumbling in chains to a stuffy chapel for supervised prayer, and babbling her confession to a priest – making it unintelligible for cover. (After all, she was supposed to be mad.) And taking sacrament – greedy for the scrap of bread – from a hooded priest whose face she never saw – part of privileges given the prisoner guest now that her "madness" seemed to have subsided. It was more that her madness turned steel cold on the outside while a kernel hatred for her captors and the abductors of her child glowed hot inside warding off despair.

So *this* was life after death, after death, after death, after death... *But in that sleep of death what dreams may come?* The princely ghost asked during his nightly visits. She turned her dream face away from him, but he kept on talking. Always talking, that one.

Do something, why don't you?

That was always my problem.

"Not at the end."

Sometimes nothing is the answer. No thing. I'm beginning to see that.

"When you figure it out, let me know."

If I could free you, it could free me.

"Find my boy."

My boy. My boy too, that is.

"That is the problem. Would that he were not your boy, not a prince, naught bit an urchin rather than a pawn of kings and cardinals."

Ophelia was amazed to find words in her dreams long after they failed her during her imprisoned days, dragging on and on. How long had she been here? The skin of her hands looked shriveled, rough and old. She pictured Ari grown into tall boy, then into a young man, if he had only survived. But she feared the worst.

But a shaft of light slanted into her cell from a high window ever day, lingering longer. The good sister Ludmilla performed her magic in circumspect fashion befitting nunnery protocol, by means of spoon feeding favorable reports to the abbess. "Good news, Mother, our mad Ophelia has been quiet now for days. No more blasphemies, no ravings about regicides, patricides or mad princes, infanticides, midnight abductions or bloody bishops." Sister Ludmilla savored such words – sucking on them with ovular deliberation like rare spicy treats in her soft pink nun's mouth.

She knew that news of Ophelia's silence would work in two directions – one, as a sign that treatments work, two, as a silent alarm that their charge might perish, contrary to their instructions from the Emperor to keep the girl alive, but hidden away for now.

++++

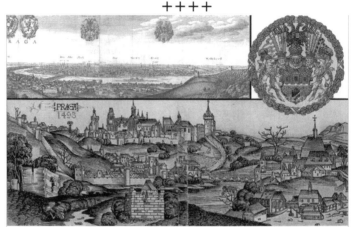

Prague in 1493, during the Jagellon Dynasty –
before Rudolf II became Holy Roman Emperor in
1576 and moved there from Vienna.

62. PRAGUE

Today there was sunlight – and the brightness of the patron saint's feast on the faces of her Benedictine keepers. Today, Sister Ludmilla had permission to allow their "guest" – as Ophelia was called – a garden stroll, under guard, but nevertheless, open and free. Ophelia breathed the early spring thaw, crocuses and new grass. Her eyes blinked constantly, tearing, head shaking, trying to see the billowy clouds above, feeling them more than seeing them. She swayed, dizzy from gentlest gusts – her ears hypersensitive to rushing sounds. She felt a chafing and realizing that she was shod only in open sandals, still feeling the burn of ankle chains. And fantastic gardens they were – exotic flowers, long rows of brilliant red tulips from Turkey, sacred flowers whose precious bulbs she had seen prized in Antwerp, seemed aplenty here, their heralding of equinox, their delicate raised blade petals – some white and yellow, new to her.

Ophelia regarded translucence of her pale blue-veined skin, the skeletal thinness of her ankles and toes in fascination, as if they belonged on another body. She felt queasy with the euphoria of trees, hedges and sky and drunk on warm breezes after fermenting so long in the dank piss smells of her penitential cell. Wind-cooled tears tickled her cheeks. She tasted their salt and knew she was alive after a long a death, not a dream, floating in strangeness, but real as the face of this black veiled nun at her side whose face she saw in full sunlight for the first time.

"There's rosemary,
that's for remembrance.
Pray you, love, remember.
And there's pansies, that's for thoughts.
There's fennel for you, and columbines.
There's rue for you, and here's some for me."

"There, there." Sister Ludmilla steadied her with a firm arm around her waist.

"Ari. Where is Ari?"

Sister Ludmilla patted Ophelia's forearm with her free hand. "In time, my lady. In time all will be revealed. Have faith. I am given little news in my humble station, but have faith."

And beyond, Ophelia glimpsed paradise through a gap in cypress trees, she saw a city of red roofs and steeples snaked through by a silver shining river, sprawling along its banks like a napping cat, a magical city that she had never seen before and where she could not recall arriving. She felt her knees shaking, a strange, comical reaction, she thought, to strangeness and terror that made her feet tingle and her skin go prickly. "Where are you my little prince? Where am I?"

Sister Ludmilla ushered her to the gap for a better look. "Prague," the sister said, very softly so that the guard behind them could not hear. Then she gestured subtly towards gray fortifications, a towering cathedral and the palace walls looming on all sides.

"Castle St. George," said Sister Ludmilla, and Ophelia realized that the good sister was speaking in a German vernacular strange, yet familiar, like old Danish, yet not. The sister sat them down on a bench. She took a small book from her generous black sleeves and began to read from it. Ophelia recognized the verses. Her own? How could that be? She leaned to look at the book's title, partially covered by the nun's pale, work-calloused hand. The sister obliged and showed her the book cover. Ophelia caught her breath at seeing the publisher's mark - *At the Sign of the Four Winds* – Vola's print house in Antwerp – and the poetry, Ophelia's own. There was her title: "*Sonia's Dream –an epic romance* by Olivia de Santille." So, Vola had survived! And done it!

"Where did you get this book?" Ophelia's own voice sounded distant and strange to her.

The nun returned the book to her sleeve. "Shh! Not permitted. I am to read only holy verses and catechism." She glanced at the guard, who stood a good distance across the garden from them behind a hedge, his back to them, apparently relieving himself.

Sister Ludmilla tapped the book. "We know this is you, Lady Ophelia – those of us who mother superior allows to write our own verses – even one of us published. I have read all the stories about you, as have a few of us – even though they say that you drowned long ago. You could be a queen. But now they say you could be tried and burned a heretic, and I am in sin speaking this way with you..."

"Sin, my dear sister, can be defined by costume." Ophelia said, half to herself. Out of the mists, Ophelia saw Vola's reassuring face gazing at her with approval. Her memory opened like an abandoned, dust covered volume. Words and pictures flew out like startled blackbirds. There was Charlotte, the runaway nun, princess of Orange. Ophelia brightened as Charlotte's visage took shape in her mind, proving, somehow, that all of what she had recalled – her flights, her fancies, her baby boy – were not ravings. Charlotte beckoning her, that forever conspiratorial smile on her rose petal lips.

The slanting light that became daylight became a blinding orb of illumination. Ophelia began to shake harder, her eyes aching, tearing, but seeing clearly.

Players. "All the world's a stage," she told her round yon virgin. "That's what we players say. Costumes make the man – or the woman. You can get in the habit of being a nun or a princess or a peasant, depending."

"I do not understand." Sister Ludmilla's lips went tight and white.

393

Ophelia plucked the waist of her sackcloth. "This is my penitent costume. But what if I got me to a nunnery."

Ludmilla's eyes widened. "But, my lady, you are indeed, in a nunnery."

"As a nun, perhaps I could leave this place on some pretext.."

"Only in pairs. We are not allowed to roam alone – even when permitted beyond the walls, which is rare."

"Beyond the walls. But what of inside the walls. Where is my boy, Ludmilla? Find that out for me, please, sister, please."

63. CARDINAL CONSPIRACY

"Madrid! Dithering fools!" Cardinal Spinola's gout was acting up and his body continued to complain about the long days swaying and bouncing in his couch over the mountains from Lyon to Prague. "Tullio, do you know why those porridge-headed advisors to Phillip think this was a good idea?

Tullio, knowing the answer, played into the cardinal's rhetoric. "Does His Eminence mean delivering the little Danish pretender and his whore-mother to King Phillip's cousin, Emperor Rudolf?"

The cardinal slapped a hand flat on the table in front of him. Thwack! "That snake of the Doria's, Enzo Palmieri is behind this."

"Your eminence?"

"Palmieri connives to go around me – and His Holiness – and make his own arrangement with the Danish nobles who want to overthrown King Fortinbras – then put the little prince, Aricin, on the throne as the Doria's puppet. Palmieri enlisted the Genoa emissary, Horatio in his scheme."

"Yes, Your Eminence. But, thanks to Your Eminence's acumen, we have thwarted Palmieri's plan. The renegade Ophelia remains incarcerated.

The cardinal puffed and shook his head. "Yes, but here in Prague, where we cannot control the situation. Diverting her and the child here was a necessary compromise. With Palmieri whispering in King Philip's ear, it was the best alternative. King Philip would not approve simply eliminating Ophelia and the boy, and didn't want the problem in Madrid, so he ordered Ophelia and her son to be transported here to Prague."

"But, your eminence, with all respect, no one in Madrid has trusted Emperor Rudolf since he refused to marry King Phillip's daughter Isabella for the good of their Habsburg empire.

The cardinal made a sour face. "Instead of siring princes, the wastrel Rudolf makes babies with his mistress, Katherina Strada, locked up in their private palace. It's like a bad fairy tale, Tullio."

"And his young male companions?"

"We do not speak of that, Tullio, nor of our having one of the emperor's confidants in our pay."

"Your eminence has told me of His Holiness displeasure at Rudolf's consorting with all and sundry of Rome's enemies – relations with the Turks."

The cardinal shuddered. "He even consorts with Jews – drinks wine with the infamous rabbi Judah Loew ben Bezalel, who they say conjures a giant clay demon that stalks the riverbanks of the Vltava, tearing off limbs of those who dare threaten the Jews who flock to Prague. Imagine, Tullio, permitting such talk! The city is a pit of heresy and hell, Tullio. The sooner we finish with this business and leave the better."

Tullio volunteered: "It is treacherous, your eminence. No one can predict this Holy Roman Emperor's next move – not even where he stands between protestant and his fellow Catholics. – only that he fears the Turks at his borders.

"Prague swarms with Jews, protestants, moriscos, necromancer, pagans, humanists and mystics – even nonbelievers – under Rudolf's misrule. Each man seems to think he can believe whatever suits him. Imagine that, Tullio."

"Like the end of times, your eminence."

"Rudolf collects thousands of books forbidden by the Vatican Index and flaunts the teachings of Mother Church in favor of his circles of philosophers, alchemists, artists, neoplatonists and other mystic riffraff. Whom does he think builds our magnificent churches and vouchsafes the power of the church? The people dropping their coins pitifully in collection baskets, or those whom God has chosen to be their estate holders, bankers and rulers?"

Tullio restrained his restiveness. "Yes. I concur, your eminence. You are right to point out these sins as Papal Nuncio here in Prague. May I inquire further as to our mission?"

"Our instructions from Rome are to see that this matter is concluded swiftly, Tullio. When we arranged for the abduction of the little pretender and his mother, I did not anticipate all these complications."

"Complications indeed."

"That meddling Enzo Palmieri of Genoa has tangled everything up. Just because he once had an audience with Emperor Rudolf … It was Palmieri's scheming that led to King Phillip ordering us to transport the mother and boy taken here to Prague instead of Madrid, or simply dispatching them both on the spot. The man confounds us, Tullio."

Tullio, as always, sat close by his cardinal, notebook open, his quill scratching, taking notes diligently.

"Ah, Rudolf collects alchemists and astronomers as greedily as he does paintings and painters. He courts the Danish astronomer Tycho Brahe shamelessly, betting the metal-nosed brute to move his observatory to Prague …"

"And Brahe's father, who is part of the Danish council of lords."

"So our spies tell me, Tullio. It was a muddle, which is why I had to intervene."

"I have written you a report on the visit of Fortinbras special emissary to Prague, your eminence..."

"A meddler. Rudolf is in one of his black sulks, holed up in his royal apartments, wandering the long corridors filled with the thousands of devices, trinkets, artifacts, inventions, antiquities and art from every corner of the world."

"Fortinbras will be disappointed, then?"

"Not at all, Tullio. The Danish king is about to recall his emissary – that wide-eyed scribbler, Horatio, back to Denmark. The king sent him here for an audience with Emperor Rudolf, a wild goose chase, really. Everyone here in Prague knows that it can take a foreign emissary months, if not years, to see Rudolf – unless they are philosophers or wizards, or come offering art treasures. "

"Or astronomers. And after that?"

"Horatio is irrelevant. Fortinbras put him here to fool the Danish council of lords that he is doing something positive. Meanwhile, Madrid has concluded the treaty that the Pope seeks, in secret, with Fortinbras, soon to be announced, bypassing Prague."

"You put Machiavelli to shame, your eminence."

Cardinal Spinola grinned and bowed his head in mock humility. "I certainly lack Machiavelli's talent as a playwright, but as a strategist... I will accept some comparison humbly."

"Better to be feared than loved, as the Florentine said."

"Our labors have borne fruit, Tullio, despite the incompetence of these courtiers and bureaucrats our efforts seem about to bear fruit. Fortinbras has all but agreed to a secret pact with Rome and Madrid.

Once it the agreement I sealed, he the Danish king will slap prohibitive levies on Dutch and English ships passing through the Danish straits between the North and Baltic seas.

"This will choke those protestant Dutch in a Spanish garrote, Tullio. Those fat burghers in Amsterdam will run out of grains and timber and metals and scream for peace. The Holy Father will be pleased."

"And what does the petty Danish tyrant get?"

"Spanish gold – that they can't afford – but worth it." The cardinal added, more importantly: Philip's cousin Rudolf will cut off aid to the Poles as part of the deal. That puts Fortinbras at liberty to overrun the rest of Poland.

"But, your eminence, the Poles are god fearing, loyal Roman Catholics."

"Fortinbras agrees to allow that. He only wants their grain and mercury – and their mercenaries. Anyway, Fortinbras will quickly get a bellyful of Poland. Quarrelsome conquer Poles will undo him soon enough."

"You could well have been a prince and a general, your eminence.

"Better than my dull brothers, who did not take the cloth, Tullio, but to each his path. Our rewards will be great as well. The Holy Father has promised us more lands in Liguria and Lombardy." The cardinal drew a breath and whispered, "and who can tell who will become the next pope, eh, Tullio? Perhaps a Spinola from Genoa?"

"I see your point, your eminence." A servant arrived with a bowl of dark new cherries from Italy, which Tullio took and served to his cardinal by a tall window overlooking the gardens of St. George Convent. As the cardinal savored them, he spied two women seated on a bench on the far side of the garden, like a pair starlings resting on a branch, one in black Benedictine nun's habit, the other in formless gray. "And what of the little Danish prince, Ari, and his mother, your eminence."

"The boy? We are merciful. I have a perfect solution..."

"Tivoli? Villa d'Este?"

"Yes, Tullio. Our dear friend, Cardinal Ippolito II, d'Este has offered to take the boy into the holy care of his foundling choir and give him musical training."

"As a *castrato*?"

"When the time comes, which will be shortly, once he's done apprenticeship."

"Excellent."

"He will have a new name and a wonderful, sanctified life."

"God willing he is one who survives the monk's knife."

"God willing. We will offer a prayer. Don't you wish you could have stayed in such esteemed company?"

"Oh, but I am grateful that your eminence took me from Ippolito's orphanage as his special one." Tullio bowed his head.

"You and I both are truly blessed, Tullio. So will it be for the little bastard pretender. Cardinal Ippolito's *castrati* have been hailed in the palaces of Rome, Florence, Venice, Genoa, Madrid, Paris and Vienna.

"And his mother? I sent the missive to Cardinal Ludovico Madruzzo as you asked."

"Splendid, Tullio. The heretic whore obviously is guilty of sorcery. Our esteemed colleague Ludovico will arrange transport to Trier for trial as a witch under the new bishop there."

"They've burned two hundred and fifty for witchery this year already, your eminence. The interrogators, judges and executioners have confiscated much gold and silver for their services. They have asked how they will be compensated for putting Ophelia to the torture and trial – in gold or worthless promissory notes? She has no property for them to take."

"I will gladly pay them myself to see this matter resolved, Tullio."

"I will notify Bishop Johann von Schönenberg that they have your support, your eminence."

"Going about as a man, exhibiting herself lewdly... seditious plays. Indeed."

"The secretary to Cardinal Madruzzo writes that the bishop's tribunals sent one hundred witches to the stake in one day last month for the feast of St. Catherine."

"Splendid, Tullio. We must do our part to help this good work. Write the bishop to include a charge of consorting with Satan in order to sink Spanish ships. Add that we have evidence of accomplices, and that Ophelia must be made to name all the others in her Satanic circle before she is executed."

"Yes. I will also draft your message to Fortinbras that both the boy pretender and his troublesome mother have been eliminated as a threat to his crown."

"You will finish it tonight, Tullio so that I may sign and have it sent by swift courier."

"Yes. Your eminence. I'll start on it forthwith."

"Pray we can bring this affair to a speedy conclusion, Tullio, and return home. This city overflows like its river with heretics, debauchees and infidels – people who think they can say and do whatever the devil puts in their heads – mock us, king, kingdom, church. They disturb natural order of things – God's intended order – under which works, peasants toiling, kings ruling, under the watchful eyes of church and those whom God has chosen to govern. We must put things aright, Tullio. Today has been a good day!"

++++

*Holy Roman Emperor Rudolph II, 1603,
engraving by Aegidius Sadeler.*

64. A CELESTIAL GLOBE

"Prague holds many memories for me, Marcellus." Horatio toyed with a gilt brass and silver globe on a Turkish inlaid table along one wall of the long chamber flanked by high, clear baroque windows through which streamed the spring afternoon's northern light.

Brilliant, undulating images tumbled through Horatio's mind from vivid paintings covering the walls and ceilings, up and down the corridor as far as he and Marcellus could see – magnificent works of Durer, Pieter Bruegel, Caravaggio, Bosch, Titian, Tiepolo, Leonardo da Vinci, Tintoretto, Holbein, Cranach, Veronese and other artists whose names Horatio did not recognize.

Rudolf II had ascended the throne only a few short years earlier, but already he had surpassed his father, Maximilian, in the richness of his collections and certainly in the gathering of the greatest minds of the era around him. Horatio was impressed. The walls and ceilings swirled with angels, devils, gods and goddesses, lovers and warriors, kings, queens, horses, processions, martyrs, prophets, maidens, wives and whores, heroes and sorcerers and scoundrels, wizards and fools in dream colors and stylized perspectives. The sacred danced with the profane.

The erotic mingled naked with the virtuous. Display cases, tables and drawers were filled with the wonders and oddities of the world, past and present – clocks, mechanical toys, cuneiforms, hieroglyphs, sacred scrolls from Egypt, India, Babylonia, Sumer, the New World, Africa burgeoned with transcendent symbols, mumbo jumbo, ancient wisdom, testaments and the secrets of every kind of magic.

"More things in heaven and earth, Marcellus, than are dreamt of in your philosophies." Horatio gestured around them. All of it the fruits of the world's most obsessive collector, Rudolf II, who – were he not Europe's most powerful regent, might be burned as its most blasphemous, heretical one, having surrounded himself with magicians, alchemists, astrologers, philosophers, artists, writers, artists, doctors of every discipline, Catholic, protestant, Jew – as long as they intrigued the moody King of Bohemia, *Dominus Mundi*, the Habsburg Lion, the Holy Roman Emperor.

"More wonders in these very halls of Emperor Rudolf's *Kunstkammer* than I could ever dream of, sir."

"Every dream in the world is found here in this labyrinth of wonders, Marcellus. But still, we see no sign of what – and whom – we seek."

Rudolf's minister of foreign affairs, Lord Gustav Rolf had received Horatio the week earlier, and examined his documents as Denmark's emissary. But like Palmieri in Genoa, he put off Horatio's request for an audience with the supreme leader.

"The emperor is indisposed," Rolf allowed, diffidently. "No one sees his majesty when he is indisposed." Rolf had drawn out the word, "indisposed," for Horatio to catch his drift. Rudolf was in one of his moods. The monarch could drop from sight for days, even weeks – perhaps in his royal apartments, seeing no one but his mistress Katherina and his confidantes, Wolfgang von Rumpf, Philip Lang and Duke Heinrich Julius of Brunwick, and at times, it was rumored, an adolescent boy or two from the royal orphanage choir.

The unpredictable Rudolf could be bathing with his comely peasant concubines at the summer house that his majesty's father had designed in the shape of Solomon's six-pointed star.

There he would nest, removed from affairs of state, among exotic gardens, serenaded by birds and roamed by beasts brought from Asia, Africa and the New World, dotted with artificial lakes stocked with exotic fish, patrolled by African Ibis and Northern Heron – all fed by an underground duct from the river Vltava. The reclusive emperor could be anywhere in Prague's rambling hilltop castle, helped to wander unseen with his entourage by wood covered passageways.

Despite this inconvenience, Horatio and Marcellus, however, did manage permission to the inner sanctum of Rudolf's arts treasures. Horatio met with the painter, Giuseppe Arcimboldo – known for his daring portrait of Rudolf as the god Vertimus, assembled, dream like, in brilliant colored vegetables.

Rudolf had also commissioned Arcimboldo as an agent to procure art treasures, particularly from the north, and Horatio had brought just the right gift – a first edition, from his Antwerp publisher – of hitherto undiscovered Durer etchings, inscribed by the artist. Horatio had heard that diplomats bearing art got preferential treatment in gaining audiences with the emperor. Horatio would still have to wait, but the Durer volume he brought as a gift to the emperor was enough to get Horatio and Marcellus a quick invitation to see the emperor's collection, with an audience they hoped soon would follow.

Just one royal footman was assigned to accompany Horatio and Marcellus. They soon diverted him to a fool's errand after the peacocks flew in through the French doors Marcellus had opened in stealth. The emperor's pet reindeer wandered in, wide eyed, bewildered at the dazzle, sniffing baubles and shaking his still-furry spring antlers. The reindeer had been a gift from Tycho Brahe, who himself kept a pet elk.

Horatio knew that the emperor had been trying for more than a year to lure Tycho to move his famous observatory to Prague from the Danish island of Hven in the Baltic Sea, ceded him by Hamlet's father – also to publish his volumes of equations and observations recording the movements of planets and stars. Tycho would visit Prague, engage the emperor in discourse – enjoying the colloquy of great minds constantly gathering at the palace – but so far make no commitment. This included his present visit, though the great astronomer was surprised and glad to meet his former student, Horatio, this time around.

Paying no to mind to the fracas up and down the corridors, Horatio examined the gilded globe, and ran a finger over the starry constellations etched on its silver surface. He called off the constellations and stars from memory, harking back to his student days at Wittenberg with Hamlet. He observed that the globe was as much a work of art as of astronomy – balanced inside gyroscopic arms, each with little globes representing the moon and known planets and their rotations.

The whole apparatus was mounted on the back of a solid silver horse in which a timepiece was inset with jewels that scattered colors from the light. "As stunning as would be the shield of Achilles described by Homer," Horatio mused as he ran a finger over the embossed surface of this ideal world.

Marcellus leaned in for a closer look. "Indeed, sir."

"Once, when we visited Prague as students, Giordano Bruno told Lord Hamlet and I of his visions. His eyes seemed as fiery pinwheels while he described "a universe of worlds – suns and planets without end, as befitting their infinite Creator, spinning like a million dancers in a giant hall to the music of infinity rising and falling."

"Out of any Italian or Spanish Inquisitor's earshot, I hope for all your sakes.

"Yes. Then and now, I fear for Bruno, as did Lord Hamlet."

"I never knew that philosophical side of our prince."

"Even as students at Wittenberg, Prince Hamlet and I sensed old ideas unraveling. Dutifully, we continued to study the orthodoxies of Aristotle and Ptolemy – and earned our honors. But around men like Lord Brahe and Fra Bruno, they seemed hollow."

Marcellus smirked. "What professors teach and students seek seldom meet..."

"We read and listened to Giordano Bruno – who lectured to us one week and sent our heads spinning like the infinite worlds revolving around infinite suns he envisioned. We did our share of rousting about, whoring and drinking, but diversions only made our visions brighter."

"Youthful thirst for new worlds..."

"Hamlet told me of Ophelia – of their journeys into fantasy together on the wings of magic herbs..."

"Such as..."

"He never said, but did quote the ancients – as does this Emperor Rudolf – always in private – the breathtaking notions of the neoplatonists, and of Hermes Trimegistus – invoking the 'Divinity-in-All-Things' of Thoth, of the Cabala, of Seshat and Ma'at."

Marcellus looked about, ducking his head.

"You need not fear open discourse in this palace, Marcellus. It is like no other in Europe in this era – like Athens and Rome of old."

"Perhaps Florence and Venice once, but less so now... I take it."

"This presumptuous mad monk Bruno travels about like a latter day prophet... declaring to all that there is but one faith unifying all the others – and everlasting faith that directs all of humankind to draw towards the light – be it the light the sun, moon, the stars, God or in each human being."

407

"For that, then, the Vatican and the Spaniards would torture and imprison him?"

"Not so much what he sees and expounds, Marcellus... They despise and fear him because too many have begun to listen too him."

"And were you and Prince Hamlet among the listeners?"

"We did not comprehend fully. We were much consumed in our own youthful pursuits. But we saw a new time dawning. One of Giordano's pronouncements, I recall now, struck our prince like a bolt of lightening. It struck me too, but I put it aside at the moment. But it came to me, shining in its compassion after the tragedy at Elsinore."

"What was that, Sir Horatio?"

"Lord Hamlet and I were walking along a parapet of the Wittenberg walls one night, talking of nonsense – of wines, of saucy town wenches, mocking our professors as hens running to and fro through the grass of their self satisfactions. Suddenly we saw him, in black robe and cowl, standing like a ghost. We stopped and stared. We thought he might be bent to leap off the wall, or bring some meteor down upon us... Instead, he raised a hand to the skies to a full, midnight moon above. 'Take heart, young men,' he said, as if answering our puerile complaints. 'Look to the light always.' Then his eyes seemed to emit their own light."

"... and that was the moment?"

"No – having fixed our attention – he walked very close to us, almost to where we could feel his breath, and said softly:

'A living earth revolves around a divine sun, amid other innumerable suns and worlds in an infinite cosmos.'

"He stopped, then took each of our hands, and then thrust his thoughts into us, like a swordsman, swiftly. I cannot recall now, if he actually spoke them to us, or simply transmitted the contents of his mind directly into ours ..."

"'and each of you contains that cosmos. Thus thou wilt present the glory and brightness of the whole universe – and the darkness of obscurity will fly from you'"

"I felt light rush through me. I looked at Lord Hamlet and his eyes were also aglow. I believe now, that Bruno's words may have changed our prince – forever. He would never dwell in the darkness of obscurity. He would triumph in the end over the shadow of murder most foul at Elsinore."

Marcellus went silent, while the two of them waited in the shadows for a pair of guards to pass. Once they were alone again, Marcellus resumed eager to learn more. Horatio had never spoken to him much about his youthful days with Hamlet. "Strange how a monk's ravings – plausible or imaginary – arouses the fear and wrath of mighty popes and emperors."

"The more vast one's vision of the world and the cosmos, the smaller it makes the mighty and powerful on this speck of earth, indeed, the more humble us all. The greater the gilded celestial globe, the more insignificant the crowns of kings, Marcellus." Horatio held the celestial globe up towards the windows, spun it and watched the light dance.

"And the more like us it makes kings," Marcellus added.

"The powerful rarely consider their place in the universe, beyond the thrones on which they sit so precariously."

"As does our 'Emperor' Fortinbras?"

"Stars surely will align against us, Marcellus, unless we persuade this emperor in Prague to block the pact proposed to Fortinbras by the Holy See."

"... of Enzo Palmieri's design?"

"No, Marcellus. Palmieri has quite a different scene. It is cardinal Spinola and the pope we must fear."

"But you, sir Horatio, are Fortinbras' emissary... Are you not?"

"Fortinbras uses me as but a messenger boy at this point. Rome and Madrid know it. I know they are about to strike, because King Fortinbras has recalled me to Denmark. We run quickly out of time to find Ophelia and our little prince – if they are still here, or were here at all, as our sources advised."

"Would that we could undo this tangled plot... Cut the Gordian Knot."

"Or may seal Ophelia's doom."

"The players are here and ready to do their part, sir, if can come to her aid."

"First we must find her, Marcellus, and more so, the little boy somewhere in this citadel."

The sound of doors opening from far down the corridor, footsteps, voices: Horatio put the celestial globe back on its table. He and Marcellus drew their daggers and stepped into a side alcove behind velvet drapes, as four men approached.

Horatio recognized the man in the lead – craggy but resplendent in a red satin cape and cap – as Cardinal Spinola, whom he had seen in Genoa blessing processions, and later glimpsed at Cathedral San Lorenzo. Another familiar figure – this one in black, pudgy, hunched, obsequious even in his gait, followed the cardinal, along with two armed men – in Genoa colors, not of the emperor's personal guard – followed.

Horatio whispered. "Not a good sign, Marcellus."

65. DALIBORKA TOWER

"You have company, my Lord. Another ghost precedes you in this tower."

You need not address me as lord, Ophelia, now I've shuffled off this mortal coil.

"Habits die hard, my lord."

The specter claps hands over his ears. *Infernal fiddle screeching – like cats courting.*

"Methinks the fiddler's serenade fits the melancholic mood of this tower, as well as my own, my lord."

Cease thy scratchings, retched fiddler!

Ophelia could barely speak aloud, but mustered more energy in this dream state. "Surely, my lord, I would have thought that you and the wretched knight's specter would have struck up a fine friendship, by now out there in the land of the dead."

... and with every fishmonger? Ophelia doomed knight of Bohemia, the tower's first prisoner, condemned to death for his support of a peasant revolt a century earlier.

The music continued, sing-song, on scratchy strings in the background. Legend was that the ghost of the tower's first prisoner, a condemned knight executed a hundred years before Ophelia was born, played plaintive ballads on his twelve-stringed *lyre de brache* every night there that the guards heard in fear and often would go off duty to avoid.

The executioner should have beheaded his fiddle too.

"My lord, you are harsh. I may well soon join the doomed knight's lot soon – and yourself among the shades."

Heaven forbid that we be melancholy Danes together. I am more bereft than sharp.

"Would that I could fly through these barred windows like yourself, my Lord."

Alas, if I could but free thee, fair Ophelia.

"I cannot face the executioner without knowing of my son, my lord."

Our son, my fair Ophelia.

"Would that he were the son of a clockmaker instead of a prince. He would be in my arms now, and I not in this dungeon."

You would deny our son?

"I would deny you, my lord – or hope to free myself at last from our entanglement."

You are free of me, Ophelia, and the better for it. I broke our ties for that very reason before my end.

"I have come to realize, my late prince, that you will be forever in my life, somehow, as long as I am mother to Ari, no matter how far I travel from Elsinore. Witness this misery now...into which our son and I have been snared..." Ophelia choked back dry tears and flailed the empty air in front of her, trying to strike him.

Fear not, Ophelia. He is safe. For now, anyway.

"How can you know?"

I know such things – as a spirit – though I cannot point to his whereabouts. I am on a plane different than your own, with its own geography.

"A hint would be helpful, my lord."

I can sense time ahead – not far – like a traveler making his way along a foggy moor.

"Then what is next."

Who is next? That is the more apt question. But softly now. He comes...

Ophelia heard murmurs and the the scrape of feet climbing the spiral stone staircase leading to her cell in the tower. "Are you real?"

She shouted into the air. At least they had removed the chains after they cast her into this small cell with its narrow barred window too high to allow Ophelia to see anything but a patch of sky. Everything had been blackness, her mind creating worlds into which she floated.

"Open the cell!" The voice sounded familiar to Ophelia. "I must examine her. Bring the torch closer."

Blinding light. A man's voice. Another priest?

She had not seen Sister Ludmilla in the ten days since the hooded guards took her from the convent to this cell in the tower – still somewhere inside the vast, high walled, hilltop grounds of Prague Castle. That much she knew.

Suddenly she felt pushed back against the wall of her cell as two black robed figures stepped inside, one with flaming torch in hand.

"Stay outside!" The first figure shouted at someone in the passageway – probably one of her guards. "Close the door." She heard the creak and thud of the cell door closing obediently. "Shh!" The first figure pulled back his cowl just enough for her to glimpse his face.

"Fortunio?" Ophelia barely got out the name before "the priest" clapped a hand over her mouth.

"Hush, my child!" Then, in full, stage voice: "I am Monsignor Henricus Institor, Special Inquisitor for Tyrol, Salzburg and Bohemia. You must come with us." He announced this very loudly, in a deep voice echoing off the stone walls, then whispered into her ear as she trembled. "Put on these robes." The other figure handed her a bundle of clothes. "Quickly!"

Ophelia trembled, partly from fear, partly gratitude at this intercession – and, as she later recounted – very much from rage and shame at realizing how wretched she must appear to her old friend Fortunio – how much she had lost.

Without further word, she slipped into the proffered, unfamiliar, rough leather sandals, wrapped herself in the coarse woven Dominican robe and cowl. But then she stopped: "I cannot go on ..."

Fortunio pulled her to him and tied the sash snugly around her waist, hung a wooden crucifix from her collar and hooked heavy rosary beads to her belt. "That will do. Come on."

The other person in the cell moved behind them, in a flurry of activity that Ophelia could not decipher. Words in Latin followed – the two mock clerics chanting in counterpoint, wailing – a good act.

"I cannot..."

"Get to your feet, prisoner. Fortunio put chains on Ophelia's wrists loosely. "For show," he whispered.

"Guard!" Fortunio shouts from the door.

"I cannot..."

The other hooded cleric mutters. "Cannot what, my dear?" Ophelia jumped, rattling the chains, then wobbles – the voice, rasping, by Ophelia had heard it so often before when Isabella would play her mock Captain character on stage. Isabella brought the torch around so as to reflect in her eyes momentarily, calming Ophelia... Still.. "I cannot."

"Cannot what, my dear?"

"We cannot abandon Ari. I cannot leave this place without my baby..." Ophelia's whisper raises into a wail.

"Silence, whore!" Fortunio roared at her, booming, savage, into his part.

The guard opened the door and stared in, holding a lantern. "We are removing this prisoner to ecclesiastical detention for interrogation!" Fortunio reached inside the sleeve of his Dominican robe and unrolled a parchment covered in Latin, waving at the illiterate guard. "Come!" He yanked Ophelia forward by the chain. The second "Dominican" pushed her from behind."

Isabella whispered into Ophelia's ear. "Ari is safe." Then she pushed Ophelia again. "Move, witch!" Ophelia staggered forward, out into the passageway. The guard ahead of them, the procession marched down the long spiral stone stairs to a subterranean passage. More barred doors and gates open on command of the Dominican Inquisitor... The plan was working, thus far.

66. ANOTHER ROUTE

AUTHOR'S NOTE: *There are two alternative versions of Ophelia's imprisonment and escape, each of which has its ardent, scholarly supporters..*

In one version – believed by nineteenth-century scholars – Ophelia did not escape at all, but perished in her tower cell, but a wizard in Emperor Rudolf's "magic circle" freed her ghost to wander Prague.

Only two, partially overlapping versions of the story can be documented, and remain credible to this day.

The first version – recounted previously – incorporates accounts found in two contemporary historical documents. Neither was penned by direct witnesses, but they do cite journals of contemporaries, including two players in the Comici group.

The second version of Ophelia's escape is documented by a journal written years later by a contemporary of Ophelia – a Benedictine nun Ludmilla Frommet, from Bohemia – mentioned earlier. Apparently influenced by Ophelia's subversive thought, Ludmilla left the order after Ophelia's escape and fled Prague and eventually migrated to the Dutch colony of New Amsterdam in the Americas.

Scholars seem evenly split on the veracity of either of these two accountings, which is why the author has included both of them in this text. Nevertheless the author favors second version, which is presented below:

Life, what she had of it, started to go a little better for Ophelia after the nun took her from her cell for that first garden outing. Ophelia regained strength slowly over the weeks that followed under Sister Ludmilla's discreet care. The nun brought her extra provisions and garments to keep warm, sneaking them in piece by piece under her habit.

The good sister also continued to bring herbs and flowers that seemed to brighten her charge – watchfully tolerated by mother superior. The abeyance of instructions left Ophelia's status vague enough for a while for the nuns to regard her more like a novitiate than prisoner.

Ophelia took advantage of the sister's help and relaxed rules to request various herbs and seeds on her own as well. She used the pretext of teaching Sister Ludmilla about remedies, as well as botany – sketching various plants for her as well. Sister Ludmilla thought nothing odd about any of the requests, even of some strange looking pods and fungi as part of the collection. These she would let dry. At night, Ophelia would carefully grind down certain of these into fine powder mixtures that she tucked into folds of her sleeve and small envelopes she fashioned from scrap paper.

One night she prepared a certain potion from dried mushrooms and ground seeds – a preparation she had learned from the book of poisonous plants she had kept among her collection as a young girl at Elsinore. She saved a cup of water and poured the gray powder into it, regarding the liquid for a long while then downing it in one draft.

The fungus-derived compound pulled her into deep unconsciousness. She could feel it sucking her downward, just like the stream of long ago that had soaked her skirts and pulled her under before Fortunio had discovered her.

She could not be sure, in fact, that she would ever regain consciousness. There were so many variables of the potion's purity and dosage. Perhaps she could then meet the mystery of afterlife... Suddenly she thought of Ari and regretted taking the potion, but it was too late – so she is believed to have told Sister Ludmilla later, but we cannot be sure.

There was a plan. She had to trust that the good sister had given her message a certain woman who would be praying in St. Vitus church.

Ophelia planned to take the potion soon as she heard the Prague astronomical clock in Wenceslas Square strike the hour of midnight. She counted her long hours by the sounds of this clock that drifted distantly through the tiny window of her tower cell on the northeast corner of Hradčany Castle hill.

The clock, constructed in 1410, modeled a Ptolemaic, earth-centered universe with sun, moon, planets and the crystal sphere of stars represented in rotation around it, hour by hour, day by day. Sister Ludmilla told her about it, and Ophelia remembered seeing an etching of it in one of Vola's books. The sister helped her sort out its various odd chimes and sounds – which gave Ophelia great comfort in her cold cell by enabling her to sort out the hours and keep her bearings in time, counting the days until she could seize an opportunity for escape – giving impetus to fevered plans to rescue Ari and exact revenge on her abductors.

Ding, ding, ding, ding, ding, ding.... a bronze mechanical skeleton of Death would begin each chiming of the hour, dancing round from its pinnacle, clanging its bell, followed by three other mechanical representations of fear and loathing – dancing, chiming bronzes of a turbaned Turk, a moneylender in the form of caricatured Jew, and Vanity, admiring itself in a looking class.

Bronze figures of philosophy, religion, astronomy and history would twirl about – as Ophelia would see for herself later – then a parade of the twelve Apostles appearing in a window above the clock, then finally the ringing of the hour.

Horatio's part two Hamlet history – *Ophelia Mortuis* – describes this midnight chiming of the Prague clock in chilling detail as marking the *actual* death of Ophelia, in a failed ruse, as discovered by her rescuers who were unable to revive her. He even describes the transport of her body to an unknown, final resting place on the Baltic Sea island Hven, in the Øresund between Zealand and Scania, now Sweden, but which at that time was part of Denmark.

Horatio even gives a detailed description of hearing the midnight tolling of the Prague astronomical clock in his account. But he adds an irony. "The clock, unbeknown to a sleeping city, was chiming the end of an era – of our world nestled in Ptolemy's – and Rome's – ordered universe, that already disrupted by Tycho Brahe's discoveries and soon to be blown aside like fall leaves by his Copernican successors."

Horatio's detailed description of Ophelia's death, however, is now widely regarded as a ruse in itself, perpetuated to give Ophelia cover – like all good myths, based in part a truth that we shall explore later in this narrative.

Sister Ludmilla's diary, though less known than Horatio's works describes more plausibly, how Ophelia faked death, with the good sister's unwitting help – a strategy that makes sense when one considers that this was a popular plot twist in both comedies and tragedies in which Ophelia had performed during her years with *I Comici*.

A fragment of Ludmilla's journal describes the incident in a way eerily reminiscent of Ophelia's first, ambiguous, faked death and funeral under Queen Gertrude's aegis in Elsinore:

419

"A burial party from 'the Danish emissary' did arrive at Daliborka at dawn to fetch Ophelia's body – two pall bearers and a grave digger, with papers purportedly from the emperor himself."

Many years later Ludmilla's journal maintained, however, that this burial party consisted of Horatio, his aide Marcellus, and two players from the theatrical group – *I Comici* – probably Fortunio and Isabella done up as a man.

They placed the "corpse" in a wooden box, lifted atop a cart and were never heard from again – probably headed for the Vltava River where a boat would have been waiting to take them northward, swiftly downstream into the mighty Elbe where they would find the North Sea and Denmark, but we have to consult other sources to reconstruct her story from this point, particularly because Ludmilla's account – or what survives of it – does not account for Prince Ari, strangely because Ophelia would have been unlikely to leave Prague while her son remained captive there – or had been killed by Ophelia's abductors.

One finds points of agreement among the various accounts of Ophelia's escape, even though the strategies they describe differ sharply, for example, all accounts mention Ophelia hearing a violin playing while in the tower that grows more audible as she makes her escape – attributed to the ghost of the tower's first condemned prisoner, but so vivid as to suggest another source from inside Prague Castle, where musical performances were common.

A letter from Fortunio to his mother in Venice describes hearing a "beautiful sad melody, repeated over and over, that nearly brought me to tears," while he took part in Ophelia's escape – but suggests a live source, rather than supernatural origin. Fortunio says he heard a violin playing "*Doină* – a song from Oltenia" that he had once seen Romanian musicians visiting Venice perform in St. Mark's Square.

Though Prague being more under Bohemian influence, the Latinized area of Oltenia certainly was part of Rudolf II's empire at that time, and in fact he made Prague the greatest musical center of its time, gathering musicians from far and wide and giving generous support to choirs, orchestras and music schools.

All in all, the author gives more credence to the second version than the first, because of its better congruence with the apocryphal story of Ophelia's death which soon spread through Prague and from there to Spain, Flanders, Denmark and the Holy See.

Historians now concur on the likelihood that Ophelia's "death" hoax in Prague was carefully planned to throw her enemies off the scent, even though it denied her access to many of those who had helped her in the past.

67. A HARD FEAST

Stealing a royal child – even one of dubious authenticity – from an imperial castle presents no small challenge. Horatio pored over diagrams of the emperor's fortress, making notes with his odd stick. "It's the latest from England." He showed it to Fortunio. "Juniper with graphite pressed inside, called a 'pencil'..."

Ophelia pushed it away. "Back to planning."

Fortunately, for Ophelia, Ari was not a prisoner. Rather he had become a playmate for the emperor's brood. Horatio had learned confidentially through a trusted contact in the court, that the boy had been taken in secret to the emperor's private family quarters in eastern wing of the royal palace

There – tended by nannies – he played with the emperor's children by Rudolf's lifelong common law wife, Katherina , oblivious to the intrigue around him.

All his had come about by fortunate circumstances that thwarted Cardinal Spinola's original abduction plan.

"I won't have you putting this child – a prince – in one of your ecclesiastical dungeons," Katherina had intervened, with support from the emperor. "This is a matter of state, not the church."

Ari had called for his mother every night when he was put to bed, but otherwise his caretakers kept him diverted. There were games, open play and lessons from the best of tutors in reading, writing, numbers, music and even dance. They clothed him in silks and fed him the finest foods, all the fresh fruits he wanted, sweet meats, cakes and puddings. They all called him the Little Prince and he began to call himself Prince Ari as well, playing at leading soldiers to battle and ordering executions of various miniature lead soldiers and stuffed animals.

Isabella tried to talk Ophelia out of it after they got the news of Ari's whereabouts. "Here he was all the time, in plain sight. He is at least well cared for it seems."

Ophelia hollow cheeks flushed slightly. "Perhaps he now has the life of a little prince that I could never give him."

Isabella removed a bonnet and puffed a stray hair from her eyes. "Or a lamb to be slaughtered at the whim of the Habsburgs."

"Or Fortinbras." Horatio entered the player's wagon where the two women sat going over costumes. Ophelia startled. Strange to see him in this context.

"You!" Ophelia pointed a finger close to his left eye. He drew back. "This was all your doing – scheming with the tyrant. You have become no better than they."

Horatio backed against the wooden side of the wagon, which, Ophelia realized provided only a little more space than her cell, yet had been home to her for so long. "Please, Lady Ophelia, I am committed only to you and your child, regardless of appearances."

"Oh! So, now it's '*lady*' Ophelia?"

Isabella interceded. "Faithful Horatio has proven himself our friend, since Genoa, Ophelia. He saved us from Antwerp, and now he is aiding your escape."

"To what end?" Ophelia eyed Horatio, and flushed when he returned her stare softly, without the old haughtiness.

"He could well hang along with the rest of us, Ophelia."

"We all are in the stew together, my lady." Horatio smiled.

Ophelia felt weak, suddenly, and sat down. "I need … water."

Isabella ladled some from a bucket into a cup and handed it to her. "You should have some sustenance too." She handed Ophelia a biscuit. "It's a bit stale, but all we have right now."

"A feast." Ophelia said, breaking off a piece and crunching it down. "You are all at my feast, and I thank you. Even you, Horatio."

Carlo entered, his face gray, heavy with the weight was everyone sensed would be bad news.

He bade Ophelia to sit down.

"Is it Ari?" She peered straight at him.

He tried to avoid her eyes. "Ari is gone. I don't know any other way to say it."

Ophelia sat, numb.

Isabella came and sat close. "Gone where? Do you mean gone from the palace? "

Carlo shook his head. "Gone."

Horatio tried to steer things away from Carlos ultimate implication. "Do you mean we have been wrong about Ari being kept in the palace?"

Carlo shook his head. "No. That part was true. I can confirm this now. The emperor and Katherina had been keeping Ari in the palace, out of the cardinal's clutches."

Ophelia looked down at the floor. "And now?" She spoke softly.

Carlo climbed onto a chair. "Gone. To put it bluntly, dead. Drowned by one of Spinola's assassins."

Ophelia sat frozen, eyes wide and unfocused.

Horatio stood tall, nearly banging his head on the roof of the wagon. "How do you know?"

"Jacopo Strada – Katharina's grandfather – told me in person, privately of course. He's close to the emperor."

"How could that have happened right under the emperor's nose?"

"The emperor has been sulking. The palace is in disarray. The assassin posed as a servant ..." Carlo swallowed hard and fought back tears. "The villain killed a nanny and took the boy while he napped."

Isabella took Ophelia's hand and looked over to Carlo. "You're sure? I can't believe this."

Carlo found his breath and continued: "Signor Strada told me that Katherina is distraught. The villain drowned our poor Ari in one of the emperor's garden ponds and got away."

Horatio shook his head. He sat on the other side of Ophelia and took her other hand, but she continued staring away.

Ophelia slumped against the wall of the wagon, all the color run out of her, eyes blank, brimming with tears, but refusing to give into the the wail she felt pushing up from her gut – for if she did she might never cease sobbing.

By Umberto Tosi

Katharina Strada, lifelong influential consort of Holy Roman Emperor Rudolf II, drawn by Giuseppe Archimboldo.

++++

68. HIDE AND SEEK

Jacopo Strada had the bright idea to take little Ari off his granddaughter Katherina Strada's hands and lodge the boy safely in the ghetto with the rabbi, the one place in Prague not rife with Vatican spies. And what safer spot there than the great rabbi Judah Lowe's household at its heart near the temple? "Once the deed is done, your majesty, I will spread a tragic story of the little prince's demise." Jacopo smiled to himself. "That should confound both Rome and Madrid and lessen thy concerns."

"Fortinbras will dance. This is what Cardinal Spinola promised." The emperor gazed out a window at his gardens in full spring bloom, his back to Jacopo.

"Fortinbras will be lulled," your majesty. "It will buy time for his enemies – for the family of Lord Brahe to rally their forces, then bring forth the new prince when they are ready to take back the Danish throne."

"How will we transport the little prince to Denmark, then, without undoing everything?"

"Leave that to me, your majesty."

Jacopo's daughter had entered the drawing room of the summer palace where they talked. She had a volume of poetry, but kept it tucked under one arm as she smiled to her father and took a seat by the window. The emperor turned from the window and smiled at his mistress, who amused him with a flirtatious toss of her hair and opened her book. "And to me, your majesty," she added.

"Our two favorite schemers," said the emperor.

"In fact, our little prince, is Ari no more." Katherina gave him a Cupid's-bow smirk. "... He is little Ariel now, and every bit as fetching in our daughter Lena's dresses. The rabbi's wife, Pearl will keep our secret, even from their own congregation.

++++

"A miracle child. True genius. Plays like an angel."

"Or one possessed by the devil."

"Such music is a gift from heaven," said the rabbi.

"Shh!" Pearl, the rabbi's tall, big-boned, ginger-and-white haired wife and made the Shabbat candles flicker with her shushing.

Ariel, in peach silk bonnet, blouse and skirts, stood upon a chair near the head of the table, sawing a simple, lively *kleyzmorim* tune on her fiddle.

"Extraordinary!"

Everyone around the rabbi's table clapped and cheered when Ariel finished, most heartily, the odd, giant, bearded man with the gold metal nose. She took an exaggerated bow just as little Ari had learned to do with the troupe, whether they had dressed him for boy's or girl's stage role. Ari didn't mind being Ariel. It was just another game. The rabbi and his wife had been gentle and kind to him and their children welcoming. Ari still missed his mother, just as he had through those months at the emperor's palace – her soft voice, her affection, her scent, but her face had begun to blur in his memory.

The esteemed Talmudic scholar and mystic – Rabbi Judah Loew – known among the Jews of Prague and even those of the emperor's court as "The Maharal" – regarded the small prodigy cheerfully, like a doting grandfather enjoying a family musicale.

"The Holy Spirit breathes through angelic grace of your playing, child." He seemed modest, even self-effacing and showed no sign of the mystical powers attributed to him. In any event, his esteemed guest was a man of science, natural philosophy, not impressed by myths and legends, only by the divine dance of stars and planets in the observable night sky.

The *rebbe* noticed that this guest – the wide, imposing, blond bearded man with the metallic nose next to him – was staring curiously at the fiddle, scaled to child's size. When Ariel finished, he took the instrument gently from the little girl and showed it to his guest. "You see. It is finer and lighter than the *lyra de bracio* – four instead of seven strings, more graceful, a richer tone."

The rabbi smiled through his voluminous beard and bowed his head slightly at Ariel, who had by now helped herself to a plump, sugar cookie, laced with almonds from a silver platter on the table.

"Let me see that." The man with the bronze, gold plated nose took the instrument, plucked its strings and listened intently to the vibration. "... and you say that this little girl picked up this fiddle and made heavenly music, just like that?"

"With uncanny speed. One of Yahweh's miracles." The rabbi clasped his hands together. "Little Ariel has been with us only a few weeks, but she watched the concert master playing at the Klaus School very intently, I am told. My wife let the child try this small fiddle, just so she could take instructions – even though she is a girl, because after all she is our special guest. The girl astounded everyone when she started playing almost immediately.

The man with the gilded nose turned the fiddle over, then peeked inside through its clefs. "Looks to be a fine Italian fiddle. From Emperor Rudolf's *Kunstkammer* collection, you say?"

429

"Donated to our music school. The latest design from Italy. They call these instruments, *violini*. This one of the first to be sized for a child by the famous luthier, Gasparo da Salò in Brescia.

It was meant as a gift from the Duke of Brescia to the emperor on the birth of another son, Ludwig. But the baby was born weak and died shortly – rest his innocent soul." The rabbi took the fiddle back in one bearish hand and gave it to his wife to replace in a leather case with the horsehair bow.

"Shall we talk business, Lord Tycho?

The man with the brass nose downed another crystal glass of dark red wine, and sighed. "I am more disposed to speak of the stars, the rains of Primavera seem determined to hide them from view for another week."

"Perhaps that is a good thing. The constellations have not been favorable, according to the emperor's astrologer. I foresee trouble for the ghetto – not because I have faith in such soothsaying, but because bad omens so often give certain ambitious priests cause to bring misfortune upon the Jews."

The man with the brass nose snorted. "Doesn't take a wizard to predict trouble for the Jews at any point, rabbi."

The rabbi nodded and gazed distantly at Tycho's drained glass. A servant girl refilled it.

The rabbi cleared his throat. "My lord, I would never presume to put astrologers on a plane with you. Lord Brahe. Your countless astronomical measurements and treatises – your amazing discovery of a new star – have spread your fame far and wide as a titan of the new knowledge. You have revealed to us a universe of stars being born, confounding scholars and overturning Aristotle. You make fools of lowly astrologers..."

"And earned me enemies as well, Rabbi."

"Science is a ladder to the eternal truths of the Torah, my friend."

"It could be a ladder to the gallows, if things continue as they have been in my homeland and this usurper king Fortinbras isn't checked. I am not in his favor of late. No longer do I enjoy the largess of King Hamlet, or that I had from his late brother, King Claudius. Fortinbras seeks only our gold for his wars."

"Shall I take that as a sign that you will be accepting the invitation that our Emperor Rudolf has extended for you to establish your observatory and publish your findings here in Prague?" The rabbi put a finger to his lips. "Of course, I ask in the utmost confidence."

The metal-nosed man gazed off along the wide table, set with finest linen, the Shabbat meal over, prayers said, with welcoming nods to him, as the rabbi's special guest – one of many Christians the rabbi had entertained often, as he had himself feasted at the emperor's table, participating in learned discourse with some of the empire's greatest minds – including, during the last fortnight, this mountain of a man, prone to inspired, bottomless drunkenness and spontaneous, bawdy bluntness.

Lord Tycho Brahe, himself a fabulously wealthy nobleman of Denmark, from one of that kingdom's most powerful families, owner of vast lands, including the entire island of Hven, given him by the crown, where, they say, he had built the world's most elaborate observatory. How could it come to pass that he would consider leaving it all, abandoning his homeland for Prague?

The rabbi observed that the great astronomer had been on his best behavior throughout this evening, however, and surmised that for all the good will, his guest might by now have become a little restless.

The rabbi's wife, meanwhile, picked up Ariel, and announced the child's bedtime. "Good night Mr. Gold Nose," Ariel waved at Tycho with both hands clutching cookies, spilling crumbs on Pearl's shoulder as she carried him from the room.

Tycho howled with laughter. Then, without hesitation, as soon as a servant followed Pearl out of the dinning room and closed the door, he turned to the rabbi, his brow knitted, face darkly close so that the rabbi smelled wine breath. "They're out to kill you all, you know," he said. "You should take warning."

The rabbi sat back in his chair. "Yes. I am aware of certain threats."

"Do not be so calm, rabbi. Forget the stars, the movements of priests and plotters in Prague Castle is what to watch."

"You have something new to tell me then, my lord?"

"Beware. Rome and Madrid conspire with Fortinbras now, to forge a new alliance, and they will not let anything stand in their way – certainly not a little fiddler dressed as a girl. Certainly not a Jew, nor even a Danish astronomer."

"I have my connections too, Lord Tycho. I see many signs. Your 'Emperor' Fortinbras called his emissary Horatio back to Denmark – where he will likely face the king's executioner because of his sympathies with your rebellious Danish lords."

"...Beware of Cardinal Spinola – one of the inquisitors of Flanders. He is in Prague at the behest of the Holy See – and probably with the support of King Philip. Even Emperor Rudolf may not be able to protect you."

"More likely, as you have observed, the emperor has withdrawn again from state affairs, deep into his melancholy."

"Careful, rabbi, such talk could land you in the tower."

"My outspokenness is a measure of my trust in you, my lord."

"And in my trust of you, rabbi, I can inform you that my wife and I depart home for Denmark in two days and are ready to take the child with us."

"Meaning that your uncle has made ready to go against Fortinbras?"

Tycho nodded. The child will be kept safe from the fighting, but we need to raise our banners now to a new king. Would that his poor mother still lived to see this.

"We know." The rabbi shook his head. "Died in the castle prison, I am afraid – against the emperor's orders – and despite our prayers."

"Does the child know?"

"We will have to leave that unhappy task to you and your wife, Lord Brahe."

The rabbi's wife returned, having put the children to bed.

Tycho rose, bowed slightly to her then sat back down. "I send a carriage tomorrow. Will you and Madame Loew please have the child ready to depart?"

The rabbi looked sad. His wife spoke up. "Yes, my lord – and I pray for your safe journey home." She paused, her voice quavering. "Our family has been happy for Ariel's sweet presence."

Tycho nodded. "I can imagine." Then he cleared his throat. "Although, given the circumstances, it seems I have come for the child not a moment too soon."

The rabbi tilted his head. "How is that?"

"While you pray, rabbi, both be watchful. I have other news that I must convey – with reluctance."

The rabbi looked up. "What say you, my lord?"

"The papal nuncio is up to new mischief. This on behalf of the bankers in Genoa…"

"That would not be new."

"You are aware that King Philip is deep in debt to these bankers?"

"Yes. And King Philip owes my uncle, Isaac ben Chaim, twenty million escudos of gold, borrowed for his war in Flanders..."

"Cardinal Spinola has been spreading slander about..."

"Let me guess. The Jews."

"Yes. You have heard?"

Rabbi Judah Lowe bowed his head and said softly, as if to himself. "The blood libel. It begins again."

Tycho downed another draft of wine, and stitched his eyebrows at the rabbi quizzically."

"The blood libel has happened in Prague before – thirty years ago. I was still a boy in Poznan."

"What happened? I can guess – an expulsion."

"Worse. Another ambitious Vatican nuncio – Thaddeus – at that time spread the blood libel from his pulpit St. Vitus. He accused the Jews of abducting Christian children and draining their blood to make matzos for the Pesach. It is an old lie, and, of course preposterous. We would never commit such a heinous crime. And besides, matzos must be made only with water and flour. The child of a nobleman had gone missing at that time... a convenience for this monster to whip Christians mobs into a frenzy."

Tycho raised both hands – "I see the connection that Cardinal Spinola could be trying to make with what he thinks is the death of Prince Ari."

"Yes. Thaddeus got then Emperor Maximilian to issue an edict confiscating all Hebrew books from the ghetto to examine them for cryptic messages. Then the soldiers come to expel us from the Ghetto, followed by the mobs. They killed thousands of men, women and children, looted the ghetto of all its wealth and set fire to our houses."

Tycho finished his wine and rose to leave. "I understand the Cardinal's financial motives well. By this slander, he means to get King Philip's debt to your uncle dissolved amid the chaos sure to ensue here. That will benefit Madrid's other creditors, including his own brother in Genoa."

The rabbi rose – seeming almost to levitate so that Tycho shook his head and looked to his cup of wine. "Not this time, my lord. I have made preparations..."

"How..."

"I best not say, even to you..."

"Perhaps the emperor can intercede?"

"Oh, he *will* intercede... of that I am certain."

"But his mood. He has not left his summer house since the solstice, doing God knows what."

"That will be fine. I am sending him a unique visitor that will be sure to get his attention..."

"I would hope so... But the child? Is that why you invited me to this Shabbat, and let me see the little prince – princess – fiddle – while your Ghetto is about to burn."

"I always value your company, Lord Brahe. But this time, I do ask the favor, that you and your charming wife, Kristen, take the child, with you – along with your own six children... on the riverboat when you make your return to Denmark. For the little princess' safety and our own."

"Denmark? But. You know that my father and uncle soon may move against Fortinbras?"

"Little Ariel will be safer there with your knights right under Fortinbras' nose than here in Prague. I guarantee you that."

"And when do you propose this?"

"Now. After the child goes to sleep. My wife has everything packed.... She is with your wife now."

The rabbi sank into reverie as Tycho consumed yet another flagon – having switched to a stout Bohemian beer. Then he opened his eyes and moved back to his chair at the head of the table where Ariel had been playing.

"In the cabala, there is wisdom – not always in action – often in no action – in seeking the light behind the light, the light of dreams and other worlds."

"I believe only in the lights I see – countless – in the skies, mysteries of the divine that shine from the dark heavens, telling me their stories each night, patient for my humble understanding."

"This too is the wisdom of waiting."

"We must spread a story – that the little prince has met an untimely end, my friend. Let Fortinbras believe he has won. Let the papal schemers and Madrid's minions drink the wine, laced with their own foolish pride, and when they are sufficiently intoxicated with hubris, seeing nothing but their vain reflections, then it will be your time, Lord Brahe, and that of your men to move – and succeed."

Vladislav Hall in Prague Castle, drawn by Aegidus Sadeler.

####

69. VLADISLAV HALL

*(**AUTHOR'S NOTE:** It is known that Ophelia encrypted many of her letters and journal entries. She became adept with the codes of her day, including use of twin, cypher-engraved copper disks – a technique invented by fifteenth-century Genoa humanist architect Leon Battista Alberti in wide use among royal emissaries, messengers, agents, merchants and military commanders during her time.*

Most Ophelia scholars believe she acquired her encryption skill from Pieter Orneck of Breda, her lover and late fiancée, with whom she worked undercover for the Dutch rebels during her time in Flanders, and probably fled Breda with the necessary copper disks after his assassination.

The disks were thought lost until recently when they were discovered among other Ophelia paraphernalia at a flea market in Arhaus by a Danish cheese maker and amateur historian named Søren Wausau. It is not clear for whom Ophelia had intended the decoder disk, or if she ever shared it, but Waamaus loaned the priceless disks to the nonprofit, Ophelia Historical Society in Copenhagen, which set a cryptographer to work on papers in their archive, along with translators. I extend my appreciation to Hilda Hansagaard for her help in obtaining and decrypting these precious documents. Thanks to this help, I have been able to piece together the following mosaic largely in Ophelia's own words of what is considered the most critical period of her life in exile.)

++++

Chatter echoing as I mingle, every day, the same:
"Five gold pieces for that fake?"
"She was a whore... What more need I say?"
"He had it coming."

438

*"Papal nuncios will make the emperor's magic
circle a ring of fire."*

"He conjures Dr. Faustus' devil ..."

"You mean the blood red cardinal..."

*"It is auspicious. "The sun and moon are in
Taurus...*

"Venus is in the house of ..."

"... nuns.., To that I can attest... "

"Again, Flavio, you rogue?"

*"Every night, I enter – as a washerwoman to pick
up linens, and I do three nuns before dawn, or before
the abbess sounds the bell and sends me running,
skirts hiked to my hips. T'was a moonless night it was
that saved me last time"*

*"Silks from China, the finest, of a thousand
designs..."*

"My word: This is genuine ..."

"Porcelain from Amsterdam ..."

"Poppy bulbs from Asia Minor..."

*"The stench of these Old Towners could drive the
Turks back to Istanbul."*

"Katharina Strada is expecting again ..."

"Kroll has discovered the Philosopher's Stone."

"With it Rudolf will rule the world..."

"Or himself – transcending the world..."

"He rules a kingdom but is slave to his moods."

"As are we all?"

So goes the daily fugue of Vladislav Hall, echoing
through its vastness, off its vaulted ceiling on the days
of public fair during which I ply my murky trades.

It is an airy place, tall enough to grow a forest
within it, cavernous enough to accommodate knights
jousting on horseback during festivals.

The hall, a wonder of the age, is a cathedral to commerce, perched atop Hradčany Castle hill, flanked by towers, churches, palaces, observatories, alchemist workshops, squares and gardens that look out over Prague's wide silvery Vltava River.

No one knows I am Ophelia. No one knows Olivia. Those carefully chose few with whom I speak at all, know me only as Oliver Curry– an itinerant Irish vagabond offering discreetly bagged herbs, seeds and other assorted flora from nearby Bohemian forests – magical, curative, poisonous, decorative. (I do not inquire as to their ultimate use. But I assure their purity and most of all, their efficacy.)

Every morning at first light, I leave my humble sleeping quarters and thread the narrow cobblestone streets of the Lessor Quarter along with men who toil at the foundry and women who spin, sew and sell flowers. I walk, keeping to myself, among carpenters, masons, printers, glazers, street vendors, smiths, sweepers, scavengers, thieves and haulers. We seem like an army of the dead summoned forth to tidy things up at world's end. I've saved enough to buy a horse, but don't want to stand out.

I cross the wood-covered Powder Bridge with its rectangular piers. I can feel the river moving beneath, and hear it – siren like – calling my soul, calling Ophelia, but Ophelia is long dead. Her body marches onward, taking practiced, stolid male strides. Oliver is seasoned now, more wily, no longer the brash youth exploring Antwerp, driving his wagon by vineyards and the fields of lavender around Lyon.

Once I traverse the bridge, I see the great towers, spires, pinnacles and walls of Prague Castle looming from Hradčany Hill across the river, regal, imposing, a citadel on its summit, ruling the city and the empire.

This is my Sonia Castle now – of stone, brick and mortar. Prague Castle stands mighty, not of sand, a citadel of power, as I am reminded passing through the main gate straddled by two bronze giants wielding cudgels the size of trees.

Its towers and spires remind me of my childhood dream castle in the dawn's glow, but fleshy and muscular like the deities of Franz Floris' giant Feast of the Gods panel I remember from the palace of a merchant prince of Antwerp.

Hradčany beckons me – a castle of my darkest dreams – teaming with schemers, soldiers, killers – the ambitious, avaricious and the powerful, bloody prelates and cold eyed administrators who run the empire while Rudolf plays its capricious gods. I love the Hradčany dreams and hate its tyrant.

Reaching the other side, I climb the steep stairways up to the gates of the Northern Wing and enter the castle grounds. The sentries look bored – country boys in ornamented silver plated helmets and breastplates etched with the Golden Fleece, symbol of the Habsburgs.

They know me by now – or think they do – and barely check as they stroll past the flat-topped Bishop's Tower from where astronomers depart wearily after star gazing through the night, leaving their notes to the mathematicians who buzz over the measurement all day like worker bees.

Then I pass Powder House, where the alchemists and their assistants toil in the laboratories intent not so much on making gold (Emperor Rudolf has plenty of that) but of finding the Philosopher's Stone and with it the secrets of uniting worlds above and below in immortality.

I keep an eye out for one particular seeker – the Oswald Kroll, with his dreamy eyes, German face and long, pensive drooping blond mustache. He is my best customer for exotic plants, although through intermediaries that I hope to bypass soon. He is chief alchemist and physician to the emperor – and, I hope soon my entrée to the royal sanctum.

Every morning, looking up, I am fascinated in spite of myself. Prague Castle is both adversary and dangerous lover – nothing like my Sonia of sand, love and adolescent longings, except in its towering silhouette.

Late spring now – the women wear garlands on fair days, brightening Vladislav hall – be they merchant wives, maidens, harlots, peasants or peers. The men sport rings of roses round the crown of their hats – unaware pagans all, and glad to down the first steins of spring beer to revel, as did their ancestors before Christendom.

I have lost track of the days, and of how long I wandered, blind with tears, trackless, fighting, thieving, risking without thought. Seasons have turned. Has it been a year? Is it two? Three?

Isabella and Carlo could no longer stay. Venice called them home – for May festivals, by invitation of the doge that could not be refused. They pleaded with me to come with them, even though Ophelia, ragged and pinched, no longer served them well in the roles she had played. I walked away. I know they cried for me.

In the blackness of new moons, I transformed to this incarnation – no longer a stage presence or a simple disguise. I am a scarred, death-visited soldier returned from the bloody fields, containing all the screams and horrors, released nightly in nightmares and drunken outings till finally numbness arrives, welcomed.

Purveying herbs for physicians, magicians and quacks is not the most lucrative of my trades, however, only the most useful, allowing me entry regular enough so that the emperor's guards, as well as papal, Ottoman, Spanish, Italian and other spies pay me little mind. This allows me freedom to practice my most rewarding art, with fine skill well learned on the road, if I do say so – picking pockets and purses.

Third – least lucrative, most secret and darkest of my arts – call it also a mission – is to be that of assassin – changer of the fate of a king who altered mine so brutally. Vengeance will be mine, for it is fallow and I see no smiting God to do this work.

Priests and philosophers say that at death the immortal soul leaves the body. But I have it the other way around. The soul can die, and still the body carries on, heart pumping, breathing, feeding itself, drinking, farting, shitting, peeing – with that I must take care to be in private. This body makes its way in the world on its own, as if it had no past or future, ignoring that my soul perished of grief with the murder of my son, as might that of any mother.

Now I am no longer mother, nor am I maiden, never a wife, nor nun, Madonna or whore, princess or peasant – actor perhaps. That I mastered. Looking back, I have never been what was expected of me – not at Elsinore, not in the wider world. Isabella knew me, but few others.

She knew I could be my truest self playing many roles, but never one. Now, with Ari gone, I have let all that go. I play only this one role – a vengeful Oliver. I cannot be even what I expected of myself, much less, what others expect of a fine young woman.

Now I am no woman at all. I am leaner, still tall and sinewy, my body relentlessly recovered from my ordeals, scarred here and there, to be sure.

People see a blond young man, in the latest cap, pantaloons, doublet and cape – not too fancy, mind you, simply enough to connote some degree of rank – useful for gaining entries and privileges – and, of course, always in black.

They never see my raven amulet, hanging inside my shirt on its gold chain. I still wear it, a memento of Prince Hamlet, dead like me now, except that I still have a body. I probably have become too boyish to attract his lustful attention. I rarely see his ghost now, so I cannot ask him.

My blood, my churning stomach, well muscled – risen from the dead. I am a fearless, iron body, returned from a gray grave of grief and feel nothing – except rage. And like many a Prague squire, I am well armed – dagger, sword, hidden pistol, not to mention the vials of snake venom, toadstool extract and – my favorite from Elsinore days – distillate of yellow henbane.

One of these potions, on one of these days – I am determined to deliver with secret deadly effect to our great emperor – tried and convicted by my vengeful heart of infanticide – the abduction and murder of my baby boy, my torture and imprisonment, none of this done by his own corpulent manicured hand, but ordered by it I am sure.

I will take a poison draft as well. The irony of ending my life like Prince Hamlet, with regicide and death by poison is not lost on me. I understand the madness of my gentle prince now and how the furies possessed him despite all his efforts.

And it is this fury, not fear of the executioner's white hot pincers that motivates my suicidal intentions. I drink my own venom so as to follow the debauched tyrant to the other side – to hell if necessary – and give him no rest even in death – if perchance that other shore exists at all. Only then will my vengeance be complete.

70. THE MAGIC CIRCLE

"...Come, you spirits
That tend on mortal thoughts, unsex me here,
And fill me, from the crown to the toe, top full
Of direst cruelty!"

I remember those lines from a play-in-progress by a young English actor who joined our troupe briefly in Antwerp before moving on. Will ... something, he called himself, quick of wit and a terrible flirt; don't recall his last name. The lines chilled me in Antwerp, but provided a perfect sheath for the bloody dagger that was my state of mind during those days in Prague.

Ari appeared to me in a dream last night. I had not dreamed of him for a very long time. He is still four years old, but by now he would be on his way to becoming a lanky, straw-haired, mischievous lad, like the pages I see running about Vladislav Hall delivering messages to the courtiers and merchants.

My dream was one of those so vivid that it makes waking life seem a somnambulistic afterwards. Ari sat astride an elk in a castle corridor, looking at ease. The elk gazed at me like a tree in its way, pursing its sensuous lips, tilting its great antlers, awaiting my utterances.

Instead, my Ari spoke in the voice of that older boy, in the half-man sonority of preadolescence trying to seem grown up. I could not decipher his words, only that he was speaking to me. Yet I saw him still a babe in appearance, only bigger. Or was the elk a miniature? Above us, a dome opened revealing a million stars. Ari gazed up at them, then back to me.

My Ari in black tights, tunic and cap, a miniature of his father –- resembling the boy Hamlet of my own childhood memories. My Ari's words filtered into my mind at last. He told me that he had commissioned the stars to watch over me, and that I must listen to them.

"And, I am not?" I questioned him.

"Shadows, mama. Shadows," was all he answered. "Beware of shadows."

He gave me a rose. He said it all, matter of fact, like he was telling his mommy that an aunt had taken him to the seashore for the day.

I awoke bereft. I felt anger too – at this dream that brought me illusion followed by death of loss upon awakening. I steadied myself. No distractions. This was the day, I would finally gain entry to the palace, thanks to Aegidius and his best friend, with whom I now shared a bed.

I hear Aegidius downstairs banging pots and pans in Spranger's kitchen. They don't keep servants, but Aegidius has a lover – a boy from Bremen who seems happMinerva y to help around the house.

The house belongs to Bartholomeus Spranger, court painter to the emperor at the moment. It is a creaky, awkward Baroque conversion of an old Gothic mansion that perches like an old man on a cliff overlooking the Vltava River, just outside Prague castle walls. I find it convenient. Too many nosy neighbors were beginning to ask questions around my rooms in Old Town.

Besides being an old friend, Aegidius has an arrangement with Spranger for room and board in return for selling prints of Spranger's work on the days of fair in Vladislav Hall. Profits are modest, but it spreads Spranger's fame far and wide, for this is a city constantly visited by merchants, peers, priests, bankers, diplomats and military satraps.

I pay no rent. Spranger, immediately smitten – I could see, when Aegidius brought me to dinner – begged me to pose for his latest opus major – a large canvas he called "Minerva Triumphs Over Ignorance." I get to stand, semi nude, in armor and silks, on the prone back of a handsome, muscled, naked soldier Spranger has hired. It suits my mood. Would that I could so prevail over the ignorant, though the soldier model, actually proved to be a rather cultivated young man from Mantua.

Spranger populates the canvas with angels and spectators already drawn in. One thing has led to another.

This was a special day, as I said, but I wanted it to seem ordinary, like so many others when I would dress as Oliver again – my two companions thought this a delightful game, willing kept secret.

I slipped from the sheets silently to wash myself and dress, leaving Spranger asleep on the other side of the the wide bed we had been sharing some weeks now. I don't love him – perhaps I will never love another – but he is passionate and attentive, and seems to worship me in our intimate moments as if I really were his Minerva – Athene to his wandering Odysseus.

He said he wanted me to pose for a new work after this, in fact – as Omphale, Queen of Lydia, who kept mighty Hercules as her slave for a year, in payment for the hero's accidental slaying of one of her servants. I would be attired only in Hercules lion skin, carrying his cudgel, while our Hercules model would be wear naught but a filmy feminine nightdress, true to the Greek myth.

Spranger seems fixated on this legend, and when he doesn't call me Athene, he calls me Omphale.

He reads me one history of the legend that says, in fact, that the Hercules and the Amazon Queen Omphale fell in love during this year, and remained together, having children. I would enjoy that – I tease him – but "no children! Find a cow and impregnate her."

++++

I didn't plan it this way. I thought I would gain entry to the emperor's palace rooms through the physician alchemist, Oswald Kroll, to whom I had been supplying herbs at the little stand I managed to share with a perfume vendor at the great hall. But Kroll has not been seen for weeks now and is rumored to be in the Russia acquiring gemstones for the emperor's other alchemists to grind to powder.

My excitement grew when Bartholomeus announced that the emperor had appointed him *valet de chambre* – in addition to being court painter, putting my lover in charge of His Majesty's vast art collection as a personal secretary.

I started plotting to use this connection for access.

The more I thought about this, however, the more troubled I felt. My new friends could end up on the gallows if anyone suspected them of colluding with me in this plot.

Meanwhile, Aegidius provided me an immediate opportunity to scout the emperor's chambers, if not to do the deed as yet. Aegidius had just finished an ambitious, elaborate drawing of Vladislav Hall. I watched him working on this large drawing for weeks while I did my business at the hall.

It was the reason we met again, here in Prague, in fact. Every day, as I made my rounds of the hall, I would see him working on it as an easel near his vending table. He would watch for hours, sketching every person and detail. I tried to stay out of his direct line of vision. But eventually he noticed me.

Our eyes locked. He stared at me quizzically at first, regarding this familiar looking fellow in black. When he walked up close, I saw his eyes fix on my raven pendant, then light up in recognition.

"Olivia?" I nearly pushed him into the crowd and stabbed him right there.

"Do I know you, sir." I arched my eyebrows and rested one hand firmly on the hilt of my sword.

"Oh." He tilted his head. He winked so subtly I almost missed it. "Of course. Pardon me."

I started to walk away.

"Wait, please *'sir'*," he said. "May I please sketch you, *sir,* for my *opus magnum?* I would pay." He did have a generous commission for the work.

We danced around, playacting a few days. Then we talked in private and reminisced about Antwerp. He had taught me a lot about drawing and etching, after all... and I had always liked him – a young man I could trust not to make advances. Fortunio and he had become lovers then, making him a part of our player family for a short while.

My playing the role of Oliver hardly surprised him. Aegidius recalled my male and female role playing very well, and had become an ardent attendee to our Comici shows...

We met often during the weeks that followed. I had always trusted him, remembering his courage in helping Vola and I during the Antwerp mutiny massacre.

I told Aegidius my secrets, perhaps foolishly, but with relief in the telling as well. He told me of his adventures since Antwerp – including many narrow escapes.

"To live is to lose, as well as gain. By age twelve, I had lost all my seven brothers and sisters and my father to plague.

My mother survives to this day and hates me for being on this earth instead of those she loved better, yet I pay to keep her in comfort at St. George's, while I remain a precarious boarder."

Aegidius always had a flare for the drama. I asked him to join our troupe in Antwerp. He didn't get that I was teasing him and I let it go.

"I have a friend, I want you to meet," he told me one day after we both had finished our work at Vladislav Hall. "He is well connected to the emperor's court, and a favorite of Rudolf himself."

My ears perked up.

"Not that influence would be a sole reason to meet him, knowing you, Olivia."

"Oliver." I corrected him.

"Oliver... yes. He is a charming, brilliant and if I must say, handsome fellow."

"You like him?"

"Not in that way. But you might."

"Who is this 'prince' you think will sweep me off my feet and make me wear a dress?"

"You know his name from the etchings I sell at Vladislav Hall – and most likely from the fame that precedes him."

"I like the etchings... but fame does not impress me."

"Bartholomeus Spranger. I told him about you..."

"What?" I nearly pushed him almost off our path.

"He is very trustworthy. Don't worry. He needs a model and you are perfect. He has invited you to dine at his palace."

"A palace?"

"You could call it that."

71. A VENOMOUS DAGGER

I stared at the brass knocker on the heavy walnut, arching chamber door. It is the size of small squash, and curving to fit the hand. Grasping it, my hand caresses the well worn naked brass buttocks of a comely woman kneeling in the act fellatio on an old man who – to those who have seen certain paintings, as have I – faintly resembles Pope Sixtus V.

This is the door to the inner sanctum of a monarch who must have has a sense of humor, I thought, in spite of myself. To get in there, Aegidius led me first through the formal rooms up long flights of stairs from Vladislav Hall's cavernous meeting space. Playing Virgil to my Dante, Aegidius kept me informed. Here, he said, *sotto voce*, as we passed into a high chamber lined with tall regal chairs and a bank of hardwood desks – all carved ornately – is where the governor general – Gustav Bierchek, a Vatican loyalist – meets with his deputies and conducts the everyday business of Rudolf's Holy Roman realm. "His Majesty, meanwhile, pursues knowledge on a higher plane, while indulging in carnal delights appropriate to a Caesar."

The chamber was empty except for the clerk who examined our papers and let us pass – and the guards, who were everywhere, discreetly positioned. I dispensed with my sword, but brought my dagger, hidden on my person with the venomous vials I planned to use if the opportunity presented itself. I tried to picture how I would get close enough to the emperor to do any harm, much less poison the monarch. It seemed highly unlikely we would be invited to the emperor's table, at least not on this visit.

But there was always Spranger. Soon, I hoped, I could come and go with him – but as Oliver, or Olivia? I would have to work that out. Spranger liked the show of it. It was a little game we would play after I would arrive at his house as Oliver, then peel off my male attire while he watched in our boudoir, revealing my "secrets." But how well would he go along with this in public – before watchful eyes at the palace where he had so much at stake?

This was the first time the thought came to me that I might not be able to do what I so passionately intended. This would not be like that day in the woods outside of Breda, when I stabbed the life from that attacker. I was in a fury then, defending my child. But am I capable of 'murder most foul' – even in my cold blooded state?

Thus conscience doth make cowards of us all.

"I am no coward, my lord. But I am no fool either." I had neither seen nor heard from my long dead prince since my incarceration. But there he was again, floating in the throne room of Elsinore. I tried in vain to wake out of this dream.

I will admit you are more man of action that ever was I, fair Ophelia.

"You keep your tongue and dagger sharp even in death, I see."

I come to caution you, Ophelia. Consider ...

"I am beyond cautions, and – as you well know – dithering only delays what is fated."

Do not presume to speak for fate, Ophelia. Your grief and anger are blind and make poor guides. Look to your better judgment, then by all means act.

At this point the prince did that annoying business of turning translucent and disappearing. But this time the Emperor Rudolf appeared in his place, looking pleasantly paunchy, his Habsburg high forehead furrowed and lower lip pouty.

He sat on a white stallion like in those heroic paintings, and riding next to him, laughing, sat Ari, astride that elk again.

"Follow us," they said in odd unison, riding off. I tried to follow but my legs were mired in sand, and I awoke, perspiring, in a tangle of Bartholomeus' silk sheets. A fair morning light filtered through the drapes illuminating my lover sitting cross-legged at the foot of the bed, gazing at me, as if about to sketch me yet again.

"Ah, my Omphale awakens!"

I lay back and stared up at the vaulted ceiling, silent.

Thus began this, the first day I would be allowed to venture into the chambers of the world's most powerful, and enigmatic monarch – the first of many, the first of a journey – like all of my days since Elsinore – of unimagined revelations.

72. HIS MAJESTY'S SINS

To: His Holiness, Pope Clement VIII,
Vicar of Christ on Earth,
Supreme Pontiff of Rome
  and the Holy Roman Catholic Church
From: Cardinal Abaga Oneglia Spinola.
 Congregatio pro Doctrina Fidei, C.D.F.,
  Apostolic Nuncio to Prague and Bohemia

Regarding:
  His Majesty Rudolf II,
   of the House of Habsburg,
   King of Bohemia,
   Archduke of Austria,
   King of Hungary and Croatia,
   King of the German States, and
   Emperor of the Holy Roman Empire.

Sent 12 Maggio, 1584 anno Dominus
via Pontifical Swiss Guard Courier, encrypted,
  for His Holiness only.

Your Holiness:
It is with the great regret that I submit this vexing,
yet critically vital report on the situation here in
Prague.
Firstly: On the subject of His Majesty's person.
I feel compelled to state, with due respect, that
supreme monarch of this great empire has abdicated
from his Divine right to rule. Put simply, Emperor
Rudolf II has abandoned God's Church on Earth.
His majesty neither speaks nor writes of God, nor
does he suffer any icons or sign of Christ, God the
Father and the Holy Trinity in his presence, other than
those in his vaunted art collection.

His Majesty shuns church services, processions and ceremonies, even on holy days. His Majesty curses the clergy and the faithful habitually, according to his courtiers.

Instead of our Holy Bible, His Majesty studies and discusses forbidden pagan texts incessantly – translations of ancient Greek, Egyptian, Persian and Arabic writings, the Cabala, the Emerald Tablet of Hermes Trimegistis and other writings listed in the Vatican Index.

His majesty neglects affairs of state. The emperor consults with magicians, alchemists, astronomers, philosophers, heretics, even infidels of every sort instead of ecclesiastic advisors.

If Your Holiness will pardon my frankness – His Majesty also cavorts with harlots and concubines at his palatial baths. His Majesty indulges in excesses of the mind as well as the body. The emperor grants audiences to dangerous heretics and infidels for lengthy colloquy – including Giordano Bruno, John Dee and Michael Sendivogius. His majesty's doors are open to our enemies – even those who advise Queen Elizabeth of England and the Protestant princes, while remaining closed to men of the cloth, including this Papal Nuncio and his staff.

While I have kept His Holiness informed about the emperor's abandonment of the faith over these past months – as well as King Rudolf's questionable mental state – matters have reached a critical juncture. His majesty's depredations no longer can be tolerated as merely objectionable regal self-indulgences. The emperor now acts upon his heretical beliefs and is taking actions of state that threaten the vital interest of our Holy Church and the Sacred Alliance of Rome that Your Holiness has built with great effort ...

++++

455

"Wait a moment, Tullio." The cardinal held up a pale hand.

Tullio stopped reading the letter aloud and laid it on the marble-topped table where he sat with his superior.

"Do my words sound too lurid, too accusatory?"

Tullio cleared his throat. "The situation, as you say, Your Eminence, is grave, and calls for strong language ..."

"And actions! Proceed, Tullio." The cardinal sat back in his customary, red-velvet-lined mahogany chair in Prague nuncio's palatial residence in St. George's Abbey adjoining St. Vitus' Cathedral.

Tullio read onward in his reedy voice – enumerating more of the emperor's reputed sins and listing new allegations.

++++

" ... *His Majesty pretends to respect Your Holiness' and the interests of the church, while working to undermine them. His diplomatic emissaries conduct official business as usual. His majesty gives lip service to the Holy Alliance of Catholic Kingdoms, Principalities and Nations to Expiriate All Heresy, as Your Holiness urges.*

"*Covertly, however, Emperor Rudolf sends members of his 'magic circle' of artists, writers, alchemists and physicians to the courts of both Catholic and Protestant rulers – ostensibly to exchange art and learning, but secretly to persuade them to join a new alliance he envisions. This new alliance is to be united by the Hermetic principle – the heresy of a single, true divinity underlying all sects and religions, given by God – a basis for making common cause in pursuit of knowledge and the secrets of nature, the Philosopher's Stone granting eternal youth and enlightenment – tantamount to devil worship.*

"Your Holiness! This is an unprecedented, worldly blasphemy that threatens the power of Christ's Church on Earth, as well as that of Rome's staunchest allies – including Emperor Rudolf's own cousin, Philip II of Spain. Respectfully, I submit, Your Holiness, that it is time to act decisively and end this emperor's misrule once and for all!"

++++

The cardinal slapped the table top. "This drunken emperor means to ruin the church, and even the empire of his cousin, Philip of Spain that has supported us so staunchly in Flanders and against the Protestant English.... He must be stopped!"

"I have faith in Your Eminence to do this," Tullio bowed his tonsured head in the cardinal's direction. He smelled victory.

"This will be our triumph, Tullio. Pope Clement is in failing health. Who knows, after this victory, we could well be next to sit upon the Throne of St. Peter!"

Tullio nodded, as he always did, obsequious smile painted on his face. He separated blank pages from those already written, adjusted the dangling sleeves of his black monk's habit, and sat forward, quill and ink at the ready. "How does His Eminence wish to proceed?"

Cardinal Spinola stood, pushed back his chair and moved about the chamber, murmuring as if reciting breviary to himself.

"Now comes the delicate part, Tullio." He walked to the curtains and the door, making sure all was secure. He lowered his voice. Tullio put down his quill and bent to listen. "We need to inform His Holiness about the little Danish prince, placing the blame squarely on the Emperor, and avoiding any hint of failure on our part."

"Yes, your eminence. And His Majesty is, in fact, solely to blame. We could not have known, nor prevented his taking the child under his person protection, nor spreading word that the boy had died."

The cardinal sat back down at the table and fumed. "A lie that we believed and told to His Holiness, come to find out now that the boy is alive!"

Tullio cleared his throat. "May I make a suggestion, Your eminence?"

"Please do."

"We should inform His Holiness exactly in that way – as another deception by the emperor, part of His Majesty's plan to subvert the church."

"Quite so, Tullio. And that strengthens our case for action."

Tullio set one sheet aside and made notes.

"Word this carefully, Tullio, without specification to His Holiness, only to signal to him that we have set the inevitable in motion. The emperor will appear to die of natural causes. This has been arranged through the agent we have placed among his valets."

"The friar, Boniglio?"

"Yes. The monsignor at St. Vitus arranged for him to be installed as our special friend in the palace more than a year ago. He is one of Emperor Rudolf's *valets de chambre*. The emperor likes his wine and beers. And he takes soporifics for chronic insomnia. When the soporifics do their work, our friar will do his work – administer a poison that will make it appear as if the Emperor died in his sleep due to his chronic ill health."

"The preparation has been distilled, Your Eminence – concentrate of henbane."

The cardinal nodded. And Friar Boniglio is to be eliminated quietly at the monastery upon completion of his task, by the way. No, no! Do not note that down. You already have your instructions."

Tullio put down the quill, his face blanched. Then his smile returned. "The vial of poison in the ear – an ironic touch. If the emperor's physicians do discover that His Majesty was poisoned, it will be blamed upon Danish spies."

"Shall I add anything more to His Eminence's letter about the succession to Emperor Rudolf once the deed is done?"

"Yes. Thank you, Tullio. Assure His Holiness that the rules of imperial succession favor us. The governor general will take power." The cardinal referred to the likelihood that Archduke Gustav Bierchek – governor general of Bohemia – and a most reliable Roman Catholic – would take power as regent of the Holy Roman Empire the moment Emperor Rudolf met his untimely end. This was due to the incapacity of Rudolf's eldest son, Julius – raving mad – whom the emperor and Katherina had locked away in an asylum after the raging prince butchered his mistress – daughter of a prominent merchant.

Tullio's eyes brightened at the cardinal's reference to royal scandal. "His Holiness will joyful. God blesses his holy church in strange ways sometimes!"

"Only one piece of our puzzle to be put in place now, Tullio." The cardinal frowned and gave his factotum a hard stare. "The Danish pretender – the boy, Ari, who slipped from our grasp due to the emperor's duplicity: We must find and dispose of him once and for all.

"Yes, your eminence. Our agents in Denmark as well as Bohemia have been working on this and have good information on the boy's possible whereabouts."

"Good information is not enough! We must have the boy in chains, bound over to us. No more delays!"

Tullio hunched over. "I will convey that to our agents, Your Eminence." He made a show of writing this down, then looked up. "Shall I include the news about Prince Ari in your missive to His Holiness?"

"Don't call him 'prince,' Tullio. Refer to the little bastard only as a pretender!"

"Yes, your eminence: the Danish *pretender*." Tullio paused before adding: "Do you wish to report the little bastard's status to His Holiness in this letter?" Tullio smirked. He relished skirting sarcasm.

"No! Tell His Holiness only that Fortinbras believes the pretender to be dead, and now has joined our fight without reservation. Say that Norwegian-Danish monarch moved to enforce our new agreement. Tell his Holiness that Fortinbarss has cut off the English and the Dutch trade with the Baltic States through Denmark's straits."

Tullio copied down a torrent of words, then looked back at the cardinal with a smile. He dared not point out that His Eminence had no confirmation of what he was telling him to write. "Done, Your Eminence!"

"Now, make final copies, Tullio, so that I may sign and set my seal upon them. Then deliver it to the Swiss Guard courier to start his journey at dawn.

Thunder rumbled outside and drops began pelting the chamber's tall windows. The cardinal shuddered and grabbed his shoulders.

"I miss Genoa. Nothing be rain, rain, rain. Nearly summer, and I still feel Prague's dampness in my bones, Tullio. Will this wretched raining never cease?"

73. POTIONS AND POISONS

The emperor had another bout of terror dreams. This had become a nightly occurrence, disturbing what few hours of sleep that His Highness has been able to achieve lately. All week, the emperor dreamed of a towering clay giant rising from the mud of the Vltava, destroying Prague Castle, throwing its occupants into a raging bonfire.

I could sympathize with the monster.

The emperor does not confide in me, but I knew about the dreams through his physician and alchemist Oswald Kroll, to whom I now was prime supplier of hard-to-find herbs, seeds, fungi and roots, even rare stones.

For a year, I had explored every tree and fold of the surrounding woodlands. I learned where to find their every herbal treasure. Then I augmented native finds with secret plantings of my own, cultivating a clandestine apothecary from exotic cuttings and seeds I garnered, traded or filched from Prague's parade of foreign visitors.

Kroll was in a dither. His Majesty – said to be in a dark mood – was pressing him to concoct a more effective sleeping remedy and fashion him a new amulet to ward off disease and demons – and quickly.

I had been right down a castle corridor from Kroll's alchemy workshop every day that week, in the atelier of my artist and secret lover, Bartholomeus.

Bardo – that's what I was calling him by now – had been keeping his doors barred while he and I worked. It wouldn't do for someone to walk in and see "Oliver" posing as a nude Venus for the artist, as he brushed oils lustily onto an ambitious new canvas.

It had been chilly that morning, but I felt the tickle of sweat on my back. Bardo enjoyed the secrecy and risk as much he did my feminine form stripped of its male disguise right there in the heart of the emperor's busy castle. I, less so.

I had overheard enough to be curious about the ongoing crisis over His Majesty's ominous nightmares. I consulted my usual sources of gossip around town and out on the floor of Vladislav Hall. From these, I pieced together much of what was happening inside the emperor's chambers. Out of habit the emperor looked for ulterior significance in every experience and event, and this was no exception.

The emperor, as he often did, consulted astrologers and soothsayers, wise men and magicians about the monster in his dreams – among them Giordano Bruno – still in Prague at the time – and Rabbi Loew – the Maharal of Prague's Jewish section.

Bruno warned His Majesty the monster in his dream was an omen. The forces of darkness, greed and intolerance – seeing the light of new learning – were growing. Unchecked, they would pull all the kingdoms into a war of unparalleled destruction that would leave Prague in ruins. Bruno advised the emperor to redouble his efforts to create the grand alliance of Catholic and Protestant states that His Majesty envisioned.

The Maharal, in turn, told His Majesty the story of the Golem, an invincible giant formed of clay by a humble rabbi, and brought to life by means of a holy inscription. I loved the story myself when Kroll related it to me. When the Jews of his city were threatened by a terrible persecution, the rabbi loosed the Golem, who destroyed all who came against his people and tore their walls, homes and castles asunder.

I was told that the emperor blanched upon hearing this tale – for it described his dream exactly and he had not told Rabbi Lowe any details of it beforehand. The emperor asked the rabbi many questions. "Why did the monster in my dream destroy Prague Castle? The Jews here have prospered along with everyone under our protection."

In a soft voice, the rabbi then respectfully enlightened His Majesty about recent events – the Papal Nuncio's "blood libel" falsely accusing the Jews of kidnapping children for their blood, the edict to confiscate all Jewish books for the Inquisition to examine for Satanism, the arrests of hundreds of Jews for no reason and the pending order of expulsion of all Jews from the city by His Majesty's Governor General Hargarthy.

The emperor flew into a rage. As soon as the audience ended, His Majesty summoned his chamber of deputies, including the governor general, and threatened them all with arrest for circumventing his authority. The emperor rescinded all of the governor general's orders regarding the Jews of Prague forthwith.

"It seems, I told Bardo after hearing the tale, "that the rabbi's Golem did its job without having to lift one of its giant clay fingers."

In spite of myself, I felt a measure of admiration for the emperor after this incident. It muddied the icy water of my vengeful intentions. I had allowed myself to see the emperor as a man more than as a tyrant – just as I had know King Hamlet as a child. I wondered if this kindly, retiring Rudolf I was seeing now could have ordered my abduction and had my child killed. The emperor had not even been aware that his own governor general was about to persecute and expel the Jews of his own city. Could the same have been true in my case? Was I allowing such thoughts to cloud my vision and deter me from my mission?

I had little time to think more upon this, however. As I had anticipated, Kroll summoned me to his workshop and asked for my help in obtaining key ingredients of the amulet he busied himself making for His Majesty.

By now I had become a fixture here in the castle – a minor player among the emperor's collection of artists, thinkers and oddballs. I continued to carry my vial of venom in a secret pocket as I went about my duties, but new knowledge weakened my resolve. I had not lost my desire for vengeance, but its focal point blurred. I do not consider myself indecisive, though the reader is free to think that. I had learned discretion and the value of observation and thought in my long, perilous journeys, if nothing else.

The counsel of Bruno and the Rabbi Loew not withstanding, the emperor reiterated his demand that Kroll provide him with a new amulet –- designed to ward off disease and psychic threats. Kroll and his assistants worked night and day formulating and preparing the ingredients to be pressed together and tightly wrapped into a capsule that the emperor could wear comfortably under his garments. They had no trouble procuring the necessary, ground powder of emeralds, amber, red and white arsenic and dessicated toad. But Kroll turned to me for two of the key plant extracts he needed – saffron and dittany.

He had neither in stock and both happened to be in short supply everywhere, particularly dittany. I knew that Kroll did not want common, native, purple-flowered dittany, but woolly stemmed, gray-green dittany from in the rocky hills of Crete. My good fortune. I had plenty of both ingredients.

I had managed to grow a patch of Cretan dittany on the dry, eastern slope of a forest outcropping, then harvest, dry and store its leaves and stems that past autumn.

I could have charged Kroll a premium, but gave him a pouch full of it, gratis. His good will and the access to the inner palace this would provide me were worth more than silver. Besides, I had been lining my pockets for a good while with cast-off garnets, emeralds and rubies that the royal alchemists kept for grinding at the royal workshops that I supplied with herbs herbs, fungi and ambers from the forests and hills.

74. DEADLY DIVERSION

Just when everything seemed to be propelling me towards the emperor and my final objective, fate pushed me off the path one afternoon with the apparition of two demons from my past – the cardinal Spinola – and his factotum, Tullio. I could not believe my eyes seeing them right there in Prague Castle where I had toiled daily. Specters of evil rose from the graveyard of my memories where I had thought them buried.

I had heard that the pope had sent another nuncio to Prague – a member of the Curia this time, not the usual archbishop. I cursed myself for not realizing that the papal emissary was the former grand inquisitor himself, Cardinal Spinola.

I recognized the pair instantly, with recalled the night of my cousin Sylvia's lavish dinner for the cardinal – the last that I would be with child before I was seized from my bed by four masked brutes and taken away bound and gagged – to suffer weeks of fear and agony in the dark of rough carriages, not knowing where they were taking me or where they had taken my Ari.

I remembered the Tullio's weasel face up close – that terrible night, and hearing the cardinal giving orders after they dragged me outside. Then another horror catching sight of Tullio in the moonlight, nodding to one of the cardinal's thugs, who slit the throat of that sweet child, Francesca, when she ran outside to my rescue.

Now, spying the pair again – fortunately, from the shadows of a corridor where they could not have seen me – the venomous snake of my rage coiled, hissed and readied to strike at new prey.

I had been in a fine mood the day that the cardinal and Tullio appeared. I had just been leaving the Emperor Rudolf's Kunstkammer, having indulged my passion for examining its treasures. Spranger often sent me there to comb the collection for exotic items he could borrow and draw for his painting. Dawdling, I had been examining navigation instruments, saddles, clocks, automate, zoological specimens, skeletons, ancient bronze armor, folios of drawings, sacred relics, horns of various beasts – including, so said the inscription – of unicorns. There were runes, whales' teeth, a crystal lion, insects frozen in amber for me to admire.

I spotted the cardinal and Tullio on my way back to Bardo's studio through the palace corridors. I stopped short. They were seated in an antechamber to the Hall of Deputies, decorated by grand images of the four elements, the twelve months, all presided over by Jupiter. I concealed myself behind a separating wall, and spied on them through a peep hole I knew to be embedded in one of the paintings of cavorting Roman deities. I could see impatience and envy coloring the Cardinal's face as he scanned the works of art surrounding them.

I knew right away that they had been stalled – as were most dignitaries, except artists – trying to see the emperor. Predictably, they had been diverted to a mere deputy. I heard the cardinal ranting. He was no common plenipotentiary from Naples or Sardinia.

"That's it. Let us depart and return to the St. George's abbey, Tullio – and deny them further pleasure from their discourtesy." The cardinal's voice rasped with rage. I guessed that he had referred to the convent of St. George next to the castle cathedral, where I had been detained, and where Cardinal Spinola no doubt now occupied the quarters for important church officials and visitors.

I followed them – at a safe distance – and confirmed my suspicions. It continued to rain. Dusk faded quickly into a night of thunderous downpours, aiding my stealth. I stole into the convent and found Sister Ludmilla, saying evening prayers in her cell by the wavering light of a single candle. She blanched at the sight of me, whom she had presumed long dead, incredulous at first, seeing this apparition of me in male attire.

I put a finger to my lips. Quietly, between convulsive sobs, I told her much of my story since she had last seen me – leaving out my affair with Bardo and my activities at the castle – and especially my obsession with vengeance against those responsible for my captivity and Ari's death. After we had talked a while, I pleaded with her to obtain a set of nun's vestments for me. I was soaked from the rain, and – I told her – I needed a temporary disguise to keep myself safe. Then I would be on my way. I did not tell my dear Ludmilla – who had already risked herself to help me in the darkest hour of my life – to what dark use I intended to put her sisterly garments.

75. CARDINAL SINS

My feet knew every flagstone of the corridor that led from the St. George nuns' quarters to the more luxurious chambers of the abbey reserved for higher clergy and their honored guests. Guards used to drag me down this corridor during my detention here to the rooms where a thick, high voiced priest, who made me "confess" my "sins" and recite the Nicene Creed over and over while strapped to a chair, my arms pulled up over its back, *strapado* style.

He called it indoctrination to save my soul, and took care not to injure me in obvious ways. I never made sense of any of it, but I observed, and thought of Ari and of my flowers and Sister Ludmilla – and nurtured a hatred of priests and kings.

This night, I walked the corridor free and in secret. I looked like just another Benedictine nun carrying a silver tray of victuals and wine that I had stolen from the cloister's kitchen while the cook was at prayer. I stride with my head bowed forward, my long black robe secured by a sensible woolen belt, my features shrouded by my black veil and high-necked, white wimple. Anyone did happen to get a look at my face would likely remember only my nasty scar. Tricks of the theatrical trade learned with my players – using a transparent gummy adhesive, I had drawn a lurid gash down my left temple and across my cheek, highlighted in a red pomegranate powder brushed well into its crease.

I found the cardinal's quarters easily.

I knocked. A muffled voice responded from behind the thick oaken door.

"Sister Judith. I bring His Eminence cheeses, fruits and fine wine from the vicar."

The door opened and the monk whom I recognized as Tullio let me in. He barely glanced at my face. "This way," he said, and led me through an ante-chamber into a larger room with a high, arched ceiling. The cardinal – still in his red robes, but bareheaded – sat at a table in the center of the room.

"One of the nuns, Your Eminence, bringing us evening sustenance – from the vicar, she says."

"Fine, Tullio. Have her set it on the table near me." I recognized his voice, with its distinctive predatory growl masked in formal joviality, badgering me with questions at the banquet in Lyon. If only I had been more vigilant – not lulled by the illusion of having found security there in my mother's ancestral home.

The cardinal ignored me as I set the tray on one side of his table. I bowed, wondering if he expected me to kiss his ring. Keeping his back to me, he kept staring at the rain coming down against the windows across from him, his face glowing yellow and orange from the flames roaring in the massive fireplace to one side of the room.

"Thank you, sister Judith. That will be all. I will escort you out." Tullio glided to my side.

"I can pour the wine for Your Eminence," I ventured. "The vicar said to tell you that he selected it specially from our cellars – a fine vintage claret from the Liguria."

I guessed right. The Cardinal from Genoa had a taste for fine wines from his home country. "Yes. Please, sister."

The wine had already been decanted into an ornately etched, crystal pitcher into which I had emptied my vial of venom. I poured a splash into a fine stem glass for the cardinal to taste. He sipped, considered, sipped again and nodded his approval.

"Yes, sister. Fill my glass. It is a fine wine indeed." He held up the glass, still not looking directly at me.

I poured a second glass for Tullio.

"You may take your leave now," said the cardinal between sips.

I complied, bowed again and backed away from the cardinal, watching the tray. To my relief, I saw the cardinal continuing to sip the wine as Tullio let me to the door and into the corridor. I had planned to retreat to an alcove, then count off time, then steal back into cardinal's quarters to slit their throats should the poison have not finished them completely off.

The poison that I had added to the wine did its work, I would find them both in grisly death. I had to be sure. I hoped for quick death, even though I thought that too merciful, because I did not relish slitting their throats.

When I returned to the room, I saw Tullio first — sprawled on his back, a chair from the table turned over. He dark eyes stared up lifeless at the shadows from the fireplace that danced on the high ceiling. The cardinal remained seated in the chair where I had left him, facing the windows, his back to me. I inched closer and saw his head back against the chair, his mouth open, eyes staring upwards. Relieved, I stepped up to the table.

A powerful hand gripped my wrist and nearly pulled me off my feet. I gasped, and struggled to break free, digging the nails of my free hand into his bald scalp. He half rose and released me. I made for him then saw that he had drawn a pistol from God knows where, cocked at the ready in his right hand, while he steadied himself against the table and sat back down with a grunt.

"Sit." He waved the pistol at an empty chair. I made for it slowly, stalling for time. I dared not try to flee or rush at him. Even if he shot wide, the pistol's report could bring help.

I sat gingerly where he had pointed. He stared at me.

"I suppose the emperor is behind this." He almost chortled. "I underestimated the fat self-indulgent rogue. I should have seen this coming. How ironic."

"Your eminence." I fought for words to distract him.

"Who gave you the order, sister? You have committed a monstrous sin and will burn for this."

"I do not know of what you speak, your eminence." I used my most timid, pious voice. "I heard a clatter and rushed back here to see what had happened. Are you both sick? Shall I fetch a physician? This is terrible, Your Eminence. Terrible!" I made the sign of the cross and bowed my head, faking sobs, stalling for time, my eyes darting for a way out.

The cardinal waved his pistol. I wondered why he had not killed me outright. *He gets only one shot*, I realized. *And he is woozy.*

"Don't even think of escape. Sister..." He tried to laugh, hoarsely. "*You* are *no* nun. You're likely a cutthroat – a man, no doubt. Remove that veil, blackguard!"

I shook my head slowly in fake piety. "I cannot, Your Eminence, before God!"

He pointed at a bell cord hanging near the fireplace. "One pull and my guards will come running."

I stiffened. Then stared him in the eye, emboldened by the realization that he had not called for help as yet, perhaps fearing a wider conspiracy. "Go ahead! How do you know that the emperor's agents won't come in here and finish the job?"

He kept silent for a while, taking inventory of himself. His gut must have been afire by that time. He brought the pistol close to my face. "I could kill you right now and take my chances with your cohorts. But I will spare you. Tell me who ordered this, and I will see to it that you go free."

"My orders come from Aricin, Prince of Denmark." I paused. It was the first time I had ever referred to my son formally as a prince of Denmark.

The cardinal tried to laugh again, but had started to look bilious. I could see his eyes wavering. "Ah, then the emperor must have sent you. I am no fool."

I puzzled at his answer. "You are a murder as well as an abductor. I hold you to account for my son's death! You may kill me, but you are bound for eternity in hell."

I stared to rise. If he fired the gun, I would have at least a chance.

He waved the pistol at me again, his hand trembling. "Ah! It is you. Ophelia! All this time, we thought you dead!" He squinted and regarded me intensely. "Yes. I thought there was a look. A shame about that scar."

I slipped my hand inside my robe and pulled my dagger slowly from the scabbard I had secured under my cloth belt. I could see his eyes glazing more. Then he laughed. "Foolish girl!"

"What do you mean?" I pushed my chair slowly backwards with my feet as I talked and waited for my chance.

"Ask your apostate emperor! He is the one who hides the pretender from Holy Mother Church!"

"Hides?" I gasped. "Is my Ari alive?"

"Foolish, *foolish* girl. You have been made a foil and you will burn for it."

"Not before you die for your deceit, murderous bastard!" Seeing him waver, I lunged full force off my chair, my dagger drawn, pushing the pistol aside with my body as he fired it off into the fireplace. Reflexively, I plunged the knife into the side of his neck. Blood spurted forth as he fell to the floor in the throes of death.

I scanned the room quickly, once more, anxious to exit before anyone who might have heard the pistol shot showed up. I emptied every drawer, shelf and box onto the floor. I broke vases and statuary. It calmed me. My choleric cooled to an icy determination. Deliberately, I tempted fate and ransacked the suite, turning over chests and chairs, pulling paintings off the walls, scattering what I found on shelves and in the cardinal's desk all over the ornate

Persian carpeting, pocketing coins and what few items caught my eye. Might as well make this affair look like a common burglary, I reasoned. But my real motive was the satisfaction I too in violating the cardinal's private quarters, thrusting my hands into his possessions like an public executioner disemboweling a condemned wretch – the way the cardinal had reached into my life and taken everything from me.

On my way out, I spotted a small, blue-enameled desk, decorated with puffy clouds and cherubs in an alcove that I had missed – the secretary, Tullio's perch, no doubt. As I moved to overturn the desk, an open folder on it caught my eye. I brought one of the candles over to examine the papers more closely and saw that it contained documents pertaining to Denmark, King Fortinbras, Prince Hamlet and myself – Ophelia – going back many years.

I thought to set it afire, but did not want to endanger the nuns in the cloister. I had no time to read all the papers. But two items aroused my curiosity – first, a parchment scroll and second, a set of fine linen sheets covered in what looked to be coded calligraphic script.

I opened the scroll and discovered Father Beppo's testament to my long-ago, phantasmal marriage to Prince Hamlet. I almost laughed, tearful, shaking.

I had little use for it now, but stuffed it under my vestments anyway – as a relic of an Ophelia long dead. I did the same with the coded sheets – folding them under my habit against my bosom.

My mind should have spinning with the horror of the two murders I had committed. That came later. I confess, instead, to have felt nothing steely satisfaction as I made to leave – mingled with giddiness at having learned that Ari might still be alive – just as I had pictured him in my dream.

I slipped out of the Cardinals quarters silently and glided down the long dark corridors, then out a side entrance – learned of from Ludmilla – into a garden and across it to an old, unused passageway where I found my "Oliver" clothes, bundled and dry. A quick change, and I exited through a tunnel, a house basement, up to a street, thence home.

76. OMINOUS SILENCE

All that following week, I agonized over the papers I had taken from the cardinal's suite. I expected heralds and pamphlets, police, beadles and troops stopping people everywhere, shutting down Prague once the bodies were discovered. I went over what had happened again and again. Had I left signs of myself behind? I felt horror at having committed murder, but, strangely, neither guilt, nor shame. Doubts? Yes.

What had I accomplished? Was Ari still alive? Had I exacted unjust vengeance? The cardinal would have squashed me like an ant given another chance. How many innocents had sent to the torturers? How many to the stake in the name of gentle Jesus?

I felt possessed by the mystery of those papers I had found.

"What are you reading?" I froze. I had not noticed Bardo standing by my desk, his hands smudged with colors, taking a moment away from his work.

I stammered. "Oh... it's a ... game ... part of a game of cyphers..." I coughed and pushed the papers aside, regaining my composure. "The emperor asked Johannes Kepler to create a puzzle game for his children. Herr Kepler gave me these to see if I could make sense of it all..."

Bartholomeus laughed and shook his head. "Perhaps Christendom's greatest mathematical wizards put to making up children's game?"

I forced a laugh. "... One never knows what the emperor's pleasure will be. Monarchs never grant favors without demanding a price."

"Oh, but the prince isn't always dear – for instance when His Majesty asks the great astronomer Tycho Brahe to cast astrological charts in return for his patronage?"

I was anxious to change the subject. "I hear that Lord Brahe may accept the emperor's offer to move his observatory to Prague after all."

But Bartholomeus dropped the small talk and bent to examine the papers more closely. I put my arm over one of the pages, a silly, schoolboy tactic that didn't stop him.

"Ah. The papal seal." He pointed to the crimson wax seal at the end of a page. He arched an eyebrow. "Part of the game? Find a pope the on a page?"

I said nothing. I could feel my face flush.

He separated the pages and examined the one that was blank. It was of a coarser paper, bearing neither embossing or a seal. "Did 'Herr Kepler' give you this one with the others?"

"Well. It was off to one side." I realized how foolish that sounded. "Sort of clumped together though..."

Bartholomeus fetched a damp rag from a table cluttered with paints and brushes next to his easel – his home studio. He flattened out the blank sheet on my desk and began dabbing it with the moist cloth. Slowly I saw ciphers begin to appear on the paper.

"The character key!" I blurted, embarrassed at my oversight. "I should have guessed right away!" I had overlooked the obvious in my anxiety and haste.

The document I had taken was one in progress, probably being prepared by the cardinal's satrap, Tullio, who had kept aside a key in invisible ink for reference in case he needed to make last minute changes. Pieter used to do this too.

"It's a Vigenère code," said my artist lover. I was seeing a new side to him. Perhaps I should be suspicious, I thought. "A polyalphabetic cypher. The key gives you the 'cipher alphabet' being used to substitute for conventional letters."

"Yes. Thank you." I tried to sound business like. "I'll get to it now ..." I slid the papers back in front of me and hunched over them protectively.

"Looks a bit advanced for children – even royal children." He shrugged, then put a hand on my shoulder, reassuringly. "This painter needs to get back to his canvas, in any case." He strolled back into his studio.

Quill in hand, I opened my journal and began using the key to decipher the cardinal's document. Who could tell how much time I would have to unlock its secrets before I would be discovered?

77. BISHOP'S PAWN

The cardinal's missive opened my eyes wide to the game in which I had been the pawn. I could see all the pieces on the board now – Kings, Queens, bishops, knights. I realized that I had made a move beyond the humble station in which I had sought refuge. There would be no hiding. I would have no choice but to make another, or lose any chance, however narrow, of seeing my child ever again.

I found no mention of Aricin by name, but ample references to "the Danish pretender."

Why the euphemism, in an encoded communication. The cardinal had made no bones about the breathtaking conspiracy to assassinate the emperor. So why be so coy about Ari? What was that crafty evil red bird trying to hide from his pope?

The cardinals' last words kept repeating in my head. Old feelings surged through me. My baby,, alive? Could I dare indulge such hope again? I had to follow this thread. Ari's life could have depended on it. Whom could I trust? Who were my true enemies? The emperor – threatened himself by the villains who sought my end – no longer fit the role of my archenemy.

How could I warn His Majesty without implicating myself in the cardinal's murder? The emperor that I came so close to assassinating myself could now be my most powerful ally. I trembled and felt chills. How could I trust my own judgment again after making so many mistake?

Look to the lights that have guided you so far.

"Better that I had contemplated consequences before acting so rashly." I whispered to the prince's shade so that Bartholomeus could not overhear me.

Thou hast outdone me, Ophelia! Thou art that 'man of action' than I aspired to be.

Lord Hamlet, in his fashionable black cloak, floated in front of my desk, impossibly nonchalant.

I hissed. "Begone. You grow too bold – visiting me in broad daylight."

I know that you saw our son in your dreams, and more real than I, as real as yourself and your lover. The ghost pointed to Bartholomeus, busy detailing an angel's wings on a canvas, his back to me.

"Thou protests too much, my lord. Jealous?"

Prince Hamlet feigned indifference, shrugging as unconvincingly as when he was alive. Then he floated nearer, his face up close to mine. I imagined I could feel his breath on me as he spoke. *Give your dreams credence. You saw our son. Yet, I have not seen him even once on this plane of spirits.*

"That is but a frail reed upon which to carry my burden of hope, my lord."

But a few days ago you had not even that reed. You must test it.

78. OPHELIA'S GAMBIT

The soldiers came for me soon enough. Or, rather, they came for Oliver. I was trading pearls on the busy floor of Vladislav Hall that morning – small ones from the Persian Gulf that the royal alchemists grind to powder or reduce to carbonic elements in vinegar for their experiments. It's a shame to destroy so many translucent darlings. The modest handfuls to which I helped myself from time to time were never missed from the castle's well-supplied laboratories. I had an abundance of choice little pearls that day, enough to trade up for what looked to me like a violet Kasmiri sapphire of exceptional quality.

"A lovely garnet, if a bit *common.*" I told the quivering, wispy bearded tailor who showed me the sapphire discreetly. He likely had filched it from the pocket of a doublet he was mending for a client, then panicked. I relieved him of the sapphire, and handed him a small pouch of the pearls.

"You should have no trouble selling these over there at the alchemist table." I nodded to a cluster of traders at the far end of the hall. "Tell them you got the pearls from Persian traders in return for sewing their pantaloons. The alchemists will pay you gold. They make the stuff in their laboratories like farmers make cheeses." The tailor pocketed my pouch of second rate pearls eagerly and disappeared into the crowd.

I turned away and nearly bumped into two of the emperor's elite guards, dark-eyed Hungarians, muscled like dray horses, always in black, matching their black mustaches, pistols and daggers in their belts – not the daydreaming, blue-uniformed, local guards who policed the Vladislav Hall fairs every day.

These two moved with far too much authority to be mere police – but neither did they display the sadistic haughtiness of ecclesiastical interrogators.

I knew they had not grabbed me for trading in stolen pearls and sapphires. That would have been something for the blue guards – who usually look the other way for a small bribe – not imperial agents.

"Oliver Spranger! Come with us." What? They think that I am Bardo's wife now? The duo flanked me, and gripped each of my arms just above the elbows. No chains, at least. They could have lifted me right off the floor and carried me if I did not keep up as they steered me straight through the milling traders, across the floor to the palace chambers entrance.

I had been expecting something like this since I shared the contents of the cardinal's deciphered letter with my lover. He copied the letter down, word for word and I hid the original – bearing the Vatican official seals – somewhere only I knew, sealed in a glass jar, buried under one of my forest herb garden spots. I "confessed" to Bardo that I took the documents from the cardinal's quarters after finding his eminence and his satrap dead.

I knew my story was flimsy, and that Bardo didn't believe it – especially being as I had described my abduction to him – including the murder of Francesca.

Bardo had read the letter several times. "I must warn the emperor." He face turned ashen. I anticipated this. Bardo was, after all, the emperor's *valet de chambre*, and court painter.

"They will arrest me. I'll be accused of murdering the cardinal. I will be tortured, tried and burned."

"None of that, I hope. The emperor's guards will come for you, Ophelia." He had taken to calling me that in private now that we had become close, relishing the risk more than I. "For show."

"For show?"

"The archduke and the archbishop cannot suspect that they have been compromised. They must think the emperor remains in the dark about the cardinal's incriminating letter to the pope. This will be to keep you safe from Vatican agents. They will think your arrest is routine, and even if they guess who you are, they will not challenge the emperor's authority openly."

"Why have the church authorities kept the murders a secret?"

"I suspect that the governor general has covered up the whole affair while he investigates. He must be terrified that the Vatican plot to kill Emperor Rudolf and make him regent has been uncovered, for that will truly cost him his head."

"But how would the governor general know I had been in the cardinal's chambers, and, even then, have guessed my true identity?

"He would not need to know about you. But he certainly knows about the cardinal's communications with the Vatican, that an intruder killed him and that letters bound for Rome had vanished — never given to the Swiss Guard courier that next morning."

"I don't like it, Bardo. I'll be rotting in a cell again – under the emperor's so-called protection, just like before."

"When I speak to the emperor – soon – I will seek assurances. You, very likely, saved the emperor's life, and he will want you brought to him – for reward, not punishment."

"I will believe this when you show me the emperor's fabled unicorn."

"Do you believe your son to be alive?"

"Tenuously, my dear Bardo, with trepidation."

"If he does still live, the emperor will know of it – and be agent to reunion of mother and child, I believe. And be ready to do whatever he asks of you in return."

"If I am able..."

"That will be your choice, but think hard upon it. I know His Majesty to be unpredictable, often vexing, but always fair."

"Not the emperor I imagined, then..."

"I will return to my atelier in the emperor's palace now, and ask to see his highness as a matter of urgency."

"And he will see you? Just like that?"

"I have undertaken many missions in the service of His Majesty, Ophelia. Most I dare not divulge. I can assure you that if I say it is urgent, the royal doors will open."

With misgivings, I nodded.

"Wait a day here after I leave, then come out of hiding. Go about your business in Vladislav Hall. It will be best if the emperor's men take you in a public place so that Vatican agents see it and wonder."

I wanted to run – take my little hoard of gems and gold coins, hire a boat and slip away down the Vltava River lost among the barges and fishermen, letting the current take me north, far into German lands, into the mighty Oder to the North Sea, from thence board a ship, across the vast water to the New World, perhaps.

But what of Ari? Was I standing on the threshold of a new life? I pictured him somewhere in a garden like the one where I used to pick flowers at Elsinore. My arms ached to embrace his loose limbed, lanky boy body, smelling of grass and dust from playing outside, and hear him giggle. Or would this be another trap?

79. GARDEN OF PARADISE

"Highly unorthodox!" I drew a breath for emphasis, not due to my tight-lipped guards quick-marching me across the castle grounds. I cast an eye out for avenues of escape as I kept up the patter. "You fellows are making a big mistake." Both of them remained silent, gripping my arms as we proceeded down a neatly hedged gravel path, past green lawns set with geometrical beds of peonies, violets, columbines and pansies.

" ..and there are pansies; they're for thoughts," I chanted, but the my somber escorts were not the thinking kind.

"There's fennel for you, and columbines.—There's rue for you, and here's some for me." I kept on, repeating my long lost lyric, though not out of madness this time, only hoping that my captors might think me so.

The week of rains had ended. The sun brought out the garden's every hue to life. I drew the fragrances of wet leaves and blossoms into myself.

Plucky brown pheasants caught my eye, darting among the shrubs sending me messages. Songbirds whistled unseen from the trees and squirrels chattered their busy nonsense. Everything around me carried a secret message that only my soul could comprehend, if it chose to return. But I was given no time to smell the roses of paradise. My guards kept shoving me towards the incomprehensible. A gust of fragrant air whisked the fountain's spray on my face and whispered sensualities in my ear – perhaps mocking this wretched prisoner with all that would be lost with the fall of an executioner's ax.

"Highly unorthodox," I blustered bravely again, "You two escort me to paradise, *before* hanging me and not after." No laugh. Not even a smirk from either of them. Maybe they only laughed at Hungarian jokes.

I had seen the Queen Anne Summer Palace – the emperor's favorite retreat – but only majestic from a distance, separated from the rest of Prague Castle by an incline rising from across the bed of a gentle stream, and set off by stables, artificial ponds and these gardens behind a high, wooden wall so that the emperor could stroll unseen from the rest of the castle grounds. Yet, here I found myself, transported – albeit under duress – into the beating heart of imperial power and largess, ideals and corruption, pride and elegance.

And at once, I felt at home here, God help me, as I once did in gardens of Queen Gertrude's summer palace in Jutland.

I realized that my two armed escorts were not out for a stroll, nor were they taking me to prison or before any magistrate. If they were taking me to be questioned by the emperor himself, as I had hoped, this would be an unlikely venue as well.

They hustled me, incredibly, straight towards the main entrance to the palace. This was truly forbidden ground. I knew that only the emperor, his immediate family and a few of His Majesty's confidants ever were allowed entry the Queen Anne Palace.

It had been built by his majesty's grandfather, Ferdinand and named after his grandmother Anna of Bohemia. Close up, it outshined its reputation – its keel-shaped, mint-hued copper roof. It reminded me of an ancient ceremonial galley – or Cleopatra's barge – capsized on a hill, the crown jewel of this private paradise.

As we crossed the garden, passed its sculptured fountain, I could see the balconies and porticoes flanked by Ionic colonnades, classical statuary. Friezes depicted Greek myths and heroic deeds – the tragedies and follies of gods and goddesses, kings and queens: *Bas reliefs* graced each spandrels – of Leda and Zeus, Jason reaching for the Golden Fleece, Zeus and Ganymede – scenes that I remembered from Ovid's *Metamorphoses*.

My guards marched me up the main stairs – where I would have feared to set foot alone – along a colonnade, under a portico to a set of massive teak wood doors. They stopped me for a moment at the door and ran their hands brusquely over me, checking me one more time for weapons. I had taken care to go about unarmed that day. My escorts had shown no interest in my sapphire or other valuables – another proof that they were not ordinary sheriffs or castle guardsmen.

The doors opened – held by two servants in livery – and we entered. The two guards let go of my arms and backed away. It took a moment for my eyes to adjust from the sunlight to the cool dimness inside the foyer. Still more heroic sculptures greeted me under an arched Roman ceiling, painted with angels, or cupids. My attention turned to a figure approaching me – not the emperor, nor a guard, nor servant, nor a magistrate, nor an executioner – I thank the gods.

Instead, a woman approached me. Striking., she stood tall, about my height, but more buxom – with coppery curls peaking from under her slouching linen cap.

She fixed me with the large luminous golden eyes of a lynx – serenely watchful, but not threatening. She reminded me of my mother Lara, and looked to be about the age my mother would have been then, had she lived. I had to restrain an impulse to embrace her – noting her fine, aquiline nose, wide set eyes and the graceful confident sway of her gait – that northern Italianate look of my mother's line,

I recognized her from a sketch that Bardo had made of her as "Primavera" - bare breasted wearing a crown of flowers and a cloak of leaves and white roses. I remember feeling a twinge of jealousy at seeing it. She looked older than in the sketch.

"Ophelia! Welcome to our home." She extended her hand. I didn't know whether to shake it or kiss it, whether to bow or curtsy. Her informal greeting and her use of my real name rattled me.

Katharina Strada, as the granddaughter of the art dealer and polymath Jacopo da Strada as well as the emperor's favorite, was easily the most powerful woman in the empire. She wore a crown of fresh flowers much like in the sketch I had seen – a queen in her bearing and grace, though uncrowned and untitled.

I saw her innate nobility and well understood how the emperor would prefer her company to that of a spoiled princess. She seemed a woman of great poise, and I knew her for one of great intelligence and learning.

"Come. Don't be shy." She took my hand without waiting for me to extend it, or even to curtsy. She led me across the marble floor and through a set of gold-embossed Romanesque double doors into her quarters. "First you must rest. I will have the servants draw you a bath. They will provide you with attire more befitting of your ..." She searched for the word "...station." By this I believed she meant to say, "gender."

I shook my head. Her words rang in my head. I had a good idea what she meant, but not what it was to cost me... to entail. I felt an urge to run from this heavenly place. Was I to be plucked, oiled and dressed like a Christmas goose? And served up to whom or what – the intrigues and murderous plots of a royal life that I had fled in Denmark, that had stalked me for seven years across half of Christendom?

"Afterwards we will dine with His Majesty. Then we will talk."

"What will be served?"

"Delicacies, a summer afternoon feast of smoked meats, trout, mushroom pies, cheeses, potatoes, pastries and fruits fresh picked from the royal orchard."

I had meant what purpose, not what victuals, but I didn't question further. What use was there indeed except for me to accede and discover what lay in store for me -- at least not imprisonment and execution – not for now, at any rate.

80. AT THE EMPEROR'S TABLE

There would be no audience with the emperor – *per se.* Nothing public. It came to me half way through the mid-afternoon feast in the summer palace's exquisitely appointed, but comfortably modest royal family rooms. An audience – before the emperor's throne, or any other parts of the castle – amid the prying eyes, spying ears and long noses of courtiers – would be out of the question considering what had transpired and what the emperor had in mind at that point.

I could only guess at that. I simply had to wait and converse politely. I was a little out of practice. Olivia and Oliver and their fellow players seldom saw kings and queens except as performers – and I still was that. But Ophelia had grown up amidst kings, queens and duchesses – as the prince's playmate, welcomed to their private tables like a visiting niece.

I kept my eyes respectfully averted from the emperor's, while my mind scrambled for scraps of evidence that might tell me about Ari. The emperor seemed to already know my story – but drew details from me as the meal progressed. I gleaned that he must have some purpose already in mind for both my son and myself in taking me so closely – if momentarily – into his royal confidence.

"Tell us more about your travels, Ophelia," said the emperor in a surprisingly youthful tenor that did not fit with his sad eyes that followed the motions of a serving girl who removed what we had not consumed of roast rock partridge and white sausages, and brought in the trout roe pies with sprigs of fresh mint served on fresh plates an a fresh set of gold forks, spoons and table knives imported from Florence.

I waited for the maid to exit before continuing my story. Might as well tell his highness everything in the most innocent, respectful, beguiling way that I could muster – my tales of Elsinore, Leiden, Brade, Antwerp and Lyon – with emphasis on the artists, players, writers and printers I had met, for I knew those would be of special interest to the world's greatest collector of them and their works. I did not speak of Prague or my abduction and incarceration, nor of my clandestine activities of late.

There was no staff present, to speak of, save that maid and one elderly, somber butler – a lifetime family retainer who silently sampled a morsel of each dish before serving it to the emperor. I did not even see the cook and his assistants who must have been preparing our lavish meal in the royal family kitchen. Their young children apparently took their meals in the nursery that day.

I sat at in the middle of a long table, with the emperor at its head – bare headed, and in simple silken garb, not his regal attire – and Katherine at the other. We ate delicately, sipped wines from the Rhone Valley – a deliberately thoughtful selection, I surmised. The emperor seemed fascinated with my journey – what I had seen of the siege of Leiden and the bloody mutiny in Antwerp.

He spun off what I related into art, astronomy, books, the novels of Cervantes and Rabelais, poetry herbal medicine, botany, but not one word about affairs of state, religion or war, save what I had seen directly. We talked freely. Katherine added lively comments throughout. In public she was spoken of only as His Majesty's seldom-seen concubine, but in this setting she acted much more like his queen – speaking her mind with easy confident.

The maid began bringing sweet pastries, though I had eaten each course sparingly. Finally, I could hold my tongue no longer. "With deepest respect, Your Majesty, may I inquire? ... "

The emperor raised his head, exhaling the closest thing to a laugh I had heard from him. "Yes, my child...Thy son is alive. The young Danish prince is well and safe, according to the most recent reports we have received from my most trusted couriers."

"Most recent? From where?" I blurted, must have blanched, and felt faint.

Again, his highness anticipated my inquiry, "Oh, he is not here in the castle – not in Prague at all, nor in Bohemia."

"Then, if I may ask, your Majesty –I beg ... I must know... Has my Aricin been abducted again?" My hands trembled. I felt a knot in my stomach. "To Rome? To Madrid? To Elsinore?"

"To Denmark, yes." The emperor locked eyes with me before I could bow my head. He must have seen my desperate apprehension.

"Abducted, no! Not at all!" The emperor sat back in his chair and exhaled a short burst of laughter. "Your prince thrives, and is being treated as a prince should be. Spoiled, we would venture..."

I covered my face with my hands. "Please, Your Majesty, do not taunt me. I must know..."

"Do not doubt us. Have no fear. Thy child is kept well guarded, safe from the clutches of the Norwegian tyrant." His Majesty's face darkened. "It is *King Fortinbras* who should be afraid now, after colluding with Cardinal Spinola to take our life."

I recover enough to uncover my face and sit up in my chair. "Your Majesty, please forgive my vexation, born of searing grief – of a mother who has been led to believe that her son perished."

"As we did believe you had perished, Ophelia..."

"Forgive me, Your Majesty, but I did perish in your tower."

The emperor sighed, sipped his wine, took his gilded fork and pushed flakes of pastry around on his golden plate.

Katherina dabbed her mouth and leaned back in her chair. "You, my child, were the unfortunate guest of His Majesty's traitorous Governor General Hargarthy – working behind our backs for the Vatican – and if I may speak frankly – his majesty's cousin Philip, who did not wish to dirty his hands."

Lady Katherina's I-told-you-so tone told me that she was addressing her man, not me. She turned more towards me, then. "And here you are, not only alive, but having risked your life to defend our emperor against powerful enemies."

She and the emperor would never know how close I had come to regicide myself – seething with misdirected hatred.

The emperor skewered a fat pastry flake on his fork brought it to his lips. Smiling, he nodded to his consort and looked back at me. "What is past is past."

But Lady Katherine wasn't quite finished. "Yes, my emperor. Past – and a good thing for all concerned that your loving consort demanded that Ophelia's little boy be brought here to safe haven among our own children instead of staying in the papal nuncio's hands."

I turned towards Katherina. "Then, may I as, was my son right here all that time. Is he still here, or already in Denmark, as His Majesty said?"

Lady Katherina shook her head. "Only for a short while, Lady Ophelia. After your presumed 'death,' we thought it wise to move your prince Ari far from the prying eyes of those who would be intent upon finishing their mission for Fortinbras.

"If it pleases you and Your Majesty, please do tell me to whence..." I was getting frantic.

The emperor interjected. "The learned Rabbi Loew – the one they call 'The Maharal' – cared for the boy for a little while in his house – the least likely place anyone would think to look for him." The emperor paused and sipped some wine.

"Enough of this bandying about!" His Majesty moved to rise and his butler stepped up to hold His Majesty's chair. "Lady Ophelia, thou wilt see thy son soon enough. Be content and ask no further of us." The emperor glanced back at his butler signaling that he wished to remain where he was at the moment. The butler took two paces back. "Before any further action, my child, thou must pledge thyself to the purpose of our having thee as our guest today – besides royal gratitude, of course."

My heart slowed its thumping only a little as his majesty went on, and I saw the curtain rise on the emperor's new play. The emperor had method to his madness. There were no niceties beneath this table cloth, and no ceremony. I knew was to be of imperial use – like any soldier – one of this drama's protagonists, like it or not, if I wanted to see my child again. And when that reunion took place it would not be as I pictured it, nor the life as I had so often envisioned it – but one all too familiar to me nevertheless.

I had no one to blame but myself – my inattention to peril in Lyon, thinking I had been at last in the safe bosom of family, my misapprehensions, my rages and torments. But the past must be taken off the table as surely as the emperor's dutiful maid now unobtrusively removed our plates and utensils.

Regardless of my judgments, what I saw unfolding would be of my own making as much as the emperor's. I had set the wheels in motion for the final act. I had been the one to alert the emperor to the ill intentions of his enemies and single them out.

The emperor got down to business. "We need an ally in the north – to be part of our new, grand alliance – and the era of peace and learning that we envision. You will be that ally, ruling as Queen mother when thy son is crowned rightful heir to the Danish throne."

"But, with respect, your majesty, how... I am but a reed too slim to bear the weight of royal responsibilities"

"We have observed thee. We have learned of thy exploits. Your emperor has listened and watched you through this meal as well. We have concluded that thou, Lady Ophelia, art most eminently suited for all that will be asked of thee.

By now I could hardly restrain the trembling of my knees under the table. "With respect, Your Majesty, I ask only to be reunited with my son."

"In time, my child. Soon." The emperor held up a beefy hand. He paused to make short work of a plum custard pastry that the serving woman had brought. He dabbed his pouty sensual lips with a red silken cloth emblazoned with a gold lion. "Lady Ophelia, do not hide thy light under a bushel. These past weeks, thou hast more than demonstrated the essential qualities every monarch needs to rule justly and well – fair Ophelia. Thou hast shown courage, resourcefulness and wisdom beyond your years. Most importantly, Lady Ophelia, thou hast shown an iron will – decisiveness. No monarch can rule for long without it."

I bowed my head. "I thank Your Majesty – such generous words... but, respectfully, I have never sought..."

"England's Elizabeth rules thusly, as does our adversary, the Valide Sultana in ruling the Ottoman Empire as regent mother of the young, feeble Sultan Murad III. She overcame hardship, like you."

I had heard that story from Isabella – about the Venetian maiden – a Spanish Jew – captured and enslaved in the sultan's harem, who rose by shrewdness and luck to rule the great Turkish empire. "Your Majesty, I am hardly to be compared with queens and empresses, nor do I seek more than a quiet life to raise my son and write my verses in peace, as I am able."

The emperor brushed pastry flakes off his beard, ignoring my protestations. "Even so. All thy other qualities aside, thou hast demonstrated to us another – even more vital quality – one that elevates a ruler from mediocrity to greatness." He smiled to himself. "Audacity, Lady Ophelia, audacity!"

I felt my body burning. I wanted to rise from the chair in which I felt myself being bound by the emperor's intentions, and run away.

"Decisiveness – regardless of the risks! A ruler – to keep his head in more ways than one, must be capable of ruthlessness, of dark deeds – when necessary.

"Thee, Lady Ophelia, will rule Denmark well – and in good faith to our new alliance. And when the times arrives, so will it be for thy son. This we know, and have confirmed with our most esteemed astrologers!"

Lady Katherina smiled indulgently at His Majesty – and with Your Majesty's most trusted Lady as well!"

His Majesty's words rang in my head. I had traveled so very far from Elsinore, yet felt myself being pulled back to its reality. I could more resist than could Prince Hamlet with all his brilliance and noble intentions. My flight into other lives had be instructive, but in the end, preparatory for what now was to come.

81. HEAVEN'S ISLAND

As a child, I remember that, if skies were clear enough, I could see the Isle of Hven from the ramparts of Elsinore, its white cliffs shimmering through mists on the Baltic Sea horizon. I imagined it a magical isle of wizards, spirits, elves and dragons. That was before Lord Tycho Brahe made the isle his bastion of astronomy, built his great observatory, Uraniborg, on it, recording the every visible point and movement in the heavens with the help of the most advanced instruments and one hundred students he paid hardly at all.

++++

Now, I drew near the island shore in a skiff piloted by one of Admiral Boisot's men. In the darkness, he seeks entry to the narrow inlet from where we had seen a signal lamp beckon us, swaying erratically as a firefly. A full moon silvered the chalky cliffs this night. The air smelled of salt and seaweed and memories of my childhood seaside summers.

It had been less than a month since my encounter with Emperor Rudolf. I had traveled three hundred leagues or thereabouts by water to get from Prague to Hven. I traveled incognito, mostly by barges loaded with hops and grains – guarded by the same two men who had brought me to the Emperor's summer palace – dressed as common seamen and posing as my brothers.

We moved with the currents down the Vltava River, finally merging into the wide, velvety Elbe River, though German principalities, bustling with boats and barges, exiting to the North Sea.

I was surprised to be met there by the ship of Admiral Boisot, my old spy master and still commander of the Dutch rebel *Watergeuzen* fleet that had lifted the siege of Leiden. Plainly, the admiral had sided with the those out to overthrow King Fortinbras and join the new alliance. I had little doubt that the emperor's gold had helped persuade him as much as emperor's tenuous ideals.

Boisot seemed older and more battle weary than in our last encounter. But he spoke with the same authority. I learned from him that a well organized rebellion against Fortinbras was already underway – led by the Danish Rigsgraad – The Council of the Realm – of which Tycho Brahe's father Otto and their family were the richest most powerful lords – all of them having had enough of the Norwegian tyrant, his levies and military adventures.

But the rebellion and war were far from my mind that night. By morning, I would see my Ari again at last if I could keep from rousing him from sleep immediately upon the midnight hour of my arrival at Uraniborg. As we drew close, I caught my breath, seeing its geometrical towers and walls looming in the moonlight. It seemed to me a fantasy dreamed in unison by Turks, Bohemians and Vikings.

I barely slept that night – my first on land for weeks –- counting the hours till dawn. I had a guest room to myself on the second floor of Lord Brahe's castle – trying to sleep while the master of the house observed the stars all night with his devoted apprentices.

From here, I felt closer to the stars than ever in my life. I could sense the heat of Lord Brahe's passion to understand the mysteries of those starry heavens and with them, those within ourselves.

I recalled Giordano Bruno's words, and, now, with greater comprehension, the remark by the emperor Rudolf that day in his summer palace – that those who seek to understand nature are the true titans of our age and will be remembered as such long after kings are forgotten.

But it was the mystery of my son that I sought to resolve at long last with my arrival. My waking mind would not rest all that night. It hovered over me and over the bed of my boy, asleep among the Brahe children just down the hall from me in Tycho's family living quarters.

Finally, I managed to doze, and in what seemed an instant, opened my eyes and saw daylight filtering though the curtains of my room. I pulled on my clothes and bounded down to the kitchen where I figured Ari – or any child – would go first thing in the morning.

There he was, standing a few paces from the cook. He stood half again taller than I had seen him last, and lankier, but with the same luminous azure eyes and buttery yellow hair.

He stared at me, blinking. Of course! He might well have forgotten me, having been but a wee lad when we were parted. I waited there a moment, smiling back at him from across the room while the cooks rattled pans and prepared the morning meals. With a pang, while I waited for him to react, it crossed my mind that my Ari by now probably addressed Kirsten Hansen – the astronomer's common-law – wife "mama" just like the rest of the children in the house.

"Ari! My darling. Mama is so glad to see you!" I moved slowly to him and opened my arms. He didn't hug back, but didn't resist my tender embrace – cautious, though I wanted to squeeze him with passion. Tears ran down my cheeks.

When I let go, he stepped back politely put out a hand. "Mother," he declared. His boy's voice was flat. "They told me you would be coming. I am very happy to see you too. Welcome to my realm."

I squinted.

"You may call me Lord Ari."

"I may thrash you as well, young man." I laughed.

He laughed. The ice was broken.

My Ari, you are indeed my dear prince, and I am your mother to love and guide you. One day soon you will be king of this rich land, the fates willing – a just and noble ruler for all.

Later that day, I would meet with members of the council, gathered in secret on the island. I would have little time to get comfortable, or for idyllic playtime with my son, for now. It would take time with him, I knew. Let him be content here for now – among Lord Brahe and Kristen's children, playing and, being schooled by the great astronomer's most gifted acolytes.

But no such peace for me. The emperor had dropped me into a boiling stew. There could be no retreat. My son would likely never fulfill any future if King Fortinbras prevailed.

I listened intently while the council's ministers reported on the progress of the rebellion on which our lives depended. The war reports had a familiar ring for me, and I did not shy voicing my opinions, from asking pointed questions, and otherwise asserting myself with confidence. If I were to be their regent queen, I would have gain their respect from the start.

The *Rigsgraad* knights had raised an army, already in the field – mostly of farmers, workmen and defecting Danish soldiers, along with mercenaries raised by the Swedish branch of the Brahe family. Our rebels caught Fortinbras off guard, with the bulk of his army bogged down in Poland. The *Watergeuzen* had blockaded Arhaus and captured the Danish straits.

The rebel legions, meanwhile, had captured Elsinore – long abandoned, but of symbolic importance – while a force from the Free Pancreatic City of Bremen marched into southern Jutland in support of the Danish uprising.

The rebel army moved to encircle *Kronenberg Fortinbras* and from there, take Copenhagen in what would be the decisive battle of the uprising.

We had convened Tycho's capacious, domed meeting room on the first floor of Uraniborg, built of inlaid mahogany and oak and cluttered with fantastical astronomical instruments. I took my place on a raised dais on one side of the room and surveyed delegates on benches all around in their formal cloaks and plumed hats.

I stepped to the dais. "I will join the battle myself," I announced. The stout old men of the council sat up straight and glowered at me. "I have armor and knowledge of arms," I said. "But most of all, I will carry the flag and address our soldiers, and show them that their queen mother is with them, going into this battle – with honor, ready to lay down my life with theirs, never wavering until victory."

A man, younger than the rest, who I had not noticed at first, stepped forward and began to applaud. "Hail to the Queen Mother!" He mounted the three steps to stand beside me on the dais platform and bowed ceremoniously before me. It was Horatio.

With that, the rest of the council members rose and cheered.

Horatio had become the council's chief war minister, it seemed.

"Our noble Queen Mother, Lady is learned and courageous. My Lady has been tested in battle as well as affairs of state. I can attest to these truths personally," he declared. "Under her banner we march to restore Prince Aricin, the son of our great Hamlet to his rightful place on the Danish throne – restoring the peace and productive life of our kingdom!" More applause.

I took stage again: "Victory will be ours, the Norwegian tyrant vanquished, the Danish people unburdened and Elsinore returned to its glory!"

More cheering. I thanked Horatio under my breath.

Horatio stood straight, respectfully a few paces behind me, and whispered: "You came at the perfect time, your highness. You were born for this."

I turned my head to him and smirked at his use of the title, though I knew that I would have to get used to it in public. "We have much to discuss, Lord Horatio," I told him softly amid the continued cheering.

Horatio answered in a soft voice no one but I could hear. "Not all of it will concern 'matters of state,' I hope and pray, your highness."

"*Everything* in our lives from henceforth, is to be a matter of state, my dear Horatio," I responded as softly "even matters of the heart."

THE END

By Umberto Tosi

Uraniborg, the observatory built on Hven Island by Danish Astronomer Tycho Brahe.

####

SELECTED BIBLIOGRAPHY

- Allen, Prudence and Salvatore, Filippo – 1992 paper "Renaissance and Reformation" - *Lucrezia Marinelli and Women's Identity in the Italian Late Renaissance.*
- Andreini, Isabella – *"Lettera del Nascimento delle Donne"* in *Woman Poets of the Italian Renaissance: Courtly Ladies and Courtesans,* ed. Anne Laura Stortoni/Mary Prentice Lillie, 1997.
- Attwood, Margaret, 1997, Lecture – *Ophelia Has a Lot to Answer For.*
- Blackwell, Richard J. ed, 1998 - *Giordano Bruno: Cause, Principle and Unity: And Essays on Magic (Cambridge Texts in the History of Philosophy).*
- Blaisdell, Charmarie – *"Religion, Gender, and Class: Nuns and Authority in Early Modern France"*, in Michael Wolfe (ed.) *Changing Identities in Early Modern France* (London, 1997),
- Brooks, Jean R., 1991, essay – *Hamlet and Ophelia as Lovers: Some Interpretations on Page and Stage.*
- Cadden, Joan, 1993 – *The Meanings of Sex Differences in the Middle Ages*
- Cox, Virginia, 2011 – *The Prodigious Muse: Women's Writing in Counter-Reformation Ital.*
- Dane, Gabrielle, 1998, essay - *Reading Ophelia's Madness.*
- Dickie, John, 2008 – *Delizia! The Epic History of Italians and Their Food.*

- Donnelly, Marian C., 1984 – *"Theaters in the Courts of Denmark and Sweden from Frederik II to Gustav III"*. Journal of the Society of Architectural Historians.
- Dreyer, John Louis Emil (2004) [1890]. *Tycho Brahe: A Picture of Scientific Life and Work in the Sixteenth Century.*
- Gianetti, Laura, 2009 – *Lelia's Kiss: Imagining Gender, Sex and Marriage in Italian Renaissance Comedy.*
- Gordon, Mel, 1983 – *Lazzi: The Comic Routines of the Commedia dell'Arte.*
- Gürkan, Emrah Safa, 2012 – *Espionage in the 16th Century Mediterranean: Secret Diplomacy, Mediterranean Go-Betweens and the Ottoman-Habsburg Rivalry.*
- Jones, Julia, 2000 – *A Primer to Giordano Bruno: New Age Prophet, Mystic and Heretic.*
- Kann, Robert A.,1980 – *A History of the Habsburg Empire.*
- Klein, Lisa, 2006 – *Ophelia.*
- Marinella, Lucrezia, 1653 – *The Nobility and Excellence of Woman and the Defects and Vices of Men.*
- Marshall, Peter, 2006 – *The Magic Circle of Rudolf II: Alchemy and Astrology in Renaissance Prague.*
- Motley, John Lothrop. *The Rise of the Dutch Republic, 1566–74.*
- Parker, Geoffrey, 1972, 2004 – *The Army of Flanders and the Spanish Road, 1567-1659: The Logistics of Spanish Victory and Defeat in the Low Countries' War.*
- Robin, Diana Maury/Larsen, Anne R; Levin, Carole (2007). *Encyclopedia of Women in the Renaissance: Italy, France, and England.*

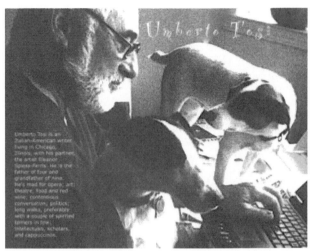

Umberto Tosi – author of *Ophelia Rising* – is contributing editor of *Chicago Quarterly Review*. His published fiction includes: *Gunning for the Holy Ghost, Our Own Kind, Satan the Movie* and *My Dog's Name* – a novella quartet set in Los Angeles, where he was a writer and editor with the *Los Angeles Times* for a dozen years. He was also editor of *San Francisco Magazine*, managing editor of Francis Ford Coppola's *City Magazine*, editor-in-chief of the Diablo Magazine Group, as well editor at digital publisher MightyWords.com. He has published hundreds of articles and stories in regional and national magazines and reviews. His other published books include the cold war spy biography, *High Treason* (GP Putnam & Sons), *Sports Psyching* (J.P. Tarcher), and the Christmas novella, *Milagro on 34ᵗʰ Street*, Umberto Tosi was born in Boston. He resides in Chicago, and is father of four, all grown.

- Rocquet, Claude-Henri, 1991 – *Bruegel or The Workshop of Dreams.*
- Setton, Kenneth Meyer,1984 – *The Papacy and the Levant, 1204-1571.*
- Shakespeare, William, 1602 – *Hamlet, Prince of Denmark.*
- Showalter, Elaine, 1985. *Representing Ophelia: Women, Madness, and the Responsibilities of Feminist Criticism.* In *Shakespeare and the Question of Theory,* Ed. Patricia Parker and Geoffrey Hartman.
- South, Preston G., 1901, – *Hamlet and Ophelia: essay from The Secret of Hamlet, Prince of Denmark.*
- Voet, Leon, 1969 – *The Golden Compasses: a history and evaluation of the printing and publishing activities of the Officina Plantiniana at Antwerp,* Vol. 1.
- Wedgwood, Cicely. 1944. *William the Silent: William of Nassau, Prince of Orange, 1533–1584.*
- Wells, Stanley/Sarah Stanton, eds. 2002. *The Cambridge Companion to Shakespeare on Stage.*
- Zemon Davis, Natalie, 1965, 1975 – *Society and Culture in Early Modern France.*

- Rocquet, Claude-Henri, 1991 – *Bruegel or The Workshop of Dreams.*
- Setton, Kenneth Meyer,1984 – *The Papacy and the Levant, 1204-1571.*
- Shakespeare, William, 1602 – *Hamlet, Prince of Denmark.*
- Showalter, Elaine, 1985. *Representing Ophelia: Women, Madness, and the Responsibilities of Feminist Criticism.* In *Shakespeare and the Question of Theory,* Ed. Patricia Parker and Geoffrey Hartman.
- South, Preston G., 1901, – *Hamlet and Ophelia: essay from The Secret of Hamlet, Prince of Denmark.*
- Voet, Leon, 1969 – *The Golden Compasses: a history and evaluation of the printing and publishing activities of the Officina Plantiniana at Antwerp,* Vol. 1.
- Wedgwood, Cicely. 1944. *William the Silent: William of Nassau, Prince of Orange, 1533–1584.*
- Wells, Stanley/Sarah Stanton, eds. 2002. *The Cambridge Companion to Shakespeare on Stage.*
- Zemon Davis, Natalie, 1965, 1975 – *Society and Culture in Early Modern France.*

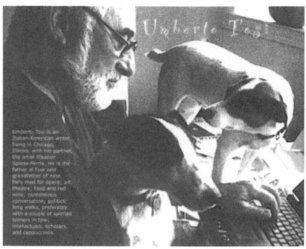

Umberto Tosi – author of *Ophelia Rising* – is contributing editor of *Chicago Quarterly Review*. His published fiction includes: *Gunning for the Holy Ghost, Our Own Kind, Satan the Movie* and *My Dog's Name* – a novella quartet set in Los Angeles, where he was a writer and editor with the *Los Angeles Times* for a dozen years. He was also editor of *San Francisco Magazine*, managing editor of Francis Ford Coppola's *City Magazine*, editor-in-chief of the Diablo Magazine Group, as well editor at digital publisher MightyWords.com. He has published hundreds of articles and stories in regional and national magazines and reviews. His other published books include the cold war spy biography, *High Treason* (GP Putnam & Sons), *Sports Psyching* (J.P. Tarcher), and the Christmas novella, *Milagro on 34ᵗʰ Street*, Umberto Tosi was born in Boston. He resides in Chicago, and is father of four, all grown.